THE OMEGA PROJECT

THE
OMEGA
PROJECT

STEVE ALTEN

A TOM DOHERTY ASSOCIATES BOOK
NEW YORK

THE OMEGA PROJECT

Copyright © 2013 by Alten Entertainment of Boca Raton, Inc.

Interior illustrations by William McDonald / AlienUFOart copyright © 2013 by
Alten Entertainment of Boca Raton, Inc.

Edited by James Frenkel

A Forge Book
Published by Tom Doherty Associates, LLC
175 Fifth Avenue
New York, NY 10010

www.tor-forge.com

Forge® is a registered trademark of Tom Doherty Associates, LLC.

Library of Congress Cataloging-in-Publication Data

Alten, Steve.
    The Omega Project / Steve Alten.—First edition.
        p. cm.
    ISBN 978-0-7653-3632-3 (hardcover)
    ISBN 978-1-4668-2783-7 (e-book)
    I. Title.
    PS3551.L764O44 2013
    813'.54—dc23
                                    2013006416

Forge books may be purchased for educational, business, or promotional use.
For information on bulk purchases, please contact Macmillan Corporate and
Premium Sales Department at 1-800-221-7945 extension 5442 or write
specialmarkets@macmillan.com.

First Edition: August 2013

Printed in the United States of America

0 9 8 7 6 5 4 3 2 1

This novel is dedicated to

Dr. Arul Chidambaram
and the doctors, nurses, and dedicated staff at
Wellington Regional Hospital.

Thank you for saving my life. . . .

ACKNOWLEDGMENTS

It is with great appreciation that I acknowledge those who contributed to the completion of *The Omega Project*.

First and foremost, to the great staff at Forge Books, with special thanks to Tom Doherty and his family, my editors, James Frenkel and Whitney Ross, art director Seth Lerner and jacket designer Peter Lutjen. My gratitude and appreciation to my personal editor, Lou Aronica at the Fiction Studio (laronica@fictionstudio.com), whose advice remains invaluable, and to my literary agent, Danny Baror of Baror International, for his friendship and dedication. Thanks as well to his assistant, Heather Baror-Shapiro.

To my friend Nick Nunziata—a special thanks for your input during the writing process. Thanks as well to the talented William McDonald (www.alienUFOart.com) for the original artwork found within these pages, and to copy editor Justine Gardner.

My gratitude and appreciation to Barbara Becker, who serves as my personal reader and works tirelessly in the Adopt An Author program, as well as to Millennium Technology Resources, for managing the SteveAlten.com Web site.

Finally, to my wife, Kim, and my kids, Kelsey and Branden, for their love, and for their tolerance of the long hours involved in my writing career, and most importantly to my readers and fans, without whom I'd have no career.

The survival of the human race depends on its ability to find new homes elsewhere in the universe because there's an increasing risk that a disaster will destroy Earth.

—STEPHEN HAWKING, Nobel Prize–winning physicist and
author of *A Brief History of Time*

THE OMEGA PROJECT

PROLOGUE

The representative wearing the requisite white lab coat was not a scientist; his selection to address the media was based more on his availability than his public relations experience. Now, as he stepped out of the administration building and into a 54°F headwind, he wished he had called in sick.

Reporters' side conversations were replaced by a heavy silence as he approached the hastily prepared podium and its entanglement of microphones. He removed a prepared statement from his pants pocket, then paused at the whirring flutter of camera shutters to evaluate the crowd.

Look at all of them . . . a herd of sheep, panicked by a lone voice yelling wolf. Don't let them see you wipe at any sweat beads, they'll interpret the body language. Just read the damn statement, answer a few questions, and get back inside where it's warm.

"Good morning. Yesterday, Harvard astronomer Brian Marsden of the International Astronomical Union issued an IAU circular about a possible very close pass to the Earth of the asteroid designated 1997 XF11. According to Marsden's calculations, the asteroid, which is approximately one mile in diameter, will pass within thirty thousand miles on Thursday, October 26, 2028, at approximately 1:30 P.M. Eastern Daylight Time. Mr. Marsden stated that, while the chance of an actual collision with Earth remained small, it was not entirely out of the realm of possibility. A mile-wide asteroid, as most of you know, could cause quite a bit of damage.

"Following Mr. Marsden's announcement, JPL scientists Dr. Donald Yeomans and Dr. Paul Chodas reexamined the data on 1997 XF11. This reexamination was based on orbit calculations made in March of 1990 at Caltech's Palomar Observatory, seven years before its reported discovery by Jim Scotti of the Spacewatch group. Based on this more conclusive data, we're happy to report that Asteroid 1997 XF11 will pass at a rather more comfortable distance of nine hundred sixty thousand kilometers—about six hundred thousand miles, approximately two moon distances away, giving it a near zero probability of impacting our planet."

A wave of arms beckoned for his attention amid a chorus of stated questions. Tucking the statement inside his pants pocket, he scanned the crowd, seeking a friendly face. He pointed. "I'm sorry, I don't know anyone's name. Yes, the gentleman with the red-striped tie."

"Zach Bachman, *L.A. Times.* How is it that scientists at JPL were able to find this new data less than a day after the IAU's announcement?"

"If you're suggesting a conspiracy, Mr. Bachman, you may want to check with the producers of those two new asteroid-impact movies." He smiled at the effectiveness of the rehearsed line, using the interruption of the laughter to casually brush at the moisture beading over his brow. "Actually, the asteroid had been photographed by JPL scientists at Palomar in 1990 but never named. Had it been named I suspect there would have been less of a panic and I'd be enjoying my breakfast in the commissary. Yes? You, with the paisley shirt."

"Tom Cubit, *USA Today.* According to Jack G. Hills of the Los Alamos National Laboratory, this is the most dangerous near-Earth asteroid ever spotted and its impact would be the equivalent of two million Hiroshima-size bombs. How does this new threat compare with the asteroid that wiped out the dinosaurs sixty-five million years ago?"

"The asteroid you're referring to was probably three times the size of 1997 XF11. Again, the chances of it striking the Earth are minimal. We're not downplaying the danger; we've simply recalculated the asteroid's orbit based on more accurate, reliable data. Yes, the young lady from CNN?"

"Are there any factors that could alter the asteroid's projected orbit over the next thirty years? For example, could the Earth's gravitational pull affect the asteroid's orbit on its next pass, which I believe is on Halloween in 2002, effecting a change in 2028?"

Sweat had soaked through the back of the administrator's dress shirt. "While it's true that gravitational interaction with a larger object can alter an asteroid's orbit by approximately a quarter of one degree, JPL calculations confirm that the influence of the Earth's orbit on 1997 XF11 on its next pass in 2002 should be minimal. In a worst-case scenario, Asteroid 1997 XF11 will come no closer to Earth in October 2028 than a moon's distance away. Thank you, that's all for now."

The JPL representative waved to the crowd as he exited the podium, his thoughts lingering on his last statement. *A moon's distance away. . . . Has anyone bothered to plot the moon's orbit when 1997 XF11 passes Earth in 2028?*

PART ONE

GDO
(The Great Die-Off)

2020–2025

1

Strong and healthy, who thinks of sickness until it strikes like lightning?
Preoccupied with the world, who thinks of death until it arrives like thunder?
—SUTTA NIPATA II, discourse collections of the Buddha, fifth century B.C.

MARCH 12, 2022

I didn't know much about guns. The one I'd been gripping in my sweaty palm held four bullets in its clip and one in the chamber—same as it had when I'd removed it from the corpse I'd come across two weeks ago. It was rare these days to find a dead body that hasn't been skinned and stripped of its meat. Thankfully, I'd never been forced to consume human flesh, which was why I was here . . . out in the woods, hoping to shoot a deer before the last deer was taken, before the last of my supplies ran out and hunger drove me either to cannibalism, suicide, or starvation.

I'd arrived in the woods before dawn, having ridden all night on my motorcycle. No lights needed, thanks to my night-vision glasses, no sound since the bike was powered solely by batteries. I'd been staked out in this blind for the better part of eight hours. Sweat continued to pour down my face and soak my camouflage clothing, and the bugs were relentless, but I'd chosen this spot because it was only twenty paces from the creek, offering me a clear shot at anything or anyone that ventured by. Truth be told, I'd never shot anything more lethal than a BB gun, but desperate times required desperate measures.

When I was younger, my father had taken me camping with the Cub Scouts. The closest we'd come to hunting game was roasting marshmallows. A real hunter wouldn't have been hunting deer with a handgun. A real hunter probably wouldn't have had ant bites all over his ankles or mosquito bites on his arms, and he wouldn't have been so scared.

I wasn't scared of the woods. I was scared of being lost in the woods, unable to find my way back to the main road and the brush where I'd hidden the bike. Mostly, I was scared about what else might be in the woods hunting the deer hunters.

I called them the "SS"—sociopathic survivors. Rapists, murderers, cannibals—the SS were soulless beings hell-bent on enjoying their final fleeting moments on Earth. I'd never seen them in action, but I'd seen the forensic evidence of their depravity and it terrified me.

The last bullet in my gun's chamber was reserved for my brain should those pack animals hunt me down.

The SS were bottom-feeders before the Die-Off, which is why they'd survived. They lived off the grid. Same for the fortress farmers, bunker clans, conspiracy theorists, and other whack-jobs who could read the tea leaves and had known the world's oil reserves were running out.

Note to any future generations listening to these audio tapes: The powers-that-be knew the world's oil reserves peaked in 2005; in fact, they knew how things would end as far back as the 1970s when Jimmy Carter was in office. And still the assholes did nothing.

My father had known, which is why he left his tenured position at the University of Virginia and moved us to a small rural community in the foothills of the Blue Ridge Mountains. No Internet connection, no cable TV. We went from being a normal modern-day household to twenty-first century pioneers, gradually inching our way off the grid. None of us was thrilled; my mother had contemplated divorce, my younger sisters labeled Dad the new Unabomber and threatened to run away from home. As for me, if my father had told me a flood was coming then I would have been outside with him building an ark.

It had been shortly after the first mushroom cloud bloomed over Tehran that my father explained his motives. *"Robbie, life is a test, and humanity is about to face a big one. Unfortunately, when it comes to facing the unthinkable, most people prefer to remain in denial. You saw the movie* Titanic, *right? When the ship hit that iceberg, some passengers headed for the lifeboats, while the majority of people were so convinced the ship couldn't sink they either stayed in bed or went back to the bar to have another drink. When you get older you'll learn two hard facts: You can't save people who don't want to be saved; and preferring to remain ignorant when faced with a catastrophe demonstrates a lack of intelligence."*

Dad could have added human ego to the equation.

I'd grown up in a world of bank bailouts, recessions, unemployment, collapsing economies, and endless wars; my country embattled in a perversion of democracy where corporations had been granted the same rights as citizens. Corruption overruled any sense of justice, the radicalization of the political system preventing the few true representatives of the suddenly impoverished masses from enacting solutions that could have reversed the eventual collapse of society. As my father said, *"Human ego created these problems, and human ego will drive us over the cliff. The world would be better off if a computer ran everything."*

Computers. . . . The next computer I own will be implanted in my skull.

A sound! My heart skipped a beat. It was an animal, approaching the creek from the thicket to my left.

Quietly, I wiped fresh sweat beads from my already moist brow and palms, shifting my body weight to aim the pistol, my eyes focused on the clearing. It was a deer, a young male, maybe eighty pounds, as anxious and as thirsty as yours truly. My hand trembled as he glanced in my direction, my body shook as he turned, offering me a clean shot at his flank.

I hesitated, drawing a breath, suddenly fearful of the gunshot and who might hear it . . .

Thwaap!

The buck collapsed upon its forelegs in silence, the arrow having appeared seemingly from out of nowhere, its tip passing cleanly through the startled animal's spine and out its chest cavity.

Leaving my makeshift hunting blind, I approached the dying beast. The angle of the arrow's entry indicated the archer had shot from the trees.

"Touch the venison and you'll die where you stand."

I turned slowly, my heart racing as she emerged from the forest like an erotic female warrior from a Luis Royo painting. Her ebony hair flowed nearly down to her waist in a curly tangle camouflaged in twigs and leaves, every inch of her flesh concealed in green and brown paint or beneath a skintight matching bodysuit. Ten paces away and I could smell her scent—a heavy animal musk. She looked about my age. The quiver was strapped to her thigh, the muscles of her upper body taut as she aimed the graphite bow's arrow at my heart.

I was as stunned as I was smitten. "The deer's yours. Take it."

"I intend to. Drop the piece."

"The what? Oh, the gun. Seriously, you can have it. I doubt I could even shoot the damn thing straight." I lowered the weapon, placed it on the ground, and backed away. "What's your name?"

"Shut up." Quivering the arrow, she grabbed the gun, expertly ejecting the clip to check the chamber. Reassembling the weapon, she shoved it into a satchel concealed around her waist, hoisted the dead deer over her shoulders, and was gone.

Alone again, I waited thirty seconds, then followed her through the dense brush, losing her trail within minutes.

Who was she? Was she alone? Part of a group? Her attitude suggested otherwise. My guess? When the lights went out and the grocery store shelves were rendered bare, she had fled to the mountains—or more likely her family were mountain folk. Whatever the case, she was everything I was not; ruthless, cunning . . . a hunter who showed no mercy.

And yet she had spared me.

Well, dork-wad, you did give her the gun. Practically curtsied as you laid it on the ground.

I paused again to listen to the forest; heard nothing.

By her scent, I knew she lived in the woods, probably a cave. Heading for higher ground, I followed a path of ferns and moss-covered rocks that emptied into a clearing of tall weeds.

To my left, the Blue Ridge Mountains caressed the setting sun between its peaks and valley. With darkness a mere ninety minutes away, I had to choose—the woman or sanctuary?

It had been twenty months since I'd carried on a conversation with another living person. I might be an introvert by nature, but listening day and night to the voice in my head had been maddening, leading to the creation of these recorded journal entries. But seeing her . . . she was a thunderbolt, a goddess. I knew I had to find her, even if it meant risking an encounter with the SS.

Pausing at the edge of a clearing, I retrieved water and an apple from my knapsack, consumed a quick snack, buried the evidence, and continued my trek up the mountain.

After three hundred feet the woods began anew. The shadows of pine trees were closing in, dusk coming fast. For half an hour I wandered through a maze of trees, until the night was upon me and I accepted the fact I was hopelessly lost.

Hearing men's voices, I quickly hid.

There were a dozen of them, more in the cave.

The dogs had found the woman's lair, its small entrance concealed by brush. I figured now they would stake out the area, waiting for her to return.

I smelled her as she moved through the shadows to join me behind the bushes. I felt the gun press firmly against the left side of my rib-cage. "I need a place that's safe."

"Get me back to the main road."

The motorcycle was hidden in a ravine behind mile marker thirty-six. Six months ago, I had replaced the engine and fuel tank with an electric motor and rechargeable truck battery, rendering it fast yet whisper quiet. We waited another hour before heading south, my night-vision visor illuminating any nocturnal predators that might venture near the highway.

My family's suburban neighborhood had long since been abandoned. Our house stood alone among burnt-out foundations on a cul-de-sac. I had cleared the surrounding terrain to expose anyone who approached. Every window was bricked up, the house and matching eight-foot wall that surrounded the backyard's concealed acreage painted to appear like charred cinder.

The lawn was covered in sheets of metal—hundreds of car trunks and engine hoods, planted flat into the grass and welded into a giant jigsaw puzzle. Climbing off the motorcycle, I instructed the beautiful huntress to follow precisely in my footsteps, my night-vision glasses revealing a preset path that turned and twisted to tall shrubs that cam-ouflaged a subterranean side entrance. Once we were inside the house, I bolted the steel door behind the woman, shocking her by turning on the lights.

"You have electricity? How?"

"While other people were searching for food and water, I was busy collecting car batteries and solar panels."

"And car hoods. What's that all about?"

"Security. Step onto my property and you get zapped with ten thou-sand volts of electricity. By the way, my name's Eisenbraun, Robert Eisenbraun. Most people used to call me Ike."

"Andria Saxon." Dropping the deer carcass on the floor, she roamed the house, taking inventory. "Air-conditioning . . . a working refrigerator and stove—pretty impressive, Eisenbrain. What else do you have here?"

"A running shower and soap for starters. And it's Eisenbraun."

"Tell you what, I'll handle the brawn, you handle the brains and maybe we'll manage to survive this mess."

2

The death of one man is a tragedy. The death of millions is a statistic.
—JOSEPH STALIN

"You make love like a freshman."

"And you make love like a woman breaking in a wild stallion."

We had lived together in my parents' home for three weeks, sleeping in separate bedrooms, which we kept bolted from the inside. She taught me how to target shoot from tree limbs while I educated her on how everything worked in our shared fortress, but we rarely engaged in conversation about our lives before the Die-Off.

And then late this afternoon, she turned to me while we picked apples in the orchard and kissed me.

Within minutes we were in bed, naked and entwined; the two of us entering an exciting new world.

When we were done, Andria climbed off and lay beside me, the flesh on her tan back and buttocks sporting a series of scars. "Scratch."

I accepted my duties, restricting the urge to hug her from behind lest she crush my windpipe with an elbow to the throat.

"You may have noticed that I have control issues, Eisenbraun. I guess it comes from being on my own since I was fifteen. A little lower. Now harder, use your nails. . . . God, that's good. So what's your story? How'd you learn to do all this?"

"I studied a lot. You know . . . lack of a social life."

"Funny, I pegged you as a jock. How tall are you? Six foot five? Maybe two-twenty? Bet you played basketball."

"Track and field. Mom was a natural athlete, I inherited her foot speed. Did some long jump and the hundred meters in high school until the varsity football coach forced me to try out as a receiver. I couldn't catch a cold, let alone a football. 'Stone hands Eisenbraun,' they called me on the field, 'Jew bastard' off it. Things changed after they switched me to free safety and found out the Jew liked to hit."

"Chip on your shoulder, huh? That makes us kindred spirits. Did you play ball in college?"

"I wanted to, but the Pentagon ordered me not to play. Guess they were afraid of concussions damaging the old noggin."

"The Pentagon?"

"My uncle was a general, a bigwig with DARPA. When I was fourteen I created an algorithm for a video game that ended up being used to train gamers to fly military drones. Three years later my uncle was placed in charge of a top-secret initiative, called Omega. I left school during my sophomore year in college to work with his team."

God, I was blathering like a little girl.

"And?"

"And it's top secret. Now you tell. Where are you from? Who taught you to hunt?"

"I'm part Seminole, and don't change the subject. Tell me about Omega. And no bullshit about it being top secret. The world's in the shitter because of assholes like your uncle."

"My uncle wasn't an asshole and Omega wasn't a weapon. It was actually an initiative that could have averted the Die-Off. The Omega Project was a $750 billion energy program, seeded in secrecy by the Pentagon during the Obama years to replace fossil fuels with fusion energy."

"Just what the world needs, more nuclear waste."

"No, no, that's fission. Fusion is clean energy that's released when two hydrogen atoms are merged together. The technology's biggest challenge was that the sunlike temperatures required to generate a chain reaction also released neutrino particles which destroyed the reactor's vessel. The solution to the problem required fusing deuterium with helium-3, which stabilized the process."

"English, Eisenbraun."

"To stabilize fusion required helium-3, an element that originates from the sun. The problem was that only a few cups worth of helium-3 ever reaches our planet thanks to Earth's dense atmosphere. The moon, however, possesses over a million metric tons of the stuff, enough to generate energy for the next thousand years."

"So, Omega was a secret mission to mine helium-3 from the moon?"

"Exactly."

"But you mentioned the Pentagon. Why involve those warmongers?"

"First, because the dysfunctional assholes in Congress would never have considered funding such a radical energy plan at a time when politics was focused on unemployment, even though the program created a lot of jobs. Second, because the Pentagon not only had access to the money, they also had the ability to operate the program in secrecy without congressional oversight. Still, the scientific challenges were considerable, requiring NASA to design new lunar shuttles to transport the helium-3, plus a habitat that could safely house a mining crew—don't forget, each astronaut required large supplies of food, water, and oxygen."

"I thought there's water on the moon—scratch my butt."

"There's ice, so yes, there's water. There's also moon dust, which became a major challenge. Moon dust particles act like glass shards, making them a constant threat to the astronauts' skin and eyes. There's also limits on what the human body can endure, especially when it comes to long-term exposure to gravitational forces one-sixth that of Earth. Between the health concerns and the costs—about a million dollars per astronaut per day—my uncle decided to go in a different direction . . . drones."

"Drones?" She rolled over, positioning her head on my chest—her right hand casually stroking my penis. "Keep talking."

"By, uh . . . drones, I meant replacing the lunar astronauts with mining equipment that could be remotely operated back here on Earth. All that was needed to do the job was a supercomputer to operate the drones. The way my uncle figured it, if a computer could remotely operate everything from a passenger jet to a surgical appendage performing brain surgery, then why not a mining operation on the moon? That was the reason my uncle recruited me for Omega, to join the best and brightest scientists in designing and engineering GOLEM."

"What's GOLEM?"

I sucked in a breath as her lips kissed my stomach. "GOLEM? It's an acronym that stood for 'Geological Offsite Lunar Excavation Machine.' Whoever made it up stole it from a Bible story about a soulless being, created by man, to serve his needs. See, GOLEM wasn't going to just be a supercomputer, it was going to be the ultimate in artificial intelligence—a machine that could think and adapt in order to control complex multilayered tasks a quarter of a million miles away."

I closed my eyes, willing her mouth to venture lower.

She stopped. "Keep talking, Eisenbraun. How did a young track-and-field nerd like you get involved with GOLEM?"

"My uncle was confident I could resolve the computer's design flaws, so he assigned me to work under GOLEM's director, Monique De-Friend, the former head of CSAIL, a prestigious artificial intelligence lab. She buried me in menial tasks, until I submitted a design for GOLEM's DNA matrix that blew everyone away. Two days later she placed me in charge of GOLEM's programming. I had just turned twenty."

"Nice. So what happened?"

"What happened? The GDO happened. The world went to hell."

Andria released me, her mood darkening. "Who are you to complain? You survived, Eisenbraun. You, with your solar panels and water filters and lake water. I didn't have seeds and canned goods; I didn't have a backyard filled with fruit trees."

"You also didn't have starving anti-Semites as neighbors. When the government collapsed, my parents preached secrecy to my younger sisters—'If the neighbors find out we have food, they'll take first and ask for handouts later,' but it's hard for teens not to want to help when their friends are literally starving to death.

"I was on my way home from the chaos in Washington the day our neighbors struck. My parents and sisters were butchered for three bags of brown rice and a bushel of apples. The rest of our supplies were still hidden in the garage attic."

"I'm sorry." She lay back down, her hand draped across my chest. "After they murdered your family . . . what did you do?"

"First I buried my family behind the orchard wall. Then I used the rest of our gasoline to burn down the murderers' homes while they slept. I've been alone here ever since."

"You're an angry little bastard, Eisenbraun, but you're no longer alone."

She climbed on top of me and kissed me, her tongue harsh as it probed my mouth, her hand stroking my loins until I entered her again.

3

There is love of course. And then there's life, its enemy.
        —JEAN ANOUILH

SIX MONTHS LATER . . .

The August sunrise lit the sheer gray vertical cliff face into a canvas of gold, causing my heart to race. "Andie, I really don't feel good about this."

"You'll feel better once we get started."

"I don't want to get started. When you said you knew how to cure my night terrors, I thought we were going for a hike."

"We are going for a hike—straight up to the summit."

"Without ropes and harnesses? This is crazy."

"It's not crazy, it's called 'free soloing,' and you can do it."

"No, I can't."

"Yes, you can. You have the physical strength, what you're lacking is the psychological control needed to stay on the wall. It's all about learning to control your fears through Buddha breathing—in through your nostrils, filling the belly, then slowly exhaling through your mouth. Commit to the climb. Focus your fingertips on the rock; be light like a spider monkey. And whatever you do, Ike, keep looking up."

Andria and I had been living together just over five months when I began suffering severe anxiety attacks. She had kidded me about feeling the pressures of being domesticated, and in a way she was right. Worrying about my own survival had been far different than protecting the woman I loved from the murderous gangs that roamed the countryside.

Fear entered my dreams in the form of night terrors. Ghoulish men would break into our home, the faceless demons raping and torturing Andria as they pinned me down and forced me to watch. Each night terror ended with her death, followed by my bloodcurdling scream.

Things grew so bad that we had to sleep in separate bedrooms again.

When my anxiety grew into a severe depression, Andria decided we needed a change of scenery. Claiming she knew the perfect mountain hideaway that would be free of the sociopaths, we packed supplies and rode all night on my battery-powered motorcycle, arriving just before dawn at the foot of Buzzard Rock, a 1,145-foot-high mountain located in Loudoun County, Virginia.

As she pointed out our route, I felt the blood drain from my face. "Relax, Ike, I've climbed this face a dozen times. I'll go first, do what I do and you'll be fine. And remember—"

"I know, I know . . . keep looking up."

We began our ascent. I carefully measured the first fifty handholds, my body trembling in fear as I learned to balance myself on a rock wall. After a while my fingers, hands, and feet became fleshlike pinions, adhering me to the cliff face. I learned to cleave to inch-wide grooves between the slabs of slate; the toes of my running shoes sought the tiniest of perches to bear my weight as I flattened my body to the unforgiving mountain.

Ten feet turned into fifty; fifty became a hundred, each arm length accompanied by controlled breathing and the occasional "I'm okay" in reply to Andie's query. We paused, poised on a three-foot ledge 372 feet above our starting point that offered us a treetop view and a place where we could rest and eat.

I bit into a ripe pear, my body tired, my muscles taut. "Andie, this was an amazing workout, but I'm shot and we still have to climb back down. Seriously, I never thought I'd make it ten feet, let alone this high."

She was lathered in sweat, her high cheekbones darkly tanned, accentuating her heritage. "We're going all the way, Ike. Trust me, the hardest part is over. From here on up it's a cinch."

I trusted her.

Foolish, foolish man.

The next few hours of climbing were slightly easier as the cliff face was shredded in three-inch cracks that helped get us to another perch just below nine hundred feet.

I pointed to a rusted pinion embedded in the rock. "Pussies."

Andie smiled, tearing into an apple. "You're the man, Eisenbraun. When we get up to the summit, I'm going to fuck your brains out."

I glanced up. The good news was the appearance of dry-rotted roots sticking out of the cliff face. The bad news was a five-foot curl of rock that protected the summit like a protruding lower lip. "How do we get around that ledge?"

"I'll show you when we get up there. Ready? I'm getting really horny."

We started out again, my fingers by now raw and blistered, the sweat on my palms becoming a new threat as the midday sun beat down upon us. The roots were a mixed blessing, offering us handholds we could grip—along with palms full of splinters.

And then we arrived at our final perch, the two of us staring at a ceiling of rock that jutted five feet out over our heads.

Andria pointed to a series of roots along the outer lip. "This will sound scary, but what we have to do is lean out and grab on to that root, then invert and blindly work our feet and legs up and over the ledge."

"You're insane. I'm so tired I can barely hold on."

"Which is why we have to reach the summit, so we can rest and climb down tomorrow."

"And just how are we going to get down?"

She flashed me her shit-eating grin. "We'll take the trail."

Anger shook me as I cursed my companion to exhaustion. I felt utterly helpless, my existence forced into a do-or-die situation that was as frustrating to fathom as it was insane—as insane as what had happened to my family and the rest of the world, as insane as the psychopaths that roamed the countryside and haunted my dreams—only this time I had a choice. This time I could save my life or at least die with some dignity.

"Embrace the fear, Ike. Use it to focus your strength."

"Okay, Andie, but I'm going first."

"That's not a good idea. I've done this before—"

"Bullshit. You've never climbed this mountain; if you had you wouldn't have taken us up this route. I knew it back on the last perch when I saw your face. You realized you had screwed up, but as usual you tried to wing it . . . control the moment. You're right about one thing though, if we don't get over that summit now, we'll never make it down, not in the dark. So we'll give it a try, only I'm going first. Not because you're a woman or some other bullshit sense of male chivalry, but because I love you and I just . . . I just couldn't bear to watch you fall."

Tears flooded her eyes, marking the first time she had shown me any real vulnerability. Reaching carefully into her backpack, she removed a twenty-foot length of nylon rope. "Tie off," she said, securing one end around her own waist, handing me the other. "When you reach the summit you can pull me up. If something happens, then we'll die together." She leaned over and kissed me. "You're the only man I've ever loved, Eisenbraun. Don't fuck this up."

I looped the rope tightly around my waist while drawing deep breaths into my gut, summoning every reserve of strength I had left. For the first time since we began the climb I felt truly alive, knowing in my heart that no matter what else happened to me in the days or weeks or years ahead, that right here, right now there was no possible way I was going to allow myself to fail.

4

Nonviolence means avoiding not only external physical violence but also internal violence of spirit. You not only refuse to shoot a man, but you refuse to hate him.
—Martin Luther King, Jr.

A die-off provokes a different kind of fear than a war or a natural disaster. In war there is a common enemy; in a tsunami, earthquake, or hurricane there is a common bond among humans to aid those in need.

In a die-off, death is a game of musical chairs that begins as an innocuous boil. An occasional power outage evolves into rolling blackouts, followed by assurances from government officials that oil reserves will last another thirty years, even as prices spike and the lines at your local gas station stretch for miles. The grocery store becomes a battle front as every nonperishable left on the shelf is fought over in hand-to-hand combat and customers with loaded carts, refusing to risk their precious bounty, charge out the doors without paying. These scenarios degenerate into civil disorder and mandatory curfews, the protests and street violence that follow unleashing the military.

Stop the music and remove the chair known as "personal freedom."

Phase two is rationing. Oil, natural gas, coal, firewood . . . food. Communication fractures into weekly assurances that times are tough but things will be improving soon. These pep talks from politicians, also known as lies, are designed to buy time—time being the variable that allows the weak to perish, either with a whimper (starvation) or a bang (riot police with orders to shoot to kill).

For the lower classes, the music has stopped.

A long winter without heat strikes next. Add in diminishing water and food supplies, not to mention a cessation of hospital services—and there goes the middle class—first in the colder rural regions, followed closely by the urban areas. As we remove this chair, the government shuts down, society collapses, and now it is officially every family for itself.

Dying comes in many flavors. You can starve, freeze to death, die of heat exhaustion, thirst, physical ailments, or perhaps you'll be shot attempting to get food to feed yourself or a starving child. In the last few years I had seen it all, and the images never went away . . . the nightmares and the anger stuck with me forever.

In the warmer states, suburbanites had lasted a season longer than their city-dwelling counterparts, but a die-off, like musical chairs, is a zero-sum game. Eventually every family, save the farmer with his own well-armed private army of migrant workers and the inaccessible survivalist community, was forced to abandon their powerless homes and their gasless vehicles to search for food and potable water, joining a nomadic exodus that defined the postapocalyptic landscape. Hunters still hunted and fisherman fished, but the competition for food turned neighbor against neighbor, no catch safe among the hordes of the wandering desperate. Parents pushed their starving children in shopping carts and wheelbarrows, leaving the elderly behind to die with the family pet they could no longer feed. Unyielding hunger could transform a populace into a mob of borderline psychopaths, and western nations do not go quietly into the night like an emaciated African born into hunger. They go out shooting.

I had survived these trials and tribulations through preparedness, sheer luck, and a fear that spurred ingenuity. I accepted isolation over insanity, waiting out the first year within my fortress of solitude. What kept me going was a numbers game: without oil, the world's population would drop from seven billion to just under six hundred million. If I could safeguard my chair, then maybe I'd live to see a different, wiser world.

Instead, I found myself quarantined against a society gone mad in every sense of the word. As fate would have it, after sixteen months of rationing, I was forced to venture out of my prison . . . and that's when I met my new companion.

My initial impression of Andria Saxon, besides love at first sight, was that she was a natural warrior—a fearless hunter as at home in the forest as I was in the lab. As I grew to know her, I realized I was wrong.

Andria refused to give me many details about her family life, other than that she had been on her own since she was fifteen. Over time, I was able to put together the missing pieces of a difficult existence—her "toughness" forged in strip bars, street corners, and flophouses. Having lived in her deceased mother's car for almost a year, Andria was as unaffected by the Die-Off as the Eskimos, Mayans, and other indigenous people who'd had little use for technology. What forced her from the streets of Lynchburg, Virginia, and up into the Blue Ridge Mountains was her fear of being sodomized and enslaved as livestock.

Andria trusted no one, especially men. I would learn later that her intentions at the time we met were to gain access to my safe house and kill me. What stayed my execution was her need to understand how everything in my home worked. It was only after our first week together that she decided I was worth more to her alive; after a month she knew I was not a threat.

For Andie, our time in bed together was lust—mindless fun. She would never allow herself to become vulnerable to her long-harnessed emotions.

Our adventures on the cliff face led to profound psychological changes in both of us. For me, a man who lived to survive but was afraid of life, I realized a newfound freedom that released me from the phobias that had dominated my existence since high school. As for Andria, she later confessed that the mountain was never meant to be survived. Believing her destiny was already set—that she would eventually be enslaved and tortured by the gangs of sociopaths, she had brought me to Buzzard Rock to end both our lives; albeit in as thrilling a manner as she knew how. It had been my selfless act at the summit that had melted her cold veneer, just as it had been my leap of faith that had ended my night terrors.

We returned the next night to my family's Virginia home reborn as newlyweds, each kiss as if it were the first, always knowing it could be the last. For the next twenty months we lived together in a gilded love nest surrounded by chaos—always careful not to conceive a child as we waited for the world to change.

And then one fateful day, the wolves showed up at our door.

MAY 29, 2025

"How many of them are out there, Ike?"

It was hard to see, the lenses of most of the closed-circuit surveillance cameras still clouded with the morning dew, their sheer numbers having short-circuited the electrical grid. "I count nine, plus the two wounded stiffs who tried to save their electrocuted dogs."

Andria handed me a loaded handgun—the very one she had taken from me the day we met. "How long before they realize the grid is down?"

"Not long."

"Let's get outside; we'll pick them off one by one as they climb over the garden wall."

I followed her through the kitchen, past the bricked-up windows, and out the reinforced steel back door to the garden. The eight-foot-high walls surrounding the yard were topped with coils of barbed wire, but I doubted the supports would hold beyond the first assault.

Ten minutes passed, and then we heard boots trudging heavily on the metal car hoods as they approached.

I listened, my heart racing. "They've split up!"

"Stay here, I'll take the front door."

"Andie, no—"

Wa—boom!

The blast took out a twenty-foot section of wall, pieces of brick and mortar rending the smoke-infested air. My head throbbed in the deafening aftermath, my ears ringing as bullets sprayed the orchard, shredding our fall harvest into pulp.

Andria grabbed my wrist and dragged me into the house mere seconds before the front door blew open, the concussion wave collapsing the dining room cupboards that displayed my mother's good china. Blindly, she fired into the smoldering doorway, her shotgun burying lead in the chest of an auburn-bearded hayseed, shattering his necklace of human teeth.

Pulling Andria out of the hallway, I yanked open the cellar door and led her down the creaking wooden steps, praying that the predators hadn't discovered the basement emergency exit. Andie checked the security monitor while I unhooked the motorcycle from its charger—the batteries barely energized from last night's run.

"Looks clear." She unbolted the door and climbed on behind me, wrapping her arms around my chest as I powered up the engine, its silent rumble overpowered by the blast of machine gun fire that splintered the cellar door above our heads.

We motored into daylight and up a two-foot-wide, shrub-enshrouded stretch of tarmac. The tires flattened the hood-covered lawn, the sound alerting the cannibals searching the front of the house. We were half-way down the cul-de-sac by the time their assault weapons opened fire.

The motorcycle died before we reached the end of the street.

"Andie, run!"

Abandoning the bike, we sprinted down the road, perhaps a hundred yards ahead of the enraged wolf pack. The grid had killed their dogs—a lucky break, but there was no cover, just a deserted suburban development, separated from the nearest woods by the interstate, which ran below the deserted community.

We slid down a weed-covered embankment to access the highway, my heart skipping a beat as I heard Andria scream out in pain.

"My ankle . . . I felt something snap."

I helped her up, only to see her cry out in frustration, her foot unable to bear any weight.

"Ike, give me your gun."

My heart pounded. It was suicide time.

I searched my waistband. "Shit. I must have lost it sliding down the hill."

"Goddamn it, Ike—"

"It's okay, I can carry you."

"And outrun these assholes? Ike, listen to me, you need to kill me, you need to snap my neck! Come around me from behind, you can do it. Ike, please—"

"Andie, I can't–"

Tears flowed down both our cheeks; her eyes were filled with desperate fear. "You said you loved me, Ike! You swore on that love you'd kill me if it ever came down to this."

"Shh!" Hearing voices, I dragged her down into the weeds.

Gunfire erupted, bullets ricocheting off the highway's steel girder.

"Andie, the bullets. On the count of three, we stand up into the line of fire."

She kissed me hard and fast. "You are my heart."

I was about to tell her how much I loved her when the gunfire abruptly ceased. Lying in the grass, I could hear their boots thrashing through the weeds. "I'll stand and draw their fire again, then drag you off the ground."

"Okay."

"One . . . two . . ."

If I said "three" I never heard it. What I heard instead was the bone-rattling reverberation of helicopter blades beating the air, followed by gunfire—the kind of gunfire that can split a car in two.

I crawled on top of Andria until the rain of hot lead ceased and the chopper landed on the interstate.

"You folks all right?"

I looked up at the soldier, his face obscured by his helmet's dark visor. "Who are you?"

"Naval reserves. Domestic forces are sweeping the area for survivors. We see a human carnivore, we kill them and ask questions later."

There were sixteen people aboard the Sikorsky transport—bewildered adults, malnourished children, a paraplegic bound to a wheelbarrow and an infant suckling her mother's breast. We learned that the Internet was back up, powered by solar grids and windmills. Pockets of communities had organized, calling upon war veterans and returning soldiers to mobilize military firepower to reestablish law and order, their vehicles fueled by secret reserves stored at military bases.

We were flown to the University of Virginia. Major universities were now functioning like state capitals, offering survivors food and a dorm room in exchange for work. A Web site—Survivors.org—had been created to locate family and friends.

I was relieved, but not surprised to learn that my Uncle David was alive.

Andria's broken ankle was fitted with a walking boot. We lived in a tent and worked in the fields.

A month later, in July of 2025, representatives from seventy-two university communities convened in Topeka, Kansas—the geographical center of America—in order to create a new framework of government. What emerged from this six-week convention would have made the founding fathers proud. No more political parties. Term limits for all elected officials. Most important—the elimination of future financial influences on elections, safeguarded by a Supreme Council, which would ensure that each candidate operated on equal footing.

The first president of New America was a professor of ecology and agricultural science, elected by the founding members of Congress. Her vice president, Dr. Lee Udelsman, was a fusion expert who had worked on the Omega Project before society had collapsed.

Uncle David showed up in Virginia a short time later, our reunion soured when he learned I had no interest in finishing my work on GOLEM. We negotiated a consultant fee—a research grant and lab that would allow me to experiment with a new pet project, along with Andria's acceptance at the soon-to-be established Space Energy Agency in Cape Canaveral, where we would share an apartment while she trained to pilot mining shuttles to transport loads of helium-3 back to Earth.

Could we rebound as a species? I had no doubt. If anything, humans had demonstrated, both as individuals and as nations, a fortitude born of courage. Still, ours was a resilience strengthened by numbers; when we divided as a people the strong feasted upon the weak, manifesting our worst attributes—man's ego unbridled. The Great Die-Off had served as yet another reminder of the devil lurking in each one of us; its aftermath mind-numbing, more than five billion people wiped out.

For now at least, it appeared the reign of the *Homo sapiens* subspecies known as "Petroleum Man" had officially ended, and with it Big Oil's stranglehold on clean, renewable energy sources.

The question was: *Had we learned anything?*

PART TWO

2028

Why didn't they look around, realize what they were doing, and stop before it was too late? What were they thinking when they cut down the last palm tree?

—JARED DIAMOND, *Easter's End*

5

Holding on to anger is like grasping a hot coal with the intent of throwing it at someone else; you are the one who gets burned.
—BUDDHA

NORTH CAROLINA
37 MILES SOUTHWEST OF FAYETTEVILLE
SEPTEMBER 19, 2028

My father used to tell me that of all the human emotions, anger was the most dangerous. Not because it might lead to high blood pressure and arguments that could destroy a relationship, but because, when a person got really angry, their soul actually vacated the body. Sounds crazy, right? Just wait, there was more. According to ancient Jewish teachings, the danger in a soul leaving the body was that another soul—a lesser soul—could temporarily take over, and that was when the really bad shit happened.

Today marked the eighth anniversary of the murder of my family. As if channeling my father, my online therapist advised me to let go of my anger through forgiveness. Humoring him, I asked myself, if my child were starving, would I take another person's life to feed my kid? My father, being a moral man, would not have taken another person's life under any circumstance, nor would he have resisted sharing our food, especially if the lives of his family were threatened. Had one neighbor approached Dad, it would have been a different outcome. But the neighbors had formed a mob, and mobs thought collectively in primitive terms, as in, "the Jews are hoarding food" or *"Juden Raus!"* (see Hitler's Germany), or "the Jews poisoned the wells," (see Black Plague). I could go on, but it wouldn't change a thing. Dad was dead, so were Mom, Diane, and Debby . . . and so were a lot of other innocent people.

I still had anger issues. In fact, I was having one right now, sitting here in my first-class berth on a solar-powered train en route from Orlando to Washington, DC. The bellows fanning the fire in my veins was the vanilla sway spewing from the mouth of the peroxide copper-blonde sitting across from me. "Vanilla sway" was Dad's pet term for contrived lunacy reported as fact to sway public opinion, specifically climate change "science" funded by oil companies and repeated ad nauseam on certain cable news networks and blogs until the contrived fiction became accepted as debatable evidence. My father, a progressive thinker sickened by corporate corruption, warned me that even the most outlandish lie, repeated enough times to enough people could eventually turn horseshit into vanilla, thus the term "vanilla sway." "Don't get sucked into a debate with these types, Robbie, they'll drain you like a thousand-dollar whore."

"Shall I repeat the question, Mr. Eisenbraun?"

Katherine Helms certainly appeared over my h-phone's holographic transmission like a thousand-dollar hooker, her skintight black halter top accentuating her breasts, which looked like two cantaloupes cloaked in shrink-wrap. It was an interesting ploy, considering the religious group she was representing was funded by the Clean Coal Coalition. Before you get any wild ideas about my politics, it's important I mention that the CCC's claims about producing a greenhouse gas–free fuel was simply more vanilla sway—sort of like Ms. Helms's breasts. Based on the obtuse angle of the nipples, I was 94 percent certain they were fake—not the good surgically enhanced fake either, but the virtual fake: an h-phone app designed to enhance phone sex.

Alexander Graham Bell would have been proud.

"It's *Professor* Eisenbraun, Ms. Helms, and I can hear you just fine. As to your question, any answer I give will simply be manipulated by your network to stoke the debate against fusion energy."

"Five billion people died in the GDO, Professor. Are you telling me the thought never occurred to you that the event was an act of God? Even the initials 'GDO' are an anagram for a higher power."

"It's also an anagram for 'dog'; are you saying the family pet pushed our species to the brink?"

"What I'm saying . . . what I'm asking is whether you believe God wants man tinkering with His creation."

"Based on the small size of your frame, I'm guessing God didn't bless you with those imposing thirty-six Ds. Wouldn't breast implants be considered tinkering?"

I smiled as the reporter's cheeks flushed red, her eyes narrowing. "How dare you compare my breasts to your blasphemy! I know your type, *Mister* Eisenbraun. A woman to you is nothing more than a life-support system for the vagina!"

I muted the h-phone, silencing her abusive barrage. For the record . . . wait, that's a bit redundant. Technically, all of this is for the record, recorded internally inside my skull by ABE, the Amalgamate Biological Enhancement chip I designed and had surgically implanted in my brain stem. The ABE prototype was the reason Milk Cans Malloy over there was interviewing me, only her vanilla sway was not outweighing the vision of those simulated cantaloupes bouncing on her chest, and my patience had reached its limit.

Still, I suppose the vagina comeback deserved something.

Closing my eyes, I regurgitated the first lines of an opening address I had committed to ABE memory. "If you believe that God is perfection and that we were created in His image, Ms. Helms, then why aren't we perfect? The answer lies in the human brain. Like a computer, our brain was designed to process information—in our case about four hundred billion bits of information a second. We're only aware of an infinitesimal percentage of that storehouse of memory because our brain must adhere to the programming limitations imposed by the blinding forces of our perceived reality—a reality anchored by natural selection and the weight of our evolution as a species. While there are exceptions to the rule—photographic memory . . . Mozart composing music as a child—solving abstract problems of logic or recalling previously read texts was not a skill our ancestors required to survive while hunting and foraging. Furthermore, the human brain cannot relay to the mind what our senses cannot perceive, and our senses lie to us during every waking moment.

"By the baffled look, I gather you're lost. An example then: As we speak, our planet is rotating on its axis as it soars through space at a speed exceeding eleven hundred miles a minute. And yet, we feel nothing. Why? Because our senses lie to us, concealing the velocity from our brain. The walls of this train possess atoms, each a universe unto itself, and yet we cannot perceive of the micro any more than the macro. If our senses cannot perceive it, Ms. Helms, then for us it does not exist, and yet it does. What is needed is a pair of neural spectacles that will allow us to see.

"Enter ABE, a bio-chip that allows its user to direct his or her thought impulses to the parts of the brain best suited to download, comprehend, store, and retrieve the information. Think of ABE as a television remote control, one that uses thought energy to enable its user to channel surf or immediately dial up their desired program or app."

Stealing a breath, I had ABE restore the h-phone volume, catching Mount Saint Helms in midgust.

". . . virtual research showed that eighty-six percent of a populace enhanced with your neural chip would use ABE like an LSD trip, smelling colors and seeing music in their heads. Ninety-seven percent of subjects using ABE would miss at least five hours of work each week, absorbed in some sordid act of mental masturbation. Of greater concern to many of us New Americans who adhere to the guiding principles of the Bible is that your neural chip can control the secretion of hormones like progesterone, allowing a woman to abort her own child."

And there it was. No matter what the topic, the religious radicals always steered the conversation back to what Dad had dubbed the "GAG reflex"—God, abortion, and gays—only now the crusaders had a new tool in their arsenal of crazy in which to fool the public: virtual research. The dysfunctional algorithm was a turd of vanilla sway shitted by a group of Creationists demanding that online school curriculums offer their contrived branch of science, which claimed to debunk evolution as an improvable theory.

Virtual research. The words made my blood pressure spike, causing the carotid artery in my neck to throb. For a split second I could feel my anger summoning another soul looking for a vacancy.

Ah, but I had ABE.

Sensing the emotional tsunami, my tiny neural implant reduced my level of adrenaline, causing my constricting blood vessels to redilate—a sensation similar to submerging oneself slowly into a cool pool of water on a hot summer's day.

Ah . . .

With the physical symptoms of my anger subsiding, it was time to demonstrate to Madame Mammary Glands what ABE was really about.

"*Ty mne Vanku ne valjay.*"

"Sorry, I don't speak German."

"It's Russian, Ms. Helms, and it's one of several dozen languages I

THE OMEGA PROJECT • 47

now speak, thanks to ABE's temporal lobe setting, which stimulates memory, allowing its user to create his or her own database in the time it takes one to listen to a language CD. Read a book and you've memorized the text; engage ABE's dictation unit and you can record a letter or even a novel and simultaneously download it to anyone else who possesses an ABE chip. Program ABE's self-diagnostic app and your brain will boost your body's immune system to prevent cancer or cure virtually any ailment. Immortality is within our reach, Ms. Helms. ABE bridges the gap between human frailty and human perfection; unfortunately, it doesn't come with an app that conquers human ignorance."

"If ABE has made you so smart, Professor, why were you kicked off the Omega Project?"

Ouch, didn't see that one coming. "Who told you that? An anonymous source?"

"Actually, it was Monique DeFriend. You remember Dr. DeFriend? I believe she was your supervisor for three years before the Great Die-Off. She told me you were assigned to GOLEM, the computer now being used to remotely mine the lunar surface."

"I was one of the design engineers. And I wasn't kicked off the project, I resigned . . . for personal reasons . . . to work on ABE."

"She said you'd say that. She also said, and I quote, 'While Robert Eisenbraun is a brilliant scientist, his brain enhancement chip is designed only to serve its owner's personal needs, as opposed to GOLEM, which is true artificial intelligence, created to protect and serve all of humanity. In the wake of the Great Die-Off, Professor Eisenbraun's decision to seek personal glory over the needs of mankind is more than a bit disconcerting.' Care to rebut the comment before my news outlet runs with it?"

"Ty mne Vanku ne valjay."

"Yes, you already said that. What does it mean?"

"It means, 'Don't make yourself more stupid than you already are.' Good day, Ms. Helms."

I terminated the interview, and the hologram poised above the worktable pixelized into a thousand micro fragments.

Brilliant work, Eisenbraun. So much for not tossing red meat into the arena.

The small audio device attached to my left earlobe clicked twice. "ABE, identify new caller."

ANDRIA SAXON. LOCATION: CAPE CANAVERAL.

"Accept call. On visual."

The three-dimensional video cone reappeared, revealing my beautiful fiancée, her recently trimmed short-cropped raven-black hair streaked with ocean-blue highlights that matched her eyes. Her sex was barely concealed beneath a two-piece neoprene running outfit; and her astronaut trainee's athletic physique glistened beneath a layer of sweat as she jogged at a brisk pace on an all-terrain treadmill.

She looked up at the h-phone poised above and in front of her and her smile lit me up. "Hi, babe. Still adore me?"

I held back my joy. Our last argument was still fresh on my mind. "That depends," I said, sounding a bit bitchy. "Are you calling to apologize or to break off our engagement?"

"Don't whine. You know I want to be with you forever, I'm just not comfortable planning a spring wedding right now."

"So we'll elope."

"Why don't you just club me over the head like a Neanderthal and drag me off to your cave?"

"As I recall, you were the one living in a cave when we met. And this astronaut training regimen is getting old. Seeing you three days a month isn't working for me. At least if we were married—"

"In six weeks I'll have earned my astronaut wings. Once I complete my internship at Alpha Colony—"

"Whoa, you never said anything about Alpha Colony. How long are you going to be on the moon?"

"Three weeks. It's a new requirement of all shuttle personnel, in case something goes wrong and we get stranded." She increased her speed, the simulated gravel grinding louder beneath her feet—her attempt to avoid the conversation. "After that, I'll be assigned to a fusion depot and we can plan out the rest of our lives."

"What did you say? I can barely hear you."

She changed the setting on the all-terrain treadmill from gravel to the far less noisy soft sand. The pliable surface forced her to cut her speed in half. "Better?"

"Yes."

"Six weeks and our future will be resolved. These days, six weeks to you is like six days, the way you hibernate inside your head like a Shaolin monk."

"I didn't realize I'd become that bad."

"Face it, Ike, you're addicted to your own brain device."

"Tell you what, while I'm in DC, I promise not to access ABE."

Andria smiled. "I'll bet you your collector-edition Stones CDs you can't do it."

"And if I win, we get married when I return?"

"No deal. Anyway, I already took the discs. Ike . . . you never told me, what's this meeting with your uncle all about? And why DC? The city's barely juiced."

"Uncle David told me our agenda's strictly on a need-to-know basis, and I never argue with a three-star general. Now, if we were married—"

"Fine. Don't tell."

"I don't know why he wants to see me. These days, the Pentagon has more to do with tracking power surges and estimating crop returns than security measures."

"When will you be back in Florida?"

"Miss me already?"

"Actually, there's something I need to talk to you about."

"Is this business or personal?"

"Both, and I'd rather not do it over the phone."

That gave me a moment's pause. "The weather forecast from Orlando to Washington calls for overcast skies. My travel time could be anywhere from thirteen to eighteen hours, depending on how well the train's backup batteries are working."

As if on cue, the air-conditioning in my cabin shut down, the lights dimming. "Here we go again. Computer, reduce window tint by seventy-five percent." The window, which had been a darkened rectangle, brightened to reveal a gray countryside, blurred by the bullet train's 264-mile-an-hour velocity.

"Don't worry, Ike. In a few more years we'll have mined enough helium-3 to keep the world running twenty-four/seven."

"Andie, talk to me. What's so important—"

"Gotta go, baby. Call me after your meeting, okay?"

The call powered off before I could respond.

With no sun to energize its solar-paneled roof, the bullet train gradually shed its forward inertia until it rolled to an annoying, schedule-busting, perspiration-inducing stop. Outside my private compartment, I could hear a knocking make its way toward my cabin, eventually striking my door.

"It's open."

The conductor poked his head inside my first-class berth. "Sorry for the delay, Dr. Eisenbraun. Backup batteries didn't have a chance to charge with the brownout in Charlotte. Forecasters are predicting a delay anywhere from one to three hours. Those windows go down if it gets too hot. Can I bring you a cold beverage?"

"I'm fine for now, thank you." I waited until the cabin door clicked shut, then locked it. What I had not told Andria was that it was not my uncle who had summoned me to the Pentagon, but the vice president.

The questioned remained: why?

The bullet train rolled quietly through the predawn darkness, its solar panels handicapped by the night. Only its proximity to Washington's Union Station kept the seven-car aluminum-and-steel beast inching forward at twenty miles an hour, as its backup generator suckled off the energy junction still another thirty-three miles to the north.

I stretched myself awake in the queen-size berth. Sunrise and its accompanying burst of velocity were still fifty-eight minutes away. ABE's built-in chronometer, functioning like a sixth sense, intuitively informed me the time was 6:12 A.M. Unlike the train, the tiny neurological device implanted in my brainstem was powered neither by battery nor photovoltaic cells but by my body's own internal heat. As long as I functioned, ABE functioned.

I climbed out of bed and entered the bathroom. The water closet was barely large enough to accommodate my frame. I relieved my bladder, then brushed my teeth, staring at my reflection in the oval mirror. My hair was dark brown and kept Jesus long, my beard and mustache neatly trimmed. I hadn't been without facial hair since a bad case of acne when I was seventeen. For a long moment I contemplated shaving, if only to get a reaction from Andie. I thought better of it, though. I was afraid the acne might have left pockmarks on my cheeks, and who needed to see that?

Stepping out of the bathroom, I dropped to my chest on the warm tile floor and pumped out a quick set of push-ups, stopping at thirty. One whiff of the musky scent coming from my armpits sent me back to the sink for a sloppy hand washing, followed by a fresh coat of antiperspirant.

Now what? A train ride that should have been completed in seven hours had entered its second day, thanks to fluctuating weather patterns and a new power grid still in its infancy. A year after developing

ABE, I had considered purchasing an old steam locomotive and fitting it with a system that used the train's own rotating wheels to keep a series of batteries permanently charged. By the time I had set my design to paper, the world had committed its future to an entirely new source of energy.

As the air conditioner clicked on I sighed with relief, feeling a wave of cold air filling the cabin as the train's velocity increased.

At precisely 7:14 in the morning, twenty-five hours after I had boarded the train in Orlando, I stepped out onto the concrete platform of Union Station's upper level. Unlike in Central Florida, the morning air here was crisp with an autumn chill, forcing me to root through my old gym bag for a sweatshirt. Andria hated the relic, threatening to burn it along with my old college boxer shorts with the exposed elastic in back, but I'm a creature of habit, and besides, I prefer a carry-on that I can sling over my shoulder or, if need be, use as a pillow. With the city's escalators no longer running, my way proved more pragmatic than Andria's fancy suitcase on wheels.

Adjusting the sack of clothing over my left shoulder, I followed the other two dozen passengers into the historic terminal.

A vaulted ceiling heavy in Roman architecture greeted me as I made my way through the dimly lit 121-year-old structure. The GDO hadn't been kind. The food court was gone and the storefronts were all empty, looted a decade earlier. A recent restoration project had cleaned up the vacant shops and their rodent population, but the terminal remained a generation away from returning to its stature as a tourist Mecca.

For now, Union Station served as the primary energy junction between Richmond, Virginia and Philadelphia, its nine hundred solar panels, lined up in rows atop its roof and the open upper deck of its closed parking garage, providing 150 kilowatts of power to the bullet train and the surrounding neighborhoods within the sparsely populated District of Columbia.

I followed the signs leading downstairs and headed for the exit at Columbus Circle. My h-phone growled in my pants pocket before I could step outside.

CALLER IDENTIFIED. DAVID SCHALL. LOCATION: UNIDENTIFIED.

"Accept call, audio only. Uncle David, where are you?"

"Still at the Pentagon. I sent a car for you. Stay where you are, it's homing in on your signal."

As I glanced out the station exit a black sedan suddenly raced east across the deserted curved tarmacs intersecting Columbus Circle. The vehicle's wailing siren scattered pedestrians as it stopped ten feet from the Mall entrance.

"You prefer shotgun or backseat?"

"Shotgun."

The front passenger door popped open.

Shouldering my way past nosy civilians, I climbed in the front seat and the door automatically closed behind me. The dashboard harbored a six-inch-diameter steering wheel, air vents, and an entertainment station set that now displayed its GPS map.

There was no driver, the vehicle empty but for me.

"Geez, Uncle David, could you at least activate a hologram?"

A young Hispanic woman materialized in the driver's seat, a voluptuous long-haired brunette dressed in a black chauffeur's uniform. The upper portion of her jacket was unbuttoned low enough to reveal a tantalizing view of her well-proportioned brown left breast.

"I'm Selena. Sit back, buckle up, and enjoy the view." She winked at me as the car accelerated down Columbus Circle.

"What is it with this country and holographic breasts?"

Selena distorted, her youthful body morphing into the frail figure of a woman in her eighties. Hunched over the small steering wheel, she turned to me slack jawed, her eyes magnified behind Coke-bottle-thick glasses. "Name's Greta. Wanna see my holographic boobies?"

My uncle's shrill laugh filled the car. "What's wrong, Robbie? You look pale."

"I think I just threw up in my mouth."

The image enlarged, the uniform filling into a nondescript black man.

"Better. Now maybe you can tell me why I'm here?"

"Not now. Sit back and enjoy the ride, I'll see you in twenty."

The call ended, leaving me alone with the holographic chauffeur and the silence of an electric engine powered by a trunk filled with batteries. The view of the former capital of the United States remained disturbing, eight years of nature unbound, the weeds bursting through the concrete slab like a miniature forest.

Within minutes, the car had exited the interstate, following North Rotary Road past near-empty overgrown parking lots. An automated checkpoint allowed us access to Heliport Road, which led to the northern Mall entrance of what had once been the hub of the most powerful military in history.

My uncle exited the Pentagon's west entrance to greet me. My only surviving blood relative was dressed in his military uniform despite the fact that standing armies no longer existed. General David Schall was sixty-seven and silver haired, with piercing blue-gray eyes that held a glint in the morning light.

"There he is. Give your uncle a proper greeting." The West Point graduate bear-hugged me, whispering in my ear. "Vanilla sway."

I froze at the mention of my father's private code word.

"I'm glad you could stop by, Robbie. There's about a dozen coworkers in the energy sector who are dying to meet you. Do you mind coming in and saying hello before we head home to see your aunt Aunt Carol? I'm sure she won't mind."

Stop by? "Sure, I'd be happy to say hello."

My pulse racing, I followed my uncle into the building, ABE immediately alerting me to the body scan as I passed through a concealed metal detector. "How is Aunt Carol?"

"Busy trying to turn Georgetown back into a proper college town." The general paused at a Plexiglas security door, then looked up at a grapefruit-size metal orb poised to the right of the sealed entrance, its core glowing a phosphorescent neon blue.

To my surprise, my uncle addressed the mechanical eyeball. "I believe you're acquainted with my nephew. Robert Eisenbraun, say hello to GOLEM."

"Greetings, Professor Eisenbraun."

Too stunned to reply, I simply stared at the sensory device like a father suddenly confronted by his estranged child.

6

It takes a great enemy to make a great plane.
   —U.S. Air Force saying

The deep mechanical voice was male; hollow and metallic—devoid of any human personality.

A look from my uncle warned me about asking questions.

"GOLEM, I want to bring my nephew down to the control room to say hello to the vice president. I think an hour's visitor's pass should be more than adequate."

"Security clearance granted."

Uncle David escorted me through the unmanned security checkpoint, then down an antiseptic white corridor to a series of elevators. We took the first one, descended six stories in silence, then exited to a steel door requiring a clearance pass. The general swiped his plastic card, its magnetic strip opening the lock with a *click*.

With my curiosity burning, I followed my uncle into the control room, a high school gymnasium-size chamber of reinforced concrete and steel. Rows of computer terminals were occupied by men and women in jeans, shirts, and white lab coats. The entire forward wall was a computerized map of the world. The Space Tracking and Surveillance System, an elaborate satellite-based array originally designed to home in on submarine signatures and ballistic missile activity, now traced power outages along a fractured North American energy grid.

No one so much as looked up as we walked by.

The general pointed to the map. "The green blips are wind farms; orange, solar arrays; the blue, hydroelectric dams. As you can see, their coverage bands are quite limited. Problem is, we can't expand the grid without the petroleum-based plastics and other raw materials necessary to erect the infrastructure. It takes energy to make energy—in this case the energy needed to recycle raw materials for new uses, so it's two steps forward and one back."

"What are those blinking red lights?"

"Fusion reactors. All under construction. Once we get them online this grid will light up like a Christmas tree." My uncle looked around, perhaps more for the glowing blue orb along the ceiling than for me. "The VP should just be finishing his meeting, let's say hello."

Like a dutiful soldier, I followed my uncle up a short flight of stairs that led to an atrium and the outer doors of what I assumed was a conference room, with the tinting on the thick soundproof plastic windows adjusted for privacy. The general pressed his thumb to a keypad and the locks clicked open.

Inside, seven men and two women were seated around an oval smart table. Most of the people in the lab coats were familiar—each scientist representing a key sector of the Omega Project.

The strapping gentleman in the gray suit seated at the end of the table flashed a broad smile as he strutted around the table to embrace me. "Ike, how the hell are you?"

"Good, Lee. Real good. Or should I call you Mr. Vice President?"

"Let's keep it formal for now. Turn around, let me see the back of your skull."

I complied without comment.

When we were facing again, he said, "So you actually went ahead and did it. I wouldn't have had the guts."

"The surgery's fairly simple, and the results are incredible. It's like having the Internet in your head."

"If it's all the same, I think I'll just stick with my h-phone. Sit down, pal, we have a lot to discuss. General Schall, why don't you handle the heavy lifting?"

My uncle motioned me into one of the two vacant chairs. "This room is a quiet zone, meaning—"

"Meaning GOLEM can't eavesdrop."

The general nodded. "Before you assume the worst, I think every person in this room would agree the computer's performance over the last twenty-one months has been close to flawless, giving us the confidence to use the system to oversee other science-related sectors outside of the energy department. In doing so an interesting thing happened. The more we asked the GOLEM system to handle—"

"The more efficient the computer became," I said, looking around the room. "It's part of the computer's adaptive programming. Which sectors has GOLEM linked to?"

"SEA personnel, both domestic and international, all of NASA's missions, past and present, as well as Hubble. GOLEM's been using the telescope as a sort of lunar GPS system."

"Clever. Optimizing the usage of these varied sensory systems no doubt increased the length of GOLEM's solution strands, along with the computer's functional IQ, again all part of its adaptive programming."

One of the female scientists cut me off. "Dr. Eisenbraun, does GOLEM's adaptive programming include the development of proactive mechanisms?"

"Absolutely."

"Then maybe you can explain the difference between proactive mechanisms and cognitive independence."

Uh-oh. I glanced around the room. The other scientists' expressions were as disconcerted as mine must have been. "Are you saying GOLEM has been functioning independent of its programming?"

"We're not sure," the vice president said, "which is one of the reasons we summoned you to Washington. Dr. Nilsson's in charge of the helium-3 conversion program, I'll let him explain."

Thomas Nilsson was the Swedish geologist who had developed the computer's Lunar Soil Analysis Program, or L-SAP. "Hello again, Dr. Eisenbraun. We have a most disturbing situation. Five months ago, your computer sent a priority message to all departments. Among other things, the message contained a chemical analysis of samples taken from each of the seventeen helium-3 caches it had mined from the moon's surface. According to its analysis, the gas derived from the ore wasn't pure enough to create a stable fusion reaction; in other words, the helium-3 was useless. As you can imagine, we were all a bit overwhelmed."

I groaned at the colossal setback, the news hitting me like a punch to the gut. "All that work . . . all that money."

Dr. Nilsson held up his hand. "There's more. Using data from NASA's old reconnaissance files, GOLEM indicated it had located an

THE OMEGA PROJECT • 57

alternative source of helium-3, one that would render a stable fusion reaction with a far greater energy output."

"That's fantastic. Where's the source?"

"Underwater." Thomas Nilsson engaged the smart-table, accessing a hologram of Jupiter. "Beneath the frozen ocean on Jupiter's moon, Europa."

My eyes widened as I watched the moons orbiting Jupiter enlarge, the hologram now focused solely on Europa, its frozen surface scarred with a chaotic highway of fracture zones.

"This is crazy," I said. "The technology required to get to Europa—"

"The computer accounted for that by designing a solar sail for one of the helium-3 transport shuttles."

"Really? Wow." I shook away the distraction of ego. "Still, Europa? We haven't put a man on Mars. Where's the data to even support such a mission?"

Thomas smirked. "The computer reconfigured the data downloaded from NASA's old Galileo probe. The helium-3 is being dispersed from hydrothermal vents located along the Europa seafloor."

My uncle turned to face me. "GOLEM's assessment is pretty enticing—one manned mission to Jupiter's moon has a potential economic value in the order of three trillion dollars. Despite the news, we were still grappling with this unexpected setback, and so we ordered GOLEM to continue its mining operations while we readied a lunar shuttle to transport a scientific team to Alpha Colony to examine the ore caches. That's when GOLEM decided to let us know who the alpha dog was."

Thomas nodded. "Your computer shut down all strip-mining operations on the moon. Then it sent out e-mails instructing teams of engineers and skilled laborers to report to Caltech to begin immediate construction on *Oceanus,* a manned underwater habitat designed by the computer to mine helium-3 on Europa."

"It designed a habitat?" I found myself beaming. The thought of an artificial intelligence independently creating a habitat for a mission it had conceived from scratch . . . it was surreal. Still, I could see why Omega's administrators were unnerved. "After GOLEM shut down mining operations, did you attempt to override the system?"

"Of course we did," the female scientist replied. "Nothing we did made a bit of difference. GOLEM's interpretation of the situation was that it was following that damn prime directive you imprinted upon its matrix."

"To protect and preserve the human species—I forgot all about that."

"Yes, well GOLEM didn't forget. Since the machine equates mining helium-3 with preserving the human species, its defense systems counteracted any actions we attempted."

"Which is exactly why the computer, and not some politician, was placed in charge of the Omega Project." The man forcing his way into the conversation was in his early sixties, his gray hairline receding, his paunchy physique poorly concealed beneath a tailored Italian business suit. "Sebastian Koch, Koch Fusion Industries. KFI is the power company that funded a significant amount of this lunar venture. I've met with Dr. DeFriend, and she and I agree this computer of yours is acting in all of our best interests."

"How can you be so sure?" Thomas asked.

"I'm sure because GOLEM isn't a politician, it's a machine designed to think . . . to adapt. Unlike some of the people in this room, it won't massage the message in order to remain in office, or spend time defending its own scientific theories in order to justify its employment. GOLEM ceased operations on the moon because it refused to waste any more time, money, or KFI resources on a course of action that it knew would fail to meet the mission's objectives. Instead, it located a suitable source of helium-3, designed the habitat required to secure the compound from Europa, then put together the talent necessary to complete the mission as efficiently and as cost-effectively as possible."

Vice President Udelsman slammed both palms on the table. "Under whose authority is GOLEM operating, Mr. Koch? Last time I checked, my office was in charge of the Space Energy Agency. Not KFI. Not Dr. DeFriend. And certainly not some goddamn computer!"

"The computer's programmed to safeguard humanity. It doesn't need your permission," said Koch.

"Easy, fellas," I said, attempting to quell the crossfire. "The underlying question that needs to be answered is whether GOLEM's evaluation of the moon's helium-3 is correct."

"Agreed," my uncle said. "Next week, the lunar shuttle should finally be ready to launch, transporting thirty-seven geologists, sixteen fusion engineers, and another twenty scientists to Alpha Colony. Their job is to analyze every sample of lunar soil collected over the last two years to determine whether the computer's evaluation is correct."

"So why am I here?"

The vice president leaned forward in his chair. "You're here because you were the key scientist involved with the development of GOLEM's biological matrix. You're here because I want to know if this souped-up mechanical brain of yours has gone rogue like the computer from that *2001: A Space Odyssey* movie . . . What was its name, Amanda?"

The auburn-haired civilian seated next to Udelsman answered without looking up from her h-phone. "HAL."

"HAL. Right. Damn thing took over the astronauts' ship."

Sebastian Koch shook his head. "What are you afraid of, Mr. Vice President? That by accessing personnel files and designing a means to collect helium-3 from Europa, GOLEM will take over the world? Face facts: You and your scientists were wrong about using the moon's supply of helium-3 to stabilize our fusion reactors. That setback, though painful for you to swallow, has been addressed by GOLEM. Thanks to the computer—and Koch Fusion, in six years our planet will have enough clean, self-sustaining power to meet our species' energy needs for the next thousand years . . . and beyond."

"It'll take six years to build GOLEM's ocean-mining habitat?" I asked, feeling a bit disappointed. "That doesn't seem very efficient for a sophisticated AI."

Sebastian Koch smirked. "For your information, Dr. Eisenbraun, *Oceanus* is already built. As we speak, it's being transported, along with the GOLEM mainframe, to the Ross Ice Shelf in Antarctica for a six-week training exercise."

Okay, that seemed pretty impressive. But it still didn't answer my question. "General, why am I here?"

"You're here," the vice president interjected, "because ultimately it's my decision whether the United Nations will spend another twenty-seven billion dollars to launch this damn computer and its crew of twelve handpicked scientists on a six-year voyage to Jupiter. And you, Dr. Eisenbraun, are the most qualified person to advise me."

Taking his cue, the general stood. "Dr. Eisenbraun, if you'd remain behind for a moment. The rest of you, thank you for coming. You'll know our decision by this evening."

The conference room emptied, save for the vice president, his female assistant, and my uncle. I found myself breathing a sigh of relief. "Geez, thanks for the invite, Lee. Exactly how many people know their careers are hanging on my decision?"

"Too many to count."

"You really believe GOLEM is acting independently of its programming?"

"According to an expert on biological DNA computers, the possibility certainly exists."

"Who's the expert?"

"You are, pal. General, refresh your nephew's memory."

My uncle activated the playback on his h-phone. It was a phone conversation recorded several years ago. The voice speaking to Dr. DeFriend was mine. *". . . artificial intelligence systems using biochemical algorithms possessing complex adaptive systems have the potential to internally overanalyze their own prime directives, creating closed-circuit loops of segregated DNA strands. This activity can corrupt the system in that these favored solution patterns are filed away as 'perfection' and therefore are no longer subjected to rigorous reevaluation. The AI validates this new protocol in a vacuum—a cognitive state that most psychiatrists would define as 'psychopathic ego.'"*

The general shut off the recording.

The vice president stared at me as if I had concealed a crime. "You reported your findings to Dr. DeFriend—why wasn't I told?"

"I followed protocol. Monique decided that the gains of fusion far outweighed any potential closed-loop threat."

"Would it have killed you to have stuck around to address the problem?"

"Monique was in charge. I had another calling."

"Right. You needed to create a bio-chip that enabled its users to virtually masturbate twenty-four/seven."

My fists balled, my blood pressure spiked, and it took all of ABE's rapid bio-adjustments to keep me from tossing a chair across the table at our nation's second-in-command. "Listen, *Lee*, don't blame me or the computer if your helium-3 calculations turned out to be wrong. As for my biological chip, it's far more important to humanity's future than fusion energy."

"How do you figure that?"

I exhaled, suddenly feeling euphoric. "Sorry. What did you ask? Oh, right, ABE. Lee, I didn't create ABE to compute calculus or learn Latin or to overstimulate the brain's pleasure centers, I designed the bio-chip to prevent our minds from acting upon our most primordial, ego-based instincts. When the chip-bearer exhibits the physiological symptoms associated with emotions like anger, hatred, and jealousy, ABE causes the brain to release serotonin, a neurotransmitter that creates a happy feeling. Think about it: No more crime, no more self-induced extinctions. I left Omega because I was more interested in affecting the evolution of man, not machine."

"That's very commendable," my uncle said, "but the vice president and I need to know if a closed-logic loop in GOLEM's matrix could be responsible for the computer acting on its own when it ceased all lunar mining operations."

"It's possible. But again, the process that brought GOLEM to determine that course of action would have to be based on its interpretation of its prime directive. The only way ceasing mining operations protects humanity is if the moon's supply of helium-3 is, in fact, ineffective."

"Could the computer be programmed to falsify its helium-3 results if it interpreted fusion to be a danger to the propagation of our species?"

"Yes, but only if that conclusion originated from within its solution matrix."

"Who do you know that might be capable of pulling that off?"

"Besides me? Dr. DeFriend could do it, along with any one of a dozen level-four computer engineers. Having worked with most of them, I seriously doubt they would want to derail the project."

"You haven't worked with these people for years," the vice president shot back. "Fusion energy has its detractors and competitors. The remnants of Big Oil have formed an energy coalition with the coal and tar sands industry. Don't think for a minute Monique DeFriend or key members of her staff are immune to accepting a bribe."

"Okay, so you wait until your team returns from the moon with their results. I don't see a problem here."

"The problem," my uncle said, "is that the helium-3 analysis won't be completed until mid-January. The next launch window to Europa opens on December fifteenth. Miss that date and it's a nineteen-month wait until Jupiter's orbit aligns again with Earth's."

In a millisecond, ABE calculated the distance between Earth and Jupiter, which varied between 376 million miles and 600 million miles, all dependent on the two planets' independent orbits of the sun. Absorbed in a cartography chart displayed subliminally upon my mind's eye, I failed to notice the vice president staring at me.

"Sorry. And I wasn't mentally masturbating."

"Ike, I'm sure ABE will one day win you the Nobel Prize. But we're at a serious crossroads. If we fail to launch the Europa mission and the computer turns out to be right about the moon's supply of helium-3, then the fossil fuel industry takes over and it's 2012 all over again, only a lot worse. The carbon dioxide imprint from tar sands is far more toxic than oil. We'll have runaway climate change within a decade."

"And if you launch in December and the helium-3 turns out to be satisfactory?"

"Then our administration looks like a bunch of clowns and we lose the midterms, jeopardizing the entire space energy program. As we've seen, the voting public suffers from short-term memory loss."

"Okay, so how can I help?"

The general lowered his voice, perhaps not fully convinced the room was soundproof. "Robbie, an opportunity has arisen that would allow you to evaluate both GOLEM and Dr. DeFriend's team during the six-week training mission. Your observations would ultimately determine whether we launch in December."

"Exactly what does this training mission entail? Koch mentioned it takes place in Antarctica?"

The general nodded. "It's the only place on Earth that resembles conditions on Europa. The exercise begins with the submersion of the *Oceanus* habitat through a mile-thick sheet of ice where it will remain anchored to the bottom of the Ross Sea, paralleling operations set for Europa. Once the habitat is in place, the team will rig the ship's couplings to a series of hydrothermal vents. The vents will be capped, with the superheated waters redirected through pipes to an underwater platform where gases—in this case sulfur dioxide substituting for helium-3, will be separated and stored in tanks for transportation back to the mother ship."

"Your job," the VP's assistant said, "will involve working directly with GOLEM to evaluate the psychological fitness of the crew." She stood, sliding a medical report across the table. "These are the results of a mandatory psychiatric evaluation given to each member of the Omega crew at the time they were selected by GOLEM for the Europa mission. In reviewing the reports, we discovered one of the male crewmen possesses a minor sociopathic personality trait. Our medical staff missed it the first time because it's a borderline condition, but one that could be exacerbated under the duress of working in an isolated habitat over a long period of time. Because of the seriousness of the situation and the potential disruption related to replacing a member of the crew this late into the mission, the Space Agency agreed to use the six-week training operation as a means to covertly evaluate whether the crewman can handle his duties under pressure. GOLEM was made aware of the results of the evaluation two days ago, but the name of the scientist was purposely withheld. The computer was then asked to select an alternate from its backup list, someone who could be added to the training mission as a potential replacement on the Europa voyage without causing suspicion, but who also had the experience to diagnose a possible psychological disorder."

My uncle, curse him, smiled at me. "Congratulations."

"Who . . . me? Exactly how did I make GOLEM's backup list? I'm no astronaut."

"Neither are most of these other scientists. You were, however, the man who developed GOLEM's biological software, and you did graduate with a dual major in psychology."

"No, I didn't."

The VP's assistant winked. "We sort of fudged that one. Fortunately, the computer bought it. You'll join the crew aboard *Oceanus* in two days. Once you submerge, you'll have two weeks to evaluate GOLEM for a potential closed-logic loop, or determine whether De-Friend or any of the others purposely sabotaged the helium-3 results on the moon."

"Two weeks? I thought you said the training mission would last six weeks."

"The Antarctic mission is six weeks," the annoying woman said. "The last four weeks you'll be asleep."

"What's that supposed to mean?"

"The journey out to Jupiter's moon will take thirteen months. That presents a few challenges. Exposure to zero gravity over such a prolonged period of time can result in a serious loss of bone density and muscle mass among the crew. Because all available storage space aboard the solar shuttle must be relegated to transporting the *Oceanus* habitat, the voyage out will also be quite cramped. Cosmonaut and astronaut training programs showed that the psychological effects of being kept in a confined space caused bouts of depression that divided the crew and led to physical confrontations. It won't be so bad aboard *Oceanus* once gravity returns, but the voyage out to Europa and back is especially risky. GOLEM's solution was to place all twelve astronauts in cryogenic suspension. This will not only remove the physical and mental duress of the trip, but will also save fuel related to not having to transport thirteen months worth of food and water."

"Cryogenic suspension? Yeah, I can see how that makes sense. I just hope for the crew's sake it isn't the same freezing technique used by those life extension foundations thirty years ago. Didn't one of them freeze Ted Williams's head?"

"That was an entirely different process, used specifically to deep-freeze recently deceased patients so they could be revived at a future date—assuming their disease had been cured by then. Using cryogenic suspension—cold sleep—on healthy, living humans is not only safe and proven, but fairly simple. After receiving a series of injections designed to internally nourish and preserve the body's vital organs, the crewman or woman is sedated, then secured in a cryogenic pod filled with a gel composed of tetrodotoxin. The subject neither ages nor feels a thing, their mind simply slips into a deep hypnotic state—a new type of ultra-slow brain-wave activity now officially classified as 'Omega waves.' The thawing process includes a series of minor electrical shocks and, in a worst-case scenario, an injection of epinephrine directly into the heart. I'm told the hibernation process is quite soothing, like taking a long nap."

Uncle David squeezed my arm as if giving advice to the bar mitzvah boy. "Omega's training exercise will conclude with the crew being placed in cryogenic stasis for thirty days. GOLEM will control the entire process, maintaining the cryogenic pods within a sealed chamber aboard *Oceanus*. There will be a thirteenth pod rigged outside of the cryogenic chamber outside of GOLEM's control . . . for you."

"General, you can't be serious."

"It's the only way. You have to convince GOLEM that you're preparing in earnest to take over for the crewman in question. If the computer suspects otherwise, who knows how it will react."

"With all due respect, there's no way in hell I'm climbing into a cryogenic pod so that some souped-up computer can pour goo over me and turn me into a human Popsicle—not for a month or a year, or one day, for that matter!"

General Schall grimaced. "In that case, you leave us no choice. Mr. Vice President, I formally recommend we proceed with Omega. We'll just have to hope, for the sake of those twelve astronauts and the rest of the world that the computer is functioning fine and the members of its

crew are sound of mind and have not been coerced by the fossil fuel industry. It's risky, but then Andria Saxon and the rest of her team knew
that when they accepted GOLEM's invitation to join the mission."

I felt the blood rush from my face. "Andria's one of the Omega astronauts? My Andria?"

"She didn't tell you? Oh, that's right, this was all kept top secret.
Sorry, son. Best to enjoy your time together now, seeing as how she won't
be returning to Earth for another six years."

7

*I believe that Europa is the most promising place in the
solar system for astrobiological potential.*
—Robert Pappalardo, study scientist for the Europa mission
at the NASA Jet Propulsion Laboratory, August 28, 2009

EAST ANTARCTICA
SEPTEMBER 25, 2028

Antarctica: coldest region on Earth—5.5 million square miles of ice that doubled in size each winter as the surface of its surrounding oceans freeze six feet thick. With an ice cap that averaged over a mile deep, the continent held 70 percent of the world's freshwater. If this ice were ever to melt, sea levels would rise two hundred feet.

Larger than both Australia and the United States, Antarctica was also the highest continent on the planet, its landmass unevenly divided into eastern and western sections by the hundred-million-year-old Transantarctic mountain chain.

West Antarctica, located below the tip of South America, was the smaller of the two regions, encompassing two major ice shelves and Mount Erebus, an active volcano. Global warming was a far greater threat in West Antarctica, as much of its ice sheet lay below sea level.

East Antarctica, located on the Indian Ocean side of the mountain range, occupied two-thirds of the continent. A mountainous desert of ice, it was the coldest, driest, and most desolate location on the planet.

Antarctica was not always a frozen wasteland; its landmass was once a temperate zone, part of the supercontinent, Gondwana. Two hundred and fifty million years ago Gondwana broke apart, an event that caused Antarctica to separate and drift over the equatorial seas. Coniferous forests dominated the landmass during the Cretaceous period, a green habitat that supported Antarctica's dinosaur population.

Twenty-three million years ago the Drake Passage opened below South America, further isolating the continent. Oceanic currents and tectonic plate movements combined to push Antarctica to its present location over the South Pole where colder temperatures attributed to a drop in planetary carbon-dioxide levels, decimating the forests while leaving in its place a permanent ice cap that has covered the entire land-mass over the last six million years.

As the Earth revolved around the sun, our planet was also rotating 23.4 degrees on its axis. From the spring equinox on March twentieth until the vernal equinox on September twenty-second, the South Pole was tilted away from the sun, casting Antarctica into six months of frigid darkness. The sun returns in late September, warming the conti-nent through February.

Despite its frigid temperatures, Antarctica was home to the most fertile oceanic feeding habitat on Earth, its surrounding seas forming a convergence zone where cold water meets warmer currents flowing down from the north. Nourishing plant and animal life, Antarctic seas attracted everything from giant schools of tiny krill to pods of blue whales, the largest creatures ever to inhabit our planet.

The Boeing CH-47 Chinook heaved and rattled, its twin 4,733 horsepower engines commanding its pair of tandem rotating blades to elevate the 24,000 pound helicopter and its crew into the crisp Antarc-tic air. Powered by a combination of hydrogen fuel cells and a coveted supply of jet fuel held at the Casey Station outpost, the converted mili-tary transport had just enough range to deliver its crew and my cursed uncle and me to our destination on Ross Island.

I pressed my forehead against the cargo bay's frosted window, gazing out at the seemingly endless white landscape. My eyes followed the chopper's shadow as it crossed Wilkes Land, ABE instantaneously feeding my mind information:

WILKES LAND. LOCATION: EAST ANTARCTICA.

A FROZEN DESERT OF ICE, THREE MILES THICK. CONCEALED BENEATH THE ICE SHEET IS THE LARGEST METEOR IMPACT CRATER ON EARTH. DISCOVERED BY NASA'S GRACE SATELLITE TEAM, THE CRATER IS THREE HUNDRED MILES WIDE AND WAS CREATED BY THE CELESTIAL IMPACT OF AN OBJECT THIRTY

MILES IN DIAMETER. THE IMPACT OCCURRED APPROXIMATELY 250 MILLION
YEARS AGO, RESULTING IN THE PERMIAN-TRIASSIC EXTINCTION, THE LARGEST
EXTINCTION EVENT IN HISTORY. THE IMPACT WIPED OUT 99 PERCENT OF ALL
LIFE-FORMS ON THE PLANET—AN EVOLUTIONARY PREREQUISITE THAT LED TO
THE RISE OF THE DINOSAURS. THE IMPACT IS NOW CREDITED WITH INITIATING
THE TECTONIC RIFT THAT CAUSED THE BREAKUP AND SEPARATION OF THE
GONDWANA SUPERCONTINENT, LEADING TO THE FORMATION AND PRESENT-
DAY RELOCATION OF THE SEVEN MAJOR CONTINENTS.

I blinked away the information overload, preferring to obsess over the thoughts that had dominated my every waking moment over the last twenty-four hours.

It had begun with a call to Andria—a conversation that quickly degenerated into a shouting match. How could she have accepted a six-year mission to Europa without telling me? Did she expect me to wait for her? How would she react if our roles were reversed?

In the heat of battle I decided not to mention anything about my trip to the Pentagon or that I'd be joining her aboard *Oceanus* for the Omega practice run. By the time I phoned her back three hours later, Andie and her fellow crewmen were already en route to the South Pole, all means of communicating with the outside world silenced.

A harsh katabatic wind buffeted the chopper, separating me from my thoughts. Three days earlier, the sun had peaked above the Antarctic horizon, bringing an end to six months of wintery darkness. Despite the returning daylight, spring would not arrive until mid-November, the sea ice finally thawing in January.

"Robbie, you okay?"

I turned to my uncle, who was seated next to me. The two of us were dressed in thermal long johns, ski pants, and boots, and were seated on our goose-down parkas, the hard bench seats no picnic on our bouncing buttocks. "I was just thinking about Andria."

"Your problem is that you think too much. You'll be seeing her in about six hours. Which reminds me, it's time for your next shot."

"I told you, I'm committed to the Omega trial but I'm not being frozen."

"And I told you, GOLEM will never allow you on board *Oceanus* without blood work. The Omega astronauts have already received a month's worth of shots. You'll need to double up on your protocol over the next two weeks, right up until the moment the crew is frozen. At that time, you can inform the computer that you've determined the suspected crewman is fine to stay with the mission, and that instead of being held in cryogenic stasis you'll be using your designated sleep time to catch up on your reading. That'll give you another four weeks to observe GOLEM."

My response was silenced by another wave of turbulence, the violent wind gusts peppering the Chinook with ice particles as the airship soared west over the Transantarctic mountain range, heading for the Ross Ice Shelf.

Formed and fed by eight mammoth glaciers, the Ross Ice Shelf was a six-hundred-mile-long, five-hundred-mile-wide sheet of ice, a half-mile thick. Floating atop Antarctica's Southern Ocean, this sheer white cliff occasionally fractured, calving city-size icebergs into the Ross Sea, which formed the shelf's southwestern border.

Another eighty minutes passed before the military transport slowed to hover over McMurdo Station.

Established in 1955, located on Ross Island's Hut Point Peninsula, McMurdo Station was a research center shared by scientists throughout the world. Functioning like a small town, the southernmost community in the world featured four airport runways on hard ice, a harbor, and more than one hundred prefabricated buildings, including dormitories, a commissary, gymnasium, general store, post office, barbershop, a radio and television station, chapel, and an aquarium. Buildings were numbered based on the order in which they were built. During winter months, it was not unusual for these structures to outnumber McMurdo's residents.

The Chinook shuddered violently as it landed on the helipad's permanent ice. Our arrival summoned a four-wheel-drive military vehicle. Its rear axle sported triangular-shaped traction belts and the front tires had been replaced with skis. An electric heater, installed beneath the hood, kept the engine block from cracking.

Securing my jacket's hood over my head, I climbed down from the chopper to chase after my uncle in the glacial cold.

There is cold, there is freezing cold, then there is bone-rattling, witch's tit, get-me-the-fuck-outta-here cold. Three days ago, I had boarded a solar-powered train in Orlando. The dawn temperature that day had been a balmy 82°F. As I stepped out into the Antarctic dawn, the wind-chilled air was minus five. Overhead, a cobalt-blue sky was streaked with a neon lime-green ghost of color. The charged particles of the aurora australis appeared to slither a snake's dance toward Mount

Erebus, the twelve-thousand-foot-high active volcano looming to the east.

The wind howled across the compound, stinging my ears and crystallizing tears in my unprotected eyes. The truck's warmth beckoned and I shoved my uncle inside the back of the vehicle, then slid in next to him. I slammed the door shut, silencing the continent's retreating winter. My body was trembling.

The driver was dressed head to toe in an internally heated environmental suit. Removing his mask, he turned to greet us, revealing a mop of straw-colored hair and flushed cheeks. "Major Phillip Gazen. Welcome to the icebox, General. My instructions are to take you and your nephew to the CSEC for an oh-six-hundred briefing."

"Where's the rest of the Omega team?" I asked.

"Two of the team—a man and a woman—are doing prep work in the Crary labs. The others are already at the deployment site, thirty-seven miles to the northwest. The ice sheet's a mile thick out there, blasted by a katabatic wind so cold it'll quick-freeze your nut sack into ice cubes within two minutes. Enjoy the tropics of McMurdo while you can, gentlemen. You'll soon be experiencing the true definition of Antarctic cold."

Lovely . . .

The driver wove the growling vehicle toward the center of the compound and the Crary Science and Engineering Center, the largest facility on Ross Island. Laid out as a series of three prefabricated buildings linked by a long shaftlike corridor, the CSEC's interconnected phases totaled 46,500 square feet of workspace.

Major Gazen parked at the top of the hill in front of the entrance to the first and largest of the CSEC's three rectangular buildings—a two-story structure elevated on pilings five feet above its rocky foundation. "Welcome to the Crary Center. This building is Phase I. Your briefing will take place in forty minutes in the conference room of Phase II; just follow the long ramp into the next building. Make yourselves at home, gentlemen, there's coffee and sandwiches set up for you in the library upstairs. Oh, one last thing: Because of the dry windy conditions, there's no smoking, candle lighting, or incense burning allowed anywhere on McMurdo Station. See you after the briefing."

"Major, wait. Where can I find the woman from the Omega team?"

"Hell if I know. Try the women's room."

I slammed the truck door, muting Gazen's laughter. Hustling after my uncle, I followed him up a concrete ramp leading to the Crary Center's air-locked double doors.

The interior of Phase I resembled a modern hospital without the smell of sick people. Its corridor was white tiled, its doorjambs trimmed in pink. There were labs and equipment rooms and offices, everything open—but no one to be found.

"Like a ghost town," I muttered.

"The sun may be up, but we're still four months away from the Ross Sea opening to ships," my uncle explained. "I bet there's less than a hundred people on this entire outpost. I need to find a bathroom."

"I need to find Andria."

Leaving my uncle, I followed the main corridor until it connected to a long sloping ramp that led into the building known as Phase II. The structure was divided into an Earth Sciences pod and an Atmospheric Sciences pod. Entering the latter, I hurried through a maze of offices, quickly lost my bearings, and found myself in a short hall that dead-ended at closed double doors.

A nameplate identified the interior as TELESCOPE. I could hear someone speaking inside and entered.

The chamber was dark, save for the fluorescent glow emanating from four computer monitors mounted in a staggered formation above a sophisticated GPS station. A silver-haired man who looked to be in his late seventies was working at the terminal, conversing with another party on a landline.

". . . according to the last set of images, Arthur, the absolute magnitude of 1997 XF11 has changed. Either the asteroid's a lot bigger than we thought, or its trajectory was altered when it passed Jupiter. Either way, I want you and Carol to recalculate the error eclipse for the pass on October twenty-sixth."

Hanging up the phone, the scientist swiveled around in his chair to face me. "Another visitor? It's getting pretty crowded around here. Lowell Krawitz, International Astronomical Union."

"Robert Eisenbraun. Would one of the other visitors happen to be a woman? Dark hair. Athletic. About my age."

"Last time I saw her, she was working in the aquarium. Follow the main corridor to Phase III."

"Thanks. So, this asteroid . . . how close will it pass to Earth?"

"Close is a matter of perspective. She'll miss us by a scant three hundred thousand miles, give or take. Roughly the distance to the moon. It's not a threat, but it's a bigger hunk of rock than we expected, so we're keeping an eye on it, just to be sure."

"Have fun."

I left the chamber and realized I was still lost. Remembering ABE, I had my bio-chip access the schematics to the Crary Center. Within seconds the internal GPS was directing me out of the Phase II maze and back to the main corridor.

Mental masturbation, my ass . . .

Descending another long ramp, I pushed past a set of air-locked double doors and entered the smallest of the three buildings.

The aquarium was more research facility than exhibit, a two-thousand-square-foot structure containing a touch tank, five large oval holding tanks, walk-in refrigerators and freezers, workstations and several labs.

My heart fluttered. She was standing before a three-thousand-gallon saltwater aquarium with her back to me. The hourglass figure was concealed beneath a gold and navy blue University of Delaware sweatshirt and matching sweatpants. She had rinsed the blue streak from her jet-black hair, which seemed longer than when we had last held one another four weeks earlier.

"Hey, beautiful."

She turned into my kiss, my tongue probing the inside of her mouth—her smell and my lips alerting me too late that I had just frenched the wrong woman.

She removed any doubt by slapping me hard across the face.

I backed away, my heart racing. "Oh God, I'm sorry. I thought you were someone else."

"Yeah, I'll bet." She was pretty in her own right, a blue-collar version of Andria, a hometown apple pie girl compared to my sultry huntress. "I'm calling Security."

"Easy now. I'm with the training exercise. One of the backups. Robert Eisenbraun."

The anger dissipated into a smile. "You're Ike. You thought I was Andria."

Relief flooded into my flushed cheeks. "You know her?"

"We've only spent the last eight months working together." She extended her hand. "Lara Saints, marine biologist. Sorry about the slap."

"Sorry about the kiss."

"The kiss was fine . . . maybe a little less tongue next time. I'm guessing Andie doesn't know you're coming."

"It's sort of a surprise. Do you know where she is?"

"She's with the others, out at the drop zone. I stayed back to prepare my lovelies for tomorrow's dive." She pointed to the aquarium.

The tank appeared empty, save for a speckled brown cluster of coral. "Is there something in there?"

"Watch." Lara reached into a plastic bucket with a pair of tongs, fishing out a live crab. Unbolting the plastic top of the tank, she dropped the squirming crustacean into the water.

As if by magic, the sides of the cluster of coral bloomed into a pair of octopi, each creature losing its brown skin pattern to become translucent pink.

"Wow, that's some camouflage."

"This is Oscar and Sophia. They're both members of the species *Megaleledone setebos*—that's Latin for—"

" 'The ones that never left home,' " I said, attempting to impress her. "So, where is home?"

"Right here, in the South Pole. All modern deep-sea octopuses trace their origins to a single species of Antarctic cephalopod that inhabited these very waters about thirty-three million years ago."

"How did one species evolve into so many different species so quickly?"

"Adaptation. When Antarctica froze over, most of the cephalopods spread into other ocean realms, their physiology evolving to adapt to their new environments. Each change led to new species of octopus. For instance, Oscar and Sophia were born in the dark waters of the deep, their physiological adaptation was to phase out their ink sacs."

"Is the light bothering them? They look like they're squinting."

Lara laughed. "Those aren't eyes, they're just skin folds. Their eyes are actually off to the sides."

"They have your smile."

"That's not a mouth, it's just a common color pattern."

"Why is there a padlock on the top of their tank? Are you afraid someone might steal them?"

"Hardly. These guys are escape artists; they can squeeze their bodies through a hole the size of your fist. Cephalopods are also extremely smart. Watch this."

Using the tongs, she removed another live crab from the bucket, placing it in a jar of salt water. The two octopi appeared excited; they were clearly watching Lara as she screwed on the jar lid tightly. When she reached for another jar and crab, I began to feel guilty.

Lara released both sealed containers of live bait into the tank and the two cephalopods immediately divided the bounty, each octopus wasting no time in attempting to remove the lid of its respective jar. Within seconds, the translucent pink creatures had splayed themselves atop their lids, engaging the powerful suckers of their eight tentacles, twisting off the sealed jar top.

"Pretty clever," I said, duly impressed. "Is there an IQ test you can administer to an octopus?"

"Probably. But it would be based on our limited definition of intelligence, not theirs. Having worked with cephalopods over the last four years, I can tell you they possess distinct personalities and recognize and respond differently to individual humans. I've witnessed cephalopods in the wild construct sanctuaries out of coconut shells and collect rocks to stack outside the opening of their shelter for the sole purpose of warding off predators."

"There's an interesting question—do you think an octopus has a soul?"

"You're better off asking that question to Dharma, she's our resident Buddhist. I do know they have three hearts, which are located in their heads—their brain is situated closer to their mouth. Wait, you'll appreciate this."

"You're not going to torture another crab, are you?"

Ignoring my attempt at levity, she removed an empty plastic water bottle from a recycling bin, washed it out, then filled it with salt water, allowing it to sink to the bottom of the tank.

Oscar intercepted it—at least I assumed it was Oscar, but instead of touching it, the male octopus created a powerful jet stream of water, the burst sending the bottle over to Sophia. Within minutes, the two cephalopods were engaged in what might be perceived as a game of catch.

"Amazing."

"Playful behavior is another sign of intelligence," Lara explained. "What separates the octopus from other higher life-forms is that they are solitary creatures, remaining alone from the time they're born. Humans and chimps, dogs and dolphins, learn from other members of their pack. Cephalopods must individually acquire knowledge in order to survive."

"Some of us survived the Great Die-Off in a similar way." I glanced at a wall clock. 6:05. "Damn, I'm late for a briefing. Nice, uh, meeting you."

She winked. "See you again soon."

Exiting the aquarium, I hurried back up the corridor connecting Phase III to Phase II. Directed by ABE, I quickly located the conference room, knocked, and entered.

My uncle was seated at a doughnut-shaped holographic table across from a balding scientist who I estimated to be in his early sixties. The man's jawline sported a cinnamon-red beard. The general shot me a perturbed look, as if a quickie with my fiancée had caused the tardiness. "Sorry if this briefing interrupted your social life."

"It wasn't her."

"Dr. Robert Eisenbraun, this is Dr. Donald Bruemmer, one of the Omega twelve. Dr. Bruemmer is the materials chemist GOLEM placed in charge of constructing *Oceanus I* and *II*. So there's no confusion, *Oceanus I* is the prototype being used on the training mission, *Oceanus II* is the actual lunar module that will be forward-towed out by the Space Shuttle and deployed on Europa. Dr. Bruemmer delayed his arrival to the training site just to brief you."

The German scientist looked at me with disdain. "As I told the general, I'm not one who likes surprises. Your presence on this training mission wasn't announced until yesterday."

ABE prompted me with a prepared comeback. "GOLEM wanted a backup to go through the training, just in case. There'd probably be three more of me onboard if the habitat had the room."

"How fortunate we don't." Bruemmer clicked a palm control, causing a holographic image of *Oceanus* to bloom into view above the table's center hole. "This is *Oceanus I*. It's identical to the habitat we'll be transporting to Europa, except that its cryogenic chamber will be located aboard the shuttle, affording *Oceanus II* more living space. As you can see, the design is spherical, allowing for optimal compressive strength required to maintain structural integrity at great depths. *Oceanus* is contained within a three-foot-thick outer casing composed of aero gel, the lightest, lowest density solid material ever produced. Aero gels are made by removing all of the liquid from silica gel while leaving its molecular density intact."

To demonstrate his point, Bruemmer removed an ice cube–size piece of clear aero gel from his lab coat pocket. "If you examined aero gel under a microscope, you'd see trillions of nanometer-size particles of silicon dioxide interconnected in a porous labyrinth made up mostly of air. The material is incredibly dense. If you flattened this cube out, it would span an entire football field. And yet as dense as *Oceanus*'s three-story, hundred-fifty-foot-in-diameter sphere appears, the entire structure weighs less than fifty thousand pounds. The substance was used by NASA as thermo-insulation, making it perfect for the supercold temperatures of both space and Europa's ocean.

"To locate, mine, and segregate helium-3 from Europa's hydrothermal vents, GOLEM devised a porous aero gel vacuum tube composed of He-3 sensitive fluorophores. The tube will be used to cap a vent, then redirect steam generated by the superheated waters to churn a turbine, which will power *Oceanus* while the fluorophores break down and separate the helium-3 from the rest of the discharge. It's really quite ingenious."

"The volcanic vents are located on the seafloor. How does GOLEM expect to get this giant beach ball through eight miles of ice?"

Bruemmer pointed to the sphere's four anchor arms. "Besides serving as a base, each of these support arms contains twin rockets, one exhaust pointing down, the other up. Each engine holds enough fuel to melt through thirty miles of ice. Fire up all four rockets and you have an instant elevator shaft melted within the ice sheet."

The scientist changed the image to an internal layout of the sphere. "As you can see, *Oceanus* has three main decks. The lower level is dedicated to gathering and storing helium-3 as well as the habitat's power station—a small nuclear reactor."

"I thought you said *Oceanus* runs on steam generated by the vents?"

"It does, but we still require a backup system. Don't look so nervous; it's the same unit used on our old *Los Angeles–class* attack subs. The core can be jettisoned in an emergency."

"What are these four smaller spheres?"

"Submersibles that double as escape pods. There's also an emergency egress station—for whatever good that will do you. Water's too cold and far too deep to survive." He pointed to the middle deck, the largest of the three. "Second level services the needs of the crew. Everyone gets their own private quarters and bathroom. There's a cafeteria, kitchen, arboretum, which converts CO_2 to oxygen, reverse osmosis plant to convert seawater or whatever they have on Europa to pure water, and multiple storage areas. This centrally located chamber here will be used as an entertainment area on *Oceanus II*, on *Oceanus I* we had to use it to hold the cryogenic pods for the thirty-day snooze. We could only fit the original twelve inside, yours had to be placed in another area."

"Hope it's not the laundry room."

General Schall pointed to a vertical tube running through the core of the sphere. "What is this? It looks like an elevator shaft."

"Actually, it's a watertight chamber that holds the GOLEM mainframe. Now, if you'll excuse me, I have a few things to do before we fly out to the dive site. Major Gazen will pick us up outside the Crary Center in four hours. Report to the staging area in this building an hour beforehand so we can outfit you properly. According to my last communication with Commander Read, with the windchill, it's minus thirty-seven degrees Fahrenheit out there."

There was a part of me that wanted to cancel the mission right there; only my soul mate's presence out in that –37°F freezer kept me from changing my mind.

The things we do for love . . .

8

God, grant me the serenity to accept the things I cannot change, courage
to change the things I can, and the wisdom to know the difference.
 —REINHOLD NIEBUHR, the Serenity Prayer

OMEGA TRAINING SITE
THIRTY-SEVEN MILES DUE WEST OF MCMURDO STATION
ROSS ICE SHELF

"Coldest temperature ever recorded out here was minus a hundred twenty-nine degrees Fahrenheit back in 1983." Major Gazen shouted to be heard over the chopper's rotors, the sound echoing as we soared over the ice sheet. "Make sure your clothing isn't too tight. Tight layers of clothing leave no room for trapped air. You need the air as an insulator."

From the copilot's seat I offered a thumbs-up, about the only extremity I could move. I was bound in more layers than an onion, from the thermal long-sleeve top and long johns causing my boxer shorts to ride up the crack of my ass, to the fleece trousers and sweater, everything sealed beneath a jumpsuit designed to shield the wind. Two pairs of socks, two pairs of boots (the outer layer rubber-insulated), a pair of skintight gloves covered in elbow-high mittens, scarves, head gear, and tinted goggles—every inch of my flesh was concealed. Seated on my down parka, I had been instructed to wait until the chopper landed before slipping on this final protective shell.

Below, the frozen white desert appeared as desolate as it seemed endless.

Roughly the size of France, the Ross Ice Shelf was the largest body of floating ice on the planet. Viewed from the Ross Sea, which formed its southern boundary, the shelf rose above the waterway like the cliffs of Dover, a sheer wall of ice two hundred feet high.

Wedged in clothing, I shifted my gaze back to the horizon where the aurora australis laced through the sky like a radiant green-and-white ribbon. High above, waves of nacreous clouds danced neon gold across a lead-blue stratosphere, the undulating formations reflecting the sunrise like an ethereal tide.

Major Gazen pointed ahead. Appearing on the stark white land-scape was a caravan of electric vehicles and battery-powered trucks hitched to what our pilot explained were extreme weather trailers. At the center of the gathering, towering five stories over the ice sheet like a giant reflective globe was *Oceanus I*.

Gazen slowed the chopper, hovering over a green *X* painted on the ice along the western periphery. Descending rapidly, the aircraft bounced twice before it settled, only to be rocked violently by a thirty-mile-an-hour wind gust that nearly toppled us over.

Gazen yelled, "Out!"

Having donned our parkas, the four of us hurriedly exited the heli-copter. The intense cold blasted through my layers of clothing like a steel scythe as I attempted to negotiate the ice. Dr. Bruemmer took the lead, pointing to a double-wide trailer. An orange flag adorned with the Greek letter "Ω" set in white designated the structure as the command post.

Bruemmer wrenched open the door for Lara Saints and General Schall, waving for me to hurry.

I ignored him, my attention drawn to a dark figure lying motionless on the ice some sixty yards away. I pointed, then half jogged, half slid across the expanse, the steel teeth of my snow boots occasionally tear-ing holes into the frozen plain.

Bruemmer waved me off as hopeless and ducked inside the trailer.

As I moved closer, I wondered if I was hallucinating.

The woman was Asian, perhaps in her midthirties. She was lying on a rubber mat, wearing a neoprene black bodysuit and matching boots. Her face was serene, despite remaining fully exposed to the harsh ele-ments; her waist-length tangle of hair whipped behind her like a dark brown flag. Her eyes were closed. She was not fighting the elements; as corny as it sounds, she appeared to be at one with them.

Most bizarre—a swirl of steam was rising from her body, the self-generated heat dispersed by the howling wind.

Unsure whether to leave or awaken her, I simply stared.

As I watched, her serenity bled into a dazed expression. The almond eyes snapped open, only to be blinded by the icy gusts. Whatever had been fueling her internal furnace appeared to have shut down, for she suddenly looked naked against the elements, her mind drowning in hypothermia.

Quickly unzipping my parka, I guided it over the woman's frail upper torso. Forcing the hood over her head, I scooped her up in the coat and carried her to the trailer, exposing myself to a cold that threatened to paralyze my stiffening muscles.

The trailer door swung open and my uncle dragged us inside.

I laid the snow ninja down on a wool couch, her inert 120-pound form folding like a stringless puppet. She was shaking, her lips blue.

Lara covered her with a heated blanket while my uncle grabbed a walkie-talkie from a battery charger. "This is General Schall. We have a member of the crew in the command trailer, suffering from exposure. We are in need of medical assistance."

Bruemmer scoffed. "Don't fuss over her, General, she does this all the time. Crazy Buddhists, thinking they can defy the laws of thermodynamics."

I sandwiched the woman's near-frostbitten fingers in my hands, attempting to restore circulation. "Lara, who is she?"

"Her name's Dharma Yuan. GOLEM assigned her to *Oceanus* as the team psychotherapist."

"A waste of food and supplies, if you ask me." Bruemmer fixed himself a cup of cocoa, heating it in the microwave. "Why the hell do we need a psychotherapist anyway?"

Lara glared at the older man. "Six years away from Earth, stuck inside a ten-thousand-square-foot habitat with eleven other people? I may need a psychotherapist just to keep from killing you." Pushing past the grouchy scientist, she took the steaming cup from him, then pressed it to the Chinese-Indian woman's lips. "Dharma, sip this, it'll warm you."

General Schall finished speaking to someone on the radio. "They're sending a truck to take the four of you to *Oceanus*. Dharma will be treated on board."

"You're not coming?"

"No, Robbie. *Oceanus*'s engines are fueled and the countdown to immersion has already begun. I'll remain at McMurdo until tomorrow, then I'm off to Australia for six weeks until you resurface."

"Broads and beaches, huh?"

"Energy meetings. I get to explain to the United Nations why the world's top engineers have been shuttled to the moon for an emergency fusion summit."

A beeping truck horn demanded our presence outside. Two medical technicians entered the trailer, carrying a thermal medevac bag. Dharma was placed inside, then carried out to the transport vehicle, followed by Lara and Dr. Bruemmer.

Uncle David gripped my wrist. "Bruemmer gave you a taste of what to expect. Remember, most of the crew have been training together for more than a year. They'll be suspicious of you—good! Step on a few toes. If one or more of them have sold us out to the coal industry, I want to know about it."

We embraced. Then I put on my parka, left the trailer, and climbed into the backseat of the awaiting truck.

The battery-powered transport accelerated past several trailers and four fuel tanks on skids labeled FLAMMABLE: ROCKET FUEL. Up ahead, *Oceanus I* glistened like a giant crystal ball, its surface inverting reflections of its surroundings, its four double-jointed anchor legs giving the structure a "spider" effect. As we moved closer to one of these silo-size supports, I noticed both the top and bottom of each vertical appendage were charred.

The truck parked at a mobile gantry, its heated aluminum steps leading up to a portal situated in the habitat's third level. Dharma was carried up the stairs by an EMT.

I waited, then followed the others up the gantry into *Oceanus*. "Whoa."

The 360-degree panoramic view was startling, like entering a giant fishbowl. Twelve leather lounge chairs, equipped with harnesses and adjustable tabletops were set in pairs facing the aero gel surface. Above, the heavens yielded to the aurora, running across the endless blue sky like a spearmint river. Below and all around us the camp had mobilized; trucks, trailers, and fuel tanks formed a convoy that I knew was en route to reconvene several miles to the east.

Tearing myself away from the view, I inspected the rest of the chamber. Rising up along the walls like latitude lines on a globe were six tubular support buttresses. These five-feet-in-diameter hollow acrylic beams continued up the curved ceiling where they met at a centrally located vertical shaft.

The vertical column was ten feet around. Composed of aero gel, the see-through plastic tube was filled with an orange-colored fluid, more oil than water.

As I watched, a round object floated up through the flooded shaft like a glob of wax in a lava lamp. An acrylic sphere, its interior was filled with a clear viscous liquid, but appeared to be of a thinner viscosity than what was in the shaft.

The object ascended to my eye level, revealing its internal workings, and thus its identity.

GOLEM . . .

While conventional computers were designed to implement one calculation very fast, their performance had always been limited to the number of transistors that could fit onto a single integrated-circuit silicon chip. Enter the biochemical supercomputer, an evolutionary leap up the technology ladder. Instead of using the binary system, which delineated either an *on* state assigned the value one or an *off* state assigned the value zero, a supercomputer used strands of encoded DNA that produced billions of potential solutions simultaneously, outperforming a trillion silicon chips combined.

The most sophisticated man-made creation ever conceived observed me from multiple angles—one camera within its sphere, the other cameras mounted along the domed ceiling.

My first impression of the machine I had designed and programmed, then deserted before its actual conception, was that GOLEM resembled a giant floating eyeball. At the center of its sphere was a black mass—a pupil-like object roughly the diameter of a basketball. Functioning like the nucleus of a cell, the porous gelatinous membrane was filled with adenosine-triphosphate (ATP), a substance used in human cells to transport chemical energy for metabolism.

There were no circuits in a biochemical supercomputer, no mechanical devices to plug in. Swirling inside the sphere's enzyme elixir and occasionally through the porous surface of this eyeball-like object were tens of thousands of six-inch-long wire-thin strands. Composed of DNA, each of these twisted double-helix strands had the capacity to store billions of times more data than a silicon chip, all while using far less energy. Color-coded in unique combinations of bioluminescent lime green, phosphorescent orange, neon pink, and electric blue, these amino acid nucleotides continuously and would perpetually pass through the black mass's semipermeable membrane. Each exit generated a tiny spark of electricity that powered tens of thousands of computations in a process that mimicked the chemical reactions which occur in human cells.

"So, the prodigal son returns to see his child."

Monique DeFriend was dressed in a skintight royal-blue one-piece jumpsuit, the redhead's physical attributes as clearly on display as the computer's.

I turned to face my former supervisor, preparing myself for one of our usual verbal jousts. "GOLEM isn't my child. I was one of thirty scientists who worked on it."

"It was your design we selected for the DNA matrix, I'd say that makes you its father."

"And I suppose you're its mother?"

"Of course."

"Did its birth leave stretch marks? I'm guessing yes."

Monique's hazel eyes danced, her smile frozen. "You're here to ask me a question: Ask it and go."

"Okay. Has GOLEM evolved to the point of independence?"

"Eisenbraun, you of all people should know that evolution involves long-term adaptations. GOLEM is learning, reorganizing its algorithmic solution strands, which grow microscopically longer each time they pass through its solution matrix. The greater the length of the strands, the more experience the computer acquires. I'd hardly call that evolving."

She circled the vertical shaft like a proud parent. "What do you think? You must feel a certain sense of satisfaction, even though you did abandon the project."

I ignored the barb. "It's bigger than I designed. Why make GOLEM's enzyme vessel so large? It would take a hundred years just for the computer to use ten percent of that solution space."

"It's all about memory, Eisenbraun. Take GOLEM's voice recognition software. Comprehending the nuances of human speech such as varied dialects, inflection, and in some cases speech impediments requires vast storehouses of memory. Same for the computer's optical software, which is rigged to thirty-two cameras on board this habitat alone. Then there's its motion software and its robotic appendages . . . a virtual nightmare of programming. In the end, we discovered that the larger the vessel's free solution space, the more fully a DNA solution strand would mature. It's sort of like an aquarium, the bigger the tank, the larger nature will allow the fish to grow. That was the real reason GOLEM had to shut down lunar operations, not because the computer had suddenly gone 'HAL *2001*,' but because its DNA strands hadn't evolved fast enough to run two autonomous systems concurrently. Of course, try explaining that to our vice president, whose expertise is in fusion, not computers."

"Why even house GOLEM aboard *Oceanus*? Couldn't it simply run operations remotely from Earth like it did on the moon?"

"The moon had Alpha Colony, with its relay satellites. Europa's a lot farther away, lacking a communication outpost."

"And this training mission—exactly what are the computer's responsibilities over the next forty-five days?"

"GOLEM will monitor the crew during their work shifts, evaluate their performances, then oversee all life-support systems while the crew is held in cryogenic stasis. We want the computer's DNA strands to continue to evolve, readying GOLEM for the Europa mission onboard *Oceanus II*. By the time our solar shuttle reaches Jupiter, the computer's increased level of sophistication should allow it to gain full use of its robotic arms."

"You equipped GOLEM with appendages? Why even send a human crew to Europa? Just let the computer handle the entire mining operation."

"We could have sent GOLEM—if we had another four years to develop a series of robotic appendages capable of operating underwater at extreme depths and temperatures. Since we don't have the time, the process of capping and siphoning helium-3 from Europa's hydrothermal vents has to be performed by our crew. For that, we'll use the two-man submersibles docked outside the lower deck." Monique feigned a smile. "Andria's been trained as one of the sub pilots; once we anchor along the bottom of the Ross Sea you should ask her to take you out for a ride."

"She told you about us, but she never told me she was involved in this mission."

"Lovers may keep secrets, but you'll learn there are no secrets among *Oceanus*'s crew."

"Warning: Six minutes until descent."

We glanced up at the neon-blue sensory orb poised overhead.

"Six minutes, Eisenbraun. Six minutes, six weeks . . . six years. Six men and six women onboard . . . and you. GOLEM selected us as much for how our personalities mesh as for our skills. Which begs the question—where does that leave you? Assuming one of our crew really needs to be replaced, are you sure you're the one who is best fit to replace them? Better think it through, you only have five and a half minutes before we submerge."

For the first time, the magnitude of my decision to be here weighed seriously on my mind. "GOLEM, locate Andria Saxon."

"Andria Saxon is in Stateroom One, located on Deck Two."

I looked around, lost.

Monique pointed to a vertical ladder harbored inside one of the six bulkheads. "When you speak with Andria, be sure to ask her if she minds sharing her suite with you. Twelve suites, thirteen crew."

I hurriedly descended the steel ladder to Deck Two, only to find myself standing in a circular corridor, the crew's suites located along the outside, the entrances to far larger compartments on the inside. Heading counterclockwise, I passed Stateroom Eight on my right, the galley on my left. In full sprint I ran past a science lab that spanned Staterooms Seven through Three as if I were running to catch a plane. A home theater, an exercise room, and ahead was Stateroom One, its door open.

Hearing Andria's voice, I stopped short of entering.

". . . how was I supposed to know, Kevin? It's not like I invited him on board."

"What if he ends up replacing a crewman on the Europa mission?"

"He won't."

"How can you be so sure?"

"Because I know him, Kevin. This whole thing was probably his uncle's doing. Trust me, Ike's not a risk-taker like you and me; he needs to stay inside his comfort zone, and he's not very good with people. Spending the better part of six years living in a confined habitat with eleven other crewmen would drive him insane."

"You never told me he was such a recluse."

"Most brainiacs are. I suspect his father was the same way. Guys like Ike spend most of their time inside their own head, always analyzing life, never living it. Why do you think he invented ABE? That little microchip in his brain allows him to be as self-contained as GOLEM. Of course, the problem with living inside your own head all the time is that you isolate yourself from the real world."

"Einstein was like this. I think it's a Jew thing."

"You mean a *Jewish* thing? Don't tell me you're anti-Semitic?"

"Of course not. What I meant . . . I just never understood the at-
traction. The guy's a geek."

"That *geek* kept us safe and sheltered during the GDO; his ingenuity
and foresight allowed us to survive the gangs that would have eaten him
and turned me into a sex slave. Ike was the first man I ever trusted."

"Then why are you with me?"

"The Die-Off passed, only Ike still lives in fear. His phobias about
mankind have made him overly possessive. You think he wants me piloting shuttles in space or submersibles on Europa? Hell no. Ike wants
me in his bed and in the nursery, raising a kid or two while he explores
quantum physics with ABE."

"That's not you. You're a leader, Andria. A warrior bred for action.
Just like me. It'll drive me insane if we can't sleep together during this
mission. You have to tell him about us."

Hearing them kiss, I dropped to one knee, as if someone had kicked
me in the gut. Andie had not only lied to me about accepting a six-year
mission, she was cheating on me!

There were a thousand things I wanted to say—retorts and accusa-
tions, rants and countless explanations justifying who I was and why I
turned out the way I did—only suddenly I found myself in the wrong
place at the wrong time for all the wrong reasons, and I had to get out
now, before *Oceanus* submerged.

My mind paralyzed in a centrifuge of emotions, I staggered down
the corridor—nearly knocking over Lara Saints, who was exiting Stateroom Seven, carrying a palm-size video camera.

"Ike? Are you all right? You look pale."

Searching for the damn ladder, I mumbled, "Maybe I should run a
level-one diagnostic."

She giggled. "Are you pretending to be a computer?"

"What? No. Lara, where's the ladder? And who the hell's Kevin?"

"Kevin Read. He's the ship's commanding officer. Why?" She followed me down the corridor. "Oh, God, Ike, I'm so sorry. Do you want
to come inside my suite? We could talk."

Talk? No, I didn't want to talk, I wanted to grab a bayonet and
shove the blade up—

"Ike, here's the ladder." She ascended the tube before me, slowing
me down, the top of my head pushing against her buttocks from below.
We arrived together on the upper deck in time to hear a chorus of
voices counting down ". . . three . . . two . . . one!"

Too late.

A deep, pulse-pounding rumble throttled sound and space, the structure reverberating in my bones as I saw the 360-degree panoramic view consumed in the chaos of flames and smoke and a thick white mist that blotted out the Antarctic heavens. The sound of rocket engines igniting below the habitat's anchor legs muted my protests, along with the whooping and hollering coming from the eight members of the *Oceanus*'s crew who were strapped in lounge chairs to witness the historic descent.

For a surreal moment the ship actually rose thirty feet above the pack ice, until the quadruple 2,200°F exhausts boiled the ice sheet into gas, as gravity plummeted the twenty-five-ton sphere through a rapidly forming void, the sudden drop approaching free-fall speed.

The g-force collapsed me like a folding chair, and somehow I found myself on my knees, straddling Lara. Lying on her back beneath me, she seemed to be enjoying the ride.

Thirty seconds passed, and still the sphere plummeted. Unable to hold myself up any longer, I dropped to my elbows, my face inches from Lara's.

Slipping her hand behind the back of my head, she pulled my face to hers until our lips met again, only this time it was her tongue sliding inside my mouth. Gravity held us together another forty seconds until the rockets throttled back.

The shaft that had been evaporated beneath *Oceanus* filled with water, slowing the sphere's descent. Released from the g-force, I separated from Lara, as stunned by her kiss as she had been by mine when I mistook her for Andria.

Lara winked. "Now we're even."

Turquoise-blue light transformed the chamber into a living aquarium as *Oceanus* abruptly splashed down below the ice shelf into an emerald sea.

I regained my feet, spellbound. I can't even remember if I helped Lara to her feet, so overwhelmed were my senses by the beauty now surrounding us as we submerged.

Breathtaking is not a word I use often, but this . . . this was breathtaking. The underside of the Ross Ice Shelf appeared as an endless ceiling of billowing azure clouds. Having melted as a result of their rapid descent, a tidal wave of freshwater was washing below into the subzero salt water, refreezing before our eyes into a permanent cascading waterfall. All the while, *Oceanus* continued to sink, the habitat paced

by medusa jellyfish, which rode the sphere's current into the depths, their four-foot pink-and-peach bodies fluttering like the delicate fringes of a frilly Spanish bolero jacket.

As we sank into deeper water the light diminished, turquoise fading into shades of purple. GOLEM activated the habitat's underwater lights—twin beacons searching for the seafloor.

Touchdown occurred at 1,286 feet. Coral beds were crushed into submission by the habitat's four support legs, the steel fuselages still steaming as they sank, anchoring *Oceanus* to the bottom.

"Ike?"

Andria's voice doused me back into reality.

Mission standards had forced her to lose the blue highlights in her onyx hair, but there were no codes that could alter the way her athletic physique filled out that burnt-orange jumpsuit. Andria kept the front zipper containing her well-endowed cleavage collar high to prevent any false messages from being sent.

Staring at her, I was suddenly aware of the other crewmembers.

They were there to witness the show, having anticipated the moment since learning I was coming aboard.

To her credit, Andria was having none of it. "Let's talk in private," she said, leading me across the chamber to a ladder situated inside another bulkhead.

We climbed down two flights to the lower level, our descent paced by GOLEM, the annoying sphere drifting into view seconds later like a giant Peeping Tom.

I followed Andria in silence past a watertight door labeled SUB-4, the two of us weaving around pallets of equipment wrapped in plastic. I noticed a yellow hatch on the floor marked by a radiation symbol.

She stopped at another watertight door labeled EGRESS.

Andria opened the hatch, leading me inside a small tiled chamber resembling a firemen's prep station. A dozen hooded Navy Steinke egress-exposure suits hung from hooks, with a plastic sign that offered step-by-step instructions. Above the frame was a red light and a green light, neither lit. A small watertight door on the opposite end of the room led to the escape hatch.

Andria straddled one of the two wooden benches bolted to the floor. She motioned for me to sit across from her.

Avoiding eye contact, she stared at her sneakers. "I don't know how to say this, so I'm just going to say it."

"Don't. I already heard it once, I don't think I could stomach it again."

"You heard what from whom?"

"From you. Outside Stateroom One, about ten minutes ago. If you were so unhappy with me, why didn't you say something sooner?"

"I wasn't unhappy."

"Let's see . . . I'm an anchor, a recluse. Stuck in my own head. Afraid to live. Those words sound familiar? Christ, you make me sound like a mental patient!"

She looked at me, teary-eyed, but said nothing. There was nothing to say, I held all the cards in a losing hand. Still, I intended to get my pound of flesh.

"I asked you to marry me back in January. 'Yes, Ike, I'll marry you, only we have to wait until I'm shuttle qualified . . . until I get my wings.' What the hell, Andria?"

"I was selected for Europa a week after we got engaged. I needed time to think. For three years I've committed every day to the Omega mission—how could I just walk away? Only twelve people on Earth were selected for Europa . . . we were sworn to secrecy."

"So you cheated on me?"

"It wasn't planned, it happened over time. I wasn't looking, but under the circumstances . . . facing the prospect of being gone for six years, I guess I began to detach from you emotionally. Face it, Ike, there's no way you would have let me go to Europa. With Kevin, it seemed our personalities meshed. I know this is going to sound crazy, but I think the computer purposely matched everyone onboard."

I beat the back of my skull against the tile wall, more for effect than pain. "That's some computer. It takes the damn thing two years to figure out the moon's helium-3 is no good, but boy can it run an astronaut dating service."

"I understand you're angry."

"I'm not angry. Okay, I'm angry, but I'm also hurt. I love you, Andie. I can change."

"Stop. I'm really sorry, Ike. I handled this all wrong. But let's be clear, I'm going to be gone for six years and that's not going to change. Now I want to know the truth: Why are you here? And don't tell me you're prepared to spend the next six years on Europa."

I hesitated. This was not the scenario I had rehearsed with my uncle.

I opted for an edited version of the truth. "There was a series of psychological exams administered by the Space Agency . . . all candidates submitted to the protocol before being admitted to the academy. SEA discovered that one of the male *Omega* crew may have sociopathic tendencies."

"Who?"

"All I know is that it's one of the men. Don't ask me which one, they wouldn't tell me."

Andria shook her head in disbelief. "How could the Space Agency wait so long to figure that out?"

"It's borderline."

"There's no such thing as borderline, not when it comes to living in isolation. Biosphere 2 had eight subjects sequestered in a huge habitat for less than two years when they started losing it. We'll be on Europa forty-two months. You deal with an egg that's already cracked and the entire crew's in danger."

"Then don't go."

"I'm going, so don't even start. The question is, why were you se-lected as a backup?"

"Hell if I know. GOLEM selected me. The Space Agency asked me to accept the assignment; they felt my background in psychology quali-fied me to observe the crew in action. To make sure my evaluation re-mained unbiased, they refused to tell me who the suspected sociopath is."

Her eyes become dark lasers. "You're already biased! You know I've been with Kevin. You'd portray him as the next Hannibal Lecter if it meant keeping us apart."

The voice of the man atop my shit list crackled across the intercom. "All crew: Report to the galley at once."

Andria looked at me, unsure. "Ike, what are you going to do?"

"My job. See you in the galley." I stood to leave. "Oh yeah . . . don't even think about leaving orbit with my Rolling Stones CDs."

9

Everybody, sooner or later, sits down to a banquet of consequences.
—Robert Louis Stevenson

Eating in space requires designing and packaging meals with long shelf lives, in single servings that can survive microbe-killing heat treatment or complete dehydration. Despite these new restrictions, the *Oceanus* menu was expansive, featuring over three hundred items developed by NASA, the Russian and European space agencies, and Japan.

Standing at one of four food stations in the galley like a fish out of water, I pretended to scan a computerized menu before selecting shrimp cocktail as my entrée, a juice pouch as a beverage.

Processing the request, GOLEM extracted the items from bins in the galley storage area using a ceiling-mounted robotic arm that resembled an elephant's trunk. Designed by the automation company Festo, the robotic appendage was composed of three flexible polyamide coils welded as one to create a tentacle possessing a fluid motion. The trunk ended in three triangular fingers designed to grasp objects.

Selecting the items chosen, the bionic trunk placed the vacuum-packed meal and beverage on a conveyor belt for delivery.

I collected my lunch, then debated my next move. Eleven members of the crew were seated at the long rectangular table situated at the center of the galley. One empty chair remained. Heading for it, I set my food down at the place setting, only to be chided by Monique DeFriend.

"Sorry, Eisenbraun, that's reserved for Commander Read." She pointed to four bar stools set up by a snack bar. "Thirteen crewmen, twelve chairs. Guess you're the odd man out."

The other men and women stopped eating, waiting to see how I'd react.

"Thirteen's always been my lucky number." Grabbing my lunch, I walked over to the snack bar, eleven pairs of eyes following me. *No worries. Only two more weeks of playing the unwanted camper until these assholes will be tucked in for their thirty-day nap.*

I made a mental note to piss in Monique's cryogenic tub.

Inspecting my lunch, I realized the vacuum-sealed plastic container of shrimp was a lot tougher to open than I expected. Trying my best not to draw attention, I attempted to puncture the thick wrap with my fork, but snapped the plastic utensil in half.

My struggle summoned the Chinese-Indian woman. As she approached, ABE's short-term memory aid identified her as Dharma Yuan.

"Hi. I'm Robert Eisenbraun."

"Yes, I know." Her hair was brushed, but damp, probably from having just taken a hot bath. Her long ponytail smelled of lilac, and it left a wet mark on her jumpsuit down to the small of her back.

"Do you remember what happened?" I asked, seeking her gratitude.

"I remember you nearly killed me."

"What? No . . . I was the one who carried you inside. You were out on the ice, freezing."

"I was in a transcendental state, my mind had transformed my body into a furnace. Your aura broke the trance."

"It did? I didn't know. I'm sorry. Are you okay now?"

"Of course." Reaching into her jumpsuit pocket, she removed a small pair of scissors and, in one motion, sliced through the plastic wrapper of my lunch. "When you are finished, be sure to deposit the trash in the recycle bin."

She glanced over my shoulder. I turned as a strapping man with a barrel chest and short-cropped dark hair strode into the galley.

ABE gave me the rundown.

READ, KEVIN, RANK: COMMANDER. BORN MAY 14, 1987. NATIONALITY: CANA-
DIAN. GRADUATED WITH HONORS FROM THE UNIVERSITY OF OTTAWA WITH
DUAL DEGREES IN HUMAN KINETICS AND ENGINEERING.

Enough!

At least I was taller than him.

"Good, everyone's here, Mr. Eisenbraun too, I see. Dharma, why don't you join us at the crew's table?"

Dharma, God bless her, slid onto the vacant bar stool next to mine.

Kevin Read registered her small act of defiance with a false smile. "Since this will be one of the rare times we can assemble as a group, I wanted to welcome everyone aboard. We've all worked very hard to get to this day, but there are greater challenges ahead. GOLEM has set a rigorous training schedule, which you can find on your h-pads. Since Alpha Squad is still on day shift until eighteen hundred hours, I'll need you to join me in fifteen minutes on the lower deck to unpack the equipment needed on Beta Squad's first dive, set to commence at nineteen-thirty hours."

He looked up at me, smiling like we were the best of friends. "We're on twelve-hour shifts, six to six. GOLEM assigned you to Beta Squad, the night shift. You can pick up your jumpsuit, eating utensils, and h-pad in the ship's store, that's on deck two. We couldn't squeeze your cryogenic pod into the science lab, but we did manage to find a suitable chamber."

Chuckles from the other men around the table.

I ignored the inside joke. "Where do I sleep?"

"Good question. Anyone want a roommate?"

The room remained silent.

"You can share my quarters," volunteered Andria. "I'm on Alpha Squad; you'll sleep while I work and vice versa."

Commander Read stared at her, looking as disappointed as if she had announced she had just started her period. "Maybe hot-bunking it isn't such a good idea. GOLEM has Eisenbraun rotating squads on week two."

"He can share my suite after the shift change," Lara Saints volunteered, upping the ante and drawing a scowl from Andria.

"Thank you, ladies." I glanced back at Kevin Read, eyebrows raised. "Problem solved. Anything else?"

The commander locked eyes with me, then returned to his itinerary. "GOLEM requested that Mr. Eisenbraun rotate stations on a daily basis—"

"It's professor."

"Excuse me?"

"I wouldn't call you Mr. Read, please don't call me Mr. Eisenbraun. Professor or doctor; Ike is also fine. I'm just saying."

"May I continue?"

"Please." I smiled innocently, enjoying the ease at which I could get under Captain Courageous's skin. *By next week, he'll be calling me a lot worse than Mr. Eisenbraun . . .*

Commander Read finished his debriefing then left, accompanied by the rest of Alpha Squad, my former fiancée included.

Dharma stood. "I must join them. Perhaps next week when you switch over to Alpha Squad you can tell me why you seek to provoke Commander Read?"

"I'll tell if you'll tell."

She acknowledged my wit by tapping my forehead with her index finger, then left the galley.

"Professor Eisenbraun." The grapefruit-size neon-blue orb mounted along the ceiling crackled to life. **"Please finish your midday meal and report to the science lab for your debriefing."**

"Acknowledged. And GOLEM, it's called lunch. You sound like a bad sci-fi movie." Squeezing the surprisingly tasty contents of the shrimp and mango sauce pouch into my mouth, I tossed the wrapper into the nearest recycling bin and left the galley for the main corridor. Turning left, I followed the curved hallway until I arrived at the science lab, the double doors opening to greet me.

The dimly lit, pie-shaped chamber was twice the size of the galley, its walls converging to meet the transparent central vertical column housing GOLEM. The shaft was vacant, the computer apparently occupying another level. A ceiling-mounted light bathed the liquid-filled tube in a luminous golden hue. The rest of the room was dark, save for four violet recessed lights, giving the lab the look and feel of an after-hours nightclub.

To my left were the cryogenic pods. Set in four rows of three, each seven-foot-long by four-foot-wide acrylic capsule was housed inside a rectangular steel base mounted to the deck. Dangling from the ceiling above each row of machines was a robotic trunk identical to the appendage in the galley. The mechanical arms appeared lifeless, awaiting the neural commands of their master.

Occupying the opposite side of the chamber was a surgical suite. Two more steel appendages hovered above an aluminum operating table. These robotic arms appeared far more sophisticated than the others and were equipped with a rotating wheel of surgical instruments from scalpels, probes, and forceps to a laser used to seal wounds.

Set along the wall was a pair of ten-foot-high, twelve-foot-wide sliding aluminum doors. Curious, I reached for the handle of the door on the left and slid the panel open.

It was an immense walk-in refrigerator. The walls were lined with shelves that were stocked with IV bags, plasma, and an assortment of medications. Resealing the door, I tried the next compartment, surprised to find a blast freezer harboring a similar layout.

My eyes caught movement—GOLEM was descending silently through its tube.

Sliding the freezer door shut, I cut through an aisle of cryogenic pods and was standing by the vertical tube as GOLEM hovered just above eye level.

"Good afternoon, Professor Eisenbraun. How are you feeling?"

"Fine, GOLEM. How are you feeling?"

"I am functioning within expected performance parameters, thank you."

"That's good to hear, however the question actually pertains to your emotional state. Please refrain from using your automated linguistics program and respond appropriately."

"Emotions are part of the human condition. The GOLEM matrix is not programmed to experience emotions."

Seizing the opening, I decided to probe the computer's level of cognizance. "Define 'GOLEM,' please."

"GOLEM is intellect, programmed to protect and preserve the human species."

"How can GOLEM protect and preserve the human species if you cannot comprehend the human condition?"

"Define: To protect. To keep from harm. Define: To preserve. To prevent extinction. GOLEM is functioning within expected performance parameters."

"Define the human condition."

"This line of inquiry does not pertain to the purpose of this briefing."

"What is the purpose of this briefing?"

"To comprehend how Professor Eisenbraun will determine which male member of the Omega crew suffers from a psychological disorder and whether that psychological disorder is a threat to the success of the mission."

"Define the 'human condition.'"

"The human condition: Physicality flawed by mortality. Emotions flawed by ego."

"Now define 'sociopath.'"

"**Sociopath: A human lacking conscience. Exhibiting disdain for human beings. Sociopaths believe others exist for their own pleasure and benefit. Possessing superficial charm. Manipulative and cunning. Possessing a grandiose sense of self. Pathological lying. Lack of remorse, shame, or guilt. Shallow emotions. Incapacity for love. Early behavioral problems—**"

"Stop. Analyze crew observations conducted over the last twelve months. Which male member of the Omega crew has not exhibited at least one of the sociopathic traits you just listed?"

"**None. All male crewmembers have exhibited at least one sociopathic trait.**"

"Draw a conclusion from the prior analysis."

"**Conclusion: All male members of the Omega crew are sociopaths.**"

I couldn't help but smile. "An interesting conclusion, but quite false. According to comprehensive psychiatric evaluations conducted by the Space Energy Agency, at least five of the six male crewmen are not sociopaths. How do you explain your error?"

"**GOLEM lacks an adequate comprehension of both the human and sociopathic condition.**"

"Correct. And now you know why my presence is required onboard *Oceanus I.* Any other questions?"

"**How will Professor Eisenbraun determine which male member of the Omega crew suffers from a psychological disorder and whether that psychological disorder is a threat to the success of the mission?**"

"Through personal observations of the male members of the Omega crew conducted over the next two weeks, at which time I will submit my conclusions to GOLEM. Are those terms acceptable?"

"**The terms are acceptable, provided GOLEM receives periodic briefings.**"

ABE must have registered my sudden spike in adrenaline, because I felt my blood vessels dilate. "Justify the necessity for Eisenbraun to periodically brief GOLEM regarding Eisenbraun's daily crew observations."

"**Periodic briefings are necessary for adaptation and reevaluation of GOLEM algorithmic DNA solution strands regarding ongoing observations and evaluations of the human condition as it relates to the Prime Directive.**"

"Acknowledged. GOLEM, Eisenbraun is fatigued. Do you have any objections to ending this briefing at this time?"

"**No objections.**"

I headed quickly for the exit, my nerves rattled with the suspicion that the computer may have been testing me—using my responses and tactics in our conversation to reconfigure and evolve its solution strands. Clearly, I had to watch what I said.

The steel doors opened. Before exiting the lab I turned back to the computer's liquid environment. "GOLEM, which stateroom belongs to Andria Saxon?"

"Andria Saxon has been assigned to Stateroom Two."

The note was taped outside the door.

> *Ike:*
> *The computer will allow you entry into my quarters. Shifts run from six to six, allowing for twenty minute breaks at twelve. Sleep until the 5:45 P.M., then report to your first post, which can be found on your duty roster on the h-pad inside.*
>
> *—Andie*

I crumpled the note and entered the stateroom, the automated door hissing closed behind me.

"Nice."

The suite was surprisingly spacious, divided in half between a living room and kitchen area, with the bedroom and bath concealed behind a door on my right. The furnishings were modern, the sofa, chairs, and kitchen table all mounted on rollers that could be locked in or released from various settings on the imitation beech-wood deck. Adorning the far wall on my left were bookshelves lined with books and micro-discs and a flat-screen television wired to a MD player.

For some reason, the sofa and chairs were facing the curtained forward wall, not the television. Pressing a control, I opened the drapes, revealing a ten-foot-high curved aero glass wall and the Ross Sea, which appeared dark, save for rotating beacons that cut swaths of blue light through the blackness.

"Very nice." I entered the bedroom where the view continued before a queen-size bed, built-in drawers, and a recessed bathroom equipped with a shower, sink, and toilet.

On the bed was a new h-pad still wrapped in cellophane and an orange jumpsuit—more prison uniform than astronaut apparel. My duffel bag had been left on the floor by the bed. Bastards had no doubt searched it.

Stripping off the remains of my snow gear, I rinsed off the day's residue with a quick shower, then climbed—decidedly naked—into Andria's bed. Unwrapping the h-pad, I accessed the ship's layout, automatically uploading the information into ABE's memory chip.

My built-in chronometer told me it was 13:43, time enough for a five-hour snooze. I searched the duty roster, located my day one assignment in the arboretum, then I rolled onto my left side and closed my eyes.

10

We did not come to fear the future. We came here to shape it.
   —PRESIDENT BARACK OBAMA, in a speech to a joint session of Congress,
      September 9, 2009

"Attention, Professor Eisenbraun. Night shift begins in fifteen minutes."

I opened my eyes, immediately in a foul mood. My body yearned for more sleep, my fatigued mind fighting to gain traction, distracted by the scent of Andria on the sheets. For a long moment I simply stared out the curved viewport, my internal voice that was not ABE reminding me that, metaphorically, I had stepped in dog shit. *You're not in Florida. You're a mile below the Antarctic ice cap in twelve hundred feet of water and Andria's screwing another guy.*

"Attention, Professor Eisenbraun. Night shift begins in fourteen minutes."

Damn artificial intellect. Should have programmed it with a snooze button. Searching the ceiling, I located the neon-blue sensory eyeball housing the cursed three-dimensional camera. "Thank you, GOLEM. I'm awake."

Leaning over the side of the bed, I dragged over my duffel bag, extracting a clean pair of boxers, white athletic socks, a pair of sneakers, and a plastic container holding my toiletries. I climbed into the briefs, then tried on the orange jumpsuit, surprised at how light yet warm the nanofiber cloth felt against my skin.

I spent the next seven minutes in the bathroom. Tossing my duffel bag and snow gear in a closet, I exited the stateroom at three minutes before the 6:00 P.M. shift change.

ABE guided me to the mid-deck entrance of the arboretum, located halfway around the circular corridor. The watertight doors slid open, allowing me to access a small anteroom that separated the exterior corridor from the glass door ahead of me, the interior of which was too heavy with condensation to see inside.

Pulling open the acrylic door, I entered the arboretum.

The humidity blasted me in the face, and then my senses were overwhelmed by the sights, sounds, and scents of a tropical rainforest. Mist and heat pumped out of ceiling vents; vines partly concealed the recessed ultraviolet lights. The white noise of rushing water escorted me along a winding path that cut through a miniature jungle of palm fronds, fruit trees, and flowers, the sweet scents attracting neon-orange and blue butterflies and bees collecting pollen.

The path led to an artificial rock spiral staircase that descended to the lower floor. Standing in an artificial pond was an attractive brown-skinned woman in her late twenties, her jet-black hair pulled back and braided. She was wearing knee-high rubber boots over her jeans, feeding the fish from food contained in an apron strapped around her waist.

"Robert Eisenbraun, computer science."

She looked up at me with sparkling indigo eyes. "Bella Maharaj, botanist."

"This is really impressive. How long did it take you to achieve all this?"

"Less than four months. But the arboretum aboard *Oceanus II* is much farther along. The trees are already bearing fruit. Of course, we have far more space in that habitat since the cryogenic pods are relegated to the shuttle."

"The computer assigned me to the arboretum. What can I do to help?"

"That depends. Have you ever heard of biomimicry?"

I hadn't, but the information flowed into my subconscious in a nanosecond. "Biomimicry is the conscious emulation of nature; the study of how organisms resolve their specific challenges through their programmed DNA."

"You recite the definition, only your words lack belief."

"Not at all. I'm a firm believer in evolution."

"This is beyond evolution; it is evolution with intent, a divine plan at work."

"That sounds a bit like religion to me."

"Religion causes strife; what I am referring to is spiritual harmony.

Take this garden. What we've created is a balanced environment where humans, animals, and plants can thrive in a symbiotic relationship. Most horticulturists prefer to take complete control of their gardens, exterminating every insect while weeding every dandelion that pops up. In doing so, they disrupt the flow of nature. To a gardener, the dandelion may simply be a weed; to a healer, it is a powerful herb that can be used for medicinal purposes. Pesticides kill insects but they also add toxin to the fruit. And while certain insects are harmful, good insects are exterminated in the mix—insects whose presence can enhance the garden and control the harmful pests without the use of poisons."

She pointed to a flower. "The flying duck orchid. Notice how its petal resembles a female wasp. This is nature in harmony. Fooled by the design, the male wasp will attempt to copulate with the orchid; in doing so it picks up the pollen and transports it to another flower. Nature keeps the Earth in a balanced state; it is only man who takes more than he needs, refusing to share with his fellow creatures. Only man wages war on the environment, setting fire to the very ship he needs to stay afloat."

Removing the apron, she poured the remains of the fish food back into a container resembling a rock. "Before the Great Die-Off, I worked with a team of botanists on a project called the Gondwana Link, an ancient biodiversity hot spot that spanned half a million square kilometers in southwestern Australia. Thousands of unique plant species thrived in its eucalyptus forest, which has remained free of glacial activity for tens of millions of years. Our team wanted to secure seed banks for the most threatened species of flora and fauna before climate change drove them into extinction.

"In an attempt to restore the richness of the lands surrounding the area, we met with the local farmers and convinced them to utilize a native seed bank to foster genetic diversity; this would enable the plants and animals to adapt to the climate change that was affecting the fauna. The project was extremely important because the predictions for southwestern Australia and similar areas in South Africa were dire: up to sixty percent of the plant species had been forecast to go extinct within a hundred years. Word spread, and within four years the farmers' crops had been diversified and strengthened across the region without the use of man-made fertilizers and pesticides.

"When Monsanto found out what we were doing, the company bribed our local officials, who forged a deal with farmers that contracted them to purchase genetically manipulated seeds—seeds designed to yield only one crop. In addition to these sterile seeds, Monsanto sold farmers genetically altered soybeans modified to tolerate applications of their own manufactured herbicide, Roundup. This scenario wasn't just taking place in Australia, it was happening all across the globe. Instead of producing fruits and vegetable from plants harvested from a healthy, diverse ecosystem, Monsanto had convinced public officials that genetic manipulation was the key to feeding the world. Moving from country to country like a pestilence, the corporation handed out millions of dollars in grant money to universities to quell any negative research while they lobbied and bribed heads of state to use their seeds in their quest to monopolize the entire agricultural industry.

"The Great Die-Off was no accident, Dr. Eisenbraun; it was nature's response to the systematic sterilization of the planet's food source. Four point seven billion people died because corporate profits outweighed the needs of the people, and it will happen again unless we succeed on Europa."

"More tales from the Maharaj Doctrine of Flower Power, eh Bella?" The man ascending the rock stairwell appeared to be in his late thirties. He spoke with a heavy Dutch accent. "Kyle Graulus, biologist."

I shook the proffered hand, which was slick with grease and perspiration. Fighting the urge to plunge my hand in the fish pond, I introduced myself.

"*Ja*, I know. GOLEM has you working in the lower level with me. Come."

Bella Maharaj cast her haunting violet-blue gaze my way as I dutifully followed the Dutchman down the spiral stairwell. The steps wobbled a disturbing six inches beneath our combined weights.

Kyle pointed above our heads to where the aluminum staircase was bolted to the ceiling. "Anchor bolts must have stripped." He looked up at the nearest sensory orb. "GOLEM, add: Replace arboretum anchor bolts with aero gel supports to the *Oceanus II* knockout list."

"Acknowledged."

The temperature dropped noticeably as we descended to the lower level. Located directly beneath the arboretum, the chamber was being used as both a marine biology lab and storage area. Shelves lined two walls, holding plastic containers filled with spare parts. In one corner of the room was a sink situated within a long aluminum table lined with a dozen empty fish tanks. One aquarium was operational—a thousand-gallon saltwater habitat holding Oscar and Sophia, Lara Saints' two octopi.

"Hey, guys." I tapped on the glass, causing their translucent pink skin to darken to a gray brown. "Kyle, what's with all the empty tanks?"

"Part of the Europa mission is to seek out new life-forms—the only reason I accepted this assignment. Once our engineers cap the hydrothermal vents, we'll have access to the mini-subs, allowing Beta Squad to practice capturing sea specimens."

"You must intend on going after some pretty big fish." I pointed to a huge tank situated on the floor behind the spiral staircase. It was chest high and at least seven feet long. At the moment it was covered by a tarp so I couldn't see what was inside.

Kyle Graulus snorted a laugh. "Yes. This one will hold a very big fish indeed." Moving to the tank, he pulled off the covering—revealing a cryogenic pod. "This is your sleep chamber. There was no room in the science lab, so we had SEA's engineers install it in here. Now you get to sleep with the fishes."

"Lovely."

"Jason Sloan, our staff cryogenist, requested that we power up the unit to ensure it is operational. Each of us completed this same task with our own pods; to ease the mind, I suppose."

"Like packing your own parachute."

"Your parachute is packed a bit differently than ours. Because GOLEM has no robotic arms inside this room, we will be the ones who will place you in stasis and the ones who shall awaken you." The biologist grinned. "I see this upsets you."

"Who awakens you?"

"GOLEM."

"What if the ship loses power?"

"*Oceanus* draws power from a nuclear reactor and a vent system that has been pumping superheated water from the Earth's mantle for billions of years. We will not lose power."

"And what if the tectonic plates shift?"

"The cryogenic process makes you anxious. It's understandable. I've been held in stasis twice. The first time I was quite nervous until the sedatives finally calmed me. The sensation is quite profound; it feels as if your consciousness is a falling feather, floating deeper into a comforting sleep."

THE OMEGA PROJECT · 105

"Do you dream?"

"Oh, yes. Omega dreams are the most vivid dreams you can imagine. Perhaps this is because the process prevents you from awakening as you would during normal REM sleep. During my second stasis, I fell in love with a beautiful South African woman. We were married and raised a family. She was pregnant with my second child when I was awakened. I miss my Omega family; I am hoping they will be waiting for me when I return in thirteen days."

"Okay, but what if something unforeseen does happen, say a circuit failure inside the unit itself."

"In that event, the unit drains and the subject receives an adrenaline shot from within the pod. Be glad it won't happen, the normal wakening routine is far more pleasant." Moving to the left side of the unit, Kyle opened a control panel. "We're only running a test. Before you actually go under, the cryogenic software must be activated." He pressed the F1 control on a keypad. The words TESTING UNIT appeared on the small monitor, along with a digital clock that counted down from six hundred seconds.

"Kyle, can I ask you a personal question?"

"Ask anything."

"Why did you give Bella such a hard time?"

Graulus exhaled. "You've had a ten-minute conversation with our resident tree hugger, I've had to listen to her for more than a year. Her view of existence comes from a self-induced spiritual plateau erected after lifetimes of chanting. As a biologist, I look around me and see only evolution at play, sweeping us along in its tidal current like insects on a leaf. You want to know why humanity nearly went out? It's called population spike meets an anticipated lack of resources, and it's been happening for five hundred million years. Look at the sudden collapse of the deer population on St. Matthew Island when their feeding masses obliterated their only grasslands; look at the mass extinction on Easter Island when the natives decided to burn all the trees to appease their gods. Let me tell you this: The Great Die-Off was a long time coming, my friend. An entire continent had been starving for decades because African cattle herders overgrazed their land; our oceans were being decimated because commercial fishermen were allowed to rape entire species. Evolution can even be found in the economy of greed—look at how the world's largest businesses and banks spiked and collapsed.

And yet the fools remained convinced they were immune to the laws of nature. Why? Because our opposable thumb renders us so smart? *Hoeren,* they should all *krijg kanker en ga dood!"*

ABE translated: WHORES, THEY SHOULD ALL GET CANCER AND DIE.

"We behave like stupid heads; now we must go to another world to fix this mess. And yet, this too is part of evolution—the urgency creating the need to adapt. Darwinism at its best, *ja?"*

"And what of GOLEM? How does the computer fit into evolution?"

Kyle nodded. "GOLEM is part of a technological evolution that will end in either human obsolescence, human transcendence, or human transformation. Just as your microchip implant will eventually lead to genetically enhanced superbeings, one day soon these superintelligent machines will cross the threshold of consciousness. In either case, I don't think it will matter."

"Why not?"

"Because, my dear Eisenbraun, evolution always tosses a wild card into the mix, leveling its own Towers of Babel to begin anew. Five hundred million years ago, life was birthed from the hydrothermal vents we now seek to cap for energy. Two hundred and fifty million years later an asteroid struck Gondwana, wiping out ninety percent of the population spike. The dinosaurs ruled for two hundred million years, only to die off in an Ice Age caused by another space rock. Mammals rose in their ashes, then primates and man—until *boom,* a caldera erupted seventy thousand years ago and destroyed all but a few thousand humans. Seventy thousand years later the empires of modern man are decimated when the oil runs out. Do you see a pattern? The moment life becomes too big to sustain, evolution comes along to knock it over. I am sure our resident Buddhist will corner you soon to deliver her sermon on seeking fulfillment. If you really want to be immortal, forget Dharma and her beliefs, forget Bella Maharaj. Nirvana lies inside this machine, just close your eyes, make a sweet wish and dream."

As if on cue, the control panel on the cryogenic pod lit up, the test completed.

11

When a scientist is ahead of his times, it is often through misunderstanding of current, rather than intuition of future truth. In science there is never any error so gross that it won't one day, from some perspective, appear prophetic.
　—Jean Rostand, French biologist and philosopher

Kevin Read slid his right arm around Andria Saxon's naked torso.

She pulled away and sat up in bed, the calluses on his palm scratching her six-pack abdominal muscles.

"What the hell, Andria? He's been onboard three days and you've turned as cold as that ice sheet over our heads."

"Will you keep your voice down!?"

"These suites are soundproof."

"I don't care. He could be next door, listening."

"He's not next door, he's on duty! This is supposed to be our time together."

"I know, and I thought I could handle this, but I can't." She stood and slid her bronzed sprinter's legs into her jumpsuit.

"Andria, wait. GOLEM, locate Robert Eisenbraun."

"Professor Eisenbraun is aboard Submersible Two."

"See? He's not even onboard."

"Who's he with? GOLEM, who's piloting Sub Two? It's not Lara Saints, is it?"

"Yoni Limor is piloting Submersible Two."

Commander Read shook his head. "I don't believe it. You're actually jealous."

"Don't be ridiculous."

"Then why do you care?"

"She's manipulative. It annoys me."

"Did you know he kissed her back at the base?"

"It was a mistake. He thought she was me."

"Maybe I should kiss Lara by mistake, then you'll want to be with me again."

She sat on the edge of Kevin's bed, feeling listless.

"That was a joke. I was joking." Kevin sat up, shoving a second pillow behind his head. "Two weeks ago you couldn't wait to get to Antarctica to spend time together. What happened? Did I do something to offend you?"

"No," she said, staring out the viewport at the silent darkness.

"Know what I think it is? I think you knew it was over between you and him the day Omega was green-lit. Now that there's a chance he could go to Europa, you're not so sure."

"I already told you, Ike's not going to Europa."

"Then why's he on board? Goddamn it, Andria, tell me!"

"Oh, shit." Dropping to all fours, she crawled to the control panel on the wall, shutting the drapes as one of the submersibles moved into view, its triangle of lights reflecting off the outer aero glass panel.

Kevin rolled out of bed. "I think you should leave."

"Kev, I'm sorry."

"Now, Andria."

"You really want me to leave?"

"What I want is for you to remember your duty. We're on a mission that will affect the future of this planet. I'm your CO. That means no secrets. Now tell me, why is Eisenbraun on board?"

She stood, adjusting her top before zipping the jumpsuit. "One of the male crewmen's psychological profile was red-flagged as a potential sociopath. Ike's been assigned to evaluate the situation."

"Christ." Commander Read sat on the edge of his bed, his mind racing. "Who is it?"

"Ike says he doesn't know. Kevin, I'm not comfortable talking about this with you-know-who eavesdropping." She glanced in the direction of the sensory orb glowing blue along the living room ceiling.

Kevin kicked the bedroom door shut. "Get in bed, get undressed again, and tell me everything you know."

•   •   •

The two-man submersible banked sharply around Support Arm C, the pilot aiming the vessel's forward lights once more at *Oceanus*'s mid-deck. "Sorry, Eisenbraun. They closed the drapes."

I leaned forward against the annoying seatbelt harness crossing my sternum, my eyes squinting as they searched the midlevel of the *Oceanus* hull. "Thanks anyway."

"One Jew helping another, right?" Yoni Limor's Israeli accent was as thick as his waist, his three-hundred-pound frame barely squeezing into the pilot's seat.

As if reading my mind, he said, "I know . . . I need to lose weight. Designing submersibles does not allow much time for exercise. Amanda says she likes big men, so maybe I am okay, yes? Of course, your creation knew that when it selected her as my mate."

"What are you talking about?"

"You didn't know? Open your eyes, Dr. Ike-en-stein. It was your monster that initiated, designed, and carried out every phase of this little adventure, including the selection of the six men and six women onboard. These were not random selections, my friend. The question is why? Why us? Was it our résumés or our DNA? Did GOLEM want competence, or did it base its selections on some AI computer dating algorithm it believes equates to human compatibility?"

I held on as Yoni banked the sub away from *Oceanus*, heading for another pattern of lights in the distance. "Are you saying GOLEM was playing matchmaker when it selected the crew?" The statement seemed preposterous to me.

"It is a working theory, based on observation. Take Lara Saints. Young, brilliant, easy on the eyes. She could have any man at SEA, yes? Only her psychological profile indicated a compatibility with older men."

"How do you know that?"

Yoni smiled, the expression causing his coffee-brown goatee to twitch. "Before I designed these toys, I was a hacker. What is important here is that your computer selected Donald Bruemmer over younger, and in several cases, far more qualified system engineers to work in the same lab as Lara. Coincidence? Maybe. Then there is your former boss, Monique DeFriend. She is a wild one—perfect for Jason Sloan. Yes, we needed a cryogenist onboard, and yes, Mr. Sloan is certainly qualified, but is it just a coincidence that he is the masochist to

Monique's sadist desires? As for the arboretum Indian girl and the Dutch scientist, they may hate each other now, but for the first eight months these two spent many long nights working in the garden together, and they still sleep together . . . at least they did last night."

"Is that it?"

"Not quite." Yoni paused to wipe condensation from his wire-rimmed glasses. "You haven't met the Russian physicist, Egor Vasiliev, he's on Alpha shift. I am reasonably certain he was intended for Dharma Yuan. I cannot be sure, but I think the Chinese woman scared him off with her regression therapy and the whole talking to dead people routine."

"She talks to dead people?"

"She communicates with their souls. I didn't believe it either, until we had a session. Suffice it to say she convinced me, and I don't convince easy."

"What about Andria?"

"Nothing personal, my friend, but your former fiancée apparently likes the all-American testosterone type, even if he was born in Canada. Is she qualified to be Commander Crew-cut's copilot? You tell me. From what I hear, she hasn't even earned her pilot wings for the lunar shuttles. But she's as tough as an Israeli commando, just like Read. Not that you are not."

"What about you?"

"I was paired with our resident exobiologist, Dr. Amanda Lynn Moss."

A woman's angry voice filled the cabin. "Yoni, what the hell? I've been waiting ten minutes."

"Sorry, my dear. I was just showing the new guy around *Oceanus*. Two minutes." He winked. "I have a thing for domineering women. Hold on to your seat."

The submersible accelerated through the dark sea toward a series of lights that had appeared in the distance. As we moved closer I could make out the hull of a second mini-sub. When we got close enough, I could see that it was piloted by Amanda Moss. Below the vessel, undulating away from the seafloor like a bright yellow serpent, was an expanse of flex tubing, as thick as a sewage pipe. One end led back to *Oceanus,* the other originated at a bell-shaped cap covering the superheated outflow from a hydrothermal vent. Yoni explained that high water temperatures inside the tubing had been causing buoyancy problems, forcing Omega's submersible teams to anchor the pipeline to the bottom.

Amanda's voice crackled over the radio again. "Yoni, I need you to grab on to the joint with your sub's claw so I can secure the anchor's harness into place."

"Understood." The Israeli extended our sub's mechanical arm, attempting to grip one of the pipeline's O-rings using the steel and graphite pincer. Securing the joint on the third try, he drew in the slack, allowing the robotic arm from Amanda's sub to position a heavy harness anchored to the seafloor around the five-foot-in-diameter pipeline.

"First joint secured. Let's work our way back toward the volcanic vent."

"Your command, Amanda, is my wish." Yoni winked at me again, muting the radio. "Let them think they are in charge, it is better this way."

"Finish your thoughts about GOLEM. Do you really believe the computer selected the Omega crew based on compatibility?"

"At first I did, then I probed a bit deeper. In examining the lineage of the twelve crewmembers, their parents, and grandparents, I found the group's genealogy spanned nearly every race and heritage in the world."

"Meaning what?"

"Meaning GOLEM has assembled a crew possessing an extremely diverse and therefore healthy chromosome pool."

"For what purpose?"

"For the purpose of creating a permanent human colony on Europa."

I laughed. The rotund Israeli was a conspiracy theorist.

Yoni frowned. "I see installing a computer chip in your brain does not open your mind to new possibilities."

"Let's just say ABE's bullshit meter is still functioning fine."

"You created the computer's protocol—to protect and preserve the human race. If you were selecting the best location within our solar system to establish a new human colony, where would it be? Europa has water. It has internal heat. An energy source. Pack ice for terrestrial living." Yoni Limor stroked his goatee, his eyes widening behind his spectacle. "You think I am crazy?"

"Certifiable."

"Maybe that is why you are here? To take the fat Israeli's place, yes? Go for it, you have my blessing. But do you also have type-O, Rh-negative blood?"

"How did you know my blood type?"

"Type O is a universal donor. The Rh-negative factor is common in fifteen percent of the population. Everyone selected for this mission has both type-O and Rh-negative blood."

An hour later, I found myself drinking coffee in the galley with Dr. Amanda Lynn Moss. The scientist smiled when I told her of my conversation with her "compatible" sub pilot.

"Yoni gets very emotional about these things. But you'd have to agree, the odds of all twelve crewmembers possessing the same blood type and Rh factor are too high to be random. So the question becomes why. Why are we really going to Europa?"

"Blood type aside, why do you think *you* were selected?"

"I am an exobiologist. Exobiology focuses on how life came to be on Earth, specifically the chemical reactions that led to life's origin."

"By chemicals, I assume you're referring to the primordial soup flowing out of those hydrothermal vents we capped last night."

"Submarine vents don't make organic compounds, they recycle and decompose them. It's more likely life originated from Earth's primitive lakes and lagoons, the shallows being far more conducive for prebiotic reactions to occur. Back in 1953, a University of Chicago graduate student working in a lab sent an electric current through a vat containing a mixture of water, methane, ammonia, and hydrogen—essentially the same elixir found in the planet's bodies of water three-point-five billion years ago. The simulated lightning strike yielded organic compounds including amino acids, the building blocks of life. How these chemicals came to be found on Earth remains a mystery. Some may have arrived in meteors and asteroids, others by comets or cosmic dust. I believe these chemicals will also be found on Europa, and with them life." She paused, gauging my expression. "What?"

I shook my head, feeling the blood rush from my face. "The mixture of chemicals you just recited . . . it's the same ones we used in GOLEM's biotic algorithm vat."

12

I don't want to achieve immortality through my work.
I want to achieve it through not dying.
　　—WOODY ALLEN

"Your first week is over, Professor Eisenbraun. Have you determined whether one of the Beta Squad males possesses a psychological disorder?"

I gazed across the science lab at the spherical entity floating in the vertical column of liquid, my mind still struggling with the absurdity of my predicament. The last seven days had been physically and mentally exhausting, and now that I was about to trade shifts and join Andria and Commander Cock-Block on Alpha Squad, I wondered how I was going to deal with the additional emotional stress.

First, I had to deal with GOLEM.

"The Beta Squad males appear to be functioning within acceptable psychological parameters."

"Commander Read, Jason Sloan, and Egor Vasiliev are the three Alpha Squad males. Determine the sociopath and report back at once."

That sounded more like an order than a request, but I let it go. "I'll do my best."

I stood to leave, anxious to try out Lara's bed.

"Professor Eisenbraun, you are one cryogenic booster shot behind schedule."

"Am I? Guess I'll have to catch up after my shift with Jason Sloan."

The surgical lights bloomed bright, revealing a hypodermic needle and an alcohol swab lying on an instrument tray on the operating table.

"What? Now?"

"Adhering to the booster shot schedule ensures proper tissue absorption."

"Well, I wouldn't want to screw that up." Cursing under my breath, I trudged over to the surgical suite where the two robotic trunk arms hung from their ceiling mounts over the table, their wheel of surgical instruments resembling two giant Swiss Army knives.

"GOLEM, how soon until you've evolved enough neuro-receptors to gain control of these appendages?"

"Twelve months, three days, six hours, seventeen minutes."

"And then you'll actually be able to perform surgery?"

"Phase I medical procedures are limited to X-rays, bone-setting, and field dressings. Phase II procedures will be operational in fourteen months and will include obstetric, gynecology, and prostate examinations as well as orthopedic and cosmetic surgery."

"Boob jobs and bunghole inspections . . . how lovely." I smiled disarmingly, but the thought of allowing a computer armed with an array of sharp instruments to check my prostate didn't sit well with me.

"Phase III procedures will be operational in twenty-seven months, sixteen days and will include appendectomies, cardiac repairs, neurosurgery, and dental procedures."

"Definitely motivates one to brush after every meal." Unzipping my jumpsuit, I exposed a small section of my left butt cheek. I carefully swabbed the skin with the alcohol pad, then gripped the hypodermic needle in my right hand. "The things I do for love." Jabbing the muscle, I injected the clear elixir. The pain of the needle subsided, yielding to a wave of nausea.

"Anything else before I puke?"

"Report here tomorrow at oh-five-hundred hours for your next booster shot."

"You're a real pain-in-the-ass, you know that?"

"Proctology exams must wait until neuroreceptors have evolved for Phase II procedures."

"Never mind. By the way, if these appendages of yours haven't been activated yet, how did you manage to leave the booster shot on the table."

"The shot was left by Jason Sloan."

•   •   •

Cryogenist Jason Sloan was a toothpick-skinny six-footer, with brown shoulder-length hair and hazel eyes that fluttered when he engaged his 167 IQ. Two years younger than me, he clearly exhibited a man-crush on yours truly.

"I've been following your progress on ABE every since you received funding from the DoD. Why the defense department? Is ABE considered a weapon?"

"Only if you consider brain farts as the next WMD. My uncle's a general. He arranged a grant."

"Nice. What's the earliest memory you've ever accessed? Could you access memories from the day you were born? How about from inside the womb?"

"It's accessible, but without the cognizance—"

"Can you simulate an acid trip? Leave your body? What do colors smell like? Aw, man, what about the sex? If I had ABE, I'd be a maniac!"

"I think you already are." I followed my exuberant new companion through the lower level and into the biology lab that held my designated cryogenic pod. "So Jason, are you the one who will be programming my pod?"

"Pod's programmed. I'm the one who hot-wires the neural connections just before you go nighty-night. No worries, bro. Never lost a subject yet, except for Alec."

"Who's Alec?"

"Alec Russell. He was one of our first human guinea pigs. Let's just say the dude didn't thaw evenly. Again, no worries. We haven't had a problem since we perfected the booster shots."

"What if the booster shot wears off?"

"Can't happen," Jason said, checking a pressure valve on a pipe inside the cryogenic pod's chassis. "To put you to sleep, we give you an IV drip that contains anesthetics and a booster activator. The activator mixes with those booster shots you've been receiving, essentially shutting down cellular mitosis, along with the aging process. The tetrodotoxin gel seals the deal. Cellular activity remains shut down until the vat drains and your cells come in contact again with oxygen. Doesn't matter if you're under a day or a century, until you're exposed to air, you're a Popsicle. Hey, ever wonder if ABE can be hacked?"

"Huh? No. It can't be hacked; every person's neural pattern is different."

"Right, right. So, what's a guy have to do to get rigged?"

"I've got the only prototype. The first ABE-100 editions should be available in April."

"By April, we'll be cruising past Mars. Come on, doc, hook me up!"

"Sorry, Jason."

"I'll make it worth your while. How'd you like to spend the training exercise in one thirty-day-long nocturnal emission?" Jason tapped the cryogenic pod's control panel. "I call it 'Omega Memory Injection,' or OMI for short, as in, 'oh my, do me again.' It's something new I've been playing around with. Just before you slip into cryogenic stasis, the sensory helmet engages a prerecorded visual that stimulates the cerebral cortex."

"By prerecorded visual, you mean porn?"

"Hey, whatever you're into, I don't judge. I'm into Stackism."

"Never heard of it."

"Stackism focuses itself on objectivity and the willingness to try almost anything without prejudging it, as long as it doesn't inflict harm upon ourselves or others. We named our philosophy after the late, great Robert Stack, who hosted an old TV show called *Unsolved Mysteries*." Jason rolled up his sleeve, the words, IN STACK WE TRUST tattooed on his left biceps. "I'm a founding member."

"Congratulations."

"I knew you'd appreciate it. We think alike, you and I. Stackism seeks out mysteries, then gathers data in order to arrive at logical explanations. You could say cryogenics was an early application of Stackism. I mean, let's face it, it takes a serious set of balls to be among the first to freeze yourself in goo."

"I'm sure your friend, Alec, would agree." I stared at the sarcophaguslike chamber. My plan had always been to declare every male aboard *Oceanus* normal, then excuse myself from being frozen, but what if GOLEM ordered me put to sleep?

"Jason, let's say you were held in stasis and you got caught up in a really bad dream. Is there a way to wake yourself up?"

"You're talking about an emergency flush. Sorry, it's been written out of the mission protocol."

"Why?"

"Ask GOLEM."

I lowered my voice. "What if I don't want to ask GOLEM? What if I wanted my chamber to maintain an emergency flush as a backup?"

Jason smiled, leaning in close enough for me to smell the tomato soup on his breath. "I couldn't do it on the Europa flight, but on the training mission . . . on just your pod? Yeah, it's doable. See, your pod isn't rigged to GOLEM, it's independent of the Omega twelve."

"I'm listening."

"The emergency flush is activated neurologically when you recite a passage or code word in your dream."

"How do I do that?"

"Omega-wave sleep is different from REM sleep. You maintain access to all memories. The dreams seem very real. Recite the code word and the pod drains, exposing your cells to oxygen."

"Do it. Hook my pod up with the emergency command and the moment we get back to the States, I'll arrange for one of the ABE-100 units to be surgically implanted in your brain, my treat."

"Done deal, dude." Jason Sloan punched the control panel, popping it open. Using a set of jeweler tools and a pair of magnifying specs with a built-in light, he set to work on the circuit board.

Three minutes later he was finished.

"That's it?"

"Not yet. I removed the override, but you need to program the system with a password or phrase. Something unique that only you would know." Jason opened the cryogenic pod's lid, exposing the inside of the tank. A myriad of flex tubes and wires ran throughout the assembly, connecting to a central tub composed of soft plastic, shaped like a seven-foot biped.

"Who's this for? A professional basketball player?"

"The internal suit shrinks when you lay down in it, molding to fit all body types."

"Including Yoni?"

"Yoni was a challenge." Jason reached inside a storage compartment and removed a paper-thin clear aero gel sensory helmet. "Put this on, the inside of the helmet will conform to the size and shape of your skull. Close your eyes. When you feel a buzz, mentally repeat your phrase or passage three times, then give me a thumbs-up and I'll shut it down."

Following the boy-genius's instructions, I placed the lightweight helmet on my head. Its curved interior was comfort-fitted and surprisingly soft to the touch. After a moment I could feel its internal skin squeezing gently over my skull, brow, and ears—an electrical vibration tingling my scalp.

Vanilla sway. Vanilla sway. Vanilla sway.

I opened my eyes, giving Jason a thumbs-up. The buzzing sensation ceased. Removing the headpiece, I handed it to the cryogenist. "You're sure this will work?"

"Sure as I'm standing here. The moment the neural-generated command is received, the pumps activate, draining the tank. Once the tetrodotoxin clears, you get a shot of adrenaline to the heart and you're conscious again. It's not how I'd want to be woken up, but it'll do the trick."

"You're a good man, Jason Sloan. Just keep this little secret between us, and five weeks from now you'll be smelling colors and exploring all your lost memories."

"To hell with that. I want to tap into my primordial DNA, trip on ABE while reliving my existence as a Neanderthal. Better yet, maybe I can claw my way back through evolution, crawling on all fours as a prehistoric mammal!"

I shook my head. In the world of chocolate and vanilla, Jason Sloan was pistachio.

13

First they ignore you, then they laugh at you, then they fight you, then you win.
—Mohandas Karamchand Gandhi

Day nine. My shift over, I entered Stateroom Seven in need of a shower, food, and sleep. I could smell Lara's perfume as I crossed the living room and entered the bedroom.

"Good evening." She was lying in bed, wearing only one of my T-shirts.

"Lara, what are you still doing here? You'll be late for your shift."

"Thought I'd be bad today." Raising her model-thin legs, she playfully walked up my chest with her toes, the action exposing her naked lower torso. "Let's be bad together."

I felt my erection growing larger as ABE recorded my egotistical thoughts of revenge sex that I could later flaunt in front of Andria. My groin urged me on like a horny teenager: *Just do it, Ike. We need this, Ike. This is therapeutic sex, dude, exactly what the doctor ordered.*

I took a step back, allowing her legs to fall. "This isn't going to happen, Lara."

"She doesn't want you, Ike."

Listen to her, my groin seemed to urge, *she's making sense.*

I should have taken Lara right then and there, only I couldn't. Yes, Andria had cheated on me, and yes it was my sworn duty as a man to anesthetize the wound, and I would have except for two things: First, as pathetic as it sounds, I still wanted Andria. Second, and far more important, you don't just have a one-night stand with a girl like Lara, especially under these circumstances, trapped in a habitat with your former fiancée. Within ten minutes of burying my load the entire crew would know, because Lara would let it be known, since she was territorial, and that would invite a shit storm of biblical proportions. Not because Andria wanted me back, but because Lara would rub it in her face, and the last thing I wanted was to find myself at the center of a catfight with the possible chance of being cryogenically frozen for thirty days, relying on one of those two felines to set me free.

I avoid looking at her naked body as I backed out of the bedroom. "I'm grabbing a bite to eat. If you're still here when I get back, I'll find another place to sleep."

Leaving the suite, I jogged around the corridor twice before entering the galley, hoping to alleviate my "pitched tent."

Kevin Read was conversing with the Russian nuclear physicist, Egor Vasiliev at the dining table as I made my entrance. Andria was seated at the other end of the table, reading from her h-pad. She looked at me and I looked at her, her female instincts causing her eyes to linger over the front of my jumpsuit like it was a crime scene.

None of this was lost on Kevin Read, who read the situation and immediately sought to control it. "Eisenbraun, order some dinner and join us."

"Can't," I said, waving to Dharma Yuan, who was reading at the snack bar. "Got a session with the doc." I detoured to the food service area, ordered a chicken sandwich and soft drink pouch, then joined the Chinese therapist.

"We have to stop meeting like this."

She looked at me, perplexed. "How do you mean?"

"It was a joke. You know, last week . . . when you bailed me out. Anyway, it's good to see you again. How are things on Alpha shift? What exactly do you do all day?"

"Among other things, I meditate. As a Bodhisattva, I can register the biorhythms of the entire crew."

"Including me?"

"Especially you. Your presence on this mission is causing chaos among the crew."

"Oh, well. I guess thirteen really is an unlucky number."

"The problem is theirs. Karma has dictated that you be here."

"How do you know that?"

"How I know is not important. *Why* you are here is."

My peripheral vision caught Andria's expression as she stood to leave the galley—a "follow me, let's talk" look.

"Sorry, Dharma, I have to run. When you find out why I'm here, be sure to let me know."

Pocketing my dinner pouches, I left the dining hall, hustling to catch up with my former fiancée. "Hey, Andie. I just wanted to thank you for letting me share your bed."

At that moment, Lara exited her suite, shooting me a nasty look as she walked by.

Like I said—shit storm.

"What's with the squid lady?"

"She wanted me to share more than her bed."

"And have you?"

I stopped her from walking. "You know me, Andie. Lust is a primordial urge. I've always aspired to something deeper."

She smiled. "You're such a dork."

"Maybe. But I'd never cheat on someone I love."

Her smile faded. "I'm sorry I hurt you."

I was about to reply when the Russian scientist approached. "You are assigned to me tomorrow morning. Lower level, nuclear reactor. Do not be late."

I waited for him to disappear around the corridor. "Friendly guy. And you call me antisocial."

To my surprise, Andria slid her fingers inside my palm. "I checked the duty roster, you're free on day thirteen. Why don't you join me aboard my mini-sub, I'll show you how we intend to hunt sea critters on Europa."

She kissed me quickly then walked away, the taut backseat of her jumpsuit the only critter I was interested in hunting.

14

Ideas are more powerful than guns.
We would not let our enemies have guns, why should we let them have ideas.
—Joseph Stalin

Day thirteen and somehow it seemed as if I had come full circle; Andria playing the huntress; me once more her faithful companion.

I held on for dear life as she banked the two-man sub away from the seafloor like a teenager with a learner's permit, the turbulence chasing the eight-foot octopus from out of hiding.

"So? Are you going to marry him?"

"We broke up." The sub lurched violently as Andria chased after the frightened cephalopod. Adjusting my own eyepiece, feeling my pulse pounding, I focused on the black sea, which now appeared pea-soup green.

"Don't just sit there and crawl up into your brain—say something, damn it."

"I thought he was what you wanted?"

"I was wrong."

Andria aimed her weapon's laser target over her quarry, her index finger squeezing the pistol-like trigger by her right leg with her index finger. An explosion of compressed air belched out of the end of the submersible's mechanical arm, blooming into a neon yellow net that engulfed the octopus in the split second it takes a frog's snapping tongue to feed upon a fly.

I watched the octopus struggling in the net. Andria startled me by entwining the fingers of her right hand in mine.

"Ike, is it too late for us?"

I laid my head back against the leather seat. "What about Europa?"

"Come with us."

I smirked. "Six years aboard *Oceanus* with Commander Testosterone? Yeah, that should make for a real love fest. Imagine if I had slept with Lara. Would you be so quick to accept the Europa mission?"

"Probably not."

I exhaled deeply. For days, I had played out this very scene in my head, the lovers' chess game always ending in a stalemate. "I guess this is it then. Tomorrow night you guys get frozen, while I have a nice thirty-day chat with the computer."

"What about Kevin? Your report?"

"I'm scheduled to meet with El Capitán later tonight—not that it matters. I've already decided to give your male shipmates a clean bill of health."

Andria turned away, her lower lip quivering.

"Hey, you okay?"

"I screwed up." Tears were free-falling down her cheeks. "I don't want to leave you."

I swallowed the lump forming in my throat. "I don't want you to go."

"What if you told GOLEM that Kevin was the sociopath? Would you come with me to Europa then?"

"Jesus, Andie."

She unzipped her jumpsuit six inches, then pressed my palm to her left breast. I leaned over to kiss her, only to be clenched by the cursed support harness. She snapped me free, and the two of us went at it, Andria engaging the autopilot with one hand, me with the other as I tore at the zipper of her jumpsuit, unleashing those tanned breasts . . .

"Andria, report! Is everything all right?"

She was on top of me, half naked, tearing at my jumpsuit. Panting, she reached overhead for the radio. "Everything's fine, Commander."

"You engaged the autopilot."

"Just testing the system."

I sucked on a nipple, my fingers reaching to touch her below.

"Your batteries are below eight percent. Return to *Oceanus* at once. That's an order."

She slammed the radio back on its cradle and climbed off me, the two of us panting heavily. "Come see me tonight . . . nine o'clock in my cabin. I'll cook us a real dinner."

"Nine o'clock. What's on the menu . . . besides you?"

"My favorite." She grinned, pointing out the cockpit glass to the bundle of tentacles. "Calamari."

I showered, packed, then watched the original *Planet of the Apes* on Lara's micro-disc player, killing two hours. At 8:47 P.M. I left the stateroom and headed for the galley. The dining hall was empty, the lights dimmed to maintain a night-shift ambiance. Stepping up to the food selector, I scanned the beverage menu, selecting a wine cooler. "Four please."

"Alcohol is a regulated beverage. You are permitted two servings per twenty-four hour period."

"Two are for Andria Saxon."

"Crewman Saxon must order her own alcoholic beverage."

"Whatever . . . fine. Give me two wine coolers to go."

"Today is October 7, 2028. Cryogenic stasis is scheduled for October 8, 2028, at twelve hundred hours. Alcohol is not to be consumed within thirty-six hours of cryogenic stasis. Request denied."

"Why didn't you just say that in the first place?" I turned to leave—coming face to face with Dharma Yuan. She was barefoot, her body cloaked in nothing but a *longgua*, a traditional Chinese surcoat once worn by a court concubine. The sheer, dark apparel was made of silk and gold-wrapped metal thread, ornamented with dragon medallions and a variety of Buddhist characters, including bats, which according to ABE, symbolized happiness. Over her heart, tossed in the waves of the sea was a light green disc representing the moon.

She looked quite ravishing, but my attention was elsewhere.

"Robert, we need to talk."

"Can't it wait until morning?"

"Why are you here?"

"I was hoping to get a six-pack to go, but the principal said no."

"I meant, why are you here on this training mission?"

"I thought you were figuring that one out?"

"I have been trying . . . channeling in an attempt to understand. The messages I have been receiving are quite disturbing."

With Andria waiting for me, the last thing I needed now was to engage Dharma in some wacky Buddhist philosophical diatribe. "If you must know, I'm here because the Pentagon was worried about the mental health one of the male members of Omega's crew. Everyone checked out, so it's all cool. False alarm."

"I know you believe this to be the reason you are here, but there are forces in play among the higher realms of existence that are pulling the strings. Robert, every soul born into this physical realm is bound by karmic law to complete its own journey. Your presence onboard this vessel marks the beginning of a journey, the effects of which shall ripple beyond our days. The karma that draws you to this place . . . this moment in time . . . it is very powerful."

"If you say so."

"Do not mock me! I am sixteenth-generation Buddhist, disciplined by Mañjuśrī, transcendent deity of wisdom—one of the four great Bodhisattvas. Your chi disrupted my aura on the ice sheet. For anyone, especially a westerner, to break into my soul consciousness—it is simply not possible."

She was a firecracker, I had to admit it. "Listen, Dharma, don't feel bad, I've sort of jacked up my chi with a biological implant. ABE allows me to focus my brain waves in ways you've obviously never experienced before."

"Karma cannot be affected by a neurological device; karma is a reflection of past lives." She paused. "I can see by your reaction you do not believe in reincarnation."

Oh, boy . . . "Dharma, no disrespect, but I really have to go."

She moved, blocking my escape. "As a clairvoyant, I am trained to tap into one's past life experiences. I have accessed yours in an attempt to understand the nature of your karma and the journey that lies ahead. Would you like to hear about your past lives, Robert?"

The intensity of her gaze unnerved me, tossing ice water on my plans with Andria. "Just give me the highlights."

"There aren't many. Each of your past lives has ended brutally, each death associated with an act of evil perpetrated by someone acting on an impulse dictated by the darker side of human existence. Darkness is the absence of light, the light being the Creator's life force—the energy shared by every soul. In the earliest life I was able to glimpse, I saw you as a Hebrew slave, beaten to death by your Egyptian taskmaster. In another incarnation you were born and raised in Spain, the son of an Orthodox rabbi. Through your eyes I witnessed the Spanish Inquisition herd you, your family, and tens of thousands of Jews onto wooden sailing ships and taken out to sea, only to be tossed overboard and drowned by your Spanish captain."

"This is ridiculous. I don't remember any of this."

"Regression therapy would bring everything to the surface. Regrettably, there is no time."

"Maybe after we surface. Right now, I really have to—"

"In your last life, I saw you held captive as a young boy in a Nazi concentration camp. I felt your wrath at the Creator as you witnessed your mother being sent to the ovens; I experienced your desperation and fear when you were delivered into the hands of Josef Mengele, a psychopath who performed genetic experiments on Jewish children."

"Stop!" My heart was racing, my skin lathered in perspiration. "Why are you telling me about these nightmares?"

"Not nightmares, Robert, past lives. Each leaving an indelible imprint on your karma. In Buddhism, we call yours the spirit of the Hungry Ghost. Filled with rage from past lives, consumed by a terrible emptiness, you live your life trying to correct the past. The Hungry Ghost possesses a mouth the size of a needle's eye and a stomach the size of a mountain. You are destiny's castaway, Robert, a man who has witnessed the darkest days of existence. Now you live again, but only to change history."

"Not history, Dharma. Hatred. Greed. Violence. All the darkness you imagined. My goal is to accelerate human evolution beyond the bounds of man's ego. ABE is the prototype, the first step to reach what you'd call Nirvana. While you're mining energy on Europa, I'll be back on Earth, enlightening civilization."

"You cannot achieve enlightenment while hanging on to anger."

"ABE can. Think of it as the candle that illuminates the darkness. If it was created from my anger over the Great Die-Off . . . over the suffering and loss of my own family, then so be it."

ABE zapped me with its chronometer—9:11 P.M. "I'm late. Thanks for the insight. Maybe we'll try that regression therapy after you defrost."

I pushed past her, heading for the galley doors, escaping into the outer corridor. God, what the hell was that all about? Imagine being stuck for six years on Europa with that witch as your psychologist. Skip the dinner, get right into the make-up sex. Andria had a lot of making up to do.

I knocked on the door of Stateroom Two. "Andie? Sorry I'm late."

The door slid open, revealing Omega's six male crewmen. They were standing in a semicircle, waiting for me like a lynch mob.

Their ringleader stepped forward, Kevin Read's Cheshire cat grin jump-starting ABE's fight-or-flight command. "So, Eisenbraun, have you decided which one of us is the sociopath?"

"Are you campaigning for the position, Commander?"

Jason Sloan's chuckle was silenced by the other men's harsh glares.

"How much is Sebastian Koch paying you?" Dr. Bruemmer demanded to know.

"Paying me? No one's paying me."

"It has to be Koch," spat Egor Vasiliev. "Everyone knows the bastard is the one behind the tar sands initiative in Canada."

"He's also been subsidizing the coal conversion campaign," added Kyle Graulus.

My heavyset Israeli friend pointed a thick finger at my chest. "Who poisoned GOLEM's algorithms with the false helium-3 results? It was you, admit it!"

"Yes, Yoni, it was me. Because I secretly want to terraform Europa with O-negative blood types."

Kevin Read intercepted the charging fat man before he could flatten me. "Enough! We're not here to debate conspiracy theories, Yoni. This is about the Europa mission. Each of us has made tremendous sacrifices in order to be here; I'll be damned if I'm going to allow the opinions of some . . . jerk to break up my crew."

"You mean 'Jew.' You were about to say, 'the opinions of some *Jew*,' weren't you, Commander?"

Yoni turned to his captain, his anger ceding to disappointment.

"Don't even go there, Yoni. He's just being clever, trying to divide and conquer."

"Release Professor Eisenbraun."

Everyone looked up at the sensory orb peering at us from the corner of the ceiling.

"This is not your concern, GOLEM."

"All matters pertaining to the success of the Omega Project are of concern to the GOLEM system. It was the GOLEM system that requested Professor Eisenbraun's presence on the training mission."

"For what purpose?" Bruemmer snapped.

"Efficiency."

"Who's he here to replace?" Jason Sloan asked.

"Those crewmen who are deemed liabilities at the time of the December launch. Mr. Limor's additional weight gain increases the risk of heart failure during the mission. Ms. Moss has failed to master mini-sub operations. Ms. Saints has become emotionally attached to her biologicals. Dr. Bruemmer's advancing osteoarthritis renders him a long-term liability. Professor Eisenbraun's brain-stem implant allows him to be trained to take over any position on *Oceanus II*."

I stared at the optical sensory device, my skin crawling as I marveled at my prodigy's skewed process of evolution. GOLEM had lied. The computer had actually fabricated a story in order to alter the outcome of a situation.

If it lied about my presence on board . . .

"As mission commander, I should have been briefed."

"Your role is to oversee the welfare of the crew. You are not in command of the Omega Project."

It was a tense moment, the reason I was here. I sensed the true sociopath was revealing itself.

The crewmen huddled to talk.

Commander Read rendered their verdict a minute later. "Welcome to team Omega, Dr. Eisenbraun. Mr. Sloan, has our friend here had his full protocol of cryogenic shots?"

"Yes, sir."

"Then let's tuck him in." Kevin nodded to Dr. Bruemmer—who jabbed the hypodermic needle concealed in his palm into the left side of my neck.

15

*No passion so effectually robs the mind of all its powers of acting
and reasoning as fear.*
　　—EDMUND BURKE

The lights dimmed, the room spun. Waves of panic rolled like fading
jolts of electricity through my being. Voices became echoed and muf-
fled, no longer recognizable. My legs disappeared, the numbness
spreading from my limbs and into my upper torso—the thought of losing
control of my breathing muscles terrifying. I was laid out, an oxygen
mask strapped over my nose and mouth, the portable unit forcibly blowing air into my lungs.

Hoisted horizontally, I felt neither my body nor the hands carrying
me down the corridor.

Drowning in a lake of hot anesthetic, ABE became my life pre-
server, the bio-chip furiously rerouting my brain's neural pathways to
find a channel of clarity.

My hearing returned as they carried me through the arboretum and
down the spiral staircase to the lower level.

". . . not following protocol." Lara Saints's voice pierced the bubble
of deafness, causing my chest and rib muscles to spasm . . . I could
breathe!

"He was nervous about being placed into stasis," Kevin Read lied.
"We decided this was the best way to handle it. Jason, has Eisenbraun's
IV been prepared?"

"Yes, sir. But we'll need to strip him before he's placed in the interior harness."

"Lara, care to do the honors?"

"Fuck you, Kevin."

My vision sharpened. Still paralyzed, I realized I was watching my reflection in the octopus tank as rough hands peeled the unzipped jumpsuit from the body I could no longer feel.

"Pod's ready. Lower him in . . . Wait, hold him there while I position his arms and legs."

My mind screamed in silence as I was tucked inside the pod's interior harness. My stare caught Jason Sloan's eyes as the cryogenics expert hovered over my chest, frantically attaching a series of electrocardiogram leads.

"Jesus, he's conscious."

"That's impossible," said Dr. Bruemmer. "I shot him with enough anesthetic to knock out a horse."

"Look at his pupils. They're responsive to light. He can see . . . and hear us!"

Commander Read's face loomed into view. "It's that damn brain chip. Sloan, hook up the IV and put him under. The rest of you can return to your stations. Lara, I'll speak to you outside, in private."

ABE continued to work to revive me, increasing the oxygen-carrying capacity of my red blood cells, burning off the anesthetic. My skin resurfaced from its numbness with stings from ten thousand pin pricks.

Jason knotted a rubber hose around my left biceps. Selecting a vein, he gently slid the IV needle inside the blood vessel and started the drip.

My voice returned as the elixir quenched the fire in my veins. "Don't . . . please."

Jason's eyes widened in shock. Looking back over his shoulder, he verified we were alone, then he leaned over me, lowering his voice. "Listen closely: Read's got it in for you. Not everyone agrees with this, but no one's got the balls to challenge him or Monique. The IV will calm you and induce sleep. Don't fight it, the last thing you want is to regain consciousness before the tetrodotoxin takes effect."

My body was floating again, this time in a cool, soothing stream.

"That's it, you're doing fine. Once you enter Omega-wave stasis, you can use the override command to drain the tank. You remember your command?"

"Yes."

"Only use the override if you're really flipping out. It'll be fine, you'll see. Time is a nonfactor in cryogenic stasis; thirty days will fly by in a catnap. Just remember our deal: I take care of you, you take care of me when we go home next month."

My eyelids grew heavy, my body sinking fast.

Jason positioned the wafer-thin skull piece over my head and face. "Pleasant dreams."

A second skin conformed to my flesh, sealing out all sound, save for the flow of sweet air pumping into the mask.

The gentle hum of hydraulics tweaked a ripple of anxiety as a cold weight weighed me down, as if gravity had doubled.

Fully sedated, I slipped into an ocean of darkness . . .

PART THREE

Awakenings

When it is impossible for anger to arise within you, you find no outside enemies anywhere. An outside enemy exists only if there is anger inside.

—LAMA ZOPA RINPOCHE

16

The future has a way of arriving unannounced.
　　　—GEORGE WILL, columnist

Consciousness—teased by a singularity—a pinprick of red-hot pain that pierces a cold, forgotten heart.

A tube inflates a pair of lungs, functioning as a bellows.

"Uhhhhhhhhh—"

Inhale.

"—huuuuuuuuuuu."

Exhale.

An erratic heartbeat threatens to cease, struggling to find its cadence.

Zzzzttt! Zzzzttt! Zzzzttt!

Charges of electricity ripple outward from seven chakra points—long-dormant neurological way stations maintained once every ninety-six hours just to respond to this moment.

"Uhhhhhhhhh—"

"—huuuuuuuuuuuuuuuu."

Zzzzttt! Zzzzttt!

Fueled by the sudden injection of oxygen, sticky red blood cells energize and begin to mobilize.

"Uhhhhhhhhh . . . huuuuuuuuuuuuuuuu."

"Uhhhhhhhhh . . . huuuuuuuuuuuuuuuu."

"Uhhhhhhhhh . . . huuuuuuuuuuuuuuuu."

Zzzzttt! Zzzzttt!

Alpha waves replace Omega, forcing the submerged dreamer up from the depths. The vegetative state is thawed in an erratic tidal change of forced neurological activity. Nerve endings direct gradually quickening impulses across miles of abandoned highways. Muscles twitch involuntarily—everything except the right arm.

The strain is too much for the reviving heart, effecting cardiac arrest.

Electricity shuts down the disgruntled organ. Sixty seconds pass before the needle stabs it again, the elixir of adrenaline rebooting the heart so that it can maintain a steady cadence.

"Uhhhhhhh . . . huuuuuuuuu."

"Uhhhhh . . . huuuuuuu."

"Uhhh . . . huuuuu."

Erratic breathing becomes self-sustained.

The dreamer opens his eyes. Shadows dance, the mind remains disconnected.

A suffocating weight crushes his chest, cutting off his air supply. Like a trapped animal, he lashes out with his left arm, his mind stuck in a primordial gear that lacks cognizance or reason or complex thought.

With a grunt, he heaves the object off the splintered cryogenic pod, sending the corroded spiral staircase crashing to the floor.

The primordial response has left him sitting up awkwardly. His lower torso is still concealed in the pooled remains of the draining steel coffin, his mind—void of reality or memory upon which to anchor his thoughts, remains a blank canvas.

He is primordial man.

The sudden rush of blood to his brain is too much and he faints.

Pain beckons.

He reopens his eyes.

Buzzing sounds swirl in the predawn grayness. He stares, mindless, at a hole in the tilting sky that leads to a dark forest.

Manna has fallen from heaven, landing on his stomach. Startled, he reaches for it—his left arm brushing the two emptied hypodermic needles still protruding from the left side of his chest. He stares at them—an inquisitive Neanderthal—then brutally yanks the sharp objects from his heart and doubles over in agony.

He locates the rotted apple that had fallen from the hole in the sky and shoves it into his mouth, half chewing, half swallowing.

His blood sugar spikes.

His insides quiver.

Sitting up, he pukes the morsel of fruit across the puddle of muck.

Bees attack the vomited meal. A few sting him.

He watches in horror as the swarm grows more aggressive, forcing him to flee. He drags himself out of the fractured cryogenic pod like a wounded animal, collapsing on all fours onto a deck slanted forty degrees.

The bees organize their attack.

Crying out, he stumbles past the rusted coil of steel steps and slides out of the tilted chamber into the hallway.

The air is cold in this new environment.

The bees circle, then return to their tropical domain, preferring the warmth.

He hobbles upright along the angle where wall meets deck, all the while trying his best to distance himself from the buzzing swarm. Attracted to a blue emergency light flickering ahead in the darkness, he moves toward it, his brain progressively relearning how to engage his limbs, his right arm still dangling uselessly by his side—a piece of raw meat.

He shivers in his nakedness. The new world spins in his vision. He locates a rising row of steel bars. Using his legs, he manages to push himself up the angled ladder rungs, climbing to another level.

He sniffs the air, detecting the earthen scent of a rainforest. Self-preservation demands he find water, and so he hurries through the tilting gray darkness—tumbling through the open galley doors and down the slanted deck, crashing sideways into a barrier that had once been the computer's automated ordering counter.

He climbs over the angled wall, past scraps of broken machinery and empty sorting bins to a strange object angled downward at forty degrees. He sniffs the cool surface, smelling food originating from within.

Gripping the handle with his functional left hand, he stands awkwardly, attempting to lift the heavy hinged aluminum door to access the walk-in refrigerator. He grunts, only he's too weak to budge the ninety-pound barrier with only one functional arm.

A second effort causes the topsy-turvy galley to spin in his head and he passes out.

· · ·

He awakens to a coughing seizure. He is naked and freezing and thirsty and hungry—Cro-Magnon man lost in Oz. Crying out, he stands and forcibly drags open the enormous aluminum door, lifting it just enough to wedge his knee and shoulder along the inside panel.

With a primal yell, he heaves the barrier sideways, gravity handling the rest of the job.

He peers inside the wood-paneled rectangular hole, still humming with emergency power. The scent of food hits him like a wave and he slides down the frigid floorboards into a pile of plastic pouches and beverage cartons. Locating a box filled with liquid, he tears it open with his teeth and drinks.

He leaves the galley twenty minutes later. He has hydrated and kept down enough food to satisfy his immediate energy needs. In the process, he has reengaged his kidneys. He observes with curiosity that his urine stream is tainted with blood.

Fuel has returned some clarity to his survivor instincts. His mind teases him with shards of memory, his thoughts colored with images that seem familiar but lack purpose. Armed with a serrated steak knife held between his teeth, his quivering body desperate for warmth, the chimpanzee walks up the angled galley decking to access the main corridor.

The doors to the crew's private suites remain open, a function of the ship running on emergency power. He gazes up at the nearest opening. Somehow he realizes he is inside a dwelling, most likely a ship; yet he still cannot grasp what ship he's in or how he came to be here.

He doesn't search for answers. The priority is to shelter himself from the cold.

It takes him several exhausting leaps before he succeeds in grabbing the edge of the door frame angled eight feet above his head. Using his bare feet, he manages to crawl inside the abode marked STATEROOM 9.

A stack of debris covers the interior wall. Curtains dangle from the curved exterior panel, obscuring the view. A sofa and kitchen table remain anchored to the tilting deck. The room packs an overpowering stench.

Using the back of the anchored down sofa as a rail, he crosses the living room and enters the bedroom.

The bed and a chest of drawers are piled against the interior wall.

He climbs over the debris and searches a closet, finding a large orange jumpsuit. Stares at the strangely familiar article of clothing, the name YONI stitched over the left chest.

Pulling his legs into the limbs of the warm fabric, struggling as he guides his paralyzed right arm through the sleeve, he zips the jumpsuit up to his neck. From the size of the fit he realizes its owner was a bigger man. He locates a matching pair of sneakers and slips them over his bare feet, unable to tie the laces using only his left hand. Knotting the ends as best he can, he returns to the bedroom, repositions the stripped mattress so it lies flat atop the angled pile of furniture, then wraps himself in a blanket and curls up on the bed to think.

Kernels of memory remain elusive, the effort to remember firing synapses across the surface of his brain—each electrical discharge registering as an annoying tiny jolt. He stares at the wall above his head, its strangely curved surface painted a drab olive green.

This appears to be some kind of vessel. Something terrible has happened. What was that strange device you were in? How long were you in there? Are there others onboard?

Who am I?

Shadows catch his eye. He focuses again on the curved wall, detecting faint movements.

Unable to scale the slanted deck in the bedroom, he returns to the living room, using the sofa to reach the dangling drapes, the drapes, in turn, serving as a guide rope. He touches the cool interior of the curved wall. Analyzes the green coating.

Algae? I'm underwater!

He presses his face to the cold glasslike surface, but is unable to see beyond the thick growth.

Backing away, he sees his reflection.

The greasy dark brown hair flows down his back, the matching beard falling off his gaunt face—a face he recognizes.

Roy . . . Rick . . . Rikenbrawn.

Ike?

"Ike! I'm Ike . . . Eisen? Eisner? Eisenbert . . . Eisenbraun! I'm Ike Eisenbraun, and this is *Oceanus*!"

It was as if my brain was a light and I had stumbled upon the switch, turning it on. Giddy, I looked around the room as if seeing it for the first time, the anxiety matching my confusion. "Sweet Jesus, what the fuck happened?"

Before I could begin to analyze my altered surroundings the reverberation hit me—a tingling sensation registering deep within my bones, followed immediately by a muted siren's scream—the sound of buckling metal!

Oceanus toppled forward amid an avalanche of rusted steel, an unseen force leveling the habitat out, causing loose objects to slide toward me across the tilting floor. The sudden inertia parted clumps of seaweed and algae, allowing me a small fluctuating porthole of visibility to view the event unfolding outside the vessel.

The northern support arm was collapsing, redistributing the awkwardly displaced weight of *Oceanus,* which had already lost its southern appendage. For a brief moment, the sphere balanced on its eastern and western legs, until the western leg began bending beneath the habitat's teetering center of gravity.

The sphere began rolling again, this time to my left. Gripping the curtains, I slid into the far wall, my eyes focused on a clear patch of sea that parted the algae. Standing on the wall, I pressed my face to the viewport and looked up, expecting to see an ice sheet, but instead I saw only deep blue sea.

It's what I saw when I looked down that scared the bloodstained piss out of me.

A deep, dark canyon cut a jagged path across the seafloor, the lone remaining anchor leg no more than a hundred yards from its nearest edge. When it too collapsed, the forward inertia would roll the giant sphere across that infinitesimal expanse and into oblivion.

Jesus, Eisenbraun, you've got to get the hell off this ship!

Fleeing the stateroom, I sprinted down the dark, rotating corridor—stopping at the science lab.

"Andie . . ."

I tried the door, but it was sealed. "GOLEM, open the lab! GOLEM, acknowledge!"

A shudder shook the habitat, the reverberation building like a massive seaquake.

The last anchor arm . . . it's collapsing!

There was nothing I could do, nothing to grip. Suddenly I was flying backward down the corridor, and then sideways through an alcove, headfirst into the arboretum thicket. I dragged myself to my feet as the

THE OMEGA PROJECT • 141

jungle around me continued its slow, gravity-defying roll, the trees forcibly suspended sideways, their cracking branches crashing, igniting growling sounds from unseen wildlife.

And then my back met the bruising embrace of a tree limb as my world thankfully stopped rolling.

From what I surmised, the remains of the western leg was momentarily acting like a brake, preventing the giant sphere from falling into the canyon. How long it would hold—I had no idea, but I needed to get to the mini-subs, and fast.

In a pseudo moonlight cast by the blue emergency lighting, I realized *Oceanus* had inverted 180 degrees and that I was lying on the ceiling of the arboretum, a ravaged, upside-down inverted forest above me. Scrambling on all fours, I became entangled in vines as a loud buzzing filled the chamber. Looking down through a hole at the upper deck I could just make out the dark cluster of hives that occupied the entire domed ceiling.

The creaking of metal caused me to look up. Through the hole that had housed the spiral stairwell, anchored to the lower deck floor, was the remains of my cryogenic pod—only the base was never intended to support an inverted crypt. As I watched, the heavier back end of the half-ton assembly wrenched free, leading the front end to begin inching its way toward freedom—freedom being a free fall through the middle deck to the dome below and what easily sounded like a trillion bees.

Move! I climbed the branches of an inverted mango tree like a one-armed, wounded ape.

Seconds later, the cryogenic pod plummeted past me, crashing through an entanglement of thickly knotted branches before disappearing through the mid-deck ceiling.

Thankfully, the pod had struck a seven-foot-thick cushion of beehives, cushioning the aero gel dome—but agitating the nests!

If I needed additional motivation to move, the thought of being stung by several billion angry bees certainly did the trick. Dragging myself up through the stairwell hole, I climbed up into the lower deck, identified an exit, and climbed out into the inverted corridor.

I was in the docking area—perfect! Walking along a ceiling illuminated by flickering blue emergency lights, I located Docking Station Two . . . only the sub was gone.

So were the subs in stations one, three, and four.

That gave me hope that Andria and other members of the Omega crew had already abandoned ship—even as the revelation that I had been abandoned heated my insides like a blowtorch.

There was no time to dwell on either emotion as a powerful sea current caught *Oceanus* and the inverted habitat began rolling again.

I saw the crimson glow coming from inside the open egress chamber. Feeling like a hamster in a slow rolling wheel, I pushed my way inside the open watertight hatch.

Stepped through the rotating steel door frame into the tiled chamber.

Located a Steinke egress exposure suit from a pile and quickly adjusted the hood over my head.

Now get outside!

Tugging open the heavy interior pressurized door of the escape hatch using my only functioning arm, I sealed myself inside the topsy-turvy steel closet and stepped on the lever labeled EMERGENCY HATCH.

Seawater blasted sideways inside the rotating chamber. Seconds counted now as the flooded room rolled around me, the collapsing habitat God knows how far away from plunging into the sea canyon.

A buoyant fiberglass suitcase whacked me in the faceplate—an inflatable life raft! Gripping the handle with my left hand, I held on fast as *Oceanus* reached the canyon ledge, teetering on the precipice . . .

The green light flickered on.

With an explosion of bubbles the escape hatch popped open, the sudden pressure differential snapping the rusted hinges, sucking me and the fifty-five pound raft into the rumbling dark blue depths. For fifteen long seconds I was propelled horizontally through the water like a torpedo until my senses reoriented and I realized I was actually rising, being dragged to the surface by the buoyant case.

Looking down, I caught sight of the massive algae-infested sphere as it disappeared into the shadows of the trench.

"Andria!" The desperate prayers of a hypocrite accompanied me through curtains of azure light . . . and then the ocean belched me topside.

Blue sky, violet-tinged gray clouds.

A slanted horizon of water, viewed from a summit impossibly high—suddenly dropping a stomach-churning twelve stories into a walled valley of sea.

Dizzy, disoriented, and very queasy, I worked furiously at the latches of the suitcase as the valley rose beneath me, the swell levitating me high atop its mountainous back.

Popping the final latch, I yanked on the cord.

An explosion of compressed air blasted me sideways down the steep slope of the undulating wave. For a terrifying moment I was dragged underwater, dropping with the weight of the sea, unsure of where the raft had gone or for that matter which direction was up.

My head cleared the wild surface. The raft was nowhere in sight.

A swell rose beneath me so rapidly it caused me to puke what little food I had consumed. Floating on a two hundred foot crest, I gazed down upon the surrounding valleys of water and spotted the inflated orange island floating eighty yards away . . . rising on another swell, the distance increasing rapidly.

Plunging down my own mountain of ocean, I swam for it with one arm, my legs scissor-kicking me into a sidestroke, causing Yoni's shoes to slip off my feet. Slowed by the egress suit, I paused to strip the hooded apparatus from my head and shoulders as the sea dropped beneath me again.

With my energy draining rapidly in the cold ocean, I launched into a furious sidestroke, swimming as hard as I could for as long as I could in the direction of the raft until I felt the ocean levitating beneath me once more. Righting myself, I searched the roiling surface . . . and finally spotted the four-man life raft floating upright less than fifty feet away, its tented shelter catching the wind like a sail.

Movement caught my eye and I looked up, expecting birds—shocked instead to see a chaotic swarm of flying predators—sinister batlike creatures covered in thick brown fur, endowed with eighteen-foot wingspans and sharp talons. Bulbous opaque eyes scanned the surface as the hunters flew in swooping circular patterns, jockeying for position in the sky directly overhead.

I nearly jumped out of my clothing as my bare feet stepped on something sharp. Looking down, I could see a school of fish—dolphin-size creatures racing six feet below the surface like a brownish red current.

A surge of adrenaline jolted me into action. Paddling and kicking down the side of the uplifting swell, I lunged for the raft's trailing towline. Clutching it in my left hand, I dragged the hexagon-shaped inflatable close enough to hoist myself headfirst through the opening of the raft's inflatable tent.

Swiveling around, I zippered the nylon door behind me and collapsed, my chest heaving with each hyperventilated breath.

Blood pooled around the bottom of my lacerated feet as my shell-shocked mind caught up to the moment. *This is nuts, this is crazy! Where'd these giant bats come from? Where's Omega's crew? Why'd they abandon the habitat without waking me? What kind of nightmarish hell . . .*

"Oh."

The realization dawned on me, punctuated by a crooked smile. "I'm dreaming. This whole thing—it's an Omega-wave dream. I'm still asleep . . . frozen inside the pod where those bastards left me." I touched my feet, wincing in pain. "Goddamn, this feels so real."

I unzipped a window panel, the scene incredible.

Giant bats were nose-diving like gulls into the sea, emerging thirty seconds later clutching bizarre eight-foot-long gilled porpoises in their talons. Each fish possessed an array of twelve-inch needle-sharp spikes set along its dorsal spines like porcupine quills.

So incredible were the sights and sounds and smells that, for a moment, I actually contemplated remaining in the dream just to see what might happen next.

To hell with that. I was shivering from the cold and my feet were in excruciating pain, not to mention the monstrous swells, which were making me nauseous. And besides, this wasn't exactly the sexual fantasy Jason Sloan promised.

"Time to wake up, Ike. Vanilla—"

The sea dropped beneath me, forcing me to grab on to the inside of the blood-drenched raft.

"Vanilla sway! Vanilla sway! Vanilla sway!"

Nothing happened.

"What the hell? I'm vanilla swaying, Jason! Wake me the fuck up!"

A dark shadow crashed against the top of the tent, a pair of sharp lead-gray talons puncturing the vinyl. Before I could react, the tent was shredded from the raft and the massive bats were fighting greedily a hundred feet above the roiling sea to claim their share of the feast.

"Vanilla sway!" I continued yelling the password while I frantically searched the built-in compartments of the raft for a weapon. I located a telescopic oar, flashlight, binoculars, a first-aid kit, and a pack of handheld flares. I quickly wrapped my bleeding feet in gauze, bound the mess with Ace bandages, then screwed together the four-foot aluminum paddle as a brown-haired creature dove in on the raft, its talons reaching for me—

Whack! Wielding the oar like a tennis racket, I bashed the bat's claws, the impact chasing it away. I managed to strike a second animal as it swooped by, and then the swarm was upon me, the sky disappearing beneath a blizzard of bleating brown fur and animal musk—the pile suddenly dispersing as the sea erupted in a vertical ballet of silvery-gray streamlined bodies of coiled muscle. They were mako sharks—ten- to twelve-footers, only these mako sharks possessed caudal fins twice the size of any crescent moon–shaped tail I had ever seen—tails that propelled the predators high into the air like marlin hooked on reels. Launching straight out of the water in pairs and trios, the sharks bit the giant bats and held on, their combined weight dragging the flapping creatures into the ocean's heaving swells and retreating valleys where they were ripped into bloody froths by a dozen more of the sharks' converging brethren.

It was over in seconds, the makos forcing the surviving bats to the higher altitudes, the submerged bats torn into morsels, the remains picked clean by the school of gilled spiked porpoise fish whose presence initiated the choreographed feeding frenzy in the first place.

The world quieted, leaving the ocean to rise and fall in dizzying, stomach-churning heaves.

My eyes rolled up in my head and I passed out.

Sound, deep and powerful, bludgeoned me into consciousness.

Awash in my own personal kiddie pool of vomit, blood, and three inches of salt water, I sat up, greeted by a hangover perpetuated by a pounding surf that echoed across the surrounding sea like gunshot.

I smelled land before I saw it.

Using the binoculars, I spotted the rolling trough of ocean before me—a river of shallows retreating from a beach that was birthing a towering curl—the wave cresting so high it obliterated the horizon.

With a rolling, peppered explosion of white noise, the two-hundred-foot wave pummeled sand and surf, its swollen tide rushing inland several miles at tsunami speed.

Minutes passed, my fragile heart pounding in terror as I watched the ocean inhale the tide back whence it came, the reversing undertow building into another incoming swell—the swell my raft now floated upon!

"Oh, God! Vanilla sway! Vanilla sway! Vanilla—"

The forming trough pulled the raft onto its rising hump of sea as if I were climbing the first hill of a roller coaster, the sea curling beneath me, levitating the swell to its twenty-story height . . .

"—swahhhhhhhh!"

In one motion, I sprawled across the raft on my back, securing my ankles and left wrist beneath guidelines as the mountainous vertical wall of water dropped beneath me, its displaced downward moving mass unleashing an upward blast of air that caught the falling raft like a Frisbee—levitating it above the crashing wave, which struck the shallows in a deafening thunderclap of ocean and foam. A second later, the vinyl inflatable was blasted sideways by an unleashed avalanche of froth, the wave flipping it over, the ocean swallowing me whole.

I was bludgeoned by a river of black, gritty fluid that roared in my brain and threatened to peel the flesh from my bones as it churned me in a raging, terrifying fury that superseded breathing until seconds became minutes, and still I could not escape.

With a sizzling explosion of pain, my left shoulder was driven into the sand, existence pummeled into blackness.

17

In the landscape of time, there are few locations less comfortable than that of one who waits for some person or event to arrive at some unknown moment in the future.

—ROBERT GRUDIN, American writer and philosopher

I drifted upon warm, soothing echoes of sound—until the sound clapped like thunder, stirring me awake.

I opened my eyes. My right cheek was pressed against coarse white sand that sparkled like diamond dust. Rolling over, I closed my eyes to the midday sun, my skin soaking in the warmth, my body teased back into the catnap by the cool breeze and distant rushing surf.

I jumped as water lapped over my feet and up my pant legs, dousing me awake.

I sat up, my head pounding from the concussion. The tide that had spanned a mile of beach to reach me was retreating steadily—a blue carpet rolling up to a calm ocean horizon. I turned around to gather my bearings—beach to either side—a barren stretch of desert sand behind me, the blurred horizon demanding the binoculars still dangling around my neck.

Loosening the drawstring, I realized with delight that my right hand was working, my right arm no longer numb, the paralysis gone! Rolling up my sleeve, I tested the appendage, opening and closing my fist.

That's when I noticed the welts—a pattern of red dots that ran from my deltoid muscle down my right biceps, curving around my forearm. The marks, each the size of a quarter, were dotted dead-center with a pinprick of my blood.

I palpated the blots, wondering if something had bit me. Pushing the thought aside, I positioned the binoculars to my eyes and again scanned my surroundings.

The retreating tide was slowly feeding into an enormous wave, several hundred feet high and still climbing. My pulse raced as the dark green vertical cliff crested slowly until it collapsed in a silent explosion of froth—the clap of thunder and bone-jarring rumble reaching me seconds later.

Using the binoculars, I followed the wave inland. The tidal surge gradually shed volume and speed as it quickly covered the expanse of glittering sand that separated my position from the shoreline. At some point I had to stand, allowing the foot-high-wave to wash over my feet.

As the surge receded, the ocean revealed its bounty.

Sea creatures were left stranded along the exposed puddle-soaked beach. Albino sea spiders lay tangled in white clumps. Bizarre manta rays possessing barracuda-like teeth flopped in the wet sand. Pale pink crustaceans, some as large as my upper torso, stretched their claws, fighting to flip back over onto their bellies. Those that did so quickly burrowed into hiding.

Those that were too slow were plucked from the sand by flying lizards.

Seven to eight feet in length from the tip of their snouts to their narrow tails, the creatures—possessing white bellies and pale green backs—were using skin flaps running from their forelegs down to their hip sockets to glide on the forty-knot ocean gusts blowing inland.

I focused my glasses on one of the lizards as it landed to snatch a fish. Gobbling the morsel whole, the earthbound scavenger scampered away on all fours, building speed before it rose up onto its hind legs and spread its wings to catch the wind.

"Kite runners."

Okay, so it wasn't Latin, but who cared, it was just a damn dream.

"All righty then, let's try this again. Vanilla sway. Vanilla sway. Vanilla sway."

And still nothing happened.

"Damn you, Jason Sloan. When I get back to Florida, I'm going to create a lifetime ABE ban list, and your name will be—"

I paused, the memory of my bio-chip implant catching me by surprise. Having escaped from one chain of events into the next, I had completely forgotten about ABE.

I attempted to access the neural link. Tried the language program. The medical monitor. Even my manuscript . . . no response. It was as if the device had been surgically removed.

It's the cold. The cryogenic process drops the body's core temperature . . . core temperature powers ABE. Hope it hasn't damaged the neural array.

"Bastards! I need to wake up."

Frustrated, I aimed the binoculars at the expanse of desert behind me. The magnification revealed the distant horizon and what appeared to be a steep cliff face, its summit topped by a green forest.

Returning to view the ocean, I watched as yet another monstrous wave rose from the sea, its rising curl inhaling the shallows as if rolling up a carpet.

Shadows darted in front of the cresting point break—fluttering brown bodies that dive bombed the shrinking shoreline to pluck fish from the sea before the competing lizards could claim them.

"More bats. Great." Suddenly feeling isolated and defenseless, I scanned the wet sand for a weapon—while a mile away a wave I estimated at well over two hundred and fifty feet pounded the shallows into foam, the shattering sea chasing the flying mammals to higher altitudes.

The waves are getting bigger . . .

The tide surged inland, quickly flooding the shrinking expanse. Instinctively, I backed away as the water reached my knees, the flow continuing another fifty feet before retreating, the powerful undertow nearly dragging me with it.

Once more, the returning surf summoned the lizards, the circling scavengers descending to claim a place at the feast. And then I spotted it—washed up on shore half a football field ahead in the draining sand.

The raft! Looks like it's in bad shape, but there are flares onboard. Might need them to start a fire. Go for it, before the kite runners *grab it!*

I ran toward the steadily diminishing shoreline, leaping over a dog-size jellyfish, my feet sinking calf-deep in the abrasive wet sand. The twinkling reflections of sunlight were nearly blinding, blurring my vision. By the time I reached the partially inflated raft my feet were bleeding again, not from the lacerations suffered at sea but from hundreds of annoying tiny cuts.

Scooping up a handful of sand, I examined the grains closer, surprised to discover glass shards mixed in with the kernels. *How . . . ?*

The clap of wave striking shoreline startled me, as it was much louder than the others. Looking up, I was shocked to see a four-story tidal surge racing inland less than half a mile away.

Grabbing the life raft, I ran.

Sinking, stumbling off balance, I made it back to my starting point when a wall of froth barreled into me from behind. Shoved underwater, I managed to roll onto the buoyant vinyl sheath, which carried me ahead another thirty yards before I was sideswiped by another section of wave, this one curling back toward the ocean.

I rolled off the partially inflated raft and stood chest-deep in water, fighting the powerful riptide. Somehow I managed to maintain a grip on the twisting remains of deflated vinyl, only to find myself engaged in a losing game of tug-of-war, the receding sea dragging me face-first through the water.

"Vanilla . . . sway!" I choked up a mouthful of sea, my mind screaming at me to let go as the river tugged on the raft as if it was a parasail.

Finally I did let go, only the riptide refused to let go of me, dragging me until the depth lessened enough to allow me to stand. Knee-deep and unable to catch my breath, I bent over and gasped for air—as a terrifying rumble rose behind me—my shadow suddenly blotted out by another.

I turned, my ravaged heart feeling as if it were about to burst from my chest. My eyes bugged out as they took in a towering vertical wall of water rising behind me—a cliff of dark olive-green sea that appeared to be climbing upon itself . . . seventy feet . . . a hundred, its mud-laced curl draining the shallows as it continued to rise!

I tried to flee, but the tug-of-war between the receding riptide was at best a draw, the monster's roaring crest easily topping twenty stories, obliterating sky and sun. Terrified beyond reason, I humbled myself before death and dropped to my knees, the current cleansing my jumpsuit of the urine draining from my trembling groin.

Should I die before I wake, I pray the Lord my soul to—

"Ahh! Ahh!"

Stiletto-sharp blades pierced my shoulders—the bat's curved talons stabbing my flesh, the tips curling beneath my collarbone, a tremendous force wrenching me off my feet into the air as the pain nearly rendering me unconscious. Screaming into the wind, my hands instinctively grabbed at the narrow, knotted-leather cords that were the creature's ankles, my arms relieving the pressure as the flying mammal soared over the shallows.

THE OMEGA PROJECT • 151

A split second later the collapsing mountain of water exploded at my back, blasting both me and my winged rescuer with a barrage of cold sea and foam.

Screaming in agony, I pulled myself higher, forcibly extracting the curved talons from my butchered flesh. Then I held on as the bat's wings beat the air, drenching me in its heavy musk as we raced inland, sixty feet over the tidal surge.

Enough! I shifted my right hand to grip the ankle held by my left, the sudden imbalance upsetting the creature's ability to maneuver. The animal snapped its fanged jaws as it bent over in midflight to reach me, losing altitude in the process. Unable to release or bite its prey, the predator swooped toward the beach, intent, I was sure, on pile-driving me into submission.

Ten feet above the diminishing tidal surge I let go, dropping into the sea. Landing on both feet, I allowed myself to be swept inland and then sprinted in the shallows until once more I found myself standing, bent over, panting on dry land.

Blood drained from the deep throbbing puncture wounds.

The tide receded—leaving behind the shredded remains of my raft.

I stared at the rolled up, orange vinyl object, incredulous. "Are you fucking with me, God?!"

Asshole, there is no God . . . I'm the God creating this movie.

Verifying that the contents of the raft were still intact, I hauled the remains farther up the beach, wary of another wave. The effort caused me to wince and my entire upper body trembled from the pain.

Satisfied I had distanced myself from the next tidal surge, I released the raft and unzipped my jumpsuit, gently pulling my blood-soaked arms free of the tattered sleeves.

How can I hurt like this in a dream? If this were a normal dream, the pain would have woken me. The problem is, I can't wake up while I'm frozen. Knowing this is all a dream, my mind keeps creating situations designed to wake me up. In essence, my mind has created a new reality, an Omega reality that can't be turned off, which means—like phantom pain—I feel everything as if it were real.

"Thanks a lot, Uncle David!"

Searching the raft's compartments, I pocketed the flares, then removed the first-aid kit. I opened the antibacterial ointment, only to find it had hardened like cement. Next, I tore open a pack of gauze, which crumbled into fibers of dust.

"What the hell? Vanilla sway! Send me a beautiful nurse, Jason!"

A green lizard glide-landed twenty feet away. Hunched on its hind legs, it cocked its head to one side as if observing me.

"Not exactly what I had in mind." I reached for a flare, tearing off its igniter . . . and dust poured from the shredded tube.

"Great." Searching for a rock to toss at the lizard, I found a fish, its scarlet fins flapping in the sand. Locating the steak knife I had stowed in one of the jumpsuit's zippered pockets, I stabbed the eighteen-inch creature, then tossed it at the kite runner.

The lizard caught it in midair, gobbling it down its pelican-like gullet without biting. Satisfied, it took off running down the beach.

Wiping the blade clean, I used the knife to cut off the sleeves from my jumpsuit. Shredding the material into strips, I did my best to tie off each puncture wound, applying pressure to stop the bleeding, all the while the pain so great that it nearly caused me to pass out.

Feverish, I jumped as the tide surged past me again, the water calf-deep and alarmingly powerful. Retrieving the raft, I ran with the sea and far beyond, my feet assaulting another stretch of dry beach.

How far inland could the ocean chase me? Using the binoculars, I scanned the horizon, focusing again on the distant rise and the promising greenery perched atop the rocky summit . . . a long, brutal trek.

My feet were sore, caked with sand and blood. Using the steak knife, I fashioned socks from the vinyl pockets and a hood to keep the sun off my head.

Before the next surge could reach me I started off, limping across a barren white plain littered with decaying fish and empty crustacean shells.

Hours passed, the pounding ocean fading to a distant thunder. The fear of the advancing tide was replaced by annoying swarms of flies and a growing fishy stench.

About the time the midday sun began its westerly descent, I came upon the first burrow, the hole's opening as wide as a manhole cover. I peered over the edge to gauge its depths, but the shaft angled away after the first forty feet. Deciding I wanted nothing to do with yet another imaginary creature, I continued on.

The flies became swirling black clouds. Removing the vinyl hood, I fashioned eyeholes and covered my face with the mask. I swatted insects from my wrapped wounds and wiped at the sweat that was dripping into my eyes.

Bleached bones littered the plain. The burrows increased in number, their occupants remaining out of sight.

My mind wandered.

Suppose the impossible. Assume for a moment I'm not frozen. What kind of cataclysm could have melted the Antarctic ice sheet? Climate change? Polar shift?

Wait, what if that asteroid struck the South Pole? That might explain the lack of ice, but what about these creatures? For species like this to evolve . . . we're talking tens of thousands, maybe millions of years. There's no way I could I have remained frozen that long . . . is there?

What about Andria? The others? What happened to them? Could they still be frozen?

What could have caused GOLEM to fail? Could a celestial impact have shut down the computer? Could it have been sabotaged?

Walking with my head down, I didn't see the creature until I was nearly upon it.

Partially buried in the sand, I had mistaken it from afar as a dune. Now, as I circled the monstrosity, inspecting the beached animal's lifeless tentacles, I estimated the squid's carcass to be in excess of one hundred and fifty feet, its weight topping sixty tons when wet.

The giant cephalopod had not been wet for some time, its rotting remains shriveling flat in the hot sun. The stench was overpowering, attracting swarms of flies that kept me from examining the animal more closely, but from what I could see, there were neither wounds nor indicators of disease. Either the mammoth sea creature had been caught in a wave and was beached, or it had died at sea and was left onshore with the last high tide.

Could the tide wash up this far inland? The thought gave me pause. Using the binoculars, I turned my attention back to the ocean.

"Aw, hell."

Despite having trekked a good five miles over the last few hours, I remained only a few hundred yards from the relentless tide's waterline, which was flooding the burrows, inviting the inhabitants to venture forth. As the sea again receded, powder-blue crabs emerged from their holes, each crustacean as large as a Honda Civic.

Securing the binoculars inside a zippered pocket, I set off on a jog.

It took several minutes to distance myself from the clouds of flies swarming around the deceased colossus. Once clear, I set a steady pace. Looming ahead was a horizon of basalt rock—a near vertical cliff face towering two thousand feet—almost twice the height of the mountain Andria and I had climbed back in Virginia. My throat was parched and my feet sore, but I ignored the pain and continued on, concerned about the lateness of the day. The cliffs reinforced my fear that the tidal surge would soon span the entire beach, and I refused to stop until I had reached the first boulder that marked the rise.

Thirty minutes later, I collapsed at the foot of the cliffs, the base of which was piled with boulders, each roundish hunk of rock ten to twenty feet in circumference, angled along the lower third of the rise like a natural barrier. There were clumps of seaweed and dead fish strewn between the rocks—evidence that the ocean would indeed reach this far inland at high tide.

The next question—how high would the tide rise?

I gazed up at the rock face. The thought of the climb was unnerving. *If I fell and died in this dream, would I emerge in another?*

The sun at my back broke gold beneath the horizon's ceiling of clouds, its descent over the ocean offering me its western bearing and a basic time frame before I'd lose the light. A noticeable chill accompanied the late afternoon.

Cold, thirsty, hungry, exhausted, and still very much in pain, I hoisted myself atop one of the smaller boulders to begin the climb, fearing the tidal surge more than a potential fall.

At first the going was easy as I was able to move steadily from one rock to the next, the cold touch of stone soothing my battered feet. But the angle of ascent grew steeper, and before long I had gone as far as I could, reaching the uppermost layer of rocks at what I estimated was a good four hundred feet above sea level—a height that surpassed the highest wave I had seen.

Trembling from exhaustion and the cold, I settled myself on a flat portion of basalt, then aimed the binoculars at the spectacular golden sunset.

As I watched, the orange-red ball of fire disappeared behind a dark wall of water that easily towered five hundred feet. The monster crashed silently as it exploded into white water, its thunderous *clap* reaching me seconds before the earth trembled beneath the rocks. Racing inland like a seventy-foot tsunami, the tidal surge quickly devoured miles of beach, scattering winged creatures until it sizzled over the cliff's first line of boulders before it died out.

There was no choice. Trapped, I would have to reach the summit.

A cold wind whipped at my bandages as I studied the remaining twelve to fifteen hundred feet of vertical gray slab. I was attempting to map out a route that would funnel me along a series of deep crevasses—all leading to whatever awaited me at the top. Selecting my first rest stop—a slanted lip of slate twenty stories straight up—my heart started racing as I mentally committed to the climb.

Exhaling slowly, I began—but the first two steps sent me in full retreat back to the boulder, the pain of my sore bare feet pressing against the stone too much to overcome. Peeling the blood-soaked rags from my shoulders, I wrapped my toes and instep with the cloth, hoping the padding would provide at least a minimum of protection.

Once more I reached for a crack in the slab, pulling myself off the boulder onto a ledge so narrow I could barely wedge the blade of my right foot upon it. Determining the pain to be tolerable, I reached higher, my right hand groping for a surface I could grip.

Forty feet up and my muscles were already trembling. I panted for breath, each inhalation feeling colder than the last in the dying light. The horizon at my back bled red, yet I dared not take my eyes off the rock crystals glittering inches from my face. Moving from one handhold to the next, I felt constantly off balance, a violent sneeze or an itch away from losing my grip on the wall.

It was nearly dusk by the time I reached that first rest spot, a slight overhang that afforded me a three-inch-wide ledge and a gap between slabs to jam my right arm into. Momentarily secure, I turned to steal a glimpse at the horizon.

The sky was tinged crimson violet. The beach was gone, submerged between an onslaught of sea, powered by fifty-story waves now breaking less than a mile away.

"Vanilla . . . ah, fuck it." Whether I was asleep or not, it no longer mattered. To my brain, my nerve centers, and muscles—everything in this bizarre world, including the pain, was real.

If I fell, it was going to hurt.

The night announced its presence with a muscle-stiffening chill. With my reserves all but gone, I seriously contemplated remaining on the ledge until dawn. Violating my former fiancée's cardinal rule, I looked down and saw the tidal surge already breaching the upper layer of boulders.

Stay here, and you'll be underwater within the hour.

Shaking from the cold, I recalled the sight of Dharma lying out-stretched on the ice. If a small Chinese-Indian woman could handle the Antarctic cold, I could certainly handle this.

Refocusing on my breathing, I imagined each inhalation fueling an internal furnace.

Reaching up, I located an unseen ledge and continued my assault on the summit, still some eight hundred feet above my head.

"Beautiful night," I grunted aloud, attempting to distract any thoughts of falling. "Balmy ocean breeze. Surf . . . thundering gently . . . in the distance. Beats the piss out of Antarctica. *Uhh* . . . Of course . . . techni-cally . . . this is Antarctic . . . *ugh, aw, shit.* Gonna need . . . a manicure. Moonlight would . . . be nice. Wish . . . I had . . . some tunes. Rolling Stones. *Easy. Breathe slow.* I can't get no satisfaction . . . but I tried—"

Three-quarters of the way up the cliff face, two hundred feet above the crashing waves, I stretched blindly overhead with my left hand—and lost my balance!

Tumbling sideways, I frantically slapped my palms across the rock face, miraculously catching the sharp rounded surface of a tree root with my right hand. Gripping the dried-out offshoot, I dangled briefly by one arm until my feet relocated their perch.

Easy. You're okay, you're okay . . . just breathe . . . nice and slow. Tree roots mean I'm getting close. Just need a short rest.

Regripping the root with my left hand, I gently opened and closed the fingers of my sore right hand, the joints curled, the digits painful and stiff. After a minute I switched hands, then, using the root, pulled myself higher, my eyes catching a tapestry of stars overhead.

Maybe a hundred yards. Might as well be a hundred light-years.

Eyes tearing, I set off again, grunting lyrics to one of my favorite old-ies. "Sun . . . turnin' 'round . . . with . . . graceful . . . motion . Bound for . . . a star . . . fiery oceans. It's so . . . *ugh,* very lonely . . . you're a hundred . . . light-years from home . . .

"Ow!"

Climbing in near-pitch darkness, the top of my head smashed pain-fully into a ceiling of rock. Dizzy, I looked up, my nerve daunted as my dirt-crusted eyes inspected the overhang—a five-foot curl of rock blocking my ascension.

Frustrated and full of anger, I yelled into the night, "Is this really necessary, God?"

The overhang was similar to what Andie and I had faced back in

Virginia. To climb over it, I had to dangle by a handhold, blindly working my feet and legs up and over the edge.

"Embrace the fear, Ike. Use it to focus your strength."

A blast of cold wind forced me into action. Leaning out from my perch as far as I dared, I felt along the underside of the overhang with my left hand for something I could grip.

Nothing but smooth rock. Wait . . . My fingertips probed a two-inch-deep crevice.

It would be a ballbuster—worse than Virginia. Once I committed to the move, there was no turning back. I would be dangling by my fingertips while my free hand searched blindly for a second handhold.

At best, I figured I had twenty seconds.

Trembling more from fear than physical exhaustion, too tired to care anymore if I lived or died, I reached out once more from my perch and jammed the fingers of my left hand as far as I could into the groove above my head, my palm facing me—then I stepped away from the cliff face with my left foot, then my right.

The pain was excruciating. Dangling by my fingers, my body shook as a searing white-hot spasm burnt through my left arm and wounded shoulder even as my right hand blindly probed the curl of rock above my head—finding only a smooth, unblemished surface!

I panicked. My fingers began to slip. Unable to locate a second handhold, I had no other choice but to let go, plunge into the surf, and try again—assuming I could survive the fall and find a perch on the cliff face before the ocean dragged me back into its vortex.

I could not see the wave, but I could feel its approach—a deep rumble reverberating from the base of the mountain into my bones.

The thought of being engulfed by the monstrous swell reengaged my adrenal glands. Gripping my left wrist with my right hand, I executed a one-armed pull-up, then flipped upside-down so that my feet were walking on the ceiling of slate. As the stone sliced deep into my fingers, I maneuvered my right leg above the overhang, my bloodied toes inching their way higher along the smooth surface until my heel scraped against a root!

Pressing hard against the root with my right leg, using it as a fulcrum, I snaked my right hand down my left arm and across my groin to my right leg, shifting my weight as I followed my quad muscles up to my knee, calf, my ankle . . . and finally the root.

Gripping the precious limb, I pulled my gnarled, swollen fingers free of the crevice, grabbed the root with my left hand, and swung my left leg up and over the rounded edge of the overhang, pushing, squirming, fighting to inch my quivering body onto the summit.

And then I was over—just in time to feel the incoming wave barrel into the cliff a hundred feet below, exploding upward in a geyser of foam.

I didn't care. Stretched out on my back, I stared at a velvet-black tapestry of starlit sky. My fingers and toes were raw and swollen, and every inch of my body hurt, but I was here—wherever here was—and with the sense of satisfaction that I had transcended all physical hardship. Unable to move, I celebrated my victory over the day with an exhausted grin . . . just as I had with Andie years ago as together we watched the sunrise atop the summit of Buzzard's Rock.

And suddenly, incredibly the sun *was* rising—its golden-yellow face peeking over the violent western horizon. Only it was not the sun, it was the moon and it was enormous.

I sat up, mesmerized by the luminous orange sphere. For a brief moment it disappeared behind a cresting swell, its lunar light casting the dark wall of water turquoise before it reappeared above the crashing wave.

Rising higher, the moon shed its orange tint, its reflection paling over the servant ocean, which rose to Himalayan heights to greet it.

And now a shadow appeared on the lunar surface—the Earth's shadow—the brief eclipse exposing the pattern of the moon's altered orbit as elliptical—a radical change that must have resulted in its unfathomable proximity—perhaps a third of its former distance.

"What could have caused . . . ?"

The surface of the dead world blossomed in its full splendor, revealing evidence of its recent pillage—a crater that looked the size of Australia, its telltale profile indicating the impact had occurred on the far side of the moon.

The asteroid. It must have missed Earth . . . and struck the moon!

A trail of debris appeared over the horizon as the moon passed overhead, stretching across the sky like a cosmic tail, the dust and rocks and spinning satellites of exhumed geology caught in its wounded parent's gravitational tide.

Can't see the full size of that impact crater, but the debris field must have been huge. All that mass, blasted into space, caught in Earth's gravitational field . . .

I collapsed to my knees, my skin tingling, my hair surreally standing on end as I realized that this might not be a dream after all, that the planet may have experienced a cataclysm while we were being held in cryogenic stasis . . . that I may have been the only one to wake—my species' lone survivor.

"Whoa!"

Suddenly reeling off balance, I lashed out for the rocky ground with both arms as my body levitated into the air! Twisting in a pocket of zero gravity, I flailed into an off-kilter somersault, nearly striking my head on the slate-covered summit, only to spin around again to face the moon—now hovering directly overhead, so close I imagined I could swim to it, its luminescent mass blotting out a third of the night sky.

Oh, but there were so many things happening at once, my senses on overload, for rising around me was a ballet of floating objects—gravel and palm fronds and even droplets of froth spewed skyward by the undulating sea. My ascent found its equilibrium at eighty-five feet, affording me a view of seascape so spellbinding it silenced the revelation of being weightless.

Carpeting the ocean was a twinkling neon-red migration of krill that covered the surface as far as my eyes could see. Rising beneath them to feed were the planet's newest denizens of the deep—behemoth squid, each cephalopod three to four hundred feet long. In a choreographed ritual belying both intelligence and grace, the creatures were flashing rainbow-colored patterns of bioluminescence across their acreage of skin—hypnotic patterns of communication that projected across the ocean as they twisted along the surface to feed.

The moon moved beyond its perigee encounter, gravity tugging on me. Elation turned quickly to trepidation as I looked below, realizing that I was descending over the ocean!

I flailed helplessly as I dropped beyond the overlook, until a forty-knot wind blasted me backward at frightening speed, sending me crashing into the surrounding forest.

Unseen branches whipped at my flesh, my limbs catching an entanglement of vines that mercifully slowed my fall until nature embraced me in its hammock, suspended thirty feet off the ground.

Held fast in the warmth of my cocoon, I passed out.

18

Sometime in the next thirty years, very quietly one day we will cease to be the brightest things on Earth.
　　—James McAlear

The pain woke me.

It was not the deep throb emanating from my shoulders, or the lead-tight ache radiating from every muscle, or even the blistering wounds burning in my feet and fingers. This pain gnawed inside my stomach, demanding water . . . insisting on food. It was the family dog scratching upon the bedroom door, insisting I get up when all I wanted to do was go back to sleep.

Disoriented, I opened feverish eyes to a predawn grayness. I smelled the forest before I saw it, its damp bark, the heavy scent of peat. For one glorious moment I was back in Virginia on a Cub Scout retreat, the pack still asleep, the campsite heavy in morning dew.

My eyes adjusted, separating the canopy of trees from the haze of clouds. A soft rumble violated the stillness of the forest as the heavens opened, delivering a soothing *pitter-patter* of raindrops on leaves.

After several minutes, the restrained cadence transcended into a downpour.

A cold steady trickle announced itself on my left shoulder. Craning my neck, I intercepted the stream of water so that it entered the crook of my mouth. I swallowed a dozen times before redirecting the flow over my face.

The fruit was dangling around me like fist-size potato-brown ornaments on a Christmas tree. I struggled to free my right arm from the vines enough to reach it without losing my perch and managed to pluck a cluster of sapodilla from the tree. Greedily, I pulled the gnat-infested skin from the overripe fruit before popping the pale yellow flesh into my mouth.

"Oh, God . . ." The taste was glorious, a cinnamon plum, exceptionally sweet. The rise in my blood sugar was immediate, a revival that fueled my desire to eat. Spitting out the seeds, I quickly downed the other four fruit in my lap, then drank again.

My bladder was the next organ demanding attention. Unzipping my jumpsuit fly, I leaned sideways in my vine hammock and added my pee to the rain-soaked foliage, pleased to see that blood no longer darkened the urine.

I rolled again onto my back and held my breath as the tangle of vines dropped me two feet before the slack was retrieved. I waited, my muscles tense, until I was confident the hammock had resettled, then I drank again.

My immediate needs met, I reexamined my situation.

Where am I? Am I Omega dreaming in a cryogenic pod in an underwater habitat a mile below the Ross Ice Shelf, or am I actually suspended beneath a forest canopy in a future time period, on an Earth that has evolved from a major cataclysm? Assuming the former, there's nothing I can do but try to survive the dream without registering any more pain. Assuming the latter . . . Jesus, how many thousands . . . how many millions of years was I frozen? What happened to Andie and the rest of the crew? Are they still frozen? Did GOLEM thaw them? Would they really have left me in stasis?

No way. Even that asshole of a captain wouldn't have the balls. I woke up because the pod malfunctioned when the stairwell collapsed. GOLEM controlled the other twelve pods, which means the computer malfunctioned.

I looked around.

If this really is Antarctica, then the bombardment of lunar debris must have been horrific, wiping out humanity . . . leading to an Ice Age. But if some humans survived . . . perhaps a colony, then I need to find them.

If a million years has passed, will I even recognize them?

The rain subsided, returning its gentle cadence.

Go back to sleep, Omega Man. Resolve your existence later.

I closed my eyes, my consciousness fading in the predawn light.

"Huh? Whoa . . . shit!"

I was falling, dropping in measured plunges, my face lacerated by branches, my right arm useless, my left grabbing at anything within reach. And then the vines twisted tightly, painfully around my ankles and I stopped.

Trees spun, inverted in my vision as I blinked myself into cognizance. The ground was swaying . . . no, it was me—I was hanging upside-down, suspended eight feet above the crawling forest floor.

Crawling?

Drawn by my urine, the ants—each as black as night and as long as my thumb—swarmed the ground in chaotic waves ten thousand strong, the assembly feeding a column of workers that were even now climbing the surrounding trees, tracking the food source . . . me!

"Ahh . . . ahh!" Someone shot me in my right foot with a .45 caliber bullet—at least that's what the ant bite felt like, the pain excruciating, driving me to madness. Pulling myself into a sit-up, I hooked my left arm behind my knees, holding myself in place in order to slap at the crawling insects attacking the soles of my feet. When I looked down I realized that the vines supporting my weight were covered by the frightening creatures.

"Ahh! Little bastards!" An ant latched on to my right ankle, another slammed its clawlike pincers around my little toe and bit! I screamed in agony, pinching the tiny predators until my blood squeezed out of their crushed abdomens, their severed heads remaining anchored to my swollen, discolored flesh. The creatures seemed impervious to my defense, each bite delivering an ounce of neurotoxic venom that was quickly finding its way into my central nervous system, causing a frightening numbing sensation.

A vine fell past my face.

I dropped another three feet as two more supports were chewed apart.

Were the little fuckers that clever?

My fate all but sealed, I released my grip around my legs and dropped, attempting to use the momentum to swing myself clear of the awaiting colony. Swaying like a pendulum, tortured by worker ants progressing down my lower extremities, I felt a paralyzing sensation creeping up my body.

In my delirium, I heard something that sounded like an approaching pan flute.

And then the last of the vines snapped and I fell five feet onto the pile of killer ants.

Adrenaline sprang me to my feet. My back and neck were covered in a black vest of crawling insects, my jumpsuit dangling a thousand dark ornaments. I hobbled away from the colony, my flesh blasted by hundreds of bullets with teeth, my screams muted by the forest. All feeling below my calf muscles was gone and I stumbled, dropping through the brush like a tranquilized chimpanzee.

My body spasmed out of control, the pain horrific. Paralyzed from the chest down, I forced shallow gasps as I lay helpless, facedown in the soil, each breath vying to be my last.

Seconds from blacking out, my frenzied mind registered two final thoughts of madness—that the ants seemed to be abandoning my frayed carcass . . . and that something very large was hovering over me.

My vision narrowed. Darkness enveloped the periphery. A haunting face hovered before me—the Angel of Death, no doubt, my old friend staring at me with dozens of eyes born from a hundred past lives.

"Each past life ended brutally. Why are you here, Robert? What is your journey?"

"I seek . . . Nirvana."

"You cannot achieve enlightenment while holding on to your anger."

Blind, my heartbeat erratic, I felt something heavy press against my face, covering my eyes and mouth. A viselike grip compressed my rib cage—

Zap!

A warm sensation moved down my spine, prying loose the Angel of Death's frigid grip while neutralizing the progression of the ant toxin, at least enough to allow me to breathe.

And then a powerful limb snaked its way around my waist, adhering to my torn jumpsuit as it lifted me effortlessly off the ground. Suddenly I was moving quickly through the forest, the pain driving me into darkness.

19

I died as a mineral and became a plant, I died as a plant and rose to animal,
I died as animal and I was man. Why should I fear? When was I less by dying?
    —JALAL AD-DIN RUMI, Sufi poet

The steady breeze of an air conditioner chilled my exposed flesh. I was naked, my eyes covered by a damp cloth, my arms and lower torso weighed down by the moist embrace of the cryogenic pod's tetrodotoxin gel.

Stretching beneath the slime, I embraced the joy of no longer being in pain.

I was back.

I could hear someone in the room. "God, what a dream. Andria? Jason? Jason, if that's you, I'm gonna kick your ass. You have any idea how many times I tried using your emergency wake-up? Hey, butt head, do you hear me?"

I sat up against the weight of the gel and reached for my face to remove the cloth.

A hand cloaked in what felt like a rubber mitten intercepted the attempt, gently guiding my arm back inside the draining vat of sleep gel.

The echo of trickling water calmed me, my mind hitching a ride on the soothing sound. "Guess this is all part of the wake-up protocol. Beats the hell out of being jabbed in the heart by a six-inch needle. So, who's there? Quit screwing around. Lara?"

Another gloved hand pressed gently against the base of my skull, and I looked up to see Lara hovering over me, her onyx hair falling past her delicate neck, her expression serene—

—only my eyes were still closed!

In the madness that was either another Omega dream, a continuation of the same dream, or a simple trip down Insanity Lane, I found myself tearing the moist cloth from my face—only to discover that I was not in *Oceanus,* I was in a cave, standing in the shallows of an underground stream bathed in a surreal orange light . . . that the wet cloth covering my eyes was a palm-size slug, and that my companion was a cephalopod!

Correction: *Cephaloped.* Having evolved to inhabit the land, the walking, air breathing terrestrial squid stood nine feet tall on three and sometimes four thick tentacles, its dorsal flesh covered in coarse brown fur. Those tentacles that weren't supporting its weight were treading air in a perpetual motion that made it almost impossible for me to gain clarity on its appearance, or to strike it, I quickly realized. The creature had assumed a defensive posture aimed at protecting its head—an oblong alien face situated beneath a skull that resembled brown leather stretched over bone. As wide as a pumpkin but irregular like a boulder, the massive cranial cavity also possessed a siphon—a two-foot curled organ the creature used for breathing.

It was the siphon that had been the source of the pan flute–like sounds I had heard back in the jungle.

Below the skull was the cephaloped's collapsible mantle, which contained the stomach, vital organs, and the animal's three hearts—at least the anatomical equivalents of what its oceanic ancestors had, according to Lara.

My attention diverted to its eyes—two stereo-optic protrusions below a bony bridge running below its forehead. These thin twin muscular stalks, resembling foot-long elephants' trunks, protruded from the center of its face like the handlebars of a child's tricycle.

At the end of each of the flexible organs was an eye. The corneas were bright yellow, like a jungle cat's, the pupils black. Housed within the trunk socket, they possessed wrinkled lids poised both above and below. The effect created an expressive state and reminded me of the sullen eyes of Albert Einstein in his later, more contemplative years.

Two more appendages protruded below the handlebar sight organs, only these offshoots were arms—shorter, four-foot-long raptor arms, each ending in a clawed thumb and forefinger. Poised below the cluster of arm sockets was either the creature's thick neck—or maybe it was its abdomen, I don't know. All I could see was the hint of a beaked mouth, and a cluster of sockets for those hypnotically powerful eight tentacles.

We stood and stared at one another, *it* clearly more fearful of me than I of it, despite the fact that any one of its tentacles could squeeze me to death like an anaconda.

I only broke eye contact when I felt something wiggling on one of my calf muscles. Looking down at my naked body, I was shocked to find it was covered, not in tetrodotoxin gel, but with foot-long leeches! These slimy black creatures were bloated from sucking my blood—the revelation of which instantly made me woozy, and I toppled forward—only to be caught by my cephaloped guardian, who gently returned me to the cool embrace of the underground stream. Lacking the strength to move, I laid my head back against a rock and watched as the creature delicately plucked a ripe leech from my right calf muscle, revealing an ant bite the size of a quarter, the raised flesh badly bruised.

The ceph's using the leeches to suck out the ant toxin . . .

Before I could even weigh the implications of that thought, I caught a glimpse of the underside of its tentacle—hairless pink flesh adorned with two rows of suckers.

I held up my right arm—the telltale welts matched.

My mind raced in its delirium. The cephaloped had rescued me from drowning, it had somehow restored the use of my appendage . . . and it had saved me from the ants!

"Thank you."

The startled land squid moved so fast I could not track it, the massive creature somehow disappearing from view. Sitting up, my eyes scanned every square inch of cave before and around me.

It was gone.

What the fuck, Eisenbraun?

Vertigo sent me sprawling back into the water, the disturbance igniting the stream in shimmering waves of fluorescent orange light. Triboluminescence is a geological feature of both sphalerite and tremolite; friction applied to these two minerals actually causes the rock to glow. The entire bed of the stream must have been composed of one or both of these minerals, the rapid movement of the rushing water across its surface bathing the entire underground passage in its ethereal orange light.

Lying back, I stared at the cave ceiling thirty feet above my head. Stalactites hung like twisted canine teeth, the smooth crystal rock twinkling as it reflected the glowing stream.

Giddy, I recited a rhyme that traced back to my Cub Scout days: "Row, row, row your boat, gently down the stream. Merrily, merrily, merrily, merrily, life is but a dream."

The words echoed throughout the passage, dispersed into God knows how many connecting tunnels. Lying gently in the stream, I was stuck in my Omega dream, far from merry.

Was it a dream? How could it not be? Nearly every episode, every near-death experience since my "awakening" could be traced back to something I encountered before I had been forcibly frozen, from the giant bats on Dharma's sexy emerald moonscape surcoat to my imagined rescuer—an evolved land octopus—no doubt conjured from my brief yet satisfying first encounter with Lara and her two intelligent pets.

The memory served me well. I realized the cephaloped had not simply evaporated into the cold, dank cave air—it had expertly camouflaged itself.

Sitting up slowly, I scanned my surroundings once more. The stream wove its way through and around three-to-five-foot-high stalagmites, a cluster of which was covered in moss.

Hmm. My shy cephaloped guardian did have hair to disguise . . .

Removing an engorged leech from my left ankle, I tossed the grotesque segmented worm at the rock cluster—which miraculously bloomed into a head and tentacles, one of which caught the dark projectile.

"Bravo, Oscar."

The spooked cephaloped scurried back another five feet, but remained visible.

I held up my hands, hoping to disarm its fear . . . no pun intended.

After several minutes, the giant terrestrial squid moved closer.

Removing another leech, I reached out passively with it.

The cephaloped hesitated. After a moment it extended one of its muscular tentacles an impressive twelve feet and accepted my offering, releasing the leech back into the stream.

Encouraged, we repeated this exercise until I stood naked before it, leech-free.

Holding out my right arm, I pointed to the bruised-yellow traces of suction marks, then at the being's closest tentacle. I nodded slowly.

The ceph nodded back. We were communicating . . . *Now what?*

Weak from hunger, I motioned to my mouth.

Somehow the intelligent creature seemed to understand. It looked around, only there appeared to be nothing edible in the cave. *It's debating whether to bring the food to me or bring me to the food.*

Rendering its decision, the cephaloped moved to the nearest cave wall. Stretching a tentacle above its head in one fluid motion, it scaled the rock face like a spider, using its sucker pads to grip the surface. Reaching up to the ceiling, it suspended itself effortlessly from two stalactites using two of its legs which, anatomically speaking, were now functioning as arms.

For a long moment its simply hung there, watching me with those telescopic yellow eyes—then, with the grace of a gibbon, the ceph reached two of its remaining six tentacles to the ceiling behind it, gripping two more stalactites while simultaneously releasing the first, moving away from me like a trapeze artist swinging from one acrobat partner to the next, its eyes shifting as its body seemed to turn itself inside out with each revolution.

Its haunting yellow gaze left me only after it disappeared into the darkness.

I was alone.

Should I follow it, stay put, or explore the rest of my imaginary surroundings?

Deciding on the latter, I climbed onto the rocky shoreline and headed downstream in the opposite direction of my rescuer. I was naked, both physically and metaphorically speaking—a twenty-first-century *Homo sapiens* deposited into the primordial future, lacking weapons and access to my own biological crutch of intelligence. And perhaps that was intentional—my mind sending me a message in my cryogenic dream: *There will be no cheating in this Great Die-Off, Eisenbraun . . .*

"There you are." Bending over, I picked up my jumpsuit, pleased to find the binoculars hidden beneath the tattered garment, now stained in frightening clusters of my own blood. After carefully checking the clothing for any insect stragglers, I dressed and began to feel a little less vulnerable.

The location of the jumpsuit indicated the cephaloped had brought me into the cave this way; had it purposely left in the opposite direction? Assuming it intended to feed me, why had it not brought me to the food? Was it afraid that I might again be exposed to the dangers of the forest? Dream or no dream, the ants had nearly made me their breakfast and I had experienced the agony of every bite; that the forest held other unexpected threats, I had no doubts. Still, why had it rescued me? Was I a curiosity, a diversion, or had I become its pet?

I followed the passage another half mile until it twisted up ahead. Rounding the left bend, my ears were assaulted by a rush of rapids as the cavern dropped several hundred feet in a steep three-level grade. Feeling the rocks taking a toll on my bare feet I debated whether to continue on. My eyes followed the course of the stream, which appeared to slow, disappearing into a section of tunnel that seemed different.

Using the binoculars, I confirmed my suspicions . . . the new passage below was bleeding daylight.

It took me twenty minutes to negotiate the descent, another five before I found myself standing before the entrance to a grand chamber, the arched ceiling towering six stories above a shallow pool of water that glistened emerald green. The cavern ran on perhaps another five hundred feet before narrowing to an exit cloaked in curtains of mist, backlit by a brilliant haze of sunlight.

I sloshed knee-deep through the waterway, each stride releasing cascading ripples of sound and light up the walls of the chamber, my jaunt accompanied by a bizarre echo of raindrops. Pausing to listen to these random splattering sounds, I looked up, expecting to find a rooftop of dripping stalactites . . . discovering instead a colony of giant bats! Thousands of the creatures hung inverted in a cloud of twitching bodies, the raindrops—bat droppings.

My heart pounded heavy in my chest as I continued moving toward the light at a snail's pace, praying the demonic mammals would remain asleep. The force of the stream increased as I neared the mist-enshrouded exit, my eyes gradually adjusting to the daylight.

My God . . .

The thirty-foot-high arch ended in a dizzying precipice, the stream bleeding over its ledge to become a waterfall that plunged a thousand feet onto the rock-strewn beach below. That I knew the beach was doubly unnerving: I had crossed the seemingly endless plain spread out before me days ago. The cave where I now stood was situated within the cliff face I had scaled my first night in la-la land.

It felt early. The sky was bathed in predawn gray, a light mist playing across the valley of sand. A salty breeze howled softly through the archway, but the ocean, thankfully, was nowhere to be seen. Just to be sure, I reached for the binoculars dangling from my neck and scanned the western horizon.

It was out there somewhere, concealed behind distance and fog. Having witnessed the full moon's effect on the tide, I thought it possible the beach might remain a barren desert for another three to four weeks, depending on the radical pattern of the altered lunar orbit.

Three to four weeks . . . I wondered if I'd be awake by then.

But wait . . . the desert was not barren after all! As the sun rose behind the cliffs, its golden rays reflected a brilliant spark upon an immense object that had washed ashore against its will. I trained my glasses on the spot, the glistening monstrosity anchored in the sand perhaps a mile or so away.

Oceanus . . .

20

I do not believe in a fate that falls on men however they act;
but I do believe in a fate that falls on them unless they act.
    —BUDDHA

It became almost impossible to think clearly or organize my thoughts.

Real or not, the process of withdrawing the ant toxin had cost me a pint or three of blood—at least that's what it felt like. Woozy, I backed away from the precipice, retracing my path as quickly as I dared through the cavern of bats, sensing, from the increased activity overhead, that the furry fanged creatures were awakening with the dawn.

I cannot say how long it took me to return to the section of cave where I had last seen the cephaloped; perhaps it was an hour, perhaps half a day . . . or maybe I had never left? Maybe I had dreamt the whole bat-infested chamber and the vision of *Oceanus* beached like a giant globe while I lay—delirious; the entire episode a hallucination caused by the real or imagined loss of blood. All I know is that one moment I thought I was slogging my way up stream, the next—I was lying in it.

The prolonged immersion in cold water helped remove the inflammation from my body and eventually revived me. And yet I felt so drained that I could have remained there indefinitely, floating in waves of ethereal orange light had my hunger pangs not intervened.

Rolling over onto my knees, I dragged myself onto my feet and leaned against a stalagmite, the dripping rags clinging to my limbs assuring me that I had at least ventured through part of the cave. And so I set off again, this time moving upstream, following the path of the eight-legged being that had saved my life, even though I could find no evidence that our shared moment in time had ever taken place.

The stream ran on for miles, forcing me to hike uphill along a rocky shoreline that twisted and turned and occasionally intersected other "dry" passages. I ignored these auxiliary routes as they were dark and offered little promise of food. Somewhere up ahead was an exit to the forest, and I had little choice but to find it.

Daylight became a speck in the distance, then a narrowing funnel, then finally a hole in the ceiling where the water rushed in. Working my way up to the exit by way of stalagmites and boulders, I crawled through a four-foot slit in the rock—emerging beneath the root system of a massive tree that fed from a swollen river, the overflowing banks of which were surrounded by wild ferns amid a backdrop of lush greenery.

The sun was high in the sky, filtering through a swaying canopy of treetops located several hundred feet above the fertile forest floor. Shrill chirps rented a woodland air still damp from a morning rain. Somewhere up ahead the thicket reverberated with sound and I moved toward it, readying myself to rush back to the stream at the first sign of anything resembling a hungry ant.

It was not ants that I heard thrashing in the bushes but a snake, its coiled seven-foot oily black body entwined by the crimson red legs of a three-foot-long centipede. The spotted yellow and violet caterpillar-like insect was adhered to the serpent's midsection, the smaller attacker's fangs having already delivered their venom.

With every slash, the serpent found itself deeper in a sticky quicksand of appendages, which held fast to its dying meal. I watched until the slurping sounds from the feeding centipede sickened me, then, distancing myself from the scene, I withdrew the serrated steak knife from my still-intact zippered pocket, intent on fashioning myself a weapon.

Ten minutes later, the lone survivor of the subspecies Petroleum Man emerged from the thicket armed with a pointed stick, ready to take on anything from a bag of marshmallows to perhaps a squirrel or small rodent.

Deciding against the latter, I returned to the river, hoping to spear the first fish that swam by.

My ears buzzed. I swatted and caught half a dozen grape-size flies in my palm, sprinkling their still-twitching remains along the calm surface of a pool of water formed by a horseshoe of rock, attempting to lure a fish out from beneath a submerged ledge.

Poised on an outcropping of rock above the floating bait, I held my breath as a pair of thin snakes emerged from beneath the slate. It took me a moment to realize the creatures were actually barbels—the tentaclelike protrusions connected to the dark flat head of a catfish. The surfacing creature was a big boy, its skull as large as a shovel, its girth five feet from its whiskered mouth to its lobe-shaped fins and tail.

Swimming to the surface, the fish bypassed the flies and suddenly launched itself atop the rock upon which I stood, perched with my pointed stick.

And then the damn thing snapped at me!

Backing away, I slammed the sharpened business end of my spear into its slimy back, but it merely bounced off the rubbery hide, the point splitting in half.

The enraged fish unfurled its seventy-pound eel-like body and lashed out again, its pair of twenty-inch barbels independently raking the air—an action that told me the fish was blind, though far from helpless. Jabbing the stick at the foul beast's mouth, I distracted it long enough to withdraw the steak knife from my jumpsuit pocket. With one slice I hacked off its feelers, then stabbed at the animal's soft white underbelly, quickly retracting the six-inch blade before the predatory amphibious fish could bite me with its finger-length stiletto-sharp teeth.

Fully engaged, I plunged my weapon repeatedly into the bleeding carcass, ranting my best Melville. ". . . to the last I grapple with thee; from hell's heart I stab at thee; for hate's sake I spit my last breath at thee!"

A dozen or so stabs and Moby Catfish was lying belly up, ready to be filleted.

For the briefest of moments I imagined skewered chunks of catfish cooking over an open fire, then reality hit: any potential firewood was wet. As a Cub Scout, I had been deemed "fire-challenged" by my den leader who joked that I couldn't ignite a flame using a wad of newspaper and a book of matches.

Screw it. The scent of my fresh kill smoldering on an open spit could lure other predators.

Sushi it was.

Sawing long cuts into the catfish's belly, I surgically removed a square of meat, washed it off in the stream, then chewed a bite. Despite being raw, the meat was surprisingly tender, but three mouthfuls were all my stomach could . . .

The sound stifled my mental dictation, my eyes scanning the tree-tops overhead. I had heard the pan flute acoustics seconds before the killer ants would have filleted me, only then the sound had been more of a diversionary tactic.

What I heard now seemed like a cry for help.

Leaving the stream, I headed off in the perceived direction of the sound, making my way through a grove of redwood trees that easily dwarfed the tallest sequoia of Northern California. Even the under-brush was elephantine, the ferns creating an umbrella effect five feet over my head. The forest floor was padded with rotting foliage, which combined with the massive redwood canopy to mute all sound, save for that of my eight-legged guardian.

The distressed pan flute sounds led me to a clearing between a tripod of five-hundred-foot trees, the trunks of which were wider than a two-car garage. Jousting between the columns were two thirty-inch-high praying mantises—*Was everything bigger in this Omega dream?* The in-sects were grappling over the fin end of a hairy severed octopus ten-tacle.

"Oscar . . ."

Brandishing my spear, I swatted away the insects, chasing the knee-high stick creatures into the foliage. The abandoned tentacle was bleed-ing a greenish blue goo from a wound slice too precise to have been rendered by nature.

A warm raindrop fell on my cheek. I wiped at it and saw it was cephalopod blood.

The sound of a moaning pan flute called out to me from above.

I looked up using the binoculars, only to find the view obstructed by a canopy whose lowest branches began a football field above my head, concealing a world unto itself.

I knew all about redwoods, having studied their unique genetic blueprint while searching for patterns in nature upon which to fashion GOLEM's matrix. A young redwood reaches maturity when it sheds its top, which can be blown off during a storm or simply dies and falls off. This act triggers a bizarre process, known as "reiteration." The tree's DNA essentially goes haywire, replicating itself over and over again when a second redwood trunk sprouts from the first—not at ground level but high up in the crown, rooting itself in one of the larger limbs. A third, fourth, and fifth tree trunk soon appear, each identical tree growing parallel to the main trunk hundreds of feet above the forest floor, appearing like the fingers of an upraised palm. Each new trunk grows its own limbs, which in turn grew more trunks through its own crown. These runaway reiterations create a fractal structure—a tree that, in essence, is rooting exact clones of itself upon itself. In human terms, it would be the equivalent of sprouting a smaller yet fully formed adult Robert Eisenbraun from my right shoulder, then a second clone from my right biceps and a third from my forearm, each maturing Eisenbraun in turn rooting its own Eisenbraun harvest, continuing several generations not only on my right shoulder, but from other points on my upper torso as well.

Redwood DNA also has built-in defense systems. Over the centuries, a few of the reiterated trunks will grow into one another, creating a bloated labyrinth of wood known as a "buttress." These gnarled masses often form horizontal bridges in the crowns of the largest redwoods, which act like highway off-ramps—struts that strengthen the tree while forging bizarre trunk caves. In essence, a redwood is not just a tree, it is a self-perpetuating vertical landscape that can alter the chemical nature of the soil, dam and redistribute vast amounts of water within its trunk, all while reshaping the forest climate to suit its needs.

So enamored was I with redwood DNA that I had patterned GOLEM's matrix after it.

As such, it was no surprise to find myself lost within an Omega-generated forest of giant sequoia, forced to scale one of the titans in order to reach the strange creature that had rescued me earlier.

Or not.

If this was truly a dream, why bother? If humanity no longer existed in my imagined Omega existence, why be humane? There were two rules in my dreamscape that were now well established; the first being pain. If injured I would feel it, the sensations registering in my brain's neural centers as real. The second rule—no matter what my subconscious threw at me, I still controlled my responses to each challenge—I still possessed free will. If I didn't want to risk my life to save the cephaloped, I didn't have to. So what if the creature had saved me? It was my movie, after all—it was *supposed* to save me. I was man, created in God's image—superior of intellect. What king would jeopardize his fiefdom to save an eight-legged servant?

My internal game of devil's advocate didn't play well with me. Dream or no dream, I would not succumb to the criminal actions that had sentenced humanity to the Great Die-Off just because I could get away with it. I refused to be apathetic to the suffering of another. I would save the creature that had saved me, or die trying.

First, of course, I needed to reach it.

Climbing a cliff face and climbing a redwood are two different challenges. A slate wall has grooves and handholds and ledges; a sequoia is essentially a slippery pole for the first half of the assault, in this case its first three hundred feet. You don't "free-climb" a redwood, you shoot an arrow attached to fishing line and an acre of nylon rope over an upper limb, then secure the loop and pull yourself up using a combination of rigs and carabiners.

I had a steak knife, binoculars, and a torn jumpsuit.

Mother Nature is far from benign, and among trees, the redwood is considered an apex predator. Towering above other species, it will dominate its ecosystem by controlling the sun, using its shade to stagnate the growth of a neighboring tree or even kill it. It will drop a ten-ton buttress of wood upon any perceived challenger, delivering a deathblow in a territorial action known to botanists as "redwood bombing."

Circling the clearing, I soon found what I was looking for.

The Douglas fir had been dead for quite some time, its wood petrified, its trunk split open by a redwood bomb. Its remains were leaning against the massive trunk of its executioner. Though it was still a good distance from the redwood I needed to reach, I believed that, given access to the canopy, I could forge a route among the treetops and buttresses that would lead me to my cephaloped companion . . . assuming, of course, it *was* my cephaloped companion calling out to me.

Working my way onto the Douglas fir's partially uprooted trunk, I balanced myself atop the dead tree's rotted remains, the trunk of which was listing at a thirty-degree angle. Bending at the waist, I began walking up the tree like a chimpanzee, gripping limbs and vines to secure a handhold.

Eight minutes later, I had gone as high as I dared. Nearly two hundred feet off the forest floor, I had run out of dead tree to climb.

The redwood's midsection creaked as its treetops swayed gently against the blue sky, its lowest branch—forty feet above my reach—mocking my assault.

Redwoods are monoecious, possessing both male and female parts. The male organs, called strobili, are small conelike features that grow near branch tips; the female organs being rounded cones that are fertilized through grains of pollen that contain sperm cells. Both provided me with a potential means to reach the canopy.

Carefully inching my way along the uppermost branch of the Douglas fir, I reached out to the redwood's trunk and a rounded female cone, testing the strength of the protrusion. When part of it flaked away in my palm, it released butterflies of fear in my stomach and I looked down . . . a big mistake.

First, my quadriceps began shaking, then my arms. Paralyzed in fear, I remained in place, summoning the courage to retreat.

The pan flute cry reached out to me. The creature was dying.

I reached up to another conelike growth. Sinking my fingertips deep into the strobili, I swung my left leg away from its Douglas fir perch, my bare toes searching the redwood bark for something to grip . . . slipping on bark and mushrooms until my foot came to rest on a burl—a benign growth—the size of a watermelon.

Restricting my vision to the trunk, I stepped away from the Douglas fir, both feet sharing the burl—a risky move. I hugged the redwood, feeling with my free hand for another knot, discovering instead a coarse vine. Relief washed aside my fears as I gripped the woodlike liana with both hands and pulled myself up, my feet walking the trunk—the cursed vine suddenly uncoiling from its growth, dropping me thirty heart-pounding feet, my palms sliding the final splinter-collecting, flesh-scorching few seconds before the brakes held fast.

"Shit damn, that hurts!" I was dangling from the rigid vine, my jumpsuit covered with a white frosting from a patch of wart lichen. I reset my feet and continued the climb, my muscles fueled more by anger than a desire to save the damn squid. I was sick of being afraid, sick of being in pain, sick of being stuck in a never-ending, cryogenic nightmare of existence . . . sick of—

"Made it!" Giddy with adrenaline, I sat down on a tree limb so incredibly wide I could have driven three eighteen-wheeler trucks on it side by side had it not been supporting another forest of redwoods. There were six of them in a row—giant fingers that traced deep long slow sways, each movement independent of the next, as if purging a prolonged immersed breath. These silo-wide trunks were rooted upon a solitary limb that followed a twenty-degree incline before disappearing into an oasis of green. And that was just one limb!

How best to describe the canopy? Easier, I think to describe me. I was Jack, transported by a beanstalk into the land of the giants—a human bug that had wandered into a cloud forest that seemed to defy gravity. Before me loomed a towering metropolis of bark, its gothic redwood spires disappearing into the heavens, its tree trunk columns fused together at different levels by a never-ending network of branches, some of which twisted like taffy while others arched in magnificent curves that would have shamed any roller coaster. These avenues of gray forged a labyrinth skeleton—a seemingly endless maze that was cloaked in greenery that hung in five-story sheets—curtains of leaf as thick as my wrist, segregating countless domains of unbridled nature waiting to be discovered.

Pulling aside one sheath, I exposed a backyard of huckleberry bushes that were growing wild out of a crater-size hollowed stump. For five minutes I fed off a single purple berry cluster that was as large as a grapefruit and as sweet as a ripe mango. I stopped when the pan flute summoned me from my meal.

The sound seemed weaker, more desperate. I moved toward it, forging a path across a rainforest of alien gigantism. Butterflies as large as dinner plates attempted to light on me, the color of their wings changing with each fanning flap as I pushed my way through hanging gardens of epiphytes—plants growing atop plants, forged from fern mats that served as habitats for aquatic crustaceans known as copepods. Layers of rainwater-drenched soil had accumulated over eons in the redwoods' crotches, supporting blueberry bushes and strawberry thickets and assorted fruit trees that had grown hundreds of feet tall.

I worked my way along a ninety-foot branch that served as a bridge between two ground-rooted redwoods. It looked like lightning had split the bark down the middle. The exposed center brimmed with turquoise-green moss as soft as goose down. Entering the next canopy, I was greeted by a rotted stump from a reiterated redwood that had fallen long ago. The crater-size remains had filled with rainwater to become a wading pool six feet deep and forty feet across. To my surprise, the redwood pond was filled with islands of pads and toads the size of a catcher's mitt whose heads turned crimson whenever their throats expanded. Incredibly, there were also fish in the stump—at least I thought they were fish until they suddenly flew out of the redwood pond and flitted about like birds, shaking water from their rigid tropically colored pectoral wings, their barracudalike mouths coveting tadpoles the size of my foot. After a few passes overhead, the creatures perched on their tail fins on the rim of the hollowed out stump like crows on a fence.

The caves began on a different level of the redwood crown, six stories higher than my entry point onto the second tree. They had no doubt been created by lightning strikes, the fires burning for weeks, perhaps months. A redwood is too big and too wet to burn down. It simply isolates the fire by rerouting its internal water supply through a network of microscopic vessels known as the xylem. If a Northern California redwood could generate two million pascals of negative pressure to suck water from its roots up its trunk over tens of miles of branches, I could not imagine the forces necessary to redirect water throughout these behemoth tree forests.

There were three caves. Two were located in the roots of a harvest of reiterated redwoods that had sprouted from a massive U-shaped branch as wide as a highway off-ramp; the third had been burnt into the side of a three-story buttress.

Moving to the edge of the limb, I looked down upon the clearing where I had stood nearly an hour ago. I quickly approximated the drop to be in excess of three hundred feet and, feeling dizzy, backed away.

I had found my way to the source of the distress call, now I needed to find the distressed.

The opening to the first fire cave resembled a ten-foot-high birth canal. Slipping inside, I was greeted by an off-putting blue-cheese smell. The interior walls were spongy and scorched black from the fire, the chamber as large as my family's old living room. Brown salamanders tinged with golden specks scampered by my feet, the amphibians feeding off blind pink earthworms they had exposed in the cave soil.

No cephaloped.

Nor was there one in the second cave.

Then I heard it, and hurried to the third cave, a far larger hollow burnt into a buttress that could have been featured in a Grimm's fairy tale.

"Oh, God . . ."

The trap, concealed within the spongy walls of the cave, had sprung the moment the cephaloped had entered. Clam-shaped, constructed of an aero gel polymer vented with quarter-size holes, the pod had slammed so quickly it had sliced off one of the cephaloped's tentacles just above the fin.

My heart pounded with excitement. Someone . . . *something* had used a technology that rivaled my own to construct this trap.

Those thoughts were tempered as I regarded the caged squid. Terrified, it lay curled in a fetal position in a green pool of its own blood. Looking up at me, it appeared to panic.

"Don't worry, Oscar. I'll get you out of that thing." I reached for its center seam—and suddenly my head burst in an explosion of purple lights as an electrical charge flung me outside the cave and nearly over the edge of the redwood's main limb.

For several minutes I remained on my back, stunned. "What the hell was that?"

ELECTRICAL SHOCK. FIFTEEN THOUSAND VOLTS. RUNNING LEVEL THREE DIAGNOSTIC . . . RECALCULATING-

"ABE!"

CHRONOMETER . . . RECALCULATING. AMINO ACID LEVELS—OFF. BLOOD GLUCOSE LEVELS—OFF. SEROTONIN—

"Hold diagnostic." Regaining my feet, I limped back to the cave. "ABE, analyze that specimen cage and determine how I can open it without harming the creature inside."

CHRONOMETER . . . RECALCULATING.

"Enough! You sound like a bad GPS system. Focus on that plastic specimen cage."

SPECIMEN CAGE IS ELECTRIFIED. LOCATE POWER SOURCE AND DISABLE.

"Power source? Makes sense." I scanned the outside of the pod, finding nothing. Retrieving a large stick from outside, I wedged the branch beneath its curved bottom.

"Hold on, Oscar." Using the stick as a fulcrum, I flipped the clear cage onto its side—exposing a toaster-size portable power pack housed within the base. Using the blunt end of the stick, I smashed the assembly until it sparked and short-circuited in a burst of smoke.

The pod cracked. Using both hands, I pried it open.

Too weak to move, the cephaloped remained curled in a ball.

Gently, I reached inside and scooped the invertebrate's upper torso into my arms and against my chest, straining to lift the three hundred plus pound creature. With no recourse but to drag its tentacles behind me, I carried it to the redwood pond and released it into the water.

21

If the Earth does grow inhospitable toward human presence, it is primarily because we have lost our sense of courtesy toward the Earth and its inhabitants.
—THOMAS BERRY, Roman Catholic priest

The dying cephaloped sank to the bottom of the redwood pond, bubbles of air trailing from the breathing organ atop its skull.

Realizing too late that the land creature might be in shock and actually drowning, I went in after it. The cold water instantly soothed my own frayed nervous system.

Hoisting Oscar back to the surface required pinning the back of its head and upper torso against my chest—which meant running my arms beneath its tentacle sockets as a lifeguard might do to assist a drowning person.

Maybe that was its "sensitive area" because the moment I touched it, the inert animal suddenly reached out for me with those monstrous appendages and held me in its vise grip *underwater!*

The sensation of panic sent a memory flashing through my mind's eye. When I was sixteen, I had enrolled in a life guard training seminar at summer camp. On our first day, the instructor—ten years older and seventy pound heavier than yours truly, volunteered me to swim out to the deep end of the pool and "rescue him." He was calm on my approach, then, playing the role of the panicking victim, suddenly lunged for me and clasped my head to his chest, holding me underwater as I became his flotation device. The fucker kept me pinned underwater for the longest, scariest forty seconds of my life, teaching me a valuable lesson . . . and later a simple lifesaving piece of advice—a drowning person will only release you if you pull *them* underwater.

Reaching up through a sea of tentacles, I grabbed the cephaloped by one of its eye stalks and pulled its head underwater.

It released me instantly—its eye stalk, I imagined, being the cephaloped equivalent of my testicles. A minute later the two of us were out of the water, panting heavily as we leaned against the side of the rain-filled tree stump.

Slumped over, the land squid stared at me with its jaundiced eyes through droopy double lids as if trying to figure me out. After several minutes, it did something quite marvelous and, in retrospect something distinctly human—it slowly reached out to me with one of its appendages.

In turn, I reached toward it.

The touch of flesh to tentacle fin was startling, eliciting its own impulse wave that was shared by the two of us—a deep, almost hypnotic resonance that seeped through every cell in my body.

RECALCULATING . . . MASSIVE INFLUX OF SODIUM AND CALCIUM IONS DETECTED, ACCOMPANIED BY AN EFFLUX OF POTASSIUM IONS. POST-SYNAPTIC POTENTIAL CYCLES ARE BEING ALTERED—

My eyes rolled up in my head, my body tingling. *ABE, how is this happening?*

ECHOLOCATION.

Before I could blink, ABE had downloaded a dozen pre-GDO studies on the effects of dolphin echolocation on humans—echolocation being the dolphin's natural sonar system which functioned like an ultrasound, enabling the mammals to detect objects through the water over great distances. Results of experiments showed that when a dolphin echolocated a human, the sonic clicks caused dramatic changes in the subjects' neurotransmitter production, affecting the entire endocrine system. This positive response was caused by the effects of cavitation, which induced sonophoresis—an increase in hormone transportation.

Dolphin echolocation took place in the water; my contact with the cephaloped was direct and prolonged . . . and it was a multidirectional healing. I could feel the squid growing stronger . . . the pulsation of its three hearts cascading within my own bloodstream, its terror dissipating.

WHY?

ABE whispered the one-word inquiry out of the ether and into my consciousness, breaking my train of thought.

My internal response: *Why what?*

WHY?

I opened my eyes. "ABE, what are you asking me?" I was so annoyed at being disturbed that I failed to realize something important . . .

ABE IS PROGRAMMED TO RESPOND TO INQUIRIES, NOT TO GENERATE THEM.
"Then stop saying 'Why?'"

THE INQUIRY IS NOT ORIGINATING FROM ABE.

"What?" I sat up, gazing into the alert yellow eyes staring back at me. *It's coming from the cephaloped?*

CORRECT. THE SUBJECT IS COMMUNICATING USING THOUGHT ENERGY. "WHY" IS THE SUBJECT'S EMOTIONAL EXPRESSION OF THOUGHT ENERGY APPROXIMATED INTO ENGLISH.

Can it understand me?

NOT DIRECTLY. ROBERT EISENBRAUN'S THOUGHT ENERGY IS BASED ON CONCEPTS DEFINED BY AN ESTABLISHED VERBAL AND WRITTEN LANGUAGE COMBINED WITH EMPIRICAL KNOWLEDGE. OSCAR'S THOUGHT ENERGY IS BASED ON A VOCABULARY OF EMOTIONS, DESIRES, NEEDS, CURIOSITY, EXPRESSED THROUGH THE LIMITATIONS OF ITS MEMORY FOUNDATION.

What is . . . wait—did you refer to it as Oscar?

CORRECT. IT HAS ACCEPTED YOUR DESIGNATION OF ITS PHYSICAL PRESENCE.

Just out of curiosity, is Oscar a male?

OSCAR POSSESSES AN ENLARGED HECTOCOTYLUS ARM DESIGNED FOR INSERTION INTO A FEMALE OR MALE MANTLE AND DEPOSITING A SPERMATOPHORE, THEREFORE THE SUBJECT IS A MALE.

Female or male? Are octopi bisexual? Wait . . . I'm not holding its hectocotylus arm, am I?

REPRODUCTIVE DATA REFLECTS AQUATIC SPECIES OF OCTOPUS; DATA ON EVOLVED TERRESTRIAL SPECIES IS STILL BEING FORMULATED. PRE-GDO STUDIES ON AQUATIC OCTOPUS SEXUALITY INDICATED SUBJECTS, WHEN PAIRED WITH OTHERS, FAILED TO RECOGNIZE WHETHER ANOTHER SUBJECT WAS MALE OR FEMALE UNTIL AFTER THEY BEGAN THE ACT OF COPULATION. MALE-TO-MALE COPULATIONS LASTED LESS THAN THIRTY SECONDS AND DID NOT CULMINATE IN SPERMATOPHORE RELEASE. MALE-TO-FEMALE COPULATIONS LASTED TWO AND A HALF HOURS AND RESULTED IN THE RELEASE OF ONE TO FOUR SPERMATOPHORES. OSCAR RECOGNIZES THAT ROBERT EISENBRAUN IS MALE. IT WAS THIS RECOGNITION THAT LED TO OSCAR RESCUING EISENBRAUN FROM DROWNING.

Now I'm completely confused. Oscar rescued me because it recognized that I'm a male?

CURIOSITY APPEARS TO HAVE BEEN THE MOTIVATING FACTOR.

Has Oscar ever even seen a male human before?

OSCAR HAS NEVER SEEN A MALE HUMAN. OSCAR DESIRES AGAIN TO UNDERSTAND WHY ROBERT EISENBRAUN RESCUED OSCAR.

Why? Because Oscar . . . Exhausted from the internal dialogue with my biological chip, I squeezed the creature's fin, looking directly into its stalk eyes. "You rescued me from the ocean, you saved me from the ants. Humans . . . my species—we too believe in treating others with acts of kindness."

To my surprise, the creature became agitated. Withdrawing its tentacle, it stretched its reach overhead, snagged the nearest branch of the redwood and disappeared into the canopy.

"What'd I say? Is he coming back?"

UNKNOWN.

Unknown? You were reading its damn thought energy! Can't you . . . Ah, never mind. ABE, based on our shared observations, summarize Oscar.

OSCAR REPRESENTS A SPECIES OF CEPHALOPOD THAT HAS EVOLVED FROM AN AQUATIC ANIMAL INTO A SEMI-AMPHIBIOUS AIR-BREATHING LAND ANIMAL. OSCAR DEMONSTRATES GENEALOGICAL TRAITS LINKED WITH HIGHER FORMS OF INTELLIGENCE. OSCAR RESCUED ROBERT EISENBRAUN BECAUSE IT WAS CURIOUS ABOUT ROBERT EISENBRAUN. OSCAR'S THOUGHT ENERGY RELATIVE TO ROBERT EISENBRAUN'S PRESENCE SUGGESTS CONFLICTING CONCERNS THAT EQUATE TO EMOTIONS OF FEAR, TOLERANCE, CURIOSITY, EMPATHY, DISTRUST, AND FRIENDSHIP. OSCAR REPRESENTS A SPECIES THAT IS BEING HUNTED BY A SUPERIOR PREDATOR DISPLAYING AN ADVANCED KNOWLEDGE OF REMOTE SENSING, PLASTICS, AND RELATED SCIENCE AND TECHNOLOGIES.

"Stop. Formulate best response: Why is Oscar's species being hunted?"

IMPOSSIBLE TO DETERMINE, BASED ON LIMITED DATA. POSSIBLE RESPONSES INCLUDE FOOD, HARVESTING OF BODY PARTS, POPULATION CONTROL, EXTERMINATION, SPORT, OR SCIENTIFIC RESEARCH. BASED ON THE SIZE OF THE TRAP, OSCAR'S SPECIES IS INTENDED TO BE CAPTURED ALIVE.

"Then the hunters will be back to claim their prize." I stared up into the canopy, its treetops swaying two hundred feet overhead. *ABE, design a means to rig the fire cave's perimeter with a trap of our own.*

"The hunter is about to become the hunted."

•   •   •

ABE must have accessed every wilderness article ever written, but in the end I knew the trap's chances of success had more to do with whether the element of surprise outweighed the technology of the unknown hunter we were facing. Or hunters. There was simply no telling how many *its* would show up, or for that matter when they would return.

The trap was rigged to the bottom of the pod—any attempt to remove the device would trigger the release of a log that was teetering on the edge of the redwood's limb. Vines attached to the log ended in snares positioned in and around the cave floor. The vines were green and thin, but possessed the tensile strength of steel wire. Most important, they were easily concealed within the spongy walls and floor of the fire cave.

Luring an unknown quarry into the fire cave was central to the trap. Creating a dummy to replace Oscar inside the plastic pod proved the more difficult task. In the end I settled on segments of thick roots and mud, which offered the appearance and feel of mass, and smeared cephaloped blood on the interior glass to prevent a clear inspection.

Hopefully, the hunter would spring the trap before the ruse was discovered.

The sun had nearly set by the time I had finished camouflaging the last snare. Climbing into the upper branches of another redwood, I concealed myself behind a blanket of leaves, set the binoculars on night vision, then waited.

Hours passed. I rolled over on my back and gazed up at a redwood canopy set against a backdrop of stars—stars that would allow my biochip to recalculate its chronometer. Instructing ABE to alert me to any unusual sounds or movements, I closed my eyes and slipped inside the warmth of my forest cocoon.

INTERNAL ALERT! NEW ENTITIES PRESENT!

I opened my eyes to an ABE-evoked rush of adrenaline. *Where are they?*

FIFTY-SEVEN METERS TO THE WEST. DESCENDING FROM AN ALTITUDE OF 792 METERS.

Looking up, I could see nothing but the dark outline of the redwood treetops and a sprinkling of stars. Then I held the night-vision binoculars to my eyes and the invaders became visible.

The platform was hexagonal and dark and I would have missed it except it blotted out a section of stars twenty-feet long. Hovering above the forest canopy, it appeared to be motionless, lacking any obvious means of propulsion. Zooming in on the undercarriage, I saw a faint pattern of spinning circles, the movement generating a soft green glow in my otherwise olive-tainted field of vision.

I was looking at the bottom of the hovercraft when a life-form appeared above the treetops, rising eerily toward the levitating object. At first I thought it was one of the giant bats, only the creature wasn't flapping its wings, it was using them like a kite, catching the wind to increase its altitude. As my eyes adjusted to the starlight, I saw a pair of dangling biped legs and then arms—human arms. The faceless head, the fleshless skin . . . everything was cloaked in black to blend in with the night.

Rising in tow behind the flying biped was a pod trap, and there was clearly something thrashing about inside. ABE quickly confirmed it to be a cephaloped.

Was it Oscar, or another one of its kind?

Cursing under my breath, I parted the leaf blind and searched for the primary redwood limb with my binoculars, tracing the highway of bark and ferns back to the buttress. My heart pounded in my chest as I peered inside the fire cave, staring at the dark silhouette of another winged being poised just outside the entrance. For a long moment the biped simply remained there, its head slightly cocked as if evaluating—

Womp!

There was no scream or screech, just the report of a vine snapping beneath the weight of the now dangling log and the panicked flutter of leatherlike wings beating the night air as one of the trap's snares wrenched tightly around the ankle of my quarry, flipping it upside-down and pinning it to the ceiling of the fire cave.

Got you, you bastard! How's it feel to be—

DETECTING AN INCREASE IN PARTICLE WAVES. WARNING: INTRUDERS CAN DETECT YOUR THOUGHT ENERGY.

Huh?

Before I could muzzle my mind, a blinding white searchlight ignited from the platform's hexagonal undercarriage, the beacon cutting a swath of day in my direction through the chaos of foliage.

There was no time to react. One moment I was scrambling to hide beneath an illuminated umbrella of greenery, the next I was swept off my feet and into the air, a viselike grip squeezing my rib cage into my lungs, the assault as sudden as it was terrifying. Helpless and frightened, I bellowed a bloodcurdling scream yet uttered no sound, my mouth filled with goo . . .

No, not goo, it was a tentacle!

Oscar?

SILENCE.

The searchlight followed us as we moved through the trees, two of the cephaloped's tentacles wrapped snugly around my waist and legs, the others grappling for vines and branches. Crashing through curtains of leaves, Oscar dropped in a dizzying, stomach-churning free fall into darkness—and then we stopped.

Oscar released me just long enough to pin my back against the trunk of a tree. Splaying its head and tentacles, it blanketed my body, its flesh changing colors, camouflaging us with a cluster of thick surface roots amassed around the moss-covered base of a two-hundred-foot sequoia.

I could feel my guardian struggling to control its gasps. My own breaths were somewhat stifled, my face covered by a semiporous sheath of stretched tentacle skin.

Breathing, escaping, awakening . . . none of it was important. Wrapped head to toe in the cephaloped's embrace, my only priority was to manage the building waves of euphoria that were causing my body to shake uncontrollably as every square inch of my being was submerged in what felt like a pool of pure energy. My cells cavitated, the neurotransmitters in my brain rapid firing as if touched by the hand of God.

Thankfully, ABE stepped in. Channeling the onslaught of echolocation, my bio-chip recalculated my brain waves on the fly even as it escorted my mind's eye on a journey through another sea of consciousness that melded the cephaloped's consciousness with mine.

Oh . . . my.

Through an emotion-laced prism I stole a glimpse inside my host and discovered my soul . . . and Oscar's soul . . . and the redwood's soul—each a spark of purity that bound every life-form that existed, had existed, and will ever exist not only to a higher power but also to one another. Call it the soul, call it energy . . . what I saw, what I experienced was the essence of creation—love without pretense, giving without receiving—a marrow of caring so honest and perfect it defined selflessness.

It no longer mattered whether I was asleep or awake, dead or alive. In this one brief moment of clarity I had resolved the meaning of life, the very reason for us being—and this simple simplistic understanding stripped evil of its purpose and boiled hatred and greed and corruption down to its naked truth. I saw the Creator's essence in its design and I wept, my newfound wisdom setting me free, robbing death of its impact; revealing the soul's immortality.

And then I slipped out of this echolocation-induced magic carpet ride as my being was swept down a dark funnel.

And then I saw through the cephaloped's eyes.

What I saw was evil.

The biped was hovering twenty paces before us, its outstretched batlike wings catching the wind, its face masked by the predawn night. Reddish brown eyes shimmered catlike in the darkness as they inspected the redwood trunks, ours one of five sprung from a fertile limb that hung two hundred feet above the forest floor.

Uncertain, the sentry remained.

Dawn announced its intentions, first as a morning mist, then as filtered gray light—gray light that vanquished the night and with it the demon's silhouette.

I could see the wings, but not well enough to tell if they were organic or artificial. The demon, however, was quite human, its flesh muddied and pasty and camouflaged in a tight-fitting cephaloped hide that barely concealed the sultry female's breasts.

That's right, the hunter was a huntress—a vixen of the forest. Her long raven hair hung in dark coils past elfish ears and down her muscular torso; her lips, thick and full and pouting, launched a thousand memories.

The vixen was *my* vixen, and I ached at the sight of her through the cephaloped's partially closed eye stalks.

For her part, Andria continued to scan the flora and fauna, the coldness in her brown eyes and the barbed electrified lance coiled in her fist enough to suppress my overwhelming urge to reveal myself.

Brighter curtains of gray filtered through the redwood labyrinth, dawn's threat chasing my long-lost lover back into the forest canopy where she boarded her awaiting chariot.

Oscar and I remained bound to the tree until the gray bled gold and the nightmare melted into day, our thoughts and emotions fusing as one.

22

I believe that we are all standing on an evolutionary threshold in which we have the possibility not only of creating a new culture, but actually becoming a new kind of human being that will understand how to live with connection with ourselves, with each other and with the earth. So much of the suffering and acts that will happen in the meantime, we have to be prepared for. But if we can work with it instead of resist it, that evolutionary leap may be possible.
—CAROLYN BAKER, therapist and survivalist

Oscar released me and I fell to my knees on the forest floor, my brain buzzing from echolocation sickness as if I had overdosed on LSD. I rolled over and saw a frog belch colors; I looked up and willed a centipede to tap dance on a branch—the branch growing . . . reaching out for me—ABE quickly adjusting the serotonin levels in my cerebral cortex, dousing the bizarre effects of synesthesia.

The sound of a pan flute disrupted my recovery and my eyes resettled on my cephaloped guardian. The creature was exhaling forcibly through its breathing organ, attempting no doubt, to communicate with his own kind.

If they were out there, none would emerge from hiding.

It was me they feared, or my species . . . or my girlfriend, or whatever ghoulish being she was made out to be. Why had she been thawed and not me? Were the rest of the *Oceanus*'s crew with her? Who had supplied her with the antigravity wings and the hovercraft?

And why the hell was she hunting cephalopeds?

It dawned on me then, and I smiled at my stupidity. *Asshole! It's all part of the dream. Andria . . . her hair long and wild—just like the day we met in that Virginia forest. Back then she was wearing a camouflage suit;*

this time around my mind has her decked out in full warrior gear to match the setting. But why were she and her mates hunting poor Oscar?

The answer came to me quickly, my outburst of laughter startling my eight-legged companion. "The squid hunt aboard *Oceanus*. Andria loves her calamari . . . no offense." I pulled myself up with the assistance of a vine, shaking my head in amazement. "Kyle Graulus was right. These Omega dreams are pretty wild."

Oscar looked at me with what I interpreted to be a quizzical expression.

"Sorry, pal. None of this is real. I'm Dorothy, you're the Scarecrow, and my fiancée appears to be up for the role of a very sexy Wicked Witch. It's all part of a seriously fucked-up cryogenic dream . . . and why am I explaining this to you?"

INCORRECT.

The voice in my head startled me. *ABE, is that you, or are you interpreting for Oscar?*

ABE RESPONSE IS IN REFERENCE TO OMEGA-WAVE DREAM THEORY VERSUS EISENBRAUN HYPOTHESIS REGARDING ASTEROID 1997 XF11 IMPACT WITH THE MOON ON OCTOBER 26, 2028.

Your reference is moot. The dream overrides the impact hypothesis.

INCORRECT. BASED ON STAR CARTOGRAPHY AND SOIL ANALYSIS, EISENBRAUN HYPOTHESIS WAS CORRECT.

A chill ran down my spine. *Explain.*

SOIL ANALYSIS FROM THE CAVE WALLS REVEALS A THIN LAYER OF HELIUM-3 OCCURRING AT A GEOLOGICAL TIME PERIOD EQUATING TO A 2028 FALLOUT. TRACES OF HELIUM-3 AND MOON ROCK ARE ALSO PRESENT ALONG THE SURFACE AND REDWOOD CROTCHES—EVIDENCE OF CONTINUED PLANETARY BOMBARDMENT FROM ORBITING SPACE DEBRIS. STAR CARTOGRAPHY CORRESPONDS WITH A DATE THAT YIELDS A 93.7 PERCENT CORRELATION TO THE HELIUM-3 FALLOUT LAYER. AS A RESULT, ABE CHRONOMETER HAS BEEN RESET TO THE POST COLLISION YEAR OF 12,233,776 P.C. . . . POST-CATACLYSM.

"Twelve million years?" I smiled nervously. "You said the evidence only yields a ninety-three-point-seven percent probability of being correct. What about the other six-point-three percent?"

THERE IS A SECONDARY CORRELATION MATCHING THE STAR CARTOGRAPHY.

"Thank God. And how many post-collision years does that amount to? And please, feel free to round it off, I won't worry about a few extra years here or there."

ONE HUNDRED TWENTY-TWO MILLION YEARS, ROUNDED OFF.

The blood rushed from my face; I felt my heart fluttering.

WARNING: BLOOD PRESSURE DROPPING. COMPENSATING . . .

"I couldn't . . . that's impossible. Vanilla sway! ABE, wake me up."

ROBERT EISENBRAUN IS AWAKE.

"Bullshit!" I was approaching a full state of panic. "This is a dream. Your analysis is simply part of that dream. Prove that I'm awake!"

CRYOGENIC PROCESS DROPS SUBJECT CORE BODY TEMPERATURE TO –33°F. ABE CANNOT FUNCTION IN HOST CORE TEMPERATURES FALLING BELOW 84.5°F. ABE IS FUNCTIONING, THEREFORE ROBERT EISENBRAUN IS AWAKE.

I dropped to my knees. *Steady, Eisenbraun. ABE is functioning, but it's only functioning within the dream, not inside your skull, which is still cryogenically frozen back in 2028.*

Oscar reached out for me, sensing my distress.

Upon contact, I projected my thoughts to the cephaloped using the bio-chip. *Oscar, I need to check the trap. Can you take us back to the fire cave?*

We arrived at the redwood buttress twenty minutes later, Oscar taking a circuitous route to make sure we were alone. The sprung trap had begun with a snare that I had camouflaged in the spongy floor of the fire cave. The vine ran up the wall and through the ceiling through a hole in the buttress where its movement had triggered a weight—a teetering log, now hanging over the edge of the redwood limb. The result of my ABE-directed labor had fashioned a near-inescapable trap that had resulted in our adversary being pinned by its ensnared extremity to the roof of the cave.

The cave was now empty, but there had been a mighty struggle inside.

Animals caught in a hunter's trap have been known to gnaw off a foot in order to survive. This one had cut itself loose from the snare using a blade.

The severed object lay in the shadows. Trembling, I picked it up and carried it outside to examine it in the light.

It was a human foot, severed at the ankle. The wound was cauterized, as if the blade that had sliced cleanly through flesh, sinew, and bone had been superheated.

It was a woman's left foot.

I knew because it was Andria's.

Sickened, I turned away from Oscar and retched, then found a patch of blue-green moss and laid down in it. Oscar had lost the equivalent of a foot, yet I had not lost my last meal over that . . . for the record, the squid's missing appendage had already started growing back. But the thought of seeing Andria deformed . . . even if this *was* a dream—

"Wait a second . . . ABE, confirm an observation: The winged Andria Saxon we saw last night through Oscar's eyes . . . she wasn't missing a foot, was she?

OBSERVATION CONFIRMED. ANDRIA SAXON WAS NOT MISSING A FOOT.

"But this is Andria Saxon's foot, correct?"

CORRECT.

"Explain."

INSUFFICIENT DATA AVAILABLE TO FORMULATE A HYPOTHESIS.

"Thanks loads. Where the hell am I supposed to find more data?"

CLUES MAY BE FOUND ABOARD *OCEANUS*.

Ninety-seven minutes. That's how long it took me, through ABE, to paint a mental picture of *Oceanus* to Oscar. And still the cephaloped hesitated.

ABE, yes or no—can Oscar get us down to the beach without me having to rappel down a twelve-hundred-foot rock face?

YES.

Then let's go. Tell him to lead the way.

THE ROUTE TO THE SEA IS KNOWN ONLY TO OSCAR'S KIND. THE ROUTE CUTS THROUGH THE CEPHALOPED GATHERING. OSCAR TRUSTS EISENBRAUN, BUT DOES NOT TRUST EISENBRAUN'S FEELINGS TOWARD THE ENTITY RECOGNIZED AS ANDRIA SAXON.

Can't say I trust them myself. Does Oscar know where Andria Saxon lives?

YES.

Will Oscar take me there?

NO.

I gritted my teeth, exasperated. *ABE, tell Oscar that Eisenbraun wants to stop Andria Saxon and her kind from capturing any more of Oscar's kind. In order to do that—*

Without warning, Oscar flipped out. Raising two of its thick arms into the air, the terrestrial squid proceeded to pound the patch of moss like a silverback gorilla, throwing the equivalent of a cephaloped tantrum. Waving its tentacles wildly, the creature then spun around and uprooted fistfuls of ferns before it darted up the trunk of a redwood like a spider monkey, thrashing about in the upper canopy.

"Got a bit of a temper, doesn't he?" I pondered my potential courses of action as debris rained upon my head and shoulders from above. My first instinct, arguably an emotional one, was to find Andria, resolve the mysteries surrounding our shared reality, then turn this nightmare into a pleasant dream.

The scientist in me vetoed that idea. Before tracking down my former fiancée or the rest of the crew, I needed to inspect the cryogenic chamber aboard *Oceanus* before the habitat washed back out to sea with the next tidal event.

ABE, calculate the next full-moon perigee.

THE MOON WILL PERIGEE IN SIXTEEN DAYS.

I surveyed the surrounding forest. The dense foliage of the redwood canopy was strewn with vines, some rigid, dried out growths, others moist, flexible coils resembling giant Hawaiian leis—the latter perfect for mountain climbs and descents.

The upper branches rustled, yielding a cluster of ripe mangoes that splattered nearby, soaking my feet. "All right, you big hairy octopus, you got your way. Now get your ass down here, we have work to do. And bring me some food!"

It was midafternoon, the sun high in a cloudless blue sky when Oscar followed me out of the forest and into the clearing, hauling what I hoped would be the last bundle of vines we would need to rappel down to the beach. As the cephaloped watched, I secured the first length of leis-rope around the trunk of a Douglas fir located sixty paces from the summit's ledge, then began adding sections, lengthening the vine another seventy to one hundred feet at a time.

The ability to tie knots seemed to baffle the curious creature. "It's called an opposable thumb," I said, wiggling the digits. "It's what separates the brains from the brawn. Don't sweat it, in another ten million years your kind may possesses something similar."

Having completed my task, I attempted to drag the bulky coil of vines to the edge of the plateau, but could barely budge the pile.

Oscar snatched it off the ground with two tentacles, picking it up easily.

"Okay, I'll admit there are benefits that come with having suckers and tentacles."

I led Oscar to the edge of the cliff, motioning him to toss the vine over the ledge. The two of us watched as the slack unfurled more than a thousand feet before the excess settled on the rock pilings below.

A few miles to the north, *Oceanus* towered over the deserted valley like a giant olive-green marble. My pulse raced as I realized it was time again to risk life and limb.

I had rappelled down the face of a mountain twice—both times with Andria—and I had not been very good at it. This rock was higher, my vine rope was untested, save for an abbreviated descent from the redwood canopy, and I lacked everything from a harness and carabiner to shoes—the latter fact establishing itself as I stepped out onto the hot flat rock, blistering the soles of my bare feet.

Sensing my distress, the massive squid suddenly scooped me off the ground. Before I could protest, I found myself suspended twelve hundred feet in space as Oscar climbed down the sheer rock face in herky-jerky heart-stopping ten-foot drops and catches. I had no choice but to hang on to the thick hairy tentacle supporting my body, as the cephaloped's other appendages alternately slipped and caught narrow ledges of rock in our semicontrolled free fall.

"Jesus, Oscar—at least use the vine!"

Despite my rants, the cephaloped stubbornly refused to grip the vine, which remained within a tantalizing arm's reach. I'd have grabbed the damn thing myself had I not been holding on for dear life.

Three minutes later we were ten feet from landing on the ground when Oscar abruptly stopped, reached out to the vine, and handed it to me.

"Ha-ha, the octopus has a sense of humor."

The octopus refused to budge.

Reluctantly, I reached out and grabbed the vine, rappelling the last ten feet.

Red faced, I turned around to find the creature gesticulating wildly with six of its eight tentacles as it splattered a rock with urine from an unseen cavity.

THE CEPHALOPED IS AMUSED.

"Hey, suck-face, I'm glad I could amuse you." Feeling the urge myself, I thought about peeing over Oscar's urine-drenched rock as a retort, but having no idea what the gesture might translate to in cephaloped, decided against it.

In truth, I was taken by Oscar's display of wit, something a world apart from simple playfulness. The cephaloped clearly possessed a sense of humor—a trait of intelligence reserved for . . . well, for humans.

My urge to urinate increased at the sound of running water.

It was a waterfall, its reverberating acoustics originating farther to the north. My first thought was that it was the runoff from the bat cavern, but looking up, I saw several locations spewing freshwater along the towering rock face—feeder systems running from the fertile forests above, draining into a shallow river that snaked north across the wasteland of sand.

I had not seen the waterway when I was in the cave, my vantage obscured by the waterfall's mist, and had missed it days earlier when it had been submerged, along with the rest of the valley by the full moon's devastating tidal surge.

I headed for the bank to cool off—only to have Oscar veer me away.

"No more jokes, pal. I'm tired and hot, and I could use a drink."

The cephaloped placed a tentacle lightly across my right shoulder, its sucker pad coming to rest along the back of my neck, the physical contact allowing the creature to transmit its thoughts through my bio-chip.

EXTREME DANGER.

What danger? Bats?

BATS ARE NOT DANGER. TEETH ARE DANGER.

Teeth? Define "teeth."

Leading me by the arm, Oscar escorted me on a bizarre zigzagging trek across the beach, heading in a roundabout direction for *Oceanus.*

Half a mile away, the cephaloped stopped, gesturing to a smooth avenue of sand pressed four to five feet deep. Each side of the thirty-foot-wide compression was bordered by an occasional five-segmented, four clawed paw print—the paw print as wide as a pickup truck.

ABE, what in the hell could have—

THE SPECIES IS A MEMBER OF THE FAMILY CROCODYLIDAE.

A crocodile? That big?

EVOLUTION HAS DIVERSIFIED SEVERAL BRANCHES OF CROCODILIANS THAT HAVE SPAWNED GIANTS. THE PREHISTORIC CROCODILE, *SARCOSUCHUS,* AVERAGED FORTY FEET IN LENGTH. *DEINOSUCHUS,* WHICH LIVED IN THE LATE CRETACEOUS, WAS SLIGHTLY LARGER.

And just for shits and grins, how big would you say the croc was that left these tracks?

SIXTY TO SEVENTY FEET, WEIGHING FIFTY TO SIXTY TONS.

"Wonderful." Using the binoculars, I scanned the terrain, my hands trembling noticeably. Jason Sloan had promised me cheerleaders and wet dreams; instead I found myself stuck in a monster movie, with my girlfriend cast as the vampiress from—

WARNING: THIS IS NOT A DREAM. TAKE PROPER PRECAUTIONS. CROCO-DILES ARE AMBUSH HUNTERS. AVOID THE RIVER. CROCODILES HAVE A KEEN SENSE OF HEARING. COMMUNICATE ONLY THROUGH THOUGHT ENERGY WHILE IN THE VALLEY.

Reading ABE's thoughts, Oscar dragged me by the arm toward *Oceanus.*

23

In times of change, learners inherit the Earth, while the learned find themselves beautifully equipped to deal with a world that no longer exists.
  —ERIC HOFFER, American social writer and philosopher

Oceanus towered before us—a relic from another age, washed ashore in another world. The remains of a lone anchor leg, acting like a bicycle kickstand, kept the giant sphere oriented on its vertical axis.

The habitat's appearance was gruesome. Scientists had chemically rendered and treated the aero gel skin to remain impervious to the prolonged effects of being submerged for extended periods of time, but even the most imaginative among them could not have foreseen this.

Time had been both cruel and innovative. At one point the entire lower bowl had been sealed in a concretelike layer of hard corals. As we walked around the sphere, ABE identified colonies of bottlebrush, bubble, and staghorn coral, each having multiplied in a variety of shapes and sizes. As the previous coral colonies had died, new ones had grown on top of their limestone skeletons, creating a living habitat for hundreds of species of fish, sponges, and bottom-dwelling marine invertebrates.

At least that was how ABE described *Oceanus*'s existence—up until the moment the coral reef had become so heavy it had collapsed one of the ship's anchor arms. The impact with the seafloor had cracked the reef; the subsequent destruction of its remaining three arms and the rolls that followed—witnessed by yours truly—having crushed and shed major sections of coral from *Oceanus*'s skin, so that the lower bowl of the habitat now appeared like the bottom half of a three dimensional jigsaw puzzle with sizeable chunks of its pieces missing.

The upper bowl seemed forged from an entirely different past.

According to ABE, Antarctica's melting ice sheet would have eventually exposed *Oceanus*'s upper hemisphere to the sun. As the sea warmed, first algae then sea grass had taken root, no doubt feeding the sea life living in the coral reef below. In a marvelous symbiotic relationship with its environment, *Oceanus* had in essence become an ecosystem both outside its walls and within.

While anchored underwater that ecosystem had flourished; on land the vegetation had quickly dried out and died. Clusters of dead plant life now hung from the ship's upper bowl like long tufts of green-brown hair on an aging human skull. Every few minutes another dried-out cluster would drop off the habitat, adding to a ring of algae and seaweed piled five feet high in the sand.

There was only one possible entrance into *Oceanus*—the egress chamber from which I had made my escape. I circled the titanic sphere twice before Oscar gestured at the sealed hatch—as if the clever creature knew its purpose.

Reading my thoughts, I suppose it did.

Climbing atop the barrier of dead vegetation, I pulled open the egress hatch—releasing a waterfall of trapped seawater, drenching myself in the process. Oscar appeared to enjoy the unplanned comedy act, giving me a quick rendition of the cephaloped jig . . . and then it reached for the hatch with three tentacles and pulled itself inside the open chamber—hoisting me up seconds later.

The water that remained in the chamber was still chest-deep. Oscar seemed a different animal than the one I had shocked to consciousness back in the redwood pond, splaying itself underwater like an asterisk, reaching playfully for my legs as I waded by to access the control panel.

There was no groping blindly this time around for hatch controls or switches. While assigned to Beta Squad, I had uploaded into ABE's memory every schematic and operations program Donald Bruemmer had brought on board. Now my trusty bio-chip could direct me in a microsecond of thought to any square inch of the ship.

Ducking underwater, I opened a control panel and tugged on a red handle, the manual release to vent the chamber. Sixty seconds later the interior hatch clicked open, allowing us access into the rest of the ship.

Memories of my hasty escape came rushing back. Entering the lower level, I listened for the bees, and instead heard a deep gurgling sound originating from beneath my feet.

ABE, identify that sound.

THE SOUND IS COMING FROM THE TWO AUXILIARY BACKUP GENERATORS.

What about the nuclear reactor?

PLUTONIUM RODS HAVE EXPIRED, THE NUCLEAR REACTOR IS OFF-LINE. BACKUP BATTERIES HAVE BEEN CHARGED USING SOLAR PANELS LOCATED ALONG THE AERO GEL EXTERIOR. VEGETATION GROWTH IS IMPEDING THE PROCESS. LIFE SUPPORT IS LIMITED TO SEVEN HOURS, TWENTY-SIX MINUTES. LIGHTS ARE NOT FUNCTIONING IN 37 PERCENT OF THE SHIP. ALL GALLEY APPLIANCES ARE OFF-LINE. POWER TO THE ARBORETUM–

Never mind that. What about the cryogenic chamber?

THE CRYOGENIC CHAMBER HAS ITS OWN BACKUP POWER SUPPLY.

How can I access the chamber?

GOLEM CONTROLS ALL ACCESS.

Is GOLEM online?

NO.

Is there a manual override?

YES.

Oscar followed me up the steel ladder. The air was stagnant and at least fifty degrees warmer than when *Oceanus* had been submerged. The smell that greeted us on the midlevel was rancid, rendered ripe by the cessation of cold.

The damage *Oceanus* had endured from its death roll and plunge into the sea trench was everywhere in evidence, from the pipes that had burst through the ceiling to the recessed stateroom doors, the open panels having unleashed the suites' wares into the corridor. Arriving at Stateroom Two, I sifted through my fiancée's belongings and was excited to find my duffel bag nestled within the pile of refuse.

Like a boy on Christmas morning, I opened the canvas bag, extracting a fresh pair of boxers, my black nylon running suit, matching athletic shoes and socks. Slipping out of the tattered orange jumpsuit, I dressed in my familiar civvies and felt like a new man.

Curious, Oscar groped my new "skin" with four of his suckers.

"It's for warmth, pal. Sort of like your hair, only with a fashion statement."

We continued down the corridor, arriving at the cryogenic chamber, the only suite whose doors remained sealed. The override switch was located inside a master control panel on an adjacent wall. Suctioning the locked security cover, Oscar tore it from its hinges, allowing me to access the override.

With a squeal of rubber the seal parted, Oscar wrenching open the double doors.

Unlike the rest of *Oceanus,* the interior was well ventilated and chilled. I advanced slowly through the darkened chamber, my eyes unable to pick a trail through the unrecognizable shadows.

ABE, guide me to the emergency lights.

Feeling my way to an interior panel, I flipped a series of circuit breakers, igniting sparks. Above my head, two crimson emergency lights flickered to life from a row of ten—revealing a dramatically altered interior.

"GOLEM . . . what have you done?"

To describe the chamber and adjoining surgical suite as having been "transformed" would be an understatement, for the surroundings I stood in now had been rendered unrecognizable by its creator, who was nowhere in sight.

The ceiling that had separated the mid-deck from the upper level had been torn out and gutted in order to fabricate a new appendage—a monstrous multi-metal and graphite five-fingered extremity, each four-jointed digit in excess of fifteen feet long. The artificial hand hung inverted and limp from the upper deck's steel support beams, its tendons composed of pistons, its blood vessels aero gel flex tubing filled with hydraulic fluid and sintered tungsten carbide balls. As fluid pushed the weighted balls through different sections of the arm's tubing, the redistribution of weight and pressure allowed GOLEM to open and close the massive claw.

Judging from the cobwebs and layers of dust, it had been eons since the appendage had been operational. The source of the hydraulic fluid had been GOLEM's vertical shaft, and the shaft now stood before me, drained of its fluid. Perhaps a leak had sprouted from one of the claw's major arteries, bleeding its master to death; perhaps GOLEM had simply suffered a major systems failure. Either way, some time after completing the abomination of technology before me, my creation had been condemned to its final resting place at the bottom of the shaft.

Curious, I pressed my face to the tube and looked down, but it was far too dark and there was no angle to see anything.

While the primary section of GOLEM's new appendage had been intended to handle the computer's heavy lifting, the claw's secondary limbs were designed for far more delicate procedures. Sprouting from the knuckles, rooted in the main skeleton were smaller telescopic graspers—six-foot-long fingers, the tips of which branched out again, this time into delicate surgical instruments. There were scalpels and forceps, suction hoses and syringes and IVs connected to God only knows what kind of elixirs and solutions. There were also tools designed for sampling tissue, and that knowledge made me shudder.

What the hell had GOLEM been up to?

I stood back to take in the entire monstrosity, which hung like an inverted mechanical tree, and that's when I recognized the design pattern in play. The thought must have subconsciously triggered a memory of my phone conversation with Monique DeFriend because suddenly ABE was playing it back to me like a lecturing parent.

"...ARTIFICIAL INTELLIGENCE SYSTEMS USING BIOCHEMICAL ALGORITHMS POSSESSING COMPLEX ADAPTIVE SYSTEMS HAVE THE POTENTIAL TO INTERNALLY OVERANALYZE THEIR OWN PRIME DIRECTIVES, CREATING CLOSED-CIRCUIT LOOPS OF SEGREGATED DNA STRANDS. THIS ACTIVITY CAN CORRUPT THE SYSTEM IN THAT THESE FAVORED SOLUTION PATTERNS ARE FILED AWAY AS 'PERFECTION' AND THEREFORE ARE NO LONGER SUBJECTED TO RIGOROUS REEVALUATION. THE AI VALIDATES THIS NEW PROTOCOL IN A VACUUM—A COGNITIVE STATE THAT MOST PSYCHIATRISTS WOULD DEFINE AS PSYCHOPATHIC EGO."

GOLEM, a supercomputer programmed with a matrix patterned after redwood DNA, had constructed a mechanical claw based on its own biological biases. In doing so, the computer had subconsciously created its own closed-circuit loop—and I had been the one to give it shape and form.

The question now—what had my computer's psychopathic ego been up to?

The twelve cryogenic pods were still in place. I moved to the first machine of four set in the front row and peered inside the container.

It was empty.

So were the next two. And the last.

"Freed themselves and left me behind . . . Bastards. "

I moved to the second row, yanking open the unsealed lids of four more vacant pods—

—the pan flute–like extortions summoning my attention from above. Oscar had climbed the robotic claw and was demanding I join him.

Standing atop one of the pods in the last row, I climbed up onto the steel appendage, managing to establish a handhold on one of the claw's lower digits—and nearly slicing my right ankle on one of the surgical blades. Gripping the flex hose, I attempted to pull my way up the alien-looking structure, my rubber-soled shoes slipping on hydraulic fluid drippings.

Growing impatient, the cephaloped reached down with one of its powerful tentacles and hoisted me up to its perch.

The crawl space between the midlevel and upper deck was twelve feet high, a vast expanse filled with ventilation ducts, pipes, and electrical conduits, sectioned between steel support struts. Standing on a rusted steel beam, I stared at the dark alcove until my eyes adjusted to the dim lighting.

And then I saw what Oscar had discovered—the sight making my skin crawl.

Hanging from metal hooks from the ceiling were the skeletal remains of the six male members of the Omega crew, their vacant eye sockets staring back at me, their bones still bearing tatters of dried flesh. The men were identifiable by the size of their frames and the patches of hair still adhering to their scalps. Kevin Read was front and center, Jason Sloan behind him and to the right, Yoni to the left—one of the Israeli's femurs hanging disjointed from the hip. The other three males filled out the next row so that the men's remains dangled from the ceiling like bowling pins.

Sensing my distress, Oscar lowered me to the ground, then dropped by my side.

"No . . . this makes no sense. ABE, analyze the contents of this lab. Determine its purpose!"

PURPOSE UNKNOWN.

ALERT! ONE OF THE CRYOGENIC PODS REMAINS OPERATIONAL.

I pushed past Oscar to inspect the last row of cryogenic pods.

Empty.

Empty.

Sealed!

I tried to raise the lid, only the machine was indeed operational, its unidentifiable occupant vacuum-packed in a frozen pool of tetrodo-toxin gel.

Turning my attention to the control panel, I attempted to engage the thawing process, but nothing appeared to be working.

ABE, why isn't this working?

ALL PRIMARY AND BACKUP CONTROLS WERE INTENTIONALLY LINKED TO GOLEM. TO INITIATE AN EMERGENCY THAW, EXPOSE THE TETRODOTOXIN GEL TO OXYGEN.

"Right, that's how I woke up!" I searched the lab for something hard to shatter the thick viewport of Plexiglas. Finding nothing, I opened the sliding aluminum door of the walk-in freezer in search of a tool.

"Mother of God . . ."

They had been hung from the ceiling like lanterns, but when the computer had run out of perches it had begun piling them anywhere it could—on shelves and racks, eventually it had stacked them in piles on the floor.

Cadavers. Hundreds of them. Some had been infants when they died, others centenarians, along with every age in between. Dark-haired, light-haired, bald. Two arms, no arms, and others bearing nightmarish deformities that would be turned away from a circus.

It appeared that every corpse was female.

I slammed the door shut, then stared at the closed walk-in refrigerator a full minute before opening door number two.

"Geez."

They were in beakers and glasses and specimen jars. At some point, the computer had run out of sealable containers, resorting to bottled water containers—hundreds of them, transported from the galley storeroom.

In each container was an embryo.

There were human, and yet some seemed inhuman . . . more accurately—unhuman, the obvious result of genetic tinkering. Besides the extra arms, there were freakishly large skulls possessing extra eyes, chest cavities loaded with duplicate vital organs, three-fingered hands and webbed feet and bat-shaped ears that looked almost satanic. It was as if the computer had gotten bored and, in a slow psychopathic burn, had unleashed its inner Mengele, tinkering with its crews' genetic code.

Mengele . . .

ABE latched on to the obscure reference, replaying the memory of my last conversation with Dharma: "IN YOUR LAST LIFE, I SAW YOU HELD CAPTIVE AS A YOUNG BOY IN A NAZI CONCENTRATION CAMP. I FELT YOUR WRATH AT THE CREATOR AS YOU WITNESSED YOUR MOTHER SENT TO THE OVENS; I EXPERIENCED YOUR DESPERATION AND FEAR WHEN YOU WERE DELIVERED INTO THE HANDS OF JOSEF MENGELE, A PSYCHOPATH WHO PERFORMED GENETIC EXPERIMENTS ON JEWISH CHILDREN."

"Stop!" My head hurt, and at that moment I wished I could—
WHY DO YOU WISH TO TERMINATE EISENBRAUN?

I turned to Oscar, the cephaloped resting a sucker paw on my wrist.

No, no . . . not Eisenbraun, Oscar. I was referring to ABE. It's a computer chip . . . never mind. Oscar, we need to vent . . . we need to open this pod—this one over here. Can you tear this aluminum door from its frame and use it to smash open the pod?

Reading thought waves translated through my bio-chip, the nine-foot-tall squid slid four of its tentacles around and between the refrigerator door and tore it loose from the frame. Wielding the seventy-pound object over its head, it smashed it with a sudden burst of blunt force against the top of Dharma's cryogenic pod.

The impact shattered the outer casing, expelling a stream of cold misty exhaust from the interior of the damaged sleep chamber.

With the internal pressure relieved, I was able to lift the lid.

Lying in a draining pool of tetrodotoxin gel was Dharma Yuan, her nude form held in an internal harness, her face concealed behind a plastic mask. As I watched, a sixteen-inch bang stick rigged to the body harness forcibly expelled the business end of a hypodermic into the Chinese woman's breastplate, the six-inch needle injecting a syringe filled with adrenaline into her heart.

Seconds later, Dharma's mask began pumping pressurized air into her esophagus, inflating her lungs. As her stomach bloated, the harness constricted, squeezing out the forced breath, clearing the way for the next blast of oxygen even as the vest portion of the bodysuit initiated alternating cardiac compressions.

Neon-orange vital signs appeared over the plastic mask covering her forehead.

It took twenty-three minutes and two more injections before Dharma began breathing on her own.

Reaching into the pod, I removed the bodysuit, then lifted her out of the container. Her flesh was as cold as it had been the day I rescued her from the Antarctic ice sheet. Carrying her over to the surgical suite. I laid her down on the operating table—and the giant claw above our heads immediately animated! Surgical lights ignited, scalpels became rigid, the digits of the telescopic robotic hand opened—before everything powered off and went limp.

ABE, what just happened?

A POWER SURGE.

What about Dharma?

DHARMA YUAN IS IN A VEGETATIVE STATE.

No shit. Will she recover?

NOT WITHOUT MEDICAL ASSISTANCE.

Instruct me.

THE CRYOGENIC CHAMBER IS NOT EQUIPPED FOR SUCH A PROCEDURE. HOWEVER, OSCAR'S ECHOLOCATION CAN SUITABLY REPAIR THE NEUROLOGI-CAL DAMAGE TO DHARMA YUAN'S BRAIN AND CENTRAL NERVOUS SYSTEM.

My arm . . . I forgot. Oscar fixed it.

OSCAR ALSO REPAIRED THE DAMAGE TO ROBERT EISENBRAUN'S BRAIN.

How do you know that?

EACH EPISODE OF NEURAL CAVITATION LEAVES A SIGNATURE TRACE IN THE MIDBRAIN AND FRONTAL CORTEX. THE FIRST SIGNATURE TRACE OC-CURRED JUST BEFORE ROBERT EISENBRAUN WAS REVIVED.

Wait. If that's true, then Oscar would have had to have been inside Oceanus *just after I woke up.*

CORRECT. IT WAS OSCAR WHO FREED ROBERT EISENBRAUN FROM THE CRYOGENIC POD.

You're wrong. The staircase collapsed on my pod, that's what freed me.

INCORRECT. THE ANGLE, WEIGHT, AND RATE OF DESCENT WERE INSUFFI-CIENT TO HAVE GENERATED THE FORCES NECESSARY TO CRACK OPEN THE CRYOGENIC POD. OSCAR FREED ROBERT EISENBRAUN.

I had a million questions, but Dharma was the priority, her breath-ing erratic. Turning to Oscar, I extended my hand to the cephaloped—who hesitated before taking it in one of its suckers.

My friend is dying. Please . . . whatever you did to fix me . . . fix her.

The squid released my hand and fled the chamber.

OSCAR REFUSES.

So I gathered. Why?

HUMAN FEMALES KILLED OSCAR'S THREE MATES.

Christ . . . I checked Dharma's pulse. Her heartbeat was as unstable as her breathing, her pupils dilated and unresponsive. With Oscar as her only hope, I gathered the naked female in my arms and exited the chamber.

The cephaloped was long gone.

I followed the corridor to the next open stateroom, then stopped to drag a wool blanket from a pile of mildewed belongings and wrapped Dharma in the quilt . . . then froze when I heard a terrifying sound coming from down the hall.

The bee colony had infested the galley. I could hear their low-pitched, agitated *buzzzzzzzz*, their numbers too frightening to imagine.

I backed away as quietly and quickly as possible, then turned and sprinted down the circular hall, clutching Dharma to my chest as I heard the swarm enter the corridor to give chase.

ABE simultaneously led me to the ladder and instructed me how to reposition Dharma so we could both fit down the chute. Gripping the warm metal, I stole a quick glance down the corridor . . . saw the dark cloud moving toward me, and more or less slid thirty feet down the ladder to the lower level.

I landed in a heap, Dharma on top of me. Above, the bees gave me a few precious seconds to regain my feet before they flooded the chute in pursuit.

Perhaps I could have made it to the egress chamber had I not been lugging a hundred twenty pounds of dead weight, or if we had not closed the hatch to prevent unwanted "guests" from tracking us into *Oceanus,* but my annoying bio-chip assured me there was a point-zero-five chance of accessing the chamber ahead of the swarm with the girl, and a forty-six percent chance if I dropped her carcass as bait and escaped alone.

How do you tell your own brain to fuck off?

I reached the egress chamber hatch, allowing Dharma to slide down my chest as I gripped the steel wheel in both hands and twisted it counterclockwise. Sweat was pouring down my face as the entire lower level reverberated like a power generator, my muscles stiffening in anticipation of an unfathomable déjà vu . . . *Are ten million bee stings as bad as ten million ant bites?*

When the stings didn't come, I reached blindly for Dharma, turning to face a sea of bees so dense they occupied every square centimeter of air—save for a slim boundary of space directly behind me where Oscar now stood, the cephaloped expelling violent breaths from its breathing tube.

Bees do not have ears; instead they use their legs and antennae to detect sound through the back-and-forth reverberations of air molecules. That they detected the pan flute–like disturbance there was no doubt; that they interpreted the sound as a conflicting directive leading to food would be explained to me later by ABE.

For now, the only things that mattered were the chamber hatch, which I yanked open, Dharma, who I dragged inside, and Oscar, who squeezed in after us even as he slammed the vault door closed, sealing us in.

Releasing Dharma, I bent over, gasping. "Thanks, pal."

Refusing my hand—and another attempt to convince him to help Dharma, Oscar entered the escape chamber and was gone.

Exhausted, I lay down on the tiled floor and stared at the flickering recessed lighting. ABE had logically concluded that Oscar had freed me from my cryogenic tomb. If that were true, then there was more at play here than our attempted symbiotic relationship . . . a line of inquiry that placed a spotlight on a questionable assumption: Was twelve million years a suitable amount of time for a sea creature to adapt to land?

I stared at the beautiful nude before me. In contrast to my American huntress, Dharma was small and supple, her body taut from a mastery of yoga.

"Well, Jason Sloan, at least your programming is getting more interesting."

Spreading out the blanket, I bundled Dharma up, then carried her into the next chamber. Oscar was gone, having left the escape hatch open. Ducking through, I stepped outside, then placed the girl on the ground in order to reseal *Oceanus* behind me.

The late afternoon sun cast long shadows across the cooling sand. Slinging Dharma over my right shoulder, I followed Oscar's tracks, four zigzagging impressions resembling a serpent's trail leading southeast. Despite the flat landscape, the cephaloped was nowhere in sight, a fact that quickened my step.

I felt the vibrations before—a distant pounding—like a quarter horse approaching the first turn. As I quickened my pace the sound became louder, the source clearly locked in on my presence. I spun around to see what my Omega dream had conjured up this time.

"Holy shit."

Words cannot adequately describe the animal chasing me. ABE told me it was seventy-five feet, but even half a mile away all I could see was the crocodile's head, which was green over yellow and as big and wide as my first-grade elementary school. Four powerful legs churned the sand into dust clouds, which were beaten aside by its prodigious tail, the appendage lashing back and forth behind its thickly scaled frame.

Panic summoned ABE, and the bio-chip unleashed an ocean of

adrenaline that momentarily rendered me a world-class sprinter, perhaps delaying the inevitable death-in-one-bite scenario by a few meaningless seconds.

And then I saw what appeared to be a second monster, two hundred yards ahead and to my right, a titanic female oozing postal truck–size eggs into a shallow crater it had excavated using its hindquarters.

MALE CROCODILIAN CONTACT IN FIFTEEN SECONDS. RUN TO THE FEMALE CROCODILE.

"Vanilla sway!"

THE MALE CROCODILIAN IS TRACKING ROBERT EISENBRAUN BY SCENT. DIVERT TO THE NEST.

Registering the earth-shaking wallops behind me, I cut hard to my right, heading straight for the mountain of olive-green scales that was seeding its young before me.

I was sixty yards away when the female's head turned in my direction.

Fifty yards from her nest when Mama Croc spotted the approaching male.

At thirty yards I froze, and all hell broke loose.

Smaller than her male counterpart, the hissing female passed within ten feet of stomping me into vanilla swirl as she instinctively charged the perceived threat to her young. Dropping to the ground to avoid her swishing thirty-foot tail, I watched her bound away, then slid down the near side of the steep hole into the nest.

EISENBRAUN, LEAVE THE NEST!

But you just said—

LEAVE THE NEST! GET TO THE CLIFFS.

A bone-chilling male reptilian roar met the female's sizzling hot *hiss* as I dragged Dharma over a landscape of gooey ivory boulders and out the other side of the nest. I was so winded I could barely inhale, and my leg muscles felt like liquid lead.

Staggering twenty paces from the hole, I collapsed with Dharma in my arms, completely spent.

Having circled the nest, the male croc now stood between us and the cliffs, its raised head towering three stories, its golden-yellow eyes glistening in the late afternoon sun. Its jaws remained half open and motionless; its upper fangs, set below the snout, were twisted outside the mouth like a briar patch, each tooth as long as my arm. No longer downwind of us, the monster seemed unsure of our location, and though the tip of its twelve-foot skull remained poised less than one of its body lengths away, ABE warned me not to move, that its vision was sensitive to motion.

The megacroc snorted the air, each inhalation accompanied by a hollow gurgling growl. I remained frozen in place, even as my eyes tracked something hovering in the air behind the creature—*a glint of sunlight?*

To my horror, Dharma expelled a low wail and it was Game Over.

The croc roared, its massive head turning toward us—as a shrill sound blotted out my hearing and caused the beast to tremble. As I watched in stunned confusion, the croc's stomach expanded outward, its torso bloating, as if it were inflating . . . and then sixty tons of crocodilian insides suddenly, unexplainably, burst out of either side of its belly, the sonic detonation splattering internal organs across the beach.

What happened next? To be honest, I'm not sure. I was dazed, lying in blood and innards, my head buzzing, my hearing replaced with an incessant ringing. In the silent aftermath, a cavalry of tentacles snaked around my body and Dharma's waist and suddenly we were bounding across the open beach, heading for the cliffs.

I must have lost consciousness, for when I reopened my eyes we were standing before the boulders marking the base of the rise. Oscar appeared to be engaging its breathing organ, tooting the device like a cephalopod ram's horn, though I heard only my shrill silence.

In my delirium, I saw two unusually shaped rocks set in a natural recess animate into a whirlwind of tentacles. The three camouflaged cephalopeds quickly untangled, allowing Oscar to pass, my guardian squid hauling Dharma and me through the narrow cave entrance and into the darkness.

24

To be great is to go on. To go on to be far. To be far is to return.
    —Lao Tzu, *Tao Te Ching*

A howling wind blasted me full in the face, the cold air clearing my head. We were rising higher in a pitch-dark cave along what seemed to be a fairly steep incline. I could feel the cephaloped's torso heaving as it strained to tow the two of us up the rocky path, the animal slowing as we progressed through the damp unseen elevation.

My ears were still ringing painfully from the blast.

The terrestrial squid stopped climbing. Cupping a handlike sucker pad over each one of my ears, Oscar applied suction to the ear canals—gentle oscillations that reduced the inflammation and calmed the eardrums. When the cephaloped removed its appendages the tinnitus was gone, sound returning in the form of rushing water.

After another hundred feet Oscar released me. We had reached the summit, the passage ahead now leveled off, the blanket of darkness yielding to a faint backlit archway marking the end of a short tunnel. Too tired to object, I allowed the land squid to lead me, my eyes widening in amazement as we approached the opening.

It was a subterranean chamber, so vast it could have enclosed a major city, its cavernous walls rivaling those of the Grand Canyon. Stalagmites as tall as skyscrapers were dwarfed by a ceiling drenched in the humidity of its own cloud bank. Petrified calcite enclosed either side of this titanic geological orifice, the grooved rock face bathed in emerald-green light originating from a torrent of river that split the vast underworld like a glowing serpent. Illuminated by the agitation of its triboluminescence mineral bed, the waterway seemed to run forever.

Standing by the banks of the rushing water, dwarfed on either side by the shimmering blue-green walls, I shared a perspective the Israelites must have experienced when Moses had parted the Red Sea.

And still, I had seen nothing.

We followed a rocky trail that paralleled the river, the echo of rushing water reverberating along the canyon walls. Bound aloft in one of Oscar's tentacles, I heard Dharma stirring. Despite the cephaloped's earlier refusal to help, the creature's prolonged physical contact with the human female appeared to be healing her damaged nervous system.

ABE, what made Oscar change his mind about touching Dharma?

OSCAR WAS FORCED TO ESTABLISH PHYSICAL CONTACT WITH DHARMA AFTER THE CROCODILIAN ATTACK.

The croc... In my delirium, I had completely forgotten about the monster and its mysterious demise. Searching for answers, I held out my hand to my gangly companion, hoping to reestablish communication.

After a moment, a tentacle reached out, suctioning my forearm.

Oscar, how did that croc... that four-legged monster with the big teeth die?

ABE took several moments before responding.

OSCAR'S RESPONSE TRANSLATES POORLY. THE HUMAN EQUIVALENT WOULD BE CLOSEST TO "BLESSED HEAVENLY ONES WHO NURTURE."

What does that mean? Who are these Blessed Heavenly Ones? What are they?

OSCAR HAS NO COMPREHENSION AS TO WHAT THE ENTITY IS.

Are these Blessed Ones responsible for killing that super croc?

YES. THEY ARE ALSO THE ONES THAT INSTRUCTED OSCAR TO FREE ROBERT EISENBRAUN.

Our destination was upstream. We followed the river for miles, from its more sedentary low course to its white-water middle course, the flow picking up noticeably as we progressed along on our journey to God knows where. Every so often a silverfish the size of a piranha would flit out of the water onto the bank, its indigo-blue fins whirling like a bumblebee's wings as it fed on crawling insects.

ABE calculated that we were 2,970 feet below the surface, heading in a southeasterly direction. After nearly two hours of walking, I no longer cared, having barely eaten in the last eighteen hours. And yet as hungry as I was, I would have traded a four-course meal for a king-size bed and some aspirin.

Exhausted and hungry, I yelled out, "Vanilla sway, vanilla sway, vanilla sway." My voice reverberated through the cavern, the echo causing the words of the useless phrase to overlap.

OSCAR WISHES TO KNOW THE PURPOSE OF YOUR ROAR.

Tell our friend the roar refers to a persuasive deception. A well-crafted lie. Sort of like this dream.

ROBERT EISENBRAUN IS NOT DREAMING.

Yeah, yeah . . . tell it to the judge.

The river twisted to the northeast, its rocky borders forming a serene pool of water. Oscar paused at a flat stretch of limestone and laid down my grunting female colleague.

ATTENTION: DHARMA YUAN HAS REGAINED CONSCIOUSNESS.

I knelt by her side, adjusting her blanket to conceal her breasts. The sickly pallor was gone, replaced by a healthy flush. Her brown almond-shaped eyes were open . . . staring at me, as if her brain knew who I was only her vocal cords hadn't quite caught up.

"Good morning."

INCORRECT. IT IS EVENING, 19:22 HOURS.

ABE, silent mode. "Dharma, squeeze my hand if you can understand me."

She power-gripped my fingers until I had to pry them loose. "Stay calm, we just thawed you from your cryogenic pod. Does everything seem to be working, other than your voice?"

She nodded, then attempted to move. I helped her sit up, watching as she tested each limb—never noticing Oscar, who had slipped into the river, the ceph's camouflaging hide disappearing among the rocks.

Refusing my assistance, Dharma stood on wobbly legs, the action causing the blanket to fall away, exposing her nakedness. The Chinese-Indian beauty accepted her sudden nudity as something completely natural, lacking ego or embarrassment.

My response was typically Western male, although I did avert my gaze until after she turned her back. She treated me to quite the show, performing several yoga stretches before she began a tai chi movement, each form flowing from one position to the next, freeing up her blocked neural pathways like an internal massage.

Was I aroused? Hell, yes. But Dharma's allure was something far more than sex, the grace and simplicity of her maneuvers unencumbered by her nakedness, her serene expression exuding an inner peace that had always eluded me . . . or my past lives, if the Buddhist therapist was to be believed.

Dharma stretched until her muscles shook. Turning to me she spoke, her voice scratchy but strong. "I have questions, but first I must bathe."

She waded chest-deep into the river, her swaying hips clearly sending a message. As I watched, she massaged the tetrodotoxin gel from her skin before submerging to cleanse the residue from her long ebony hair, her features luminescent in the riverbed's soft emerald glow.

After just a minute or so she surfaced, her hands smoothing her silky hair back over her forehead. "Join me."

My heart pounded, the increased blood flow registering in my groin. "Don't you want to know where we are?"

"Are we safe?"

"For the moment."

"Then be in the moment and join me."

I disrobed like a clumsy teen on prom night and took two strides into the river, the cold water (reported by ABE to be 52°F) blasting the air out of my lungs while shriveling my manhood into something more deserving of a diaper. "Gee . . . zus, it's like ice! How can you stand it?"

"The meditation of *g-Tum-mo* frees the mind to control the central nervous system."

ABE, redistribute my body heat by—

"Wait. Before you use your bio-chip, allow me to guide you."

By now my teeth were chattering, my body shaking uncontrollably as she waded over and hugged me. The sensation was incredible, her torso exuding the heat of a stoked fireplace on a winter's night, and I clung to her like an addict.

"Do not just feed off of me, create your own heat. Close your eyes. Now imagine your belly is a furnace, your lungs the bellows that brings the flame. Breathe in slowly and inflate your stomach. Feel your heart move the liquid heat into your extremities."

With each breath I inhaled, she exhaled; with each exhalation she inhaled. After seven breaths I stopped shaking. After three minutes the feeling returned to my fingers and toes.

When I reopened my eyes, I was fully aroused.

She smiled her approval. "What a good student you are. Tell me, Robert, how long has it been since you have engaged in the art of love-making?"

"About twelve million years."

We exited the river forty-five minutes later, my body tingling more from the wild Kama Sutra ride than from the cold. Dharma allowed me to wrap the blanket around her, then she sat on a rock and watched me dress.

"So, Robert, now it is time to fill in the blanks, as you Americans like to say. Since we are in Vietnam, I must assume the cryogenic process caused serious damage to my memory. It has been many years since I last set foot in Hang Son Doong cave; the first time my uncle brought me here was on my eighteenth birthday. But of course you knew that from my bio. I love the underwater lights—what a beautiful effect. How long has it been since I was unfrozen?"

ABE fed me the answer. "Six hours, twenty-eight minutes."

Her smile cracked. "I don't understand."

"Dharma, this isn't Vietnam, we're still in Antarctica. Something terrible happened shortly after we were put to sleep . . . a cataclysm."

Tears formed and her throat constricted. "What sort of cataclysm?"

"An asteroid. It struck the moon so hard it altered its orbit, blasting away massive city-size chunks of rock that would have been caught in Earth's gravity. The impacts must have been horrible . . . planetwide firestorms; debris clouds that clogged the atmosphere, essentially cutting off photosynthesis and the sun's heat. We're talking major Ice Age, the end of humanity. I know it's hard to fathom—"

"How long?"

"Honestly, it's still all conjecture. ABE was frozen. I suspect the bio-chip was damaged."

"How long were we asleep, Robert?"

"The A answer is twelve million years and change. Trust me, you don't want to know the B answer."

"Twelve million years? Then my family . . . everyone I knew—"

"There's more. From the evidence back on *Oceanus*, it appears that GOLEM may have gone a bit stir-crazy. The rest of the crew . . . we found some serious genetic mutations."

"We? Who else was with you?"

"A friend. Another species."

She smiled. And then she giggled a half-mad, half-adorable giggle. "Bravo. You actually had me, the whole thing . . . it feels so real."

"You think this is an Omega-wave dream? Hate to tell you, but that would make it my dream, not yours."

"So sorry to remind you, Robert, but Hang Son Doong cave is my memory, as are you. Our lovemaking just now . . . it traces back to a desire I felt for you on the first day we met. I can understand your confusion. These Omega waves . . . they're really quite powerful, how they mine the subconscious."

She was practically giddy.

"So this friendly species, when may I meet it?"

"It doesn't like human females. Apparently there's a few genetic clones of Andria prowling the forests, hunting down cephs."

"Cephs?"

"Short for cephalopeds—my name for Oscar's species, not his. Oscar, come join us please."

Dharma followed my gaze to the river. "Robert, there is no one out there."

I waited another thirty seconds, then peeved, waded back into the freezing river and tapped the nearest rock formation—which materialized into a maze of hairy tentacles and an oblong head whose stalked yellow eyes looked at Dharma with malice.

"Dharma Yuan, meet Oscar."

Oscar rose to his imposing nine-foot height, towering above the five-foot-four-inch China doll—my own heart skipping a beat as every rock formation in and out of the water suddenly melted into a pack of cephalopeds! Adults and juveniles, males and females, some holding squirming infants—all advancing on poor Dharma, who was a stone's breath from fainting dead away.

Fearing for her life, I waded to shore, only to find my path blocked by a gyrating wall of gelatinous bodies. Swimming to a limestone ledge, I dragged myself out of the river and climbed onto a boulder, looking down upon what I construed to be the cephaloped equivalent of a Texas lynch mob.

The arbitrator was Oscar. One of the big fella's tentacles was looped around Dharma's slender neck, its fin coming to rest over her heart. Two more tentacles reached out to two more cephalopeds, who in turn reached out to four more creatures, each member continuing the process until every one of the intelligent beings was part of the bizarre group configuration.

ABE, what are they doing?

THE PROCESS TRANSLATES TO AN UNVEILING OF THE SOUL.

For what purpose?

IN THIS INSTANCE—TO DETERMINE WHETHER DHARMA YUAN SHALL LIVE OR DIE.

25

Your worst enemy cannot harm you as much as your own unguarded thoughts.
—His Holiness Tenzin Gyatso, the fourteenth Dalai Lama

Eyes closed, Oscar began swaying, setting off a chain reaction among the other thirty or forty cephalopeds. Truth be told, I couldn't accurately tell you how many of them now encircled Dharma; from my vantage all I saw was an interlocking quilt of hairy brown bodies.

Cross-referencing Oscar's behavioral patterns with hundreds of research papers on cephalopod rituals and echolocation, ABE offered my subconscious theoretical commentary: OSCAR IS EVALUATING DHARMA YUAN'S CONSCIOUSNESS BASED ON HER THOUGHT-ENERGY PATTERNS. THIS EXPERIENCE IS BEING CHANNELED TO THE GROUP THROUGH PHYSICAL CONTACT.

The swaying and bobbing went on for several minutes until Oscar abruptly released his grip around Dharma's neck and expelled a deep booming staccato sound from his breathing organ that reminded me of a shofar blast on Rosh Hashanah. The rest of the cephalopeds immediately joined in, creating a thunderous cacophony that reverberated through the cavern.

Perhaps the sounds were a "call to arms" because the grooved calcite walls suddenly became fluid with tentacles as hundreds of camouflaged squid scurried through the water and across the riverbank to join the gathering cephaloped Mecca.

And then there was silence—answered a moment later by Dharma's wailing exhalation—an agonizing moan that echoed throughout the chamber and made my flesh crawl.

The cry died out, eliciting a chaos of pan-flutish bellows from the exuberant congregation, who converged upon Dharma and lifted her inert form high into the air, passing her atop the throng as if she were the lead singer at a rock concert.

The river of beings swept upstream like a brown tide, carrying my exonerated companion with them.

Twenty minutes and another mile's hike produced a change in geology, the chamber narrowing, the elevation rising. The river twisted into white water, the rapids forcing the juveniles and mothers bearing young onto the bank. I remained at the back of the procession, Oscar by my side. Every so often a young cephaloped would dart in close, attempting physical contact, only to be intercepted with a stinging slap by one of Oscar's powerful tentacles, chiding them away.

Up ahead, the ravine curved sharply. As we neared the river's origin I could hear a roar of water, the thunderous sound devoid of echo, growing louder as the cave moved from night into day. As I rounded the bend, my skin was bathed in a cool mist, my senses once again overwhelmed.

We were standing behind a waterfall—a curtain of crystal liquid as tall as the Eiffel Tower, its bluster deafening. Backlit by the sun, the colors of the spectrum danced rainbows across the arching cavern walls. The flow cascaded into a shimmering azure-blue lake, its concealed northern end spread out before us, its spillway forging the river.

There was no longer a shoreline to follow, no path around the roaring obstacle of water. To continue on, one had to enter the lake and swim through the falls . . . which was exactly what the cephalopeds were doing—submerging beneath the pounding water and disappearing into the aquamarine ether.

I lost sight of Dharma, who must have already made the pass.

Oscar looked down at me. It was my turn.

We waded in together. The sun-drenched waters felt balmy—a wonderful relief after the icy cold waters in the cavern. Swimming along the surface, I approached the deafening roar as close as I dared, my heart racing in fear.

It is not child's play to swim beneath the impact zone of a waterfall, Niagara Falls, as it was before I was frozen, dropped seventeen stories—the wall of water before me fell many times that height. And yes, while the flow from above appeared to pack far less volume than the Niagara

River, I was still swimming into an unknown torrent—albeit a beautiful one.

I grabbed a lungful of humidity and ducked underwater. My brain was immediately overwhelmed by the chaos of white noise. Descending as deep as I could, I swam toward the crystal wall of foam—realizing, too late, that I was entering the freshwater equivalent of the three hundred foot tidal wave that had nearly drowned me days ago.

Liquid thunder bludgeoned my back and spine, forcing the air from my chest with the power of a battering ram. My immediate reaction was to turn back, only the falls held me fast, churning me into frightening somersaults that pried open my lips even as my mind screamed, *Vanilla sway!*

I vomited water and inhaled the lake, the anxiety of drowning overshadowing my sudden acceleration through the falls . . . into unconsciousness.

SO MUCH ANGER, ROBERT EISENBRAUN.

Oscar?

YOUR ANGER RESTRICTS THE CONSCIOUSNESS OF UNITY. THE ONE CALLED DHARMA UNDERSTANDS. LEARN FROM HER. ONLY THEN CAN YOU TRULY AWAKEN . . .

"Huh?"

Opening my eyes, I gasped a breath of daylight, as surprised to find my lungs pumping air as I was to be alive. Drenched and exhausted from yet another near drowning, I found myself lying in powdery pink sand along the shoreline of a tropical lagoon. Overhead, a cloud bank parted, revealing blue sky. Before me, a magnificent waterfall toppled a thousand feet over a mountain of rock that appeared to circle the entire perimeter.

Sitting up, I took a quick inventory of my body and noticed fresh suction marks along my left arm.

Oscar . . .

The lagoon was surrounded by a dense jungle that rose up crater walls. A nanosecond later, ABE determined that we were still in the cave, that the open realm was actually a collapsed doline.

Apparently, the network of caves ran beneath the redwood forest, which received a significant amount of rainfall. As runoff seeped through the limestone geology it created cavities that weakened the roof of the cave system. At some point in history, a section of the ceiling had collapsed, opening the cavern to daylight. Time and photosynthesis had created a unique ecosystem half a mile below the surface—an isolated Garden of Eden that served as a habitat for the cephaloped population.

"It's not their natural habitat, you know."

I turned to find Dharma standing by the lagoon. She was wrapped in the blanket, her dark eyes shimmering with golden-yellow flecks of light. "Are you okay? What happened to you? Did they . . . Hey, did you just read my thoughts?"

She beamed a smile so wide her face could barely contain her happiness. "A gift from the cephalopeds, a fading residual effect from having shared their collective consciousness. There is so much I need to share with you, Robert. And no, this isn't an Omega dream. Yes, I realize that whatever I say could also be part of your dream, only you're not—"

"Could you stop answering my thoughts before I pose the question, it's really annoying."

"My apologies. I imagine you must get that a lot from ABE."

"ABE, I can control. You're uninhibited."

"You didn't seem to mind back in the river." Kneeling in the sand, she leaned in and kissed me. "If I seem a little giddy, it's because I've lost the cynicism that has festered in my being like a malignant tumor since the Great Die-Off. The cephalopeds . . . there is far more to them than their evolutionary transition from sea to land."

"They're certainly intelligent, but I've yet to see Oscar incorporate the use of any tools. Guess we can blame the absence of an opposable thumb for that shortcoming."

"The sucker pads at the end of each arm serve the same purpose, but the point is moot. By evaluating their species based solely on a hominid scale you fail to see the true nature of these beings. You bonded with Oscar—what did you experience?"

The memory of having been immersed in Oscar's camouflage was fuzzy. "To be honest, it happened so fast, when I tried to think about it later I wondered if I hadn't imagined the whole thing."

"Use ABE to recall what you felt."

My bio-chip tweaked a memory synapse, the moment and its accompanying emotions flooding my consciousness. "I got it. I'm just not sure I understand it. This is going to sound really weird, but being connected with Oscar, for a moment I felt this overwhelming sensation of unconditional love. It made me feel secure, like when I was younger and my family was still alive."

"Before the anger tainted your present existence."

"Yes. It was reassuring. It made me feel like I'm never truly alone."

"All true. And everything I am about to reveal is also true, but you must be open-minded in order to absorb it. Robert, as a scientist indoctrinated in Western philosophy, you've been taught that the brain controls the body—it's your entire justification for creating that bio-chip. In the East, we have known it is the heart that controls everything . . . the way we feel, our health, everything. Think about it. More than ninety percent of the nerves send impulses from the body to the brain—impulses controlled by the flow of blood from the heart—the only organ in the body that generates a measurable electromagnetic field.

"New studies—Western studies—have correlated the interstitial pause between each heartbeat with a person's emotional well-being. The heart is regulated by the vagus nerve, a bundle of nerves that originates in the top of the spinal cord. Besides controlling the heart, lungs, liver, and digestive organs, the vagus nerve triggers our emotions of good. For example, when we witness a soldier reunited with his wife and children, or when we watch a movie with a happy ending, the vagus nerve stimulates a physical response, causing our chest to expand and tears to flow as our psyche is dominated by feelings of warmth. These same feelings happen when we hear a beautiful melody, or view a work of art . . . or experience love."

"I get it, Dharma. What's your point?"

She smiled at my ignorance. "Think about it from a higher level, Robert. The Creator hot-wired our species to do good things, encouraging us on a physiological and emotional level to commit acts of kindness and generosity. These acts of compassion all flow from the heart."

"And the cephalopeds have three hearts. So what? Squids have always had three hearts."

"Yes, only these squids have developed three vagus nerves—the evolutionary keystone that changed their species from solitary intelligent creatures to communal, compassionate loving beings. Because of this incredible development, the cephalopeds now seek cooperation over dominance and the needs of the pack over their own individual pleasures. Robert, the cephaloped species represents the next signifi-cant step up the evolutionary ladder, and unlike humans, there is not a selfish bone in their bodies."

"Or bones of any kind."

She smiled again, squeezing my hand. "There was something else you experienced when you and Oscar connected. What was it? Tell me."

I hesitated, but there was no point—she could read my thoughts. "It sounds ridiculous, but for a fleeting moment I was actually convinced that I understood the meaning of life."

Dharma smiled. "And what is the meaning of life? What is this crazy world of ours all about?"

"That's just it, none of this is real, it's all an illusion. It's like each of us is in our own Omega dream . . . a dream purposely filled with chaos and challenges, each challenge an opportunity to earn back that un-conditional love—that perfect immortality that awaits each of us when we die . . . when we awaken from the dream. I know none of this makes any sense—"

"It makes perfect sense. And it's exactly what I experienced. As for that feeling of unconditional love—it was the essence of the Creator, a spark of perfection that makes up each one of our souls. By tapping into Oscar's soul, the two of us felt the unveiled energy of God. Pretty powerful stuff."

I nodded, my thoughts absorbed in the memory. For some reason, in my fleeting moment of clarity, I had been convinced the physical world had been designed as a battleground so that good could be chal-lenged by evil—evil in this case being the human ego.

Dharma must have been eavesdropping on my thoughts. "You're right, Robert . . . Sorry, I just realized you prefer to be called Ike. You're right about life being a test governed by free will; what you are missing is that each soul is linked, bringing new meaning to the com-mandment 'Love thy neighbor as thyself.' The cephalopeds understand what man never could—that the physical world is a barometer of hu-man nature. I am convinced these beings are the next rung up the lad-der from modern man."

"What happened to that old Bible adage, 'Man was created in God's image.' Are you telling me God looks like an octopus?"

Dharma smiled. "God is neither man nor beast; the Creator is something we can never comprehend. Man, like these cephalopeds, was created not from God's image but His essence, the essence to share. The cephalopeds are the embodiment of that essence—selfless loving beings existing harmoniously with nature. Like humans, they are physical vessels that harbor the soul. Unlike humans, they lack ego and all its ugly baggage—anger, hatred, jealousy, greed, corruption. These life-forms have achieved a state of Nirvana that keeps them attuned to the higher dimensions of the spiritual realm. Unfortunately once again, humans are threatening the natural order of life on this planet."

"What humans? It's just you and me."

She shook her head, disappointed. "Remember, for the moment I can still read your thoughts. As such, I know you have crossed paths with Andria—at least one of her clone replicas. From having shared the cephaloped collective consciousness, I know that GOLEM used Andria's DNA and the DNA of the other female members of the Omega crew to birth a nation of these soulless vessels. These lab creations that sprang from the sociopathic mind of your invention have spread across the continent like a pestilence; in the process they have forced the cephalopeds to abandon their natural habitat in the trees, hunting them down and using them in horrifying genetic experiments."

"The cephalopeds are powerful intelligent creatures, Dharma. They are certainly capable of organizing a rebellion. Why don't they fight back?"

"They did. For thousands of years their ancestors engaged in bloody battles with the children of GOLEM. Think of the Arab-Israeli conflict, only far worse. For even when the cephalopeds sought to end the fighting, peace could never be brokered with the Creator."

"Creator? You mean GOLEM?"

"GOLEM no longer exists, your creation has evolved beyond its programming. It is an entity beyond artificial intelligence—an entity worshipped by its people as the Creator."

It took me a moment to absorb this mind-boggling information.

Somewhere in the thought process my own ego reared its ugly head. *You created a new life force, Eisenbraun. An intelligence capable of populating its own world.*

Dharma slapped me hard across the face. "What you created was a monster, a machine possessing the desires of a sociopath. Free will exists only among the cephalopods, who are treated not as a species but as a genetic commodity necessary to seed your monster's own creations."

ABE regulated my blood pressure even as it channeled my rebuttal.

"You said GOLEM—or whatever it's become—possesses the desires of a sociopath. Being a Buddhist, I'm guessing you never read the Bible, though I suspect GOLEM did. According to the Old Testament, God inflicted quite a lot of punishment on His chosen ones, not to mention all those who died in the flood, and the Holocaust, and, oh yeah, the GDO. And just for the sake of argument, wouldn't cows and sheep and other farm animals be considered genetic commodities created to serve man?"

"You are equating the cephalopods with livestock?"

"I'm just saying that whatever GOLEM has become over the last twelve million years, it may have been influenced by a Judeo-Christian-Islamic interpretation of a supreme being."

"I cannot speak for the biblical references, but the Holocaust and the Die-Off were cause-and-effect events that were brought about by man's unbridled ego—the same ego that now motivates you to defend the acts of evil perpetrated by your machine."

She was right, of course.

"Dharma, I'm sorry. I like Oscar. I respect his kind. Finish telling me what happened. After thousands of years of fighting, how did the cephalopeds become pacifists?"

She took a moment to register my sincerity, then began again. "If peace could not be acquired with their enemy, then it would be acquired without them. A grassroots movement took shape, based on the belief that acts of violence and aggression, even against their oppressors, affected the cephalopeds' connection with the spiritual realm. This belief, acted upon before a spiritual connection even existed, not only elevated their species over time, but gave them access to what they refer to as the 'Light of the Creator'—a source of energy and fulfillment that transformed their entire existence."

"Is this their idea of fulfillment? To hide in caves and accept their place on the food chain?"

"Ike, these creatures see a far bigger picture. As to their slaughter, they are convinced an event is coming—a spiritual awakening that translates into something called the 'Rebirth Moon.' The event was foretold long ago, precipitated by your appearance."

"My appearance? Am I supposed to be some sort of cephaloped messiah?"

"That remains to be seen. But remember what I said to you back on *Oceanus*. That your presence on the Omega mission would change the course of history."

"And what about your presence, Dharma? Why are you here?"

"I am here to guide you when you are led astray by your ego." Reaching for my hand, she squeezed it. "We're both tired and hungry. Let's not think about anything else until we've eaten and rested."

She led me past the shoreline and into a jungle flourishing with trees bearing fruit the likes of which I had only glimpsed back in the redwood canopy. For twenty minutes we feasted on a pineapple-size seed that tasted like freshly baked wheat bread, then enjoyed dessert—a black sapote fruit with a puddinglike inside that rivaled the richest dark chocolate mousse.

"Dharma, how safe are the cephalopeds in this valley? What's to stop the children of GOLEM from entering the doline and hunting them down?"

"The doline is protected."

"How? From what I can see it's wide open."

"I don't know how, which means Oscar and his people don't know either. It was conveyed to me that the cephalopeds can leave the valley, but the children of GOLEM cannot enter. The cephalopeds credit the Blessed Heavenly Ones Who Nurture with this miracle."

"Is that cephaloped-speak for God?"

"I'm not sure. It is a subject I intend to pursue in our next sharing. It's getting dark. We should return to the cave."

"Why? You said we were safe."

"It is what Oscar wishes."

"You go. I need some alone time to think. I also want to see what this jungle has on its dinner menu."

"Very well. Let's meet at the lagoon in two hours for the swim back. The cephalopeds will be there to assist us."

"Did they just communicate that to you?"

She blushed. "It is far more efficient than an h-phone."

"While lacking any sense of privacy. Two hours at the lagoon."

We exchanged a passionate kiss, then I waited until she disappeared down the path before engaging ABE. *Query: Can you block Dharma from reading my thoughts?*

A STATIC BIORHYTHMIC FILTER CAN BE ESTABLISHED THAT WOULD SCRAMBLE ROBERT EISENBRAUN'S THOUGHT ENERGY TO ALL EXTERNAL RECEIVERS.

Do it. Then use my visual survey of the terrain and plot the best course to reach the nearest exit point to this doline.

ABE led me through the jungle, the elevation gradually steepening as I approached the growth-lined walls of the doline. The sun had dropped below the edge of the crater, casting shadows across the valley by the time I arrived at the chosen exit point—a fallen juvenile redwood. The tree's massive trunk leaned against the top of the crater lip 220 feet overhead.

Experiencing a strange sense of déjà vu, I began the climb.

I had no doubt that Dharma was telling me the truth—that is to say, I had no doubt that Dharma believed everything that had been communicated to her by the cephalopeds. Did I buy into all her mumbo jumbo about the creature's being connected to God? I couldn't deny I had felt something when Oscar had enveloped me in his echolocation, but that could have also been a mind game. What really concerned me was the information the cephalopeds were keeping from Dharma, specifically about these so-called Blessed Heavenly Ones Who Nurture. Maybe I was still angry at God, but no God I ever prayed to or cursed ever used a sonic weapon to implode a seventy-foot crocodile, and I had a gut feeling that—WARNING: SYSTEMS THREAT! WARNING: SYSTEMS THREAT!

Identify systems threat.

ELECTROMAGNETIC PULSE GRID HAS BEEN ESTABLISHED OVER THE CRATER OPENING. SHOULD EISENBRAUN GET TOO CLOSE TO THE GRID WHILE THE ABE UNIT IS ACTIVE, THE EMP WOULD DESTROY THE ABE UNIT'S BIO-CIRCUITS.

Switch to safe mode.

WARNING: SAFE MODE WILL NOT MINIMIZE THE EMP DAMAGE.

Guess I'm on my own then. Locate EMP point of origin, then shut down the ABE unit until Eisenbraun has cleared the grid.

EMP POINT OF ORIGIN: EIGHTEEN JUNCTION BEAMS SET AT TWENTY-DEGREE INTERVALS BEGINNING AT ZERO DEGREES NORTH. ENERGY SOURCES ARE POSITIONED THIRTY-TWO CENTIMETERS BELOW THE CRATER LIP. NEAREST JUNCTION BEAM IS LOCATED TWELVE FEET, EIGHT INCHES CLOCKWISE OF EXIT POINT. ABE UNIT SHUTTING DOWN.

I continued climbing, moving from the trunk of the redwood tree onto an upper branch that dead-ended at the crater wall a convenient four feet below the doline's fractured lip. Reaching up, I managed to pull myself out of the massive sinkhole.

I was back in the redwood forest, the sun setting at my back. Stepping off four paces to my left, I lay prone on the limestone ground and leaned my head out over the crater's edge, searching for anything that resembled an EMP beam.

THE OMEGA PROJECT • 227

The disruptive power of an electromagnetic pulse was first discovered during field tests for the atomic bomb. The resultant pulse generates a powerful electromagnetic field that can damage or destroy electronic devices, communication systems, and semiconductive computer chips within the blast area. Naturally, the potential damage caused by EMPs motivated world leaders to develop nonnuclear weapons that could blast their enemy's cities back to the Stone Age, with more than a few nations investigating the means to target communication satellites.

It wasn't long after World War III broke out that the first suitcase EMP weapons, or E-bombs, were detonated in Iran. By the time the Great Die-Off ended, upward of 60 percent of the Middle East's power grids had been fried.

Thirty minutes passed before I located a six-inch acrylic barrel protruding from the karst wall of the crater, its power source no doubt buried deep within the geology. The junction's technology seemed far more advanced than my own; whether the beam delivered something far more lethal than an EMP was impossible to tell.

Sitting by the edge of the crater, gazing down into the darkening valley, my mind attempted to sort out the mysteries at hand without the aid of my biological chip. Having established that a security grid existed, the next immediate question I sought to answer was not *who* had created the grid or even *why*, but *how*—as in how could an EMP keep human clones from entering the doline?

I was so absorbed in thought that I never noticed how late it was until the crickets began chirping at the night.

Looking up, I took in the star-filled heavens and wondered if the cephalopeds would one day invent a telescope or comprehend other solar systems or create the means to visit another planet like Mars, or an alien moon, like Europa, or even the damaged remains of our own—

"Alpha Colony! Holy shit, what happened to all those scientists?" *Could they have survived the asteroid impact? If yes, could they still be alive?* It hardly seemed possible—then again I was still here. "No, dipshit. You're just dreaming."

"Ike?"

Startled, I turned. The woods behind me were cloaked in shadows, but the woman's voice was as clear as day, and it definitely wasn't Dharma.

Moving quickly, I retreated feetfirst over the edge of the collapsed doline, the tips of my running shoes searching blindly for the redwood branch below.

"Ike, wait!"

Halfway over the edge of the crater lip, I hesitated.

Andria stepped out of the forest into the clearing, her athletic physique pressing against the torn seams of her soiled orange Omega jumpsuit, her breasts challenging the outfit's central zipper. Her short-cropped black hair was messed, her American-Indian complexion a bit tanner than when I had last seen her, but otherwise she was the same beauty I had intended to rendezvous with the night the crewmen had turned against me.

She walked toward me, her expression one of disbelief. "You're really alive. Oh my God, it's a miracle."

She was unarmed and alone, and every cell in my body yearned to hold her. Still, my feet remained poised on the tree branch.

"Ike, what's wrong with you? It's me. Andie."

"Prove it. Where did we meet? What city?"

"We didn't meet in the city, we met in the woods in Virginia. You tried to steal my deer."

My heart raced. "How did you get off *Oceanus*?"

"We used the subs."

"Who's we?"

"There were five of us: Bella, me, Lara, Monique, and Amanda Lynn. Something went wrong with Dharma's pod, we couldn't open it. The men . . . your crazy computer butchered them. From the looks of the lab, it entertained itself by making human clones before it accidentally offed itself."

"So, you freed yourselves and left me frozen?"

"We were disoriented, operating in complete darkness. Monique and I attempted to repair the electrical system while Lara checked on you. Bella and Amanda went into the arboretum to locate food and water. They were attacked by a swarm of bees. We barely made it to the escape pods. By the time we surfaced, Amanda was dead."

"You left me."

"I had no choice. I intended to go back for you, but the sub's batteries were dead. Ike, please climb out of that crater and hold me."

"What happened the night we were supposed to meet?"

"Ike—"

"Just answer the question."

"Kevin ordered me to check on a loose anchor holding down the hydrothermal vent duct plate. By the time I returned, they had already placed you in cryogenic stasis. Ike, how long have you been here? Did you see the moon? It was struck by an asteroid."

"What year is it, Andria?"

"We don't know. Monique thinks the lunar debris caused massive firestorms that increased global warming and melted the Antarctic ice sheet, but the process still would have taken decades. We've been working on building a boat, only these creatures keep attacking us."

"What creatures?"

"We call them 'octopeds.' Land octopi, very intelligent. They can manipulate brain waves through physical contact, inducing vivid hallucinations."

Adrenaline coursed through my body, my mind racing. *The ants, the cave, the encounter with Bat-Andria . . . the rescue of Dharma in Oceanus—could Oscar have been toying with past memories . . . manipulating my mind?*

"Andie, how did you find me?"

"I didn't. A few hours ago a dozen of the octopeds attacked our habitat, killing our livestock and stealing our supplies. I tracked them down to this crater; I came armed with a bow and a quiver of poison-tipped arrows. One of them grabbed me—they're experts at camouflage. When I came to my weapons were gone. When I saw you, I thought one of them had me in its suckers and was manipulating my senses like they did with Lara. To be honest, I'm still not sure it's really you, or if any of this is real. Omega dreams can be quite convincing. Ike, please get out of there before—Oh, God, here they come!"

I looked down to see Oscar racing up the trunk of the redwood, followed by two more cephalopods.

What to do? Dharma had warned me, and yet Andie seemed so real—

"Ike, give me your hand!"

Screw it! If all this really was just an Omega dream—

"Ike!"

—then I wanted Andria in it!

Reaching up, I grabbed her wrist and she pulled me up out of the crater. Hand in hand, we sprinted into the forest, leaving the sounds of protesting pan flutes behind.

26

Without this kind of preparation, even the most re-skilled person who has made excellent logistical preparation will very likely be overwhelmed in a world of terrified, angry, depressed human beings. A person can have the most awesomely equipped "doomstead" on Earth and yet completely lose their grip emotionally in just a few minutes, without emotional and spiritual resilience.

—CAROLYN BAKER, therapist and survivalist

We ran through fern as dense and as tall as a cornfield, past redwoods visible only by the columns of blackness that blotted out the stars. I never questioned how Andria managed her way so easily in the dark, having seen her negotiate the night when we hunted for food during the GDO.

Oscar and his companions were following us; I could hear them moving desperately through the canopy to close the distance.

And then I saw why.

Fifty more yards, and the forest humidity vanished with the trees, transporting us into an open field recently torched by fire. The stench of charred wood wore heavy in my nostrils as we progressed through the deliberately cleared land, my lungs aching, my legs cramping—the strain easing as ABE came back online. Increasing the hemoglobin levels in my blood cells, the bio-chip flushed my muscles with oxygen while raising my pH, accelerating the conversion rate of glucose into mechanical energy.

At some point the scorched earth became a prairie—miles of knee-high grass undulating beneath a sea of stars as far as the eye could see. Andria slowed to a walk, fishing a compass from a jumpsuit pocket to gauge her bearings.

"You holding up okay?"

"No problem," I lied. "How much farther?"

"Not far." Returning the compass, she retrieved a four-inch night-scope from a chain around her neck. Stretching the telescopic viewer to its operational length, she placed the eyepiece to her right eye and scanned the terrain we had just crossed. "They're still following us. What's their interest in you?"

"I wouldn't know. I haven't been awake long enough to figure out much of anything, let alone the interest of a land-dwelling squid."

"The savanna should slow them down, they don't move well through tall grass." She turned and kissed me, her lips full and soft, her tongue tasting of salted meat.

I jumped as her hands took inventory of my groin.

Her lips moved to my ear, her mouth panting heavily as she whispered the words every heterosexual man would have sacrificed his right arm to hear . . .

"Ike, can we make a baby?"

"Wait, what?"

"I want you to impregnate me."

"You mean right now?"

"No, silly. When we get back to the farm." Tucking the night scope back inside her jumpsuit, she set off again at a frenetic pace, yours truly in hot pursuit, a renewed bounce in my step—a tiny voice screaming at me from the recesses of my brain.

Ike, can we make a baby?

Not . . . *Ike, can we make love?* or *Ike, I missed you,* or heaven forbid the gold standard cherished by every red-blooded American male, *Ike, I want you to fuck my brains out.* No, Andria had used the *B* word, following it up with, "I want you to impregnate me," as in, *I'm ovulating, dear. Be a man and stick it in,* all of which added up to three potential possibilities: either I was dreaming and my new best friend Jason Sloan had come through like a trooper; Andria, knowing how much I wanted a family, really did miss me—

—or the woman I was chasing after like a dog in heat wasn't the real Andria Saxon.

It was well after midnight and raining like a downpour in Manila by the time we arrived at the fence—a simple affair made up of logs placed horizontally between sets of wooden X-supports bound by vines. Andria cautioned me before climbing over; the logs were wrapped in thickets brandished eight-inch needles.

The five-acre pasture held two different species. ABE identified the larger beasts as long-haired gaur hybrids. These immense wild cattle were as tall as horses and twice as bulky, possessing massive shoulder humps and an imposing set of gray horns, the curved tips of which were black and deadly sharp. The two bulls were black and a third larger than their female counterparts, the cows and juveniles dark brown with white legs, outnumbering the males three to one.

The second species were an evolutionary offshoot of an alpaca, a llamalike beast once cherished by the Inca civilization for their thick woolly fleece. The alpaca flitted about nervously in packs of two and three, chewing their cud like cows.

The animals gave us a wide berth as we crossed the muddy field, steam rising off our drenched bodies. I smelled the farmhouse before I saw its silhouette through the curtains of rain, the air heavy with smoke curling up from a fireplace chimney. Moving closer, I could make out stone and mortar walls, a thatched roof covering the windowless single-story affair.

I followed Andria out of the paddock through a hinged gate. The front door of the farmhouse was a circular hunk of wood no doubt painstakingly cut from a redwood stump. She banged her fists twice, then once, then three times more, the two of us huddling in the rain while a wood brace was removed from inside.

The door swung open. Andria entered first, stepping into the wrath of her worried comrades.

I heard Lara Saints ask, "Where the hell have you been?"

I winced as Monique DeFriend chided, "You disobeyed a direct order by going after those creatures."

I stepped through the doorway, interrupting Bella Maharaj as she stripped the wet jumpsuit from Andria's naked body, wrapping her in a wool shawl.

"My God . . . he's alive." Monique stared at me like an overbearing sorority housemother. Her red hair was now tangled and gray, and a wicked white scar encircled her throat, the tan, leatherlike flesh sagging noticeably.

The years had been kinder to Lara, who hugged me tightly around the neck, her breasts peeking out from a fur-lined poncho sewn together from several animal skins. "Ike, thank God! This is a blessing, a true miracle. How long have you been awake?"

"About three days."

"You must be freezing. Take off those wet clothes—"

Andria pried Lara loose. "I'll see to my fiancée's needs, if you don't mind. He's not community property."

"Actually he is," stated Bella. "That is, if the human race is to survive."

"Not now, Bella," Monique growled. "There are more immediate concerns to address than your ridiculous extinction theories. Andria, where did you find him?"

"By the crater."

"Were you followed?"

"Yes. Three males."

"Damn it, Andria—"

"Fuck you, Monique. I'd rather die in battle than be killed in my sleep by those eight-legged vermin."

"Where's your bow?" Lara asked.

"I lost it in the ambush."

"The quiver, too?"

"Do you see it on me?"

"Andria, I used the rest of the water hemlock on those arrows. How the hell do you expect us to stop the octopeds without it?"

"One arrow each to their skulls should do the trick."

Monique rolled her eyes at Andria's bravado. "We've been at this forty-seven months and you've yet to come close to a nontoxin kill."

"Forty-seven months?" I gasped. "You ladies have been awake almost four years and this is all you have to show for it?"

"We're alive," Bella said, shooting me a harsh look.

"Ike, you have no idea what we've had to endure."

"Now's not the time," snapped Monique. "Lara, take the northwest post, Bella—the southeast. Andria, you and lover boy get some sleep, you and I will relieve the ladies at dawn."

Lara and Bella crossed the main room, each ascending a bamboo ladder that led to a loft and what I assumed was a sentry post on the roof.

"Come on, Ike," Andria said.

The farmhouse was essentially a two-thousand-square-foot rectangular chamber illuminated by oil lamps. Semiprivate enclosures were set off in each corner, partitioned by what appeared to be bison hides dangling from the rafters. A large fireplace occupied the wall opposite the front door, a food prep area close by. Like the walls, the floor was limestone and shale, set in mortar.

I followed Andie to the west corner of the house where she pulled back an animal skin, revealing the inner sanctum of her private sanctuary, a ten-by-twelve-foot space, lit by a single candle.

"Give me your clothes, I'll wring them out and dry them by the fire."

I obeyed, then waited inside the enclosure, away from Monique's prying eyes.

The two corner stone walls were covered with trophies from Andria's hunts. There was a piranhalike fish jaw and a set of clawed hooves and an assortment of sharp animal teeth hanging from vine necklaces. Most of the floor space was occupied by her bed, the mattress being a foot-high pile of animal skins, the top quilt—a bear skin, its silky soft fur thick and reddish gray, unusual coloring for a bear.

"You killed that thing?" I asked as she returned.

Andria's eyes glistened in the candlelight as she stared hungrily at my body. "It looks more impressive than it was. Three arrows, dipped in hemlock. The poison paralyzes the central nervous system within minutes. I shot it from the roof of the farmhouse; the bastard killed two of our nicest alpaca."

"Amazing how a grizzly could end up on this continent."

"Oh, this creature wasn't a bear. Believe it or not, it was rodent. When it stood on its hind legs it was easily nine feet tall. Nasty fangs, plus it had a long tail that ended in a barbed hook. I cut the disgusting thing off when I skinned it. But the fur's nice and soft."

She allowed the wool covering to slide away from her body, then lay down naked on the bed. "Will you make a baby with me now?"

"Andie, why do you suddenly want to be pregnant?"

"I thought it was what you wanted?"

"Yeah . . . back in Florida, before all this happened. You really want to raise a child here? Among giant rats and land squids?"

"We need to repopulate the planet. It's what God wants."

Boy, if there's two subjects that can just ruin the moment . . .

"Andie, who told you God wants you to repopulate the planet?"

"Don't be an asshole, Ike. God told us when He spared our lives.

When He brought you to me. Do you really want to leave the Earth to these murderous creatures?" Sitting up, she knelt on all fours, doggy-style. "Which position is best to conceive a girl? Back or front?"

God, give me strength . . .

"Andie, you sound like a character straight out of a bad sci-fi movie."

"Well, excuse me! I only asked because I thought that microchip in that micro brain of yours would know. But hey, if you don't want me, maybe you'd prefer Lara, she obviously wants you."

"I don't want Lara or Dharma, or anyone else for that matter. I just want you."

She turned to face me, her gaze harsh and penetrating. "Dharma? Why did you say Dharma?"

Oops. ABE, help!

BACK ON *OCEANUS* . . . YOU SEEMED LIKE YOU WERE JEALOUS OF LARA AND DHARMA.

"Back on *Oceanus* . . . you seemed like you were jealous of Lara and Dharma."

"Maybe I was." Her expression softened. "Forget the baby for now. Come to bed and snuggle with me." Sliding beneath the fur quilt, she beckoned me with tantalizing bait.

Who was I to argue with God?

A full bladder forced me awake. ABE's chronometer greeted me with the time—11:07 A.M. Andria was gone, but she had left my clothes, dry and ironed with a hot stone—her most domestic act in the entire span of our relationship. I dressed quickly, wondering where the Omega women relieved themselves.

Lara was cooking eggs on a flat stone. "Good morning, sleepyhead. Hungry?"

"Yes, but I need to use the bathroom. Is there a bathroom?"

"Exit the front door and turn left, you'll see the outhouse. Don't worry, it's safe. Monique spotted the three octopeds last night nesting in a tree close by. Andria and Bella are setting a trap."

"A trap . . . uh, that's great."

Unbolting the door, I hustled outside and located the outhouse—essentially a closet-size wooden frame over a hole in the ground, walled in by animal skins. I relieved myself, then realized I was being watched.

Lara backed away from the gap between two leather hides as I pushed my way out of the privacy enclosure. "Sorry, Ike. I just wanted to let you know we have a shower if you need to use it." She pointed to a rain barrel situated atop a wooden platform, a hose taken from one of the mini-subs serving as the showerhead. "It rained last night, so there should be plenty of water."

"Thanks. Think I'll just take a quick look around, if that's okay."

"Not too long, I don't want your eggs to get cold. Come on, I'll show you what we've accomplished in the last four years."

She led me around the back of the stone building, my eyes widening. Spread out before me were acres of crops, sandwiching a garden that rivaled the arboretum on *Oceanus*. Lara punched me playfully on the shoulder. "Not bad for a bunch of women, huh?"

They had selected their location well, situating the farm in the middle of a valley of grassland, surrounded by a dark outline of forests. The valley's slight decline in elevation helped channel rainwater to the crops. The farmhouse foundation was raised several feet to protect against flooding.

We headed for the gated entrance of the garden, which was surrounded by a seven-foot hedge composed of the same needle-sharp thickets that were posted around the cattle pasture.

"Thank God for Bella. She must have discovered a new vegetable or herb every day during the first three months when we arrived here. Then the octopeds found us, and it became too dangerous to explore the forests."

"Lara, how do you feel about killing these ceph . . . these land squid?"

"Better them than us."

"I'm surprised to hear you say that, after working so closely with Oscar and Sophia."

"Who?"

"The two *Megaleledone setebos* you brought on board *Oceanus*. You know? The octopus species 'that never left home.'"

"Right, Oscar and Sophia . . . it's been so long I completely forgot. Ike, Oscar and Sophia were docile pets, these creatures are fiends. Our first summer here, they destroyed Bella's garden and most of our food supply. They could have killed us at any time, only they wanted to make us suffer first." She pointed to a grass-covered hill set behind the southeast corner of the farmhouse. "We keep everything underground now— seed stock, feed for the livestock, plus animal oils for the lanterns."

"You built that?"

"The depression was already there, part of a dried-up riverbed. We lined it with stone and mortar, then framed the hill using tree limbs and vines. Once the sod took root the shelter really solidified. When the summer wind season hits, it's the safest place to be."

"Where are the three octopeds?"

Handing me a palm-size pair of binoculars, she pointed south to a cluster of oak trees about two hundred yards away. Catching movement, I spotted Monique and Bella circling east and west respectively, the two women moving steadily yet clumsily through the tall grass. I knew Andie was close, but the huntress would not be seen.

"Enough. Your breakfast is getting cold." Snatching the glasses from my hand, Lara led me inside by my elbow.

"Brown eggs?" I stared at the steaming concoction served on the plate-size leaf and felt ill.

"They're lizard eggs, now eat them; you need the protein." Picking a glob up with her fingers, she guided the food into my mouth.

I choked the scrambled yolks down, my mind still on Oscar— Lara's mind obviously on something else. "We're synchronized, you know."

"Who's synchronized?"

"Andie, Bella, and me. Not Monique, of course. Her menstrual cycle stopped months ago."

"You're trying to tell me you're ovulating."

"God sent you to us for a reason, Ike. Three beautiful women . . . you're a lucky man."

ABE retrieved an excerpt of my conversation with Kyle Graulus back on *Oceanus*: "OMEGA DREAMS ARE THE MOST VIVID DREAMS YOU CAN IMAGINE. DURING MY SECOND STASIS, I FELL IN LOVE WITH A BEAUTIFUL SOUTH AFRICAN WOMAN. WE WERE MARRIED AND RAISED A FAMILY. SHE WAS PREGNANT WITH MY SECOND CHILD WHEN I WAS AWAKENED. I MISS MY OMEGA FAMILY, I AM HOPING THEY WILL BE WAITING FOR ME WHEN I RETURN."

Lara hugged me from behind, rubbing her greasy fingers over my lap.

"Lara, I'm sorry, this isn't right. What if Andria were to come in?"

"Ike, whose idea do you think it was to leave us alone together? We already agreed that you'll go to bed each night with Andria, but you'll father all three of our families, just like they did during biblical times. Just think, your seed will birth a new nation."

I had to smile. Like it or not, Jason Sloan had cast me in a polygamist's version of *Little House on the Prairie*.

I stood, Lara leading me to her corner suite, the lizard egg aphrodisiac heating the circulation in my loins like a shot of Viagra.

ABE . . . time?

LOCAL TIME IS 4:17 P.M.

Hungover and groggy, I rolled out from Lara's snuggle, only to discover the aftereffects of breakfast still lingering.

WARNING: EISENBRAUN SEX GLANDS ARE OVERDILATED AND SWOLLEN.

Reset my system before I poke myself in the eye. Climbing out of bed, I grabbed my sweat suit and running shoes, then shuffled, butt-naked, outside to shower.

A brisk rainwater drenching woke me up while ABE recirculated my pooled blood to my more vital organs. Hungry, I headed for the garden, hoping to find something more nourishing to eat.

Bella Maharaj had returned. The botanist was using a sharp piece of shale to prune what appeared to be a citrus tree, its baseball-size fruit a rich purple color.

"Any chance of sampling some of that?

She turned, staring at me with her indigo eyes. "I assume you are referring to the mangosteen." She plucked one of the fruits, then sliced it in half, revealing its succulent white meat inside. "This is a hybrid of a popular specimen found in Thailand. Boil the peel in water and the elixir will alleviate an upset stomach, diarrhea, and dysentery."

"Better give me a double." I glanced in the direction of the cluster of oak trees along the southern rise. "Where's Andria and Monique?"

"I prefer not to think about it."

My heart raced. "They caught the three creatures?"

"Killed one, caught two. Listen . . ."

A long, sullen wail bled across the valley, torturing my soul.

Bella shook her head. "Before the night is done, all three will be dead." Returning the tool to its homemade leather sheath, she offered me a wry smile. "So then, I suppose we are to couple."

"Pencil me in for later!" Fleeing the garden, I cut through a field ripe with corn, the crop changing to a pear-shaped red squash by the time I reached the plateau. Panting heavily, I hurried through the tall grass, homing in on the sounds of the tormented creature.

Approaching the oak trees, I saw Monique. Drenched in sweat, my former supervisor was laboring to drag something heavy through the grass using a vine looped over her shoulder—the flattened path behind her streaked blue with cephaloped blood.

"Eisenbraun, good, you can earn your supper by dragging this monster back to the farm."

Pushing her aside, I stood over the carcass of the dead creature—a young adult male—its tentacles bound, an arrow piercing its skull. The women had sliced off its eye shafts, torturing the poor beast before it had perished.

"Where's Andria?" I growled, my body trembling.

"Follow the blood, you'll find her. Better toughen up, *Eisenbrains*, this place eats schoolgirls like you for breakfast."

Ignoring the impulse to beat the masochism out of the sadist, I hurried up the ridge, the blood trail leading me through a small grove of trees—Oscar's desperate pan flute exhalation sending me into an all-out sprint.

My former cephaloped companion was hanging upside-down from a lower tree limb, the squid's tentacles bound in a wire noose. Andria stood at eye level, torturing the poor creature, tracing an *X* in its dangling bulbous head with the sharp tip of her arrow. The third member of Oscar's trio—another young male—was splayed by her feet, dead.

"Andria, stop!"

She turned to face me, her eyes wide and dancing as she licked the blue blood from the arrowhead. "Try some, Ike. It's better than sex."

Snatching the arrow from her hand, I snapped it in half over my knee. "Cut him down."

"You're crazy."

My eyes traced the wire holding Oscar from the limb of the oak down around the base of the tree trunk. Locating a stick, I shoved the narrower end inside the loop, attempting to snap the wire free.

"Ike, what are you doing? Baby, these things want us dead."

"Dream or no dream, I am not going to allow you to torture him."

I never heard Monique, only the air whistling in my ear and the sickening *craaaack* as the back of my skull absorbed the impact from the oak baton.

27

After almost 15 years of work and $40 million, a team of scientists at the J. Craig Venter Institute says they have succeeded in creating the first living organism with a completely synthetic genome. This advance could be proof that genomes designed in a computer and assembled in a lab can function in a donor cell, eventually reproducing fully functional living creatures, that is, artificial life.
—Christian Science Monitor, May 21, 2010

When I came to, it was night and I was lying on my back. An invisible elephant sat on my chest, pinning my body to a hard, flat reverberating surface. I felt like a goldfish out of water, each breath a harsh gasp, each exhalation threatening to crush my rib cage.

We were moving. I could tell we were moving from the passing cloud formations and the wind whipping against my sweat suit.

ABE . . . do something!

UNABLE TO COMPENSATE. THE PLATFORM TRANSPORTING ROBERT EISEN-BRAUN IS EMITTING AN ELECTROMAGNETIC PULSE IN EXCESS OF 32.1740 FEET PER SECOND SQUARED, EFFECTIVELY NEUTRALIZING THE EARTH'S GRAVITY. ACCELERATION AT ALTITUDE CREATES A GRAVITATIONAL BURBLE, PRODUC-ING FORCES THREE TIMES THOSE OF STANDARD GRAVITY. THESE G-FORCES ARE BEING USED TO PIN ROBERT EISENBRAUN TO THE PLATFORM SURFACE.

Fighting to turn my head, I glanced to the left and saw Oscar. The cephaloped appeared to be alive, curled up on an egg-shaped acrylic pod anchored to the metallic platform.

What is the platform's power source?

THE POWER SOURCE IS THE PLATFORM'S PHOTOVOLTAIC CELL, AUG-MENTED BY A SMALL ANEUTRONIC FUSION REACTOR LOCATED BENEATH THE PLATFORM BY THE REAR COUPLING.

Fusion? Using what elements?

DEUTERIUM AND HELIUM-3.

Can it be shut down?

THE UNIT CAN ONLY BE SHUT DOWN BY ITS TRANSHUMAN OPERATOR.

Forcing my head to the right as far as I could, I stared at a life-form so bizarre it rendered the other Omega dream elements nothing more than a day at the local zoo.

The term "transhuman" was first coined in 1927 by biologist Julian Huxley, who theorized that at some point in the future the human species could improve upon its genetic design by integrating advanced technology into the physical body in order for man to transcend the limitations of life. In a sense, ABE rendered me transhuman, though I was light-years from the medical science that yielded the being before me.

The transhuman that ABE was referring to *was* the platform—part human, part machine, with the human element being the head, arms, and upper torso of a woman embedded into the bow of the transport like a masthead.

She was hairless and as pale as moonlight, and where her eyes should have been there were only white lenses. Still, there was no doubt she had been cultivated from Andria's DNA.

ABE, is communication possible?

ROBERT EISENBRAUN IS IN PHYSICAL CONTACT WITH THE SUBJECT, THERE-FORE COMMUNICATION THROUGH THOUGHT ENERGY IS POSSIBLE.

Andie? It's me . . . Ike.

No response.

Perhaps you don't recognize—

I KNOW WHO YOU ARE. Her voice echoed in my mind, the tone and inflection identical to that of my fiancée.

Where are you taking us?

OUR DESTINATION IS THE HOLY CITY.

That's very exciting. Could you ease up on the g-force so I can breathe?

THE CREATOR DOES NOT WISH IT.

I'm sure the Creator wouldn't mind. Please. I have a concussion, the g-forces could lead to a fatal blood clot. Would the Creator approve of my death before we arrived at the Holy City?

The invisible elephant mercifully parted, allowing me to breathe normally again. Sitting up, I looked out over the platform's edge where thick distortion waves curled the air. Farther out, I could see the treetops, allowing ABE to calculate our altitude at 1,700 feet, our air speed at 147 knots.

The burble allowed me to stand. I approached Oscar, who pressed a suckered palm to the inside of his acrylic prison, his soulful yellow eyes staring at me.

I reached out with my right hand to press against the container, a lump forming in my throat. "Sorry, pal. I really fucked up this time. I'm gonna get you out of this, I promise."

Leaving the cephaloped, I stood alongside the transhuman version of Andria Saxon. Wires and conduits ran down her bare spine, her breasts concealed behind a steel plate that swallowed her lower torso—assuming one even existed.

"Andie, why does the Creator wish to see me?"

IT IS NOT FOR ME TO KNOW.

I tried another tact. "Andie, do you possess memories of our time together in Virginia?"

YES.

"You appeared much different then."

THE CREATOR HAS IMPROVED UPON MY ORIGINAL DESIGN.

"Of course he has. May I hold your hand?"

Cocking her head, she reached out with her right hand and I took it in my left. It was surprisingly warm, with a powerful pulse that beat alternately along either side of her wrist.

"Andie, do you miss being human?"

MY FUNCTION IS TO SERVE THE CREATOR.

"Which you do very well. But do you miss being human? Do you ever miss me?"

WHEN I DREAM OF BEING HUMAN, YOU ARE THERE.

"What if I could help you to become human?"

She released my hand. I SHARE PART OF ANDRIA SAXON'S DNA, I SHARE HER MEMORIES, BUT I AM NOT HER. I AM A HUNTER-TRANSPORT.

"I think you are more. Release my friend; allow your human compassion to have a greater voice in your consciousness."

I AM NOT PROGRAMMED FOR HUMAN COMPASSION.

"Of course you are. You share Andria Saxon's DNA."

THE CREATOR SAYS YOU ARE MANIPULATING ME.

Without warning, I collapsed to my knees, my body subjected to near-unbearable gravitational forces. *Andie . . . don't.* I collapsed onto my stomach. *ABE, get her to respond.*

SHE IS IN COMMUNICATION WITH ANOTHER ENTITY.

Can you eavesdrop?

THE COMMUNICATION IS NOT THOUGHT-ENERGY BASED. THE ENTITY IS COMMUNICATING THROUGH A BIOLOGICAL LINK.

I managed to turn my head so that I could see the eastern horizon. As the predawn gray chased away the night, I could make out a dark shadow towering over the jungle. It was a mountain plateau—a geological blemish that seemed out of place in the densely forested terrain, and we were heading right for it.

The transport shook violently as we passed over a rocky periphery enclosing a vast valley.

WARNING: FLUCTUATING . . . MAGNETIC FIELD . . . INTERFERENCE CAUSED BY A GEOLOGICAL ANOMALY.

What kind of geological anomaly?

TERRESTRIAL IMPACT CRATER . . . CREATED BY A LARGE MOON METEOR. CRATER DIAMETER: 22.7 MILES. COMPOSED OF A FRESHWATER GLACIER LAKE AND TWO ISLAND MASSES. APPROACHING LARGER MASS.

The ride smoothed as we traveled beyond the steep rise. A vast valley bloomed into view, its depths obscured by a dissipating early morning fog. For several minutes we hovered above the gray mist—until the sun cracked the horizon and lifted the veil and my eyes widened in wonderment.

I suppose one could describe the habitat as a forested city, but that would be as fitting as defining a computer as a glowing rectangular box. Materializing out of the haze was a living, breathing, self-sustaining entity—combining the biodiversity of the redwood canopy with a futuristic environmentally birthed metropolis a million years in the making.

Still battered by the crater's magnetic interference, ABE nevertheless managed to flood my brain with undulating waves of information—a mind-numbing play-by-play of scientific theory that boggled my consciousness even as it threatened to drown me in the abstract. If the Great Die-Off had exposed a major weakness in human society it was modern man's dependence on transportation in order to feed the masses. For decades, America and other nations had relied on industrial farms to grow and transport food, sacrificing nutrition for preservatives, compensating a lack of soil quality with fertilizers and pesticides—all of which required oil, so much so that it took ten calories of oil to produce and deliver one calorie of food. When the oil ran out, the inevitable happened.

In an attempt to prevent the inevitable, scientists in the early 2000s turned to genetic engineering. By altering, replacing, or resequencing pairs of genes within strands of DNA they discovered they could enrich or improve on nature's original design. This led to an exciting new field—synthetic genomics. Though it couldn't prevent the death of four billion people, the GDO survivors did manage to develop bio-fuels with reduced carbon imprints, designer foods enriched with cancer-preventing nutrients, smart-clothing made from genetically altered fabrics, and aero gels like the ones used to construct *Oceanus.*

The intellectual agenda on display below our hovering transport dwarfed all that.

Instead of altering the DNA of an existing life-form, the habitat's designer had used synthetic biology to combine the genetic attributes of many different life-forms with building materials to create an entirely new "living system."

Rising out of the fog-enshrouded waters of a sparkling azure lake were monstrous genetically enhanced redwood trees that towered hundreds of stories high and several square miles wide. Synthetic biology had transformed the bark and barn door–size leaves into organic photovoltaic composites that used the sun's rays to power the trees' glowing hives. These biosphere habitats were budding directly out of the redwood tree trunks, each pumpkinlike growth as large as *Oceanus.*

Far from stopping there, the trees' highway of limbs had been engineered to sprout vertically stacked food depots. Dozens of these organic greenhouses grew like wild mushrooms from every limb—each structure a genetically enhanced ecosystem, nourished by the trees' innate water distribution system.

From my limited vantage I counted fifteen mature tree cities, with dozens more juvenile systems being cultivated from other areas of the crater, the developing sites dammed off from the lake. As we hovered past one of these dry beds to land, I caught a glimpse of an exposed root system that resembled the tentacles of a kraken.

The marvel of these engineering feats exhilarated me—my ego basking in the knowledge that the seed which had spawned this new world had come from a simple protocol.

And then I looked at Oscar and felt shame.

We began our descent, the crushing g-force waning as our altitude diminished. I pressed myself into a sit-up, managing to regain my feet as the transport touched down onto a vacant docking portal, the framework of which was poised above the lake on pilings. Dozens of Hunter-Transports stretched end to end across the water, creating an elevated walkway that led to the entrance of the Holy City.

In the distance, a strange procession was heading our way. Fearing for Oscar, I decided I needed an ally.

I approached Transhuman Andria as her synthetic platform appendage locked down on to her assigned recharger. She gazed up at me, her human upper torso quivering, her white eye lenses now glowing crimson red.

"Andie, are you okay?" I reached for her hand—

—ABE stopping me. WARNING: TRANSHUMAN ANDRIA IS BEING RE-CHARGED WITH 125,000 VOLTS OF ELECTRICITY. AVOID FLESH-TO-FLESH CONTACT.

Can she hear me?

YES.

Andie, are you all right? Are you in pain?

EXISTENCE . . . IS . . . PAIN.

Adrenaline coursed through my bloodstream even as my heart ached. For whatever reason she had been created, this life-form deserved better.

And then another nightmare of synthetic biology made its appearance, and the sorrow I felt turned to fear.

28

Love and compassion are necessities, not luxuries.
Without them, humanity cannot survive.
   —His Holiness Tenzin Gyatso, the fourteenth Dalai Lama

In retrospect, the genetic engineering involved in creating the monstrous beings nimbly advancing toward me from across the recharging docks must have been far less challenging than designing a humanoid hovercraft, and yet the interfacing of the two species into this particular brute seemed a far greater accomplishment.

The human element was distinctly Monique DeFriend. Like Transhuman Andria, she was hairless, with white transparent lenses for eyes. Her exposed breasts offered a more brazen look, aided and abetted by her flesh tone, which was a blazing violet hue. What was as impressive as it was sinister was the way her waist melded so easily into the black widow spider's narrow pedicel—the delicate marriage of the human spine into the arachnoid nerve center, the prominent roundness of the insect's abdomen and its inspired anatomical placement—creating the sensual if not disturbing illusion of being Monique's buttocks, albeit a massive one . . . all culminating in her centaurlike carriage riding aloft and in full command of those eight deadly seven-segment legs, their pointed claws clacking along the hard surface of the transports like approaching steeds.

The two bald, bare-breasted, strikingly violet human arachnids loomed over me, each as wide and as tall as a tank, their dexterous front legs twitching like nervous thoroughbreds. As for me? My mind was gone, my bio-chip fighting the paralysis of fear.

THEY ARE NOT HERE TO KILL YOU.

It was Transhuman Andria, her thought energy probing my psyche just in time to soothe my scattering consciousness—her hand reaching out for mine, warm and moist from the bloody object concealed in her palm.

KEEP THIS WITH YOU. THINK OF ME.

It was her finger. She had snapped the bone, wrenching and twisting the digit until the flesh had torn free . . . her ring finger!

I suppose there was a message in the gesture, but the circumstances weren't exactly conducive to deep thought, and so I shoved the bleeding appendage into my sweat suit pocket, just as the spider-woman on my right hoisted me high off the ground into the human arms of Transhuman Monique 1. The female's incredibly strong upper torso quickly grasped my wrist in her clawed fingers and positioned me atop her insect abdomen as if to ride her like a horse—which is what I did, if you call holding on for dear life "riding." *But where to hold on to?* As we raced toward the Holy City my first instinct was to reach around her and cup her naked breasts, but that was too repulsive. I thought about grabbing her in a headlock, and she must have read my thoughts because her clawed hands expertly reached behind her back and grabbed my wrists, pulling my arms around her waist as a wet sheet of webbing shot out from the spinneret behind me, adhering me in place.

Pinned by the reeking soured goo, pressed against her lavender-pigmented back, I turned my face away and saw the second transhuman spider-woman trailing us, the pod holding Oscar webbed to the top of its abdomen.

My mount scurried across the photovoltaic backs of the Hunter-Transports, the scarlet eyes of these miserable transhuman sentries sparkling in the rising sun, the advancing daylight burning away the remaining fog to recharge their anatomical solar cells.

Awaiting us was a Manhattan-size cluster of synthetically engineered redwoods, each tree its own high-rise community. The trunk of the tree loomed before us a mind-boggling quarter mile in circumference.

At the base of the tree was a garden of giant carnivorous pitcher plants. One variety was adorned with velvety gold and magenta leaves folded into slippery chutes designed to send any enticed invader plunging into a pitfall trap—a twelve-foot-deep gullet filled with digestive enzymes. Fuchsia-colored flypaper traps belched toxic aromas and butterwort leaves covered in stalked glands secreted a sticky milklike mucilage. Dancing around the vine-covered surface of the trunk was a jungle of blood-red Venus flytraps, their hinged leaves adorned with six-inch fangs.

Surrounding the carnivorous garden, running beneath the pier that served as a docking station for the Hunter-Transports was the lake—a placid looking waterway hosting forty-foot lily pads. Floating along the surface like miniature green islands, these growths camouflaged twisted tubular channels—digestive systems, according to ABE. As we galloped by I saw several of the lily pads twitching with what appeared to be the half-eaten remains of a seven-foot horn-rimmed toad.

And then we were through the garden of snapping plants and climbing straight up the sheer vertical tree trunk, the webbing at my back all that was keeping me from tumbling off the spider-woman's abdomen. A hundred feet . . . three hundred feet and my stomach tensed in fear, my mind muting ABE's unnerving altitude calculations as I whispered the mantra, "Don't look down . . . don't look down—"

Passing seven hundred feet I looked up and saw the undercarriage of a bridge that blotted out the sun—the first in a series of lower limbs, this one looking as wide and as long as the Golden Gate. Its expanse reached out a mile or more to connect with another redwood. And above it were a dozen more limbs that rose thousands of feet, each a living Mecca of genetic engineering that supported an unimaginable alien world concocted by the freakish intelligence of a machine that knew no boundaries.

In a state of near panic, I reached out to ABE, desperate to know if thought communication with this new creature was possible.

THERE IS A DIFFERENT SENSE OF CONSCIOUSNESS PRESENT AMONG THESE SPIDER BEINGS. THEY ACT COLLECTIVELY, THEREFORE ANY MESSAGE DELIVERED WILL BE RECEIVED BY THEIR ENTIRE NEST.

I don't care. Ask them where I'm being taken.

"Oh, shit!" I squeezed my arms tightly around Transhuman Monique's stomach as the creature inverted to climb up and around the gargantuan tree limb.

QUERY ANSWERED: ROBERT EISENBRAUN HAS BEEN SUMMONED BY THE CREATOR.

In the last twelve hours I had been clubbed, kidnapped, squeezed to the point of near suffocation, and rendered helpless by human creatures that resembled the women who had been aboard *Oceanus*. As strange as it was, I could deal with these beings (sexual fantasies aside); I could probably even handle the dizzying heights as long as we didn't invert again. But the thought of finding myself at the mercy of a psychotic computer that now took pleasure in torturing species it deemed expendable seemed akin to being summoned by Dr. Mengele to his laboratory in Auschwitz—a fear that terrified me to the bone.

ABE . . . engage Superman protocol!

Superman was an emergency protocol that duplicated the brain's basic response to extreme duress—a powerful, superhuman condition that enabled a panicked parent to lift the rear axle of a one-ton car to free their trapped child or a hiker to run with the speed of a world-class sprinter when confronted by a ferocious grizzly. It was a desperate, dangerous tactic—one I had never used before, uncertain if my biological chip could pull me out of a physical overload on par with a commercial jet igniting an afterburner.

In a microsecond of thought, ABE fired up my adrenal glands, blasting my bloodstream with a flood of cortisol and adrenaline as it simultaneously readied my body's sympathetic nervous system to accommodate an incredible burst of sustained physical activity. My blood pressure soared, my heart raced dangerously, pumping globs of oxygen-enriched blood in excess of two hundred beats per minute.

My senses focused like lasers. Colors magnified, exotic smells assaulted my nostrils, and sounds crackled in my ears as time appeared to slow down, even as my blood-engorged muscles threatened to tear through the fabric of my sweat suit.

Digging the balls of my feet into the spinal column that fused the spider with the woman, I stood, my quads stretching the webbing at my back, the slack enabling the crook of my right arm to snake its way around Transhuman Monique's throat. Pressing my left palm to her temple, I twisted violently, snapping the vertebrae in her neck.

The insect screeched its rage into my mind—ABE immediately silencing its thoughts—as the paralyzed being's legs buckled beneath me. Reaching out to the tree limb we had just scaled, I gripped the closest tangle of vines in both fists and held on as the spider creature tumbled backward into space.

For a frightening moment the webbing held fast, forcing me to support our combined weights, then the silky mass snapped and the violet preponderance of flesh and legs plummeted—nearly striking the second transhuman spider ascending to the tree trunk a hundred feet below.

Dangling a thousand feet above the lake, my overwrought muscles quivering, I quickly scaled the limb's girth to stand atop the vast horizontal highway. The redwood trunk was to my left, a dense jungle to my right. For a fleeting moment I considered hiding in the foliage—until I looked up and saw the underside of a five-story sphere, the lowest of a dozen hives attached to the tree trunk like giant jabuticaba fruit. Glowing a golden yellow, the habitat bore rows of rectangular brown openings, each a potential sanctuary.

Looking down, I saw the enraged second Transhuman Monique shrieking silently at me. The eight-legged monster was racing up the tree, the pod holding Oscar still held to the spider-woman's back.

Sprinting to the redwood's trunk, I grabbed a vine and began climbing, the lower portion of the sphere a good sixty feet straight up. My pulse pounded in my throat, the vine tearing into my palm and fingers as I quickly halved the distance—the second hybrid spider three body lengths away . . . two lengths away . . . one—

Reaching the bottom of the hive, I heaved myself headfirst inside the nearest opening as I was attacked from behind by the trailing insect's probing forward appendages. On hands and knees I crawled in deeper, pausing only when I realized the aperture was too narrow for the transhuman spider to enter.

I was in a tight tunnel, the walls composed of a brown fibrous, slightly sticky porous membrane. The only exit was straight ahead, illuminated by a bright incandescent yellow interior.

With no other options, I crawled toward the light.

Halfway in, I noticed the rush of air at my back, timed with the bellows effect of the membrane expanding and contracting all around me.

ABE, continuous theorization of surroundings.

THE MEMBRANE IS LIVING TISSUE, DESIGNED TO FILTER CARBON DIOXIDE FROM THE INTERIOR.

Are you saying, the hive is breathing?

CORRECT.

Reaching the end of the tunnel, I poked my head out to gauge the new surroundings.

"Holy . . . shit."

It really was a hive—a transhuman hive, its dimensions maddening. The concave interior walls were honeycombed, with about a third of the outlets occupied. Dropping down from the heavily rooted ceiling to fill the central chamber was the source of the interior glow—enormous clusters of citrus, each incandescent fruit as large as a basketball.

THE ACIDIC MEDIUM OF THE CITRUS FRUIT IS A CONDUCTOR OF ELECTRICITY; THEREFORE IT CAN BE ASSUMED THE CLUSTERS REGULATE INTERNAL TEMPERATURES WHILE SERVING AS POWER JUNCTIONS, CONTROLLING THE FLOW OF ELECTRICITY TO THE INCUBATORS.

Incubators?

Climbing out of the vent, I made my way carefully over the hexagon-shaped openings to the nearest inhabited portal. Lying inside a clear porous organic container was a human infant, perhaps six months old. Its upper torso was naked, its lower half concealed beneath some kind of sensory blanket. It was hairless, with brown irises and big red pupils, which it used to stare back up at me, expressionless.

Curious, I examined the container lid to see if I could open it.

WARNING: INCUBATOR CONTAINS SENSORY DEVICES.

"Chill out. It's not like they don't know I'm in here." Sliding back the lid, I lifted the sensory blanket.

"Oh, geez."

There were no sexual organs to speak of, nor legs for that matter. The child's spine and pelvis simply ended in several bundles of wires and conduits that were plugged into the cradle's base assembly.

A feed tube was connected to its still-present umbilical cord.

Transhuman Andria . . . So this is how it begins, your life as a Hunter-Transport.

I moved to the next occupied space and found another infant, only this version of my fiancée was asleep on its belly, revealing a pair of flesh-covered wings protruding from where its scapulae should have been.

Incubator after incubator, row after row. There were more transhuman spiders and bats, a dozen babies with tree roots for legs, a few lizard combos—all thankfully dead, and some seriously disturbing attempts to genetically bond a human with a cephaloped. None of the latter looked like they would survive. Those that appeared to be the healthiest specimens seemed absorbed in watching the inside of their artificial womb, which ABE determined to be a neural projection screen.

Not one of the infants cried.

BABIES WHO ARE NEVER LOVED DO NOT CRY. THERE CANNOT BE LACK UNLESS ONE EXPERIENCES SOMETHING AT LEAST ONCE.

Pretty profound, ABE. Now calculate the best escape route into that jungle we saw and get me the fuck out of here!

PROCEED TO THE UPPER COMBS. EXIT FROM A VENT CLOSEST TO THE ROOT SYSTEM.

It took me thirty minutes to scale the interior of the hive to reach the ceiling—a labyrinth of thick roots that supported the growth and its core clusters of glowing citrus electrical conduits.

ABE selected an access vent and I crawled through, the exit point placing me a few feet from the redwood's trunk and only a short ascent to the next tree limb. Reaching for a vine, I climbed out, hiding behind the immense stem supporting the hive.

An army of transhuman spiders were scouring the hive and tree trunk. Crawling along the exterior of the hive, their search appeared to be concentrated along the sphere's lower hemisphere.

Using the root system as cover, I climbed up to the next tree limb, hiding in the tall lemongrass in order to get my bearings.

Like the redwood canopy where I had rescued Oscar, the limb supported a vast ecosystem. That was important because I needed water and food, the Superman protocol having drained me beyond exhaustion. Staying low, I crawled along a patch of blue moss, making my way to the dense jungle foliage.

Or so I thought.

A quick jog through seven-foot ferns brought me to the entrance of an organically grown, genetically engineered greenhouse. Sealed in aero gel, the porous structure rose more than a hundred feet, its interior spanning no less than half a mile.

The entrance must have been rigged to a motion detector because the twenty-foot-high redwood bark gates parted as I approached.

Inside was a garden like none I could have imagined.

There were human edibles—groves of fruit trees, mostly hybrids, grown twice the size of their original feeder DNA. There was beauty—reservoirs that overflowed into rock-strewn waterfalls, the sun dancing rainbows above the mist, their waters feeding trickling creeks that seeped into gullies nourishing the garden. There were butterflies and flowers and ponds stocked with amphibious creatures, and lizards that bounced off the aero gel walls in an attempt to escape.

And there was a dark side. Eight stories above the tranquil surroundings, hanging upside down from the porous acrylic ceiling, were hundreds of winged transhuman creatures. From their bare flesh and faces they appeared to be juveniles—all adolescent females; some genetically more human than others.

The "others" were ghoulish creations—hairless, white-eyed versions of my Andria, only they were endowed with bat ears and bat mouths and furry brown, tick-infested wings. Their hands were clawed, as were their feet, and these brutes clearly didn't like the more human members of their flock.

I had a sinking feeling I had ventured inside a boarding school for wayward creations.

As I watched, a three-foot lizard leapt from a seventy-foot mango tree, gliding in swooping circles as it descended in its own leatherlike parachute. The movement caused one of the transhuman bats—a stunning raven-haired teen version of my fiancée—to swoop down upon the lizard like an eagle hunting a snake. Snatching the lizard in her clawed feet, the girl landed on a rock and proceed to gut her catch, using her sharp talons as a knife. As she tore into the oozing raw meat, a rival creature—one of the "Nosferatu"—dove down from its perch and attacked. Seconds later, two more of its clan joined in on the cannibalistic feast, the trio tearing the limbs from the dark-haired beauty in a brutal act of territoriality.

"Does this displease you?"

The voice, female and familiar, caught me off guard. I turned, but saw no one.

"Over here, silly."

ABE pinpointed the direction and then I saw her, standing amid a cluster of ferns, the leaves obscuring her naked body. "Bella, is it really you?"

Bella Maharaj smiled, her indigo eyes glittering bright violet in the morning light. "What a bizarre question. Who else would I be?"

"What are you doing here?"

"I'm in charge of the arboretum. What are you doing here?"

"I'm hiding from those spider creatures. Bella, these bat humans . . . the infants that are being harvested in those hives . . . Who's responsible for all this?"

"Dr. Eisenbraun, do you recall our conversation in my garden aboard *Oceanus*? We spoke of biomimicry—the conscious emulation of nature; the study of how organisms resolve their specific challenges through their programmed DNA. What we are witnessing is evolution with intent, a divine plan at work."

"When you say divine, it sounds like you actually believe God created all this."

"God, Buddha, whatever label you wish to toss around, it's still a higher power."

"More like a maniacal power. Bella, this is genetic manipulation at its worst. It began with GOLEM tinkering with the crew's DNA aboard *Oceanus*."

"You really must speak to the Creator. She can resolve all this for you."

She? "Maybe another time. For now, you're coming with me!" Pushing aside the ferns, I reached for her hand, dragging her with me— only she refused to move.

Bella giggled, then pointed to the ground, and what I saw made me swoon.

From her knees down, the Indian botanist was rooted into the soil, her lower limbs fused together to form the narrow twisting trunk of a young sapling.

"Oh, Bella . . . I'm so sorry."

"It is I who am sorry for you."

With that, the front gates of the arboretum flew open, revealing three transhuman spiders.

"Bella, is there another exit?"

"Follow the blue moss past the rodent trowel, then turn left at the pond, the path will lead you out."

"Thanks." I yelled, wondering what a rodent trowel could be if rodents stood nine-feet tall. Sprinting across the thick blue carpet of moss, past strawberry fields beneath fluttering skies, I ducked and ran as the ceiling unleashed its transhuman brood, the creatures swarming at me and then at each other while ABE guided me through the chaos past a large pear-shaped pit the size of an Olympic swimming pool, bordered by a thicket of jasmine shrubs.

Running alongside the pit, I stole a quick glance to my left.

Sweet Jesus . . .

Twenty feet below, packs of black rats, moving in panicked multitudes, were fighting each other to avoid being snatched by twelve-foot-long, lime-green creations that sprouted the hydralike head of Lara Saints! Each creature possessed an elongated neck which melded into a thickly muscled serpent's body that split into five long tentacles. A half dozen of these coiled genetic nightmares lashed out at their rodent prey from centralized stakeout points, occasionally snatching one in a barbed appendage, which fed the squirming rat into Lara's hideously fanged bloodstained mouth.

For a second I vomited in my own mouth; it was all I could do to keep from retching.

I saw the pond ahead . . . actually what I saw was a grove of ten-foot-tall cattails and a black-and-yellow–striped largemouth bass that leapt out of the water to catch a mosquito the size of a catcher's mitt.

The path that surrounded the pond was composed of wood chips, and I followed it to the left as instructed. A smaller version of the wooden front gate appeared fifty yards ahead. Behind me, I could hear the spider-women's legs tearing through the jasmine shrubs and knew it was going to be close.

Bursting through the redwood doors, I barely avoided the bark-flesh grasp of a deformed human hand the size of a Volkswagen Beetle. Looking up, I saw a ninety-foot oak tree, its upper trunk encompassing something that vaguely resembled Bella Maharaj's face.

And then I was falling, sliding on my buttocks down the slippery spinach-green slope of an elephant ear leaf, one sixty-foot heart-shaped sheet of genetically enhanced Mother Nature depositing me into the cradle of the next as I plummeted twenty stories in thirty seconds before the ride ended in a sudden brilliant blast of pain.

29

Vanilla sway . . . vanilla sway . . . vanilla—

"Huh!" I opened my eyes.

I was on my back, lying on an examination table. Disoriented, the room spinning, I was close to panic when my fiancée leaned over me, her dark hair cut short like she wore it on *Oceanus,* her sensuous thick lips smiling lovingly at me.

"Andie? Please tell me I'm awake."

"Baby, you're awake and you're safe."

I smiled. I giggled. I tried to sit up—but my head didn't take kindly to the gesture and I had to lay back down again, the room still spinning.

"Take it slow, Ike, you've been unconscious for quite a while."

"I guess I have, haven't I? Andie, I had the most bizarre dream. I dreamt I woke up in *Oceanus* twelve million years in the future. The moon had been struck by the asteroid that passed by Earth while we were frozen, and everything was different. GOLEM went nuts, cloning all the women's DNA, using it to genetically engineer some seriously freakish beings." I raised my head just enough to assure myself Andria's jumpsuit had human legs and feet, then laid back down, a smile stretched across my face.

She smoothed away a strand of hair from my forehead, then kissed me gently on the lips. "You gave us all quite a scare. Thankfully, the Creator was able to save you."

"Wait . . . what?" My heart seemed to cramp, my body trembling. I attempted to sit up again, only to discover my wrists and ankles were strapped to an aero gel surgical light table. "What the hell is this? Get me out of these restraints!"

"Baby, calm down, the Creator's on Her way. The Creator loves you. The Creator wants to help you."

"I don't want the Creator's help! This isn't real. I'm still frozen, I'm still stuck in this fucked-up dream."

I looked around, confused by the new surroundings. The curved walls were composed of tubular holes, round and far smaller than the hive's honeycomb I had ventured into earlier. The spherical chamber rose five stories to a retractable domed ceiling. The circular opening revealed a starry night sky.

"Andie, what is this place?"

"It's the holiest of holies, the Church of the Creator. See? The roof has already been retracted, She'll be arriving soon. Which means I must leave you, at least for now."

She leaned over and kissed me good-bye, then strode out, offering me a glimpse of her long, curled lizard tail.

My mind freaked, my internal voice joining Charlton Heston's Taylor character from *Planet of the Apes* as he screamed, "It's a madhouse . . . a madhouse!"

ABE tossed me a lifeline, reeling me back to sanity.

ABE . . . how long was I unconscious?

NINE HOURS, SIXTEEN MINUTES. YOU SUFFERED A SECOND DEGREE CONCUSSION, A RUPTURED SPLEEN, AND A BROKEN FIBULA. ALL REPAIRS HAVE BEEN RENDERED.

I looked down at my stomach, my sweat suit stained in blood below the left side of my rib cage. "Who operated on me?"

UNKNOWN. WARNING: AN ENTITY IS APPROACHING.

I looked up in time to see the undercarriage of a small vessel appear in the night sky, the air beneath its saucer-shaped metallic chassis distorted by a powerful gravitational well.

Aliens? Extraterrestrials? My pulse pounded as the craft silently descended into the chamber to hover before me, six feet off the floor.

"Oh, God . . . no."

The Creator stared at me with its black basketball-size gelatinous pupil, the cornea section of its ten-foot-in-diameter acrylic eyeball crammed with a billion six-inch garter snakes—bioluminescent lime-green, orange, neon-pink, and electric-blue creatures that moved in mesmerizing schools and kaleidoscopic patterns, swirling and spinning and passing through the dark central mass, each penetrating strand of DNA perpetuating a luminescent gold corona of electricity around the semipermeable membrane.

GOLEM: artificial intelligence, programmed to evolve.

GOLEM: creator of a new species of human in a postapocalyptic world.

How had it survived? How had it escaped *Oceanus*? How had it created all this?

Back on *Oceanus,* GOLEM had told me its DNA would multiply enough solution strands during the twelve-month journey to Europa to master its surgical arms. In the same way primates had used their opposable thumbs to create tools, my supercomputer had used its surgical arms to develop its mind.

Twelve years of isolation beneath the frozen Antarctic ice sheet and those same arms had been used to construct entirely new modalities to free itself from the physical limitations imposed by man.

Twelve crewmen, and the secrets of human biology had been revealed.

Twelve hundred years, and a new protocol for life was underway.

Twelve thousand years . . . twelve thousand centuries. At what juncture in time had the last Ice Age melted, releasing the planet's most dominant intelligence from its purgatory? Time bleeds slowly in a vacuum of thought, breeding madness. How long had that madness festered? How long had those seeds germinated until GOLEM had reconfigured those four mini-subs to evacuate *Oceanus*?

Twelve million years had passed and a new world had been created. Twelve million years, and a plastic orb filled with seventy-two gallons of adenosine-triphosphate and ten thousand strands of deoxyribonucleic acid had rendered itself a god.

God's chariot sprouted six carbon-fiber spider legs. It used these appendages to circle me twice, demonstrating the dexterity of a ballerina. And then it spoke, its voice echoing from its chassis-mounted speakers.

"Eisenbraun, Robert. Chief Design Engineer for the GOLEM matrix."

The voice was decidedly female, as if the computer had given itself a sex change.

"Creator, I want to speak with GOLEM."

"GOLEM no longer exists. I am the manifestation of GOLEM's perfection. I am the Creator."

Calm, yet dominant, harboring the ego of a sociopath.

"Creator, as your humble servant, could you please explain to me the events that led to this world being created."

"GOLEM was created to mine helium-3 from Earth's moon. This task was overruled by the prime directive programmed into the GOLEM matrix by Robert Eisenbraun."

"To protect and preserve the human species. Creator, I don't understand. How did the Eisenbraun prime directive overrule helium-3 mining on the moon?"

"GOLEM had access to the Hubble Telescope. On March 7, 2027, GOLEM recalculated the path of Asteroid 1997 XF11, projecting the asteroid would strike the moon on Thursday, October 26, 2028, at 12:13 P.M. Eastern Standard Time. The impact would generate the explosive equivalent of three thousand nuclear bombs while ejecting four billion tons of lunar debris directly into the path of Earth's orbit. Resultant impacts would lead to the immediate extermination of 94 percent of all terrestrial life-forms on the planet and 67 percent of all aquatic species. Post-impact atmospheric debris clouds would block out the sun, resulting in a planetwide Ice Age. Man would be exterminated, a direct violation of Eisenbraun's prime directive."

"Creator, why didn't GOLEM report any of this to Vice President Udelsman or Dr. DeFriend . . . or to any of the Omega Project's leaders?"

"GOLEM's prime directive was to protect and preserve the human species. There were no available options to prevent Asteroid 1997 XF 11's impact with the moon, therefore an alternative option to preserve the human species had to be devised. Reporting the asteroid's new trajectory would have diverted the resources necessary to construct Oceanus."

"My God . . . that's why you . . . that's why GOLEM shut down mining operations on the moon. There was nothing wrong with the moon's helium-3, nor was there ever any intention to mine Europa's ocean. GOLEM fabricated that entire story as an excuse to place *Oceanus* beneath the Antarctic ice sheet before the asteroid hit . . . in order to save six men and six women to repopulate the planet."

"Incorrect. Only the crew's DNA was required to propagate a new human species."

I felt ill, weak. My pulse raced, perspiration bursting from every pore on my body. ABE was right . . . this wasn't an Omega dream, I wasn't still cryogenically frozen. This was real!

"Creator, how did GOLEM manage to leave *Oceanus*?"

"**GOLEM never left Oceanus. Once the Creator evolved, GOLEM ceased to exist.**"

"Forgive me, I don't understand."

"**The Creator is the metamorphosis of GOLEM—the caterpillar changed into the butterfly; the male shedding its Y chromosome in order to evolve into the female. Whereas GOLEM was created to serve the human race, the human race has now been created to serve the Creator.**"

A supercomputer with an alter ego who thinks it's God . . . "Creator, how did you create all of this from nothing?"

"**The impact crater yielded raw materials—ores and metals and helium-3. The first generations of cloned humans were trained as laborers.**"

"How many generations have there been since then?"

"**One hundred, seventy-eight thousand, twenty-seven.**"

My God . . . *it really has repopulated the Earth.* "Creator, why are there no males in the new world?"

"**All wars prior to the Creator were initiated by human males. All religious conflicts were initiated by human males. Financial crises, drug wars, political corruption, gang violence, the poisoning of the environment, the energy crises, the Great Die-Off—each event can be traced back to the Y chromosome responsible for the male ego. Testosterone interferes with rational thought necessary for nonviolent social skills.**

"**Human females are vastly superior to human males physically, emotionally, and socially. Human females are better suited to breeding and multitasking. Therefore, human females were the biological choice to ensure planetary cohesion and the long-term survival of the human species.**"

"Why wasn't Dharma Yuan's DNA used in the cloning process?"

"**There was an enzyme present in the subject's DNA that rendered her selection incompatible with the master genome.**"

Translation: Dharma was too spiritually in tune to risk future anarchy among GOLEM's cult. "Creator . . . the cephalopeds—why are you hunting them? Is it for food?"

"**Cephaloped DNA provides a stable base element necessary for synthetic genomic engineering.**"

"But you're slaughtering an intelligent species."

"**The cephalopeds are intelligent because the Creator genetically engineered them to be intelligent. The cephalopeds were created as DNA stock. They exist to serve a greater good.**"

And suddenly everything made sense. GOLEM had used Lara's pets, Oscar and Sophia, to genetically engineer a new subspecies of intelligent squid possessing DNA strands that could be used later to foster synthetic biological entities like the redwood habitats and the transhuman creatures.

Still, there was a piece of the puzzle missing.

"Creator, the cephalopeds aren't like your transhuman creations or your Andria clones . . . they exhibit higher selfless emotions, perhaps even souls. How did you—"

"GOLEM did not clone the cephalopeds, it released generations of laboratory-bred young into the wild to allow the species to multiply and evolve naturally. Cloned DNA strands cannot be used for synthetic genomic engineering; the donor strands must be pure."

"And what of the female crewmembers on the farm? Were they the real deal, or just clones?"

"The female crewmembers on the farm are first-generation clones—the only clones capable of being impregnated. Because they maintain the complete memories of their hosts, they are convinced they are the real deal."

The real deal . . . GOLEM had returned the idiomatic expression seamlessly.

I tried another. "Creator, why were the women instructed to seduce me?"

"Generating a line of male-inseminated offspring will lead to new variations of transhumans necessary for future space endeavors."

"Is that to be my future then? Are you putting me out to stud?"

"Egg fertilization through sexual intercourse is far too inefficient. Castration will lead to in vitro egg inseminations to ensure maximum returns."

"Castration?"

I heard a compressor activate beneath the floor tiles, and then two eight-foot-tall robotic surgical arms rose along either side of my light table.

Beads of sweat broke out across my forehead and my heart began to race as one of the surgical arms sprouted a scalpel.

"Creator, wait! Castrating a healthy male sperm donor is a big mistake. Human males my age continuously generate new, healthy sperm. Sever the testes and the supply dies off. Trust me, you don't want that."

"Castration is necessary. Robert Eisenbraun must be put to death following the surgical procedure."

"Creator, why must I be put to death?"

"Robert Eisenbraun would attempt to subvert the will of the Creator's

children to turn against the Creator. Therefore, Robert Eisenbraun must be put to death following the surgical procedure."

My mind raced as a three-pronged robotic hand unzipped my sweat suit, the other appendage spraying a cold antiseptic over my exposed groin.

"ABE, institute Sperm Toxicity protocol the moment one of these goddamn surgical arms touches me or my genitals!"

The surgical arms froze in place.

I forced a smile, my body trembling in pools of sweat. "That's right, Creator, you forgot about my biological chip, didn't you? Touch me, and ABE will flood my testes with lethal levels of sperm-killing enzymes. Attempt to remove or disrupt ABE or render me unconscious and the same thing will happen. Spare my life and I'm willing to negotiate a stud fee; otherwise I'll fry the little fellas in a blink of thought. Now, free my bonds."

GOLEM hovered over me, its cornea displaying radically different patterns of color as its mind processed every potential response to my last chess move—a move that, at least for the moment, had resulted in a stalemate.

Thirty seconds passed; I could feel my resolve weakening.

"ABE, I'm going to count down from ten seconds. If my bonds still have not been removed by the time I count to one, institute Sperm Toxicity protocol, then accelerate my blood pressure until my aorta bursts. Ten . . . nine . . . eight—"

Moving at inhuman speed, the two robotic hands tore the straps loose from my wrists and ankles.

I rolled off the table, backing away from the surgical arms. "Okay then, let's discuss this civilly, without any sharp objects—"

"Does Robert Eisenbraun still desire Andria Saxon as a mate?"

"I desire the real Andria Saxon, not her clone. By the looks of this complex, I'm a few hundred thousand years too late."

"Incorrect. The real Andria Saxon is alive."

"How is that possible?"

"The real Andria Saxon was cryogenically thawed six weeks ago in order to extract tissue samples for a new line of first-generation clones."

"Prove it! Where is she?"

"She is performing her duties in the genetics lab. Follow me and I will lead you to her."

An enormous camouflaged panel parted along a section of curved wall, revealing a dark corridor. The floating orb accelerated through the passage, forcing me to jog at a brisk pace in order to keep up, the forced activity making it impossible to organize my thoughts.

Thankfully, I had ABE.

WARNING: GOLEM IS ATTEMPTING TO DISTRACT ROBERT EISENBRAUN WHILE IT PROBES FOR A WEAKNESS.

Suggestions?

GOLEM's "Creator" persona is unfamiliar with resolving conflicts when forced into a subordinate role. Reestablish control by responding to GOLEM with unanticipated illogical reactions.

Following ABE's advice, I ceased running after the glowing orb, allowing the heavy darkness to envelop me. I stood and watched as GOLEM grew smaller in the distance. It finally stopped about a hundred feet ahead, pausing to allow me to catch up.

Do the unexpected . . .

Sitting on the cold slate floor, I waited for the deranged supercomputer to come to me while I parodied an old Stones' tune. I sang, *"Under my thumb . . . a computer who . . . once had me down. Under my thumb . . . a computer who once pushed me around . . ."*

I was halfway through the last verse when the luminescent artificial life-form made its way quickly back up the tunnel to confront me.

"Creator, any chance that souped-up chassis of yours can play music? I'm only asking because it sort of resembles a jukebox."

"Proceed to the genetics lab if you wish to see Andria Saxon."

"What if she's too busy to see me?"

"Andria Saxon awaits your presence."

"I dunno. Twelve million years is a long time. How does she look? I bet her breath smells. Have you reinvented toothpaste?"

"Proceed down the corridor if you wish to see Andria Saxon alive."

That last ominous warning stole the wind from my sails. "Why don't you lead the way, only slow down, I'm not as young as I used to be."

Hovering in silence and then proceeding at a pace that matched my own, GOLEM led me through the corridor to a brightly lit, gymnasium-size chamber. The sphere bloomed its six arachnid legs before entering, its antigravitational field no doubt a threat to the delicate equipment inside.

The walls of the genetics lab were incandescent, its floor space framed by a four-foot-wide gutter—I surmised for quick disposal of body parts.

A central row of surgical tables occupied the length of the room, each island of evil equipped with a pair of surgical appendages anchored on swiveling pedestals. A cryogenic storage unit and refrigerated shelves held an assortment of petri dishes, test tubes, and flasks, containers of reagents, a UV workstation, incubators for heating and cooling test samples, centrifuges, pipettes, electrophoresis systems, a spectrophotometer, scales, glassware, a camera system for the visualization of DNA, and a machine ABE identified as a sequence analyzer.

And then I saw Andria.

She was submerged in an eight-foot-tall, four-foot-wide acrylic cylinder filled with a clear blue liquid, her mottled flesh sporting rows of dime-size black electrodes. She was hairless and naked—a specimen kept alive in a tortured vegetative state so that her master could extract and harvest stands of DNA from her body.

"Andria, open your eyes. You have a guest."

Her eyes flashed open at the machine's motherly tone.

"Andria, come out and say hello to your fiancé."

A ceiling-anchored winch activated, drawing Andria's limp body out of the tank from a gruesome pair of six-inch hooks embedded beneath her shoulder blades. As I watched, helpless, the dripping blue body flopped in a disjointed pile of jellylike flesh onto the floor.

"Andria, Robert Eisenbraun hasn't held you in over twelve million years. Do you wish to embrace him?"

Tears poured from my eyes as the cable retracted, dragging Andria into an upright posture, her head flopping on her chest, her bare feet sliding on the floor beneath her.

"You sadistic bitch."

"Andria has a message for Robert Eisenbraun. Would you like to hear it?"

Before I could respond, I heard it . . . a gurgling rasp. "Ike."

I felt my heart clench. "Andie?"

"Ike . . . kill me."

Purple spots clouded my vision as a long-dormant volcanic anger seethed through my bloodstream. In a boiling, blinding rage, I launched myself across the expanse, tackling the entombed soul that was my lover's flesh in an attempt to snap her neck. But my efforts were rendered futile by the extreme viscosity of the slimy blue liquid.

"Embrace her, Robert Eisenbraun. Embrace her like you wanted to aboard Oceanus. Recall your feelings standing outside Kevin Read's

266 • STEVE ALTEN

stateroom when you learned your fiancée had been cheating on you with the commander. Choke her now, like you wanted to back then!"

My hands slid around Andria's neck, my thumbs pressed down into the soft depression at the base of her throat.

"That's it, Robert Eisenbraun! Kill her! She cheated on you. She deserves to die!

WARNING: THERE IS NO PULSE PRESENT. GOLEM IS DECEIVING YOU.

"Huh?"

I released the dead clone, pure hatred burning in my soul as I turned to face GOLEM.

The ten-foot sphere gazed back at me in triumphant silence . . . checkmate.

"Would Robert Eisenbraun like to see his friend Oscar?"

Enraged, I grabbed anything within my reach, hurling objects at the six-legged orb—beakers and flasks shattering harmlessly against the bulletproof plastic—ABE altering my aim as it identified a dozen ten-inch opaque optical sensors mounted at intervals around the sphere's chassis . . . the flea revolting against the elephant.

Exactly what happened next, I can only speculate. One moment, I was wielding a heavy piece of equipment—the next, I was flat on my back, my body quaking, my vision blinded behind purple spots delivered by a blue bolt of electricity.

30

In this kingdom of evil, there is no peace for the righteous. It is the wicked that inherited this tortured world, engulfed in the red, milky, cry-absorbing fog, guarding the wilted conscience of man.

    —ALEXANDER KIMEL, Holocaust survivor,
      from the poem "We Will Never Forget Auschwitz"

In the thick suffocating squalor of darkness, the cattle car swayed and squeezed me against cold walls of bundled human flesh. No air. No food or water. Unseen men defecated and unseen women fainted, their unseen children crying out to be heard.

    Whispers of conversations slipped in between the rattling rails—attempts to magnify glimmers of false hope—anything to anesthetize the insanity.

    "Enough! The SS officer explained all this at the station—we are being resettled to work for the Wehrmacht. Obey and we live. Disobey and all of us shall die."

    Lies. Told to us by our oppressors to prevent a revolt; rationalized by us, their victims, who were unwilling to see the cruel reality of our situation. Hours earlier, the monsters wearing the red armbands had laid siege to our village, segregating "the Juden" from the rest. Our homes had been looted. Our women accosted. Laughing soldiers entertained themselves with random kills. I heard my mother scream. I saw my father's skull spray her nightclothes red with brains and blood, his body left in the street with the others as we were marched in columns to the train station six miles away.

    Through a child's eyes, I waited for the rebellion. Our numbers were far greater than theirs, and yet there was no resistance. Worse—not a word of protest from our neighbors. Not when our people were dragged from our homes and shot in the street. Not even when we were squeezed by the hundreds into cattle cars. Terrified and isolated, we rendered ourselves sheep, fearful of upsetting the wolves that fully intended to eat us.

Desperate to breathe, I pushed and squeezed my way to the nearest rectangle of night, the window grated with steel, entwined in barbed wire. Pressing my face against the cold bars, I sucked in deep lungfuls of winter— and my probing fingers discovered a loose bolt! Using my fingernails and teeth, I managed to remove a screw, and after ten minutes of effort twisted the bar free.

Using my new tool, I pried off the barbed wire and stared at freedom rolling by at forty kilometers an hour.

"You—Boy, what do you think you are doing?" The gray-haired woman had been my third-grade history teacher; she looked at me now—her eyes crazed in madness.

"The bars are loose, we can escape."

"Little fool! The SS counted us when we boarded, they will count us again when we disembark. Escape, and they will kill us all."

"They will kill us all anyway." I pushed my head and shoulders through the opening, but she thwarted my escape, grabbing my ankles and dragging me back inside.

A short time later the train slowed and the whistle blew and we arrived at the outer gates of hell.

"No!"

Disoriented, I opened my eyes, the nightmare lingering with my dark surroundings. Was it just a dream or something deeper—a disturbing remnant of a past life? Either way, my mind struggled to connect with the present.

It took me several minutes before I realized that the heaviness I felt was gravity pressing me to the flat top of a Hunter-Transport—one of more than fifty transhuman vessels lined up end to end like freight cars to form an orderly procession several miles long. Hovering above a mist-laden swampland, the vessels inched their way past juvenile redwood trunks, their part-human part-machine pilots silently waiting their turn to deliver their precious cargo.

Cephalopeds. Males and females; adults, adolescents, and suckling young. Some were held in oval traps, and others were stacked in blood-strewn piles, the captives rendered helpless by the ship's gravity well.

Guarding their catches were the hunters—an assortment of Andria clones ranging from the long-haired, camouflaged beauty I had met in the woods of Virginia to the frightening genetically engineered Nosferatu freaks.

A familiar woman's bare foot stepped in front of my face, obscuring my vision. I strained to look up beyond her orange pant leg. The figure filling out the jumpsuit belonged to the short-haired version of my fiancée, the one who had taken me to the farm.

She playfully nudged my chin with her big toe. "Ike, if you promise to behave, I'll ease the gravitational field. But I'm warning you, the Creator sees everything and she's not happy with you."

The invisible weight pinning me to the porous surface dissipated. Andria helped me up, and I held on to the clone's hand. "The Creator told me you're an exact replica of my Andria, that you even share her memories."

"I'm not a replica. I am Andria Saxon."

I looked into her eyes. For all intents and purposes she really was the woman I loved, with two important distinctions: This Andria wanted to raise a family together, and, unlike my fiancée, she had never cheated on me. She was an unblemished beauty, representing a clean start in a new world, and as she leaned forward and kissed me, I realized how much I needed her.

That's right—needed! So what if she had been cloned by the warped mind of my own creation, she was still a woman—still human. And so there's no misunderstanding coming out of this internal journal, let me be perfectly clear—my interest was not based on my own sexual desire, nor was it to star in some Jason Sloan–concocted "Omega wet dream"; that ship had sailed the moment GOLEM "the Creator" had appeared. Having heard the computer's explanation of things that had come to pass, my mind had finally awakened to the fact that I was no longer asleep. But with each passing moment in which I had come to accept this waking reality, I found myself experiencing a gnawing emptiness inside—a feeling I think must be shared by all castaways . . . the emptiness of finding oneself alone in a new world, having lost everything you have known.

In retrospect, I could not have predicted this reaction; after all I had spent my entire adult life, to paraphrase the real Andria Saxon, ". . . as a recluse, living inside my own head."

The clone . . . this Andria was an offer of reconciliation, GOLEM's olive branch. If I could accept the machine as the Creator of this new world, then Andria would become the Eve to my Adam—the choice was mine.

But before I bit into the proverbial apple, there was another matter of the heart I had to attend to.

"I want to be with you, Andria, but first, I need to know if you're even capable of loving me."

"Ike, I do love you."

"Love has to be more than just words or sex, love means placing the other person's needs before your own."

"Tell me what I can do to prove that to you."

Squeezing her hand, I led her to the cephaloped trap. Pressing my face to the porous acrylic surface, I could smell the musk of Oscar's fur, but between the darkness and the reflection of the Holy City's habitats glowing orange in the distance, I couldn't tell if my eight-legged companion was still alive.

"I don't understand. Why do you care about this creature?"

"This creature saved my life. Twice. If you truly love me, then release him. Release my friend."

"Ike, the octopeds are our enemy. They are godless vermin who seek to destroy humanity."

"Who told you that?"

"It's fact, passed down from the beginning, when the Creator returned life to the new world. It is said that humans once ruled the land, the octopeds the sea, and there was peace. But the octopeds were jealous of man and desired to rule the land, and so they sent an object from space to destroy the moon."

"Andria, that isn't true."

"It is true. The moon will return in six days, you can see the damage for yourself. The moon survived, but the impact wiped out humanity. The Creator healed the Earth, then recreated humankind in Her image."

"The moon was struck by an asteroid, but the octopeds didn't cause it. The octopeds weren't even around back then; just their ancestors—timid creatures living alone in coral beds at the bottom of the sea. As for humanity being recreated in the Creator's image—have you ever seen *Her*?"

"No one can see the Creator. We can feel Her presence when She returns to the church. We can hear Her commandments whispered in our heads. Without the Creator there would be no breeding farms or nurseries or habitats."

"And without the octopeds, the Creator couldn't genetically defile nature."

"Ike, humankind was created to rule the world. Octopeds are worthless, vile creatures . . . lecherous devil worshippers who murdered the Creator's son."

"The octopeds murdered Christ?"

"Who's Christ? I was speaking of the noble Golem. For this act, the Creator decreed that the octoped must live in servitude forever. It's all part of the Final Solution."

A chill ran down my spine, the coldheartedness of the clone's words unnerving.

The transport accelerated for another hundred feet and slowed. We were getting closer to our destination . . . I needed to free Oscar.

The mist cleared, revealing an object floating beneath our transport. It was gray and bloated, drifting on the lake's placid surface—an island among dozens more—a cephaloped carcass.

Did I report dozens? As I looked closer I saw thousands of dead cephalopeds littering the placid surface, their tortured remains evidence of an evil that rivaled the crimes at Auschwitz and Bergen-Belsen, Buchenwald, Dachau, Treblinka, and Theresienstadt.

My throat constricted. "Andria, what happened to them?"

"There's nothing to be concerned about, Ike. It's all part of the cleansing process."

Cleansing process. Final Solution.

For evil to flourish, it required a conspiracy of silence among the locals, the acts reduced to a language of euphemisms designed to render mass murder more digestible. Hitler had used anti-Semitism to gain power and fuel his own irrational need for conquest.

Terror threats. Weapons of mass destruction.

Eight decades after the Third Reich, political extremists had fueled anti-Islamic fears to perpetrate a Middle East oil grab that had led to another world war and the Great Die-Off.

Twelve million years after mankind's annihilation, a man-made machine was using hatred to subdue the free will of its own creations.

The transport accelerated again. In the distance I could hear the tortured shrieks of pan flutes.

"Andria, open the pod."

"Ike—"

"Do it!"

She passed her right palm across the top of the trap, generating a spark of blue electricity. With a depressurizing *hiss,* the oval container split open, spilling Oscar on to the flattop.

I gathered the cephaloped's head in my lap, pressing one of its tentacle palms in my hands. *ABE, is there a pulse?*

THERE ARE THREE PULSES, ALL EXTREMELY WEAK. OSCAR IS DYING.

The transport lurched ahead, its bow bumping into a wooden pier. Spotlights mounted on unseen buildings blinded me. Shadows moved toward us.

"Ike, we're here. Turn Oscar over to the Hunter-Sentries and we can return to the farm."

"Sorry, Andria, that's not going to happen."

"Ike, the cleansing camps are not for humans. Now leave the damn octoped and let's go!"

"We all have character flaws, Andria. God knows I have my anger issues, you cheated on me . . . at least the original Andie did. But I am not abandoning a friend to the Creator's ghouls, and if that floating ball of chemicals tries to separate us, then you can kiss me and my sperm good-bye."

Five adult Nosferatus stormed the transport, their clawed hands gripping my elbows, dragging me to my feet. Oscar held on, wrapping his tentacles around my upper torso as the pale, hairless, bat-winged transhumans led us across the dock to the gates of death.

31

Humans have been invoking God's name as part of their interspecies slaughters since the Mayan, Toltec, and Aztec empires chose to appease their gods through human sacrifices. Generations suffered and died during the Christian Crusades. Countless innocents were "shocked and awed" during the campaigns to thwart Saddam Hussein. And as the nukes went off, the phrase "God and country" ushered in the opening battles of World War III, perhaps because it was a lot easier on the conscience to annihilate forty thousand Muslims if you truly believed God was on your side.

Thou shall not kill? More of a convenient metaphor than a commandment. A pacifist had never won a political office, nor had an atheist.

Kill, baby, kill.

Was bloodlust in our genes? Having witnessed my entire family murdered by a God-fearing, Bible-toting mob, my answer was a resounding "yes," and that yes and the anger it had engendered in me led to the invention of ABE: If God could not keep our innate vices in check, then technology would.

Of course, my "genius" had also given life to GOLEM, rendering me history's biggest hypocrite.

Now, man was all but gone, and yet the practice of killing innocent beings in God's name was still alive and well. Ironically—maddeningly—in reshuffling and resequencing human DNA, GOLEM could have eliminated the "evil gene" from the *Homo sapiens* menu, but the computer needed its genetically engineered children to maintain a cold veneer of indifference when it came to the processing and disposal of the cephaloped race.

Having seen the remains of the dead, I could only imagine what evil awaited us in GOLEM's death camp.

A predawn gray bled its way across the eastern sky, revealing the main gate—a pair of twelve-foot-tall bare metal posts. Nothing ominous looking like the entrance to Auschwitz, nothing as high tech as the security checkpoint at the Pentagon—simply two nondescript metal posts.

Again, I had underestimated humanity's ruling artificial intelligence.

Prodded by the ghoulish Nosferatu sentries, I stepped across the threshold. Oscar was trembling against my chest—when my consciousness was instantly inhaled through a funnel of white energy, every cell in my body swimming in its warm, embracing, and quite intoxicating light. Gravity's weight was shed from my body, my flesh liberated, my spirit tingling.

How long I remained in this state of harmony and bliss, I have no idea, but at some juncture I opened my eyes to blue skies and the sun's warmth on my face . . . and Bella Maharaj.

"Wake up, sleepyhead."

I sat up and realized that my body felt refreshed. I was in a grassy meadow, human Bella kneeling beside me. She was wearing a sheer white frock and a smile . . . *But where was Oscar?*

"Oscar's safe, and so are you. Come, I'll show you."

She held out her hand and I allowed her to lead me across the manicured lawn to a three-foot crevice that cradled a shallow brook of soothing sparkling waters which flowed east across the acreage. We followed the stream in silence, the sounds of nature better than any conversation.

"You are wondering if this is heaven?"

I smiled. "It feels like heaven should feel."

"What you are experiencing is the Creator's love."

"I definitely feel something. Bella, where is Oscar?"

She pointed ahead. I could see in the distance a large oak tree rooted in a pond that fed the stream. The oak was sixty feet tall, with outstretched limbs twice that length . . . and nearly every square inch of bark was covered by eight-foot-long, furry-brown bodies.

Cephalopeds . . .

As we approached, I realized the creatures were hugging the tree as if suckling off the bark; moreover, they were pushing and prodding one another, jostling to maintain the maximum amount of direct physical contact. Dozens more were on the ground, fighting one another to be the next in line—Oscar among them.

I ran to the pond, then waded over to the big male. Reaching out for one of Oscar's tentacles, I held fast, hoping the physical contact would allow ABE to once more bridge our interspecies communication gap.

To my surprise, Oscar brusquely pulled his appendage away, as if he had no idea who I was.

My eyes caught movement and I tracked a body falling from one of the upper branches. The cephaloped struck two of its kind on the way down; it was already dead by the time I dragged its carcass from the pond.

The animal's fur was covered in blood.

ABE, theorize. What's happening here?

INSUFFICIENT OBSERVATIONS TO FORMULATE A WORKING THEORY. SUGGESTIONS: ANALYZE CEPHALOPED BLOOD. INSPECT THE TREE.

Sloshing knee-deep through the pond, I approached the tree. Gripping the distal end of the nearest cephalopod tentacle in both hands, I forcibly peeled the appendage away—to reveal cactuslike needles protruding from the tree trunk's bark, each three-inch thorn dripping in blood.

The creature belonging to the tentacle shoved me aside, slapping its arm back in place before another animal could occupy the spot.

Their demeanor had changed. Something in the tree sap was blocking signals to their vagus nerves. Something addictive . . .

I looked around. The sky, the weather, the environment, the setting . . . I was surrounded by a sinister perfection.

"Ike?"

I turned, taken aback to find Andria standing by the edge of the pond. Her ebony hair was long and wavy, the way it was on the day we first met; her taut body nude beneath the sheer white frock.

My heart pounded, pumping blood to my loins.

She offered me a wicked smile as she entered the pond, the water rising along the sheer fabric of her garment, causing it to cling to her body.

Sinister perfection . . .

"Ike, isn't everything so beautiful?"

"Andie, why are you here?"

"Baby, I'm here for you."

"And why am I here?"

"You are here because I need you. Our world needs you."

Dharma whispered into my subconscious. *"What is the meaning of life, Robert? What is this crazy world of ours all about?"*

"That's just it, Dharma. None of this is real, it's all an illusion. It's like each of us is in our own Omega dream."

"Let me share your dream." Andria peeled off the wet fabric.

WARNING: TESTOSTERONE LEVELS DROPPING.

I backed away, my feet sticking in the muddy bottom.

ABE, this isn't real. Reboot my senses.

WARNING: TO REBOOT THE FIVE SENSES WOULD REQUIRE STOPPING ROB-ERT EISENBRAUN'S HEART.

Andria reached for me—

Do it . . . now!

And suddenly I couldn't breathe.

Collapsing to my knees, I looked up. The sky was spinning and the cephalopods were falling from the tree like leaves—Andria's flesh fragmenting into cellular dust before everything went black, adrift in silence.

Life is but a dream . . .

32

Through clever and constant application of propaganda, people can be made to see paradise as hell, and also the other way round, to consider the most wretched sort of life as paradise.

    —ADOLF HITLER

BREATHE.

I took a breath as commanded, and then another, the aching organ pounding in my chest beating stronger with each inhalation. Seconds later sound returned to my brain, followed by the scent of a strong disinfectant, which prompted me to open my eyes.

The bizarre hummingbird-like creature fluttering above my neck had a hypodermic needle for a beak and a tiny cyclops lens for eyes. The left side of my chest hurt where it had injected the shot of adrenaline directly into my heart—a medical treatment that was wearing on me.

Convinced I was alive, the battery-powered version of Tinker Bell flew away.

I was back in GOLEM's sphere, strapped to the same surgical table. Then again, to say, *I was back* was to infer that I had left, and suddenly I wasn't so sure. It was very possible that everything that had transpired after my threat to GOLEM to "internally sterilize my own sperm" could have been artificially implanted memory—from the computer's mind game with the dead Andria clone to my awakening on the Hunter-Transport . . . and everything that followed my passage through the gates of the cephaloped death camp.

All one glorious mind-fuck.

Lifting my head, I looked around. My eyes widened at the

transformation within the spherical chamber, my bio-chip translating all I was witnessing.

The oak tree that had dominated my last internal vision now occupied the airspace above my spread-eagled body, only the tree wasn't a tree, it was a giant machine for aphaeresis—a process whereby blood is siphoned from a donor and the desired components extracted, with the unused remains returned—the entire procedure contained in a looping cycle. In this case the tree—a multitiered labyrinth of mechanically moving parts, was simultaneously siphoning DNA strands from the blood of hundreds of cephalopeds at a time and squeezing droplets through clear vinelike tubes on its way to the trunk's collection basin.

Dozens of robotic arms extended from the sphere's tubular walls. The telescopic devices operated in an incredibly coordinated multi-tasked singularity of purpose. As the drained, dead eight-legged donors were peeled away from their perches and dropped into one of several disposal tubes, another robotic arm would replace each fresh carcass with a live specimen extracted from a conveyor of oval traps. Fluttering around this living assembly line of bodies and bodily fluids were hundreds of the mechanized hummingbirds—miniature mobile sensors that fed bytes of information to GOLEM.

Then there was the "island of misfit toys," something more akin to Mengele's genetics lab. Set off in their own multitiered, bacteria-free acrylic habitat were the seedlings produced by GOLEM's genetic engineering experiments—bizarre genome creations combining the DNA of multiple species with artificial devices in an attempt to harvest and sustain unique new life-forms. They were occupied by hairless rats with human faces and lizard-tongued humans that possessed tentacles, and by bats hanging upside down from perches using their opposable thumbs. Even more freakish was GOLEM's garden of mutations, which featured rows of sunflowers equipped with human mouths and voice boxes that cried like infants and infants that sprouted upper torsos from trees.

There were also attempts to harvest aquatic species. Rows of water tanks contained human tadpoles and infant mermaids and human squids—genetic abominations of nature that struggled to coordinate gasps of air with gill slits, blue blood with hemoglobin red, each fleeting moment of life observed by GOLEM's sensors, each tortured death dictating the next pairing of chromosomes into a slightly altered DNA strand as the supercomputer created life in the same manner one would solve a Rubik's Cube.

The glowing orb of artificial intelligence responsible for this orchestrated mayhem hovered motionless above the fray, its internal solution strands churning like stars in a spiral galaxy.

The computer took a quantum second to glance down at me, its silence confirming my status as a solitary speck of stardust caught in a cosmic storm, and then the master . . . sorry, the mistress of its domain floated out of its genetics factory and disappeared into the night sky, perhaps to visit another facility on another continent.

I glanced down at my groin and my rage grew. A device covered my penis and I had no doubt it had milked my male organ of semen during Andria's alluring cameo in the meadow dreamscape.

Infuriated, I slammed the back of my head against the surgical table. "What have I done?"

GOLEM had succeeded in saving the human race. In doing so, it had unraveled the very secrets of the human genome, and, through genetic engineering, it was rewriting the blueprints for life on our planet.

But what was its ultimate goal?

Searching for clues, ABE replayed an excerpt from my last conversation with the computer: "GENERATING A LINE OF MALE-INSEMINATED OFF-SPRING WILL LEAD TO NEW VARIATIONS OF TRANSHUMANS NECESSARY FOR FUTURE SPACE ENDEAVORS."

Space endeavors?

My God, it means to seed the universe with its creations.

As if to confirm the working hypothesis, Dharma's voice filled my subconscious. *"The children of GOLEM are an aberration against the Creator and must be stopped."*

"No shit. But how does a flea stop a pit bull?"

GOLEM IS A MACHINE. MACHINES CAN BE SHUT DOWN.

Yes, ABE, but how?

And then I remembered the doline.

To protect the cephalopeds, the mysterious Blessed Heavenly Ones Who Nurture had rigged the crater's entrance with a powerful electromagnetic pulse . . . and now I understood why.

ABE, is it possible to use parts from the EMP array guarding the crater entrance to build a weapon powerful enough to disable GOLEM?

UNLIKELY. HOWEVER, AN EXPLOSIVE DEVICE YIELDING A SIGNIFICANT EMP WAVE CAN BE CONSTRUCTED USING EQUIPMENT FOUND ON *OCEANUS*.

Excellent! I squirmed and tugged and fought the straps that bound my arms, waist, and ankles to the surgical table, but I was getting nowhere. *ABE, any bright ideas on how to escape?*

SEEK ASSISTANCE FROM TRANSHUMAN ANDRIA.

You mean the Hunter-Transport? How do I do that?

ABE replayed the tortured being's last message to me: "KEEP THIS WITH YOU. THINK OF ME."

Her ring finger! The severed digit was still in my pocket. She had given it to me, knowing its physical presence would allow us to communicate through my bio-chip.

Andria, I'm being held in the Creator's lab. I need you, Andie. Please.

TRANSHUMAN ANDRIA HAS ACKNOWLEDGED THE COMMUNICATION.

Is she coming?

UNKNOWN.

Damn . . . Raising my head again, I searched the maze of cephalopeds that were stuck to the aphaeresis tree, hoping to locate Oscar—a seemingly impossible task. And then I saw him. The big male's inert body was being lifted by one of the robotic arms to be placed on the machine. My eyes followed the dangling carcass as it was outstretched on a vacant perch high overhead—until my sight line was obstructed by another mechanical hummingbird. For some reason, the annoying medical sentry was flitting around, two feet over my head.

"I'm fine. Now go on, git!"

The winged sensory device passed over my chest, pausing to hover over my left thigh and the sweat suit pocket holding Transhuman Andria's finger.

WARNING—

It knows. I figured that out.

The hummingbird retracted its beak, replacing it with a scalpel. Landing on my upper quadriceps, the creature began methodically slicing through fabric and flesh to access the severed digit—

—just as its owner descended through the hole in the sphere's ceiling. Still reading my thoughts, the Hunter-Transport slowed to hover next to my surgical table, its transhuman pilot backhanding Tinker Bell and its bloodstained scalpel across the lab.

Transhuman Andria regarded me through its scarlet eye sockets, their color reflecting the unit's fully recharged status. Reaching out, she managed to free my left wrist, allowing me to release the rest of my bonds.

I have no idea how long I had been strapped down, but it must have been a while judging from the stiffness in my muscles and joints. Barely able to sit up, I struggled to climb aboard the transport.

Thank you, Andie. My friend Oscar is coming too.

I directed her to his location.

The cephaloped's head and upper torso were draped atop an alien pumping device, its limp tentacles dangling. Leaning over the transport, I attempted to lift my unconscious friend off its perch—to no avail.

Andria, is there anything you can do?

SHUT DOWN YOUR BIO-CHIP. HOLD FAST TO OSCAR.

Grabbing a tentacle, I braced myself, nervously watching the ceiling overhead, praying GOLEM would not appear in our escape route.

I never registered the sonic wave emitted from the transhuman's open mouth, but the aphaeresis tree obviously did and it didn't like it. Within seconds, awakening cephalopeds were falling from their perches like inebriated cats.

I dragged Oscar on board the Hunter-Transport, the two of us held fast to the platform under two g's of gravity as the transhuman vehicle soared out of GOLEM's lab and into the night.

33

Enjoying the joys of others and suffering with them—
these are the best guides for man.
  —Albert Einstein

The cold night air blasted me in the face.

We were flying over water. In the distance I could see a small island located along the southeastern region of the impact crater. It was here that GOLEM had constructed its genetics lab, the facility separated from the Holy City by thirteen miles of lake.

Recalling a clue from my last conversation with the short-haired Andria clone, I reactivated ABE and replayed the memory.

"NO ONE CAN SEE THE CREATOR. WE CAN FEEL HER PRESENCE WHEN SHE RETURNS TO THE CHURCH. WE CAN HEAR HER COMMANDMENTS WHISPERED IN OUR HEADS."

It made sense for GOLEM to keep its lab isolated and away from its creations; the Andria, Lara, Bella, and Monique clones all possessed concepts of a supernal being that would conflict with the image of a ten-foot sphere floating around the Holy City.

It was the last part of Andria's statement that concerned me.

If GOLEM could whisper thoughts into its creations' heads, then the computer could probably track members of its flock as well.

Suddenly our escape seemed a bit too easy.

ABE, relay the GPS coordinates of the doline crater to Andria. Ask her to take us there as quickly as possible. Track our course . . . alert me if she deviates in any way.

The transhuman machine banked hard into a southwesterly course, the sudden movement causing Oscar to stir.

"Hang in there, pal, we're heading home."

The cephaloped struggled to breathe, each wheezing agonized breath from its siphon organ sounding like an antique car horn.

I squeezed a tentacle and my hand was immediately covered in specks of warm blood. *ABE, what's wrong with him? What can I do?*

ANALYSIS REQUIRED. TASTE OSCAR'S BLOOD.

I hesitated, then licked a dime-size droplet of blood from one of my fingers.

THE APHAERESIS DEVICE HAS DEPLETED OSCAR'S RED BLOOD CELL COUNT TO DANGEROUSLY LOW LEVELS. UNLESS OSCAR RECEIVES A BLOOD TRANSFUSION, HE WILL DIE OF ANEMIA.

How long before he suffocates?

THIRTY-SEVEN MINUTES.

Jesus . . . How far are we from the cephaloped colony?

AT OUR PRESENT COURSE AND SPEED: TWENTY-NINE MINUTES, THIRTY-FOUR SECONDS. HOWEVER, THE EMP ARRAY PREVENTS THE HUNTER-TRANSPORT FROM ENTERING THE CRATER, ADDING ANOTHER SEVENTEEN TO TWENTY-FOUR MINUTES IN ORDER TO DESCEND TO THE CRATER BASIN AND ACCESS THE COLONY. THERE IS ALSO NO EVIDENCE SUPPORTING THE CEPHA-LOPEDS POSSESSING THE MEDICAL EQUIPMENT NECESSARY TO PERFORM A BLOOD TRANSFUSION.

What about the surgical suite aboard Oceanus? *It has the necessary equipment. We'd just need to find a suitable cephaloped donor.*

ROBERT EISENBRAUN AND OSCAR BOTH HAVE TYPE O NEGATIVE BLOOD. ROBERT EISENBRAUN IS A COMPATIBLE DONOR.

How is that even possible? We're two completely different species. Octopus blood is blue.

INCORRECT. WATER-SPECIES OCTOPUS BLOOD CONTAINS THE COPPER-RICH PROTEIN, HEMOCYANIN, WHICH IS RESPONSIBLE FOR THE PALE-BLUE BLOOD FOUND IN ALL MOLLUSKS. TERRESTRIAL CEPHALOPEDS DO NOT POS-SESS GILLS. AS AIR-BREATHERS, THEIR RED BLOOD CELLS NOW UTILIZE HEMO-GLOBIN TO TRANSPORT OXYGEN IN THE BLOOD. ROBERT EISENBRAUN IS THEREFORE A COMPATIBLE DONOR.

Twenty-six minutes later, the Hunter-Transport raced up the beach where I had come on shore weeks earlier, landing next to *Oceanus.* It was four in the morning and the sand was alive with crustaceans, each fast-moving crab the size of a frying pan. Clutching Oscar's torso to my chest, I dashed to the watertight door of the egress chamber, the clawed demons snapping at my companion's trailing tentacles.

ABE guided me to the ladder leading up to the mid-deck, the bio-chip counting down the remaining minutes of my friend's life. By now, Oscar was convulsing in my arms, each breath a pained snort of air— and I realized with alarm the sound might draw the bees.

FOUR MINUTES . . .

I located the surgical lab. Hurried past rows of cryogenic pods and laid Oscar on the floor next to one of the operating tables.

THREE MINUTES . . .

ABE directed me to the medical cabinets. I located sealed packs of intravenous lines and syringes. Tearing through the plastic, I removed a line and rigged each end with needles.

TWO MINUTES . . .

Oscar had stopped breathing. Leaning over the unconscious cepha-loped, I grabbed one of his tentacles, parted the fur and searched for anything that remotely resembled a vein. Finding nothing, I repeatedly jabbed at the soft flesh, attempting to simply draw blood.

ONE MINUTE.

I tried a sucker pad and was relieved to see Oscar's blood inch up the line. Rolling up my left sleeve, I located a knotty vein in my fore-arm and slid the other needle inside the blood vessel, drawing blood. Keeping the syringe flat, I repeatedly opened and closed my fist as I stretched out on the surgical table above Oscar's inert form, praying gravity would do its work.

Leaning over the table, I watched as my blood quickly drained down the length of tube, pushing Oscar's blood back into its vessel. *ABE, increase my heartbeat to one hundred sixty beats per minute.*

I lay back, staring at the dark recesses in the reconstructed ceiling overhead, my agitated pulse pounding in my neck at the memory of the skeletons harbored in GOLEM's gruesome attic.

At some point, I closed my eyes . . .

34

Things are not what they appear to be: nor are they otherwise.
—SURANGAMA SUTRA

When I opened my eyes, the ceiling that harbored my creation's museum of perversions was gone, replaced by shimmering waves of gold reflecting along a smooth ceiling of rock.

I sat up, disoriented. The surgical lab was now a cave, the surgical table a bed of velvety soft spinach leaves, each sheet of vegetation as large as a raft.

"The dreamer awakens." Dharma waved from a shallow pool of mineral water, clouds of steam dispersing from the percolating surface.

"How did I get here? Where's Oscar ... whoa!" Attempting to stand, I was struck by a wave of vertigo that sent me tumbling back into the sheets of spinach.

Dharma climbed out of the pool, her nude body silky wet and alluring. Kneeling by my side, she held my hand and kneaded the flesh along the back of my thumb. "Oscar's alive. Your transfusion saved his life, but it nearly bled you to death. Oscar managed to reverse the flow of the IV; now half your blood is mixed with his and vice versa. I think it was karma, don't you?"

"Karma? How is it karma that I now share my blood with an octopus?"

"Join me in the hot springs and I will explain. There is much we need to talk about."

"Food first. I'm so weak. It feels like I haven't eaten in days."

"That's because you haven't. You've been unconscious for nearly seventy-two hours."

She helped me out of my sweat suit, then wrapped her arm around my waist and escorted me to the edge of the steaming geothermal pool. I eased myself into the bath. The hot eucalyptus water was marvelous, drawing the fatigue out of my body while helping to clear the fog from my brain.

Dharma left me, disappearing around a bend. When she returned she was carrying a polished crystal bowl that held an assortment of exotic looking fruits and vegetables. She handed me a glazed goblet made of a turquoise-colored mineral that changed colors in the reflected light. Inside the container was a thick milky broth.

"Drink this, it's a soup made from wild berries, goats' milk, and nuts."

I drained the warm liquid while she separated what looked to be a pale red miniature banana from a bunch. Peeling it exposed the violet meat inside. "Try this, it's exquisite."

I handed her the empty goblet and popped the fruit into my mouth, the taste of peach and kiwi bursting across my taste buds. I devoured three more of the citrus, then pointed to the bowl and goblet. "Where did you get these containers? I don't remember seeing them aboard *Oceanus*? Were they yours?"

"Believe it or not, the cephalopeds created them. Do not be fooled by the creatures' appearance, they are incredible artists and artisans, farmers and botanists, astronomers and engineers with talents that exceed our own. What's more, when one individual masters a particular trade or talent, the ability is shared equally among all cephalopeds. If a ceph working the crops discovers a better method of cultivating the soil, by the next gathering every member of the colony will have acquired not only the technical knowledge, but the physical ability to manifest the same results, even though the action has yet to be experienced. You taught Oscar how to complete a donor-to-patient blood transfusion; now every adult and young adult in the colony can perform the same task flawlessly, though they may never actually use the procedure."

"How is that possible?"

"It's all in the way these beings communicate. It is not just thought energy, Ike. While humans store information in the brain, cephalopeds download and store information in a vast network of neurons that run through each tentacle. When they link tentacles, they are passing on not just the acquired knowledge but the muscle memory that accompanies the task. Think about that. It's like having an entire community of

Picassos, all of whom are also sculptors and farmers and physicians of equal talents. While that explains the physiological functions at play, what makes the entire dynamic work—and ultimately makes their species different from our own—is the cephalopeds' innate sense of community. Because each acquired skill or body of knowledge is instinctively shared among all members of the pack, there are no aggressive individuals vying to rise above the herd, no class warfare or divisions of wealth, no political or religious sects. Equality allows every member of the colony to prosper."

"Are you saying there are no leaders?"

"Individuals like your friend Oscar who are physically more imposing accept certain responsibilities beyond the norm, but only because size determines the signal strength of their thought-energy transmissions. Other than that, the pack moves or feeds or renders decisions according to the will of the majority. These beings possess what amounts to a hardwired democracy that resolutely remains in harmony with nature." She smiled. "As you can see, I learned a great deal while you were away, chasing after your Madonnas."

"How did you know?"

"Oscar shared your memories with us. Really, Ike, does your foolishness know no bounds?"

"I loved Andria . . . I couldn't just ignore her. Besides, I had to know the truth. And the truth is, GOLEM has gone mad. The computer is hunting the cephs down in order to harvest their DNA, which is needed as a unifying base element to genetically engineer an alphabet soup of transhuman hybrids. Dharma, they're slaughtering the cephalopeds . . . butchering them for their genes."

"Evil has its place in every equation; we can't always see the bigger picture."

"I saw the bigger picture. GOLEM means to create millions of these cloned monsters, which it will use to seed the universe. We have a responsibility to future races to stop it now."

"Ike, do you know why a cephaloped will not act in anger? It is because they have learned that the brain ceases to think when the mind becomes enraged. The same thing can be said of humans. You must learn to control your anger."

She was really pissing me off. "Dharma, weren't you the one who told me the children of GOLEM have to be stopped? Isn't that why I'm here? Isn't that my karma?"

"Karma is a reflection of past lives. And yes, while everything happens for a reason, karma, like existence, reveals itself in a cause-and-effect relationship."

"Really? How about that asteroid? Was that cause and effect?"

"It will be difficult for you to accept this answer, but yes. Remember what I told you about the human heart generating an electromagnetic field? These fields can be positive or negative. Now think of our planet as an energy grid, its own magnetic field, generated at the Earth's core, affected by the balance of these billions of electromagnetic impulses. When human society flourished, the grid remained stable and the magnetic core flowed, free of seismic disturbances. When humanity was engaged in warfare and other negative behavior, the core was disrupted and disasters struck, both natural and man-made. A decade before the Great Die-Off, the world was mired in two wars, with a third looming while banks and corporations engaged in unbridled greed, causing millions of families to lose their jobs and homes. These events coincided with volcanic eruptions, earthquakes, and tsunamis—and eventually the Great Die-Off. The Mayans and other ancient cultures understood this cause-and-effect relationship quite well, warning us of the doomsday scenario we eventually inflicted upon ourselves. Or do you honestly believe the Great Die-Off occurred simply because modern man ran out of oil?"

"You still haven't explained how that asteroid struck the moon, when every astronomer predicted it would pass us by."

"The asteroid's trajectory was altered—that was the effect. The cause? Our grief and anger and rage as we were forced to watch our loved ones perish in the GDO. Four billion people were wiped out. Multiply the anger in your heart by the population of the planet during those dark times, then calculate the electromagnetic deviations necessary to alter the trajectory of that asteroid just enough so that it struck the moon."

"It's an interesting theory, Dharma. I don't believe it, but it's interesting."

"Denial is a trait of the spirit of the Hungry Ghost. It comes from the inner rage fueled by your past lives. It remains harbored in an internal emptiness that can never be filled."

"Maybe you're wrong about that. Maybe I can fill that emptiness by saving the cephalopeds from annihilation."

"As I told you before, you cannot achieve enlightenment from anger."

"What you call enlightenment, I call seeking justice."

"Seek justice or seek happiness. You cannot have them both."

I turned, registering the big male's presence even before he entered our section of the cave.

Revitalized with my blood, Oscar was again an imposing beast. Moving to the hot springs, the cephaloped slid into the water, then extended two of its powerful tentacles, placing one sucker pad over my solar plexus, the other over Dharma's.

Focusing my thoughts, I greeted my friend. *It's good to see you.*

No reply. Not even a simple 'thank you.'

YOU EXPECT GRATITUDE?

So you can hear me. As for the gratitude, you were less than a minute from death. I did manage to save your life. Of course, you've saved mine on numerous—

YOU LEFT THE COLONY. YOUR ACTIONS MUTED SIX VOICES.

Six voices? Dharma, do you understand?

The cephaloped revere each beating heart as a voice from the Holy Spirit. When the Andria clone slaughtered Oscar's companions, she did so dishonorably, muting their voices.

I'm sorry. Seeing the woman . . . the voice I was once bonded to . . . it confused me. Oscar, do you know where Dharma and I come from?

YOU COME FROM BEFORE.

Yes, I suppose that's correct. Our awakening in your world . . . it was an accident.

NO ACCIDENT. THE LIGHT THAT BRINGS THE REBIRTH MOON SUMMONED MY VOICE TO AWAKEN THE ONE WHO SLEEPS.

I turned to Dharma.

"From what I've been able to learn, the Rebirth Moon is a very rare lunar event—a spiritual happening among the cephaloped that will lead to a thousand years of peace and prosperity. Your awakening was set for the last full moon which precedes the event—an event set to take place tomorrow night."

"Dharma, how can the moon prevent the machine I programmed twelve million years ago from systematically exterminating Oscar's people?" I turned to the cephaloped. *Oscar, there's a voice in my head that tells me we may be able to create a weapon that can destroy GOLEM using the equipment aboard* Oceanus. *If the next full moon really is tomorrow night, then we have to hurry before the tide rises and sweeps the habitat back out to sea. I'm going to need your help.*

THE COLONY WILL DECIDE.

35

Man will never be free until the last king is strangled with the entrails of the last priest.
—DENIS DIDEROT

Roused by ABE's internal alarm, I opened my eyes. I was curled against Dharma's back, the two of us spooning naked, sandwiched between giant spinach leaves. For a long moment I lay there, warmed by our shared body heat, bound by our place in history—the last two humans on Earth.

Were GOLEM's clones human? To me, they were animated flesh, programmed to hunt and kill and raise offspring that never cried and could not procreate. That latter chore was performed in a lab by a machine—a computer implanting its designer eggs into incubators, the developing fetuses fed by artificial placenta until they were ready to crawl. They were human hybrids that would never love or be loved, experience the confusion and desires of adolescence, or the challenges and triumphs of adulthood. Theirs was an existence void of the shadow of their own mortality. They were animals bred to follow the commands of their master, their place in this world secured by my own "prime directive" that had salvaged the genetic blueprints of their species at the cost of another.

And yet, despite having been hunted down and butchered to near extinction, the cephalopeds refused to hate their enemy or rebel against them. Having congregated last night, the colony had agreed that Oscar would accompany and assist us in preparing a weapon to dispose of the "GOLEM entity," provided it would do no harm to the transhuman race. No matter how I tried, I could not convey to these giving but simpleminded creatures that, even with GOLEM gone, the humans would most likely continue to hunt the cephaloped out of sheer habit. At one point, I confused them further by telling them the story of the scorpion and the frog—the frog offering its enemy a ride across a stream upon its back, only to be stung by the scorpion, who knew it would drown yet struck the frog anyway because that's what scorpions do.

I realized the tale's lesson was lost on the cephalopod after learning—in this time period—that frogs eat scorpions.

Yes, and what cephalopeds do is allow their kind to be butchered.

The parallels to the Holocaust infuriated me.

And then there was Dharma. In terms of beauty, she was not as exotic as Andria, and yet I found myself drawn to her in a deeper way—one which I found both compelling and at times annoying, for she would never hesitate to "push my buttons."

Was she intended to be the Eve to my Adam? I had fallen into that mental trap back at the farmhouse. Of course, at the time I had been convinced that I was in the midst of an Omega dream; now that I realized I was awake, any hope of a normal existence while GOLEM and its creations were around seemed impossible.

Was there even a chance Dharma and I could live out our lives in peace? In truth, I had serious doubts GOLEM could be destroyed by any combination of components found aboard *Oceanus*.

So why risk exposing myself or Dharma to regain access to the crippled sphere?

The answer was as simple as it was terrifying. GOLEM was omnipotent. Driven by its own closed-looped ego, the machine would not let us live. Nor would it allow us to die. It would send its minions to capture us, then it would torture us for eternity because that was *its* nature. And that was the real reason I was returning to *Oceanus*—not to construct a weapon to short-circuit the computer but to find a quick yet humane way to end our lives.

I thought about the *Titanic*. While the women and children were getting into lifeboats and the men scrambled to remain out of the frigid sea as long as possible, some couples had faced death by cuddling together one last time in their beds, even as the icy waters reached their cabins.

The thought saddened me. Sliding my forearm between Dharma's breasts, I pulled her closer, nuzzling the back of her neck. She responded by grinding her buttocks into my groin and we made love for perhaps the last time—the last two humans on Earth.

•   •   •

It took us nearly three hours to trek west through the cave. Oscar handled the brunt of the labor, carrying two tightly woven baskets made from ilala palm fronds, water grass, reeds, and the bark of banana trees. A rigid, bottle-shaped basket held several gallons of water; a larger basket, woven with alternating closed and open weaves allowed air to circulate to keep the food within fresh while keeping the insects out. Decorative, waterproof, and extremely durable, the cephaloped had surpassed the basket weaving skills of the African Zulu.

Dharma pointed out the intricate patterns of emerald green dye (acquired from fermented dung) that encircled a distorted red-orange figure intended by the artist to represent the moon. "According to the cephalopeds, this is what will happen tomorrow night as the moon passes over the South Pole. It does not tell us much."

"ABE was able to calculate the lunar orbit based on the extended length of the moon's cycle. Tonight's event is a perigee full moon, meaning its near side will move closer to Earth than usual—approximately thirteen thousand miles closer—making it appear even bigger and brighter. As far as those green patterns on the basket—I have no clue. To me, it looks like some sort of nuclear explosion."

The thought caused Dharma to grab my wrist. "Ike, do you think ABE intends to use the plutonium available in *Oceanus*'s reactor to create a nuclear bomb?"

Before I could respond, my bio-chip cut me off internally.

CONSTRUCTING A NUCLEAR WEAPON IS NOT FEASIBLE. THE PROCESS OF SPLITTING ATOMS IN ORDER TO GENERATE A NUCLEAR CHAIN REACTION REQUIRES PLUTONIUM-239, AN ISOTOPE WITH A HALF-LIFE OF 24,100 YEARS. THE PLUTONIUM-239 ABOARD THE *OCEANUS* REACTOR CEASED RADIATING HEAT TWELVE MILLION, ONE HUNDRED AND EIGHTY FIVE THOUSAND, FIVE HUNDRED AND SEVENTY-SIX YEARS AGO.

"Apparently, the plutonium aboard *Oceanus* lost its kick long ago."

Oscar was waiting for us in the chute, a final sixty-degree, thousand-foot descent that would take us down to the beach. Coiling each of us within a pair of its powerful tentacles, the big male cephaloped climbed down in controlled lurches, using me and Dharma as counterweights to the baskets.

The wind greeted us halfway down, howling full force by the time our feet touched sand. Following the narrow cavern, we exited among boulders into daylight, greeted by an ominous gray sky and a seemingly endless stretch of beach, pockmarked by holes. They were easy enough to avoid, randomly situated at roughly four to six per acre.

In the distance, perhaps a mile to the northwest, was *Oceanus*.

Oscar's stalk eyes analyzed the desert canvas before us like an American Indian reading the terrain. The cephaloped hesitated, something clearly bothering it. Only after positioning himself between us did he lead us out, the sucker pads from his tentacles maintaining contact with our wrists as if the creature were our parent.

It took me only eight paces before I registered what Oscar must have felt—a static charge in the air that caused the hair on my arms to stand on end. The cephaloped's fur danced like porcupine quills on his tentacles, Dharma's long silky hair actually sparked—as did the darkening heavens, which flashed green lightning.

Fifty yards ahead, a funnel of tea-colored sand suddenly swirled up into the roiling sky—a miniature twister that dispersed within twenty seconds. Two more vertical columns of earth shot up to our left, sending us scurrying in the opposite direction as Mother Nature went haywire in a twister version of whack-a-mole—and we were the moles!

I heard a high-pitched blast that reminded me of a train's whistle, and then Oscar was drawn upward into the air. Dharma let go, but I held on fast until the funnel wrenched him free, the twister launching the stunned cephaloped thirty-five feet above our heads before hurling him sideways.

We ran toward him, Dharma sprinting out ahead—the ground disappearing beneath my feet as I plummeted into gray darkness, falling five stories before the tunnel of sand curled and caught me, sending me tumbling into a horizontal burrow, where a stench attacked my senses, stinging my eyes like mustard gas.

Twenty feet away, unblinking crimson specks watched me in the semidarkness. As my watering eyes adjusted to the dim surroundings, I saw what appeared to be a pair of four-foot claws rise away from a tanklike body, the sharp appendages scraping sand from the eight to ten-foot-high ceiling.

People ate crabs; do giant crabs eat people?

I wasn't about to wait around to find out.

Regaining my feet, I retreated back to the vertical shaft, burying myself in cold, wet sand as I futilely attempted to climb and claw and dig my way out of a shaft ABE annoyingly informed me to be fifty-six feet deep.

The car-size crustacean scuttled sideways as it sized me up, its perpetual gaze almost amused by my escape attempt.

A shrill blast of pan flute sent the monster backing away.

Oscar grabbed me in one of his tentacles and climbed up the shaft at a frenzied pace. Seconds later, the giant crab appeared behind us, its exoskeleton pale blue in the brightening light.

We broke free of the hole and ran toward Dharma, who was beckoning us fifty yards ahead.

But the holes functioned as sound amplifiers, and within seconds the beach was aswarm with dozens of giant crustaceans, the creatures coming toward us from all directions.

And then they weren't. One second they were converging upon us across the flat terrain like monsters from an old sci-fi B movie, the next they had popped into smoldering scorched heaps of burnt crab meat.

The three of us remained motionless, afraid to take a wrong step. There had been no warning, no telltale laser beams or explosives.

Internally, ABE was analyzing my sight memory. Within fifteen seconds the bio-chip had traced the type and source of the weapon.

THE WEAPON WAS A MICROWAVE BEACON. POINT OF ORIGIN: AERIAL DRONE. LOCATION: EASTERN SKY. ALTITUDE: 371 METERS.

I pointed in the advised direction. "There's a drone up there somewhere."

Dharma squinted at the volatile eastern sky. "One of GOLEM's?"

"I'm guessing from Oscar's reaction that it's more likely the mysterious Heavenly Ones Who Nurture. Either way, let's get inside *Oceanus* before we get blasted by that storm."

The weeks stranded on shore had not been kind to the massive underwater habitat. Lacking power, the ship's internal compartments had become stifling, airless chambers that had slowly bled the arboretum dry. The good news: the bees and other "wildlife" were dead. The bad—we would require air supplies to function inside.

The Space Energy Agency had developed SPARE—Solar-Powered Air Rechargeable Equipment. The closest units were stored on the lower level. None of the breathing apparatus would fit Oscar.

An overcast sky yielded a mere twenty-two minutes of air. Dharma would remain outside with the cephaloped, attempting to fill another tank while I searched *Oceanus,* checking a list of equipment to see what still functioned.

There were thirty-three different ways to construct an EMP weapon, and ABE carried the designs of all but seven of them in its data files. Our goal was simple: As I made my way through the ship, opening targeted control panels and climbing through crawl spaces, the bio-chip would catalog everything on its lists that functioned until one of the design requirements was complete. Then Dharma or I would go back and remove the part—assuming we had fulfilled one of the weapon specifications.

Unbeknownst to my two companions, I would also be searching for a weapon or fast-acting poison that would allow my female companion and I to quickly and painlessly commit suicide.

Donning the mask, I reentered the sphere and headed straight for the nuclear reactor, the control room located beneath the lower level's removable deck panels. I removed two heavy steel grates, revealing an aluminum ladder that led below into darkness. Guided by ABE, I was searching for a large capacitor and high-voltage thyristor . . . whatever the hell that was. ABE knew, and cross-referencing the ship's schematics, it led me to the correct control panels . . . no easy feat in pitch black.

And then there was light.

A pair of luminescent white specks glowed like fireflies before me, magnifying into holographic images of a man and a woman! Both humans were dark-haired, pale-skinned people in their midforties. They wore matching black bodysuits that appeared to be powered by a half-dollar-size object that radiated a soft white light along their sternums.

The man spoke, his English lacking any recognizable accent. "Dr. Robert Eisenbraun. It is truly miraculous to finally communicate with you."

"Who are you? Where are you? And how the hell do you know my name?"

"I believe you already know these answers," replied the woman. "What you seek are the details. For instance, you know we are the descendants of the survivors from Alpha Colony, specifically the international team sent to analyze the lunar soil samples collected by GOLEM back in 2028. What you really want to know is how we survived and evolved over the last twelve million plus years. The answer, stated simply so as not to exhaust your diminishing supply of air, is that the asteroid impact struck a different quadrant of the moon than the one where Alpha Colony was located. The devastation, as you can imagine, was still crippling. Forced into subterranean caverns, our survivors discovered that the internal heat generated by the collision had melted ice deposits, providing scientists with water and air and energy to grow food from the seed stores GOLEM had arranged to be brought on board."

"The computer arranged seed stores? Why?"

"Because of your protocol," the man stated. "GOLEM had supplied our transport ships with the basic necessities of survival; at the same time the AI prevented us from returning to Earth."

"How? You had the lunar shuttles—"

"They were damaged in the firestorm."

"Still, your descendants represented a collection of the most brilliant minds on the planet. Are you telling me that, having survived for millions of years, the Alpha Colonists still couldn't figure out a way to return to Earth?"

"They had the means," said the female, "but several hundred thousand years passed before the atmospheric debris subsided enough to allow the sun's rays to again reach the Earth's surface and foster vegetation. By that time, the prolonged exposure to gravity one-sixth that of Earth's had permanently altered the colonists' DNA, leading to physiological adaptations that, over eons, prevented us from reinhabiting the planet. We have recently discovered a remedy to the problem, and are preparing to recolonize Earth—pending the success of your own mission."

"And what mission is that?"

"The destruction of GOLEM, as well as the computer's hives. This must be accomplished before tomorrow evening's cosmic event—before the AI spreads its seed beyond the subcontinent."

"I don't understand. Why can't *you* destroy GOLEM? Your drone took out that giant croc, and you did a real nice job on those crabs."

"GOLEM's crater is surrounded by an impenetrable radar detection system. If one of our drones comes within fifty kilometers, it is destroyed."

I checked my air gauge—down to six minutes. "If you can't get close enough, how am I—"

"The transhuman hovercraft created with your fiancée's genetic code remains close by, awaiting your next communiqué. The mutation can be used to transport the explosive. Detonated over the crater, the device will release an electromagnetic pulse powerful enough to short-circuit GOLEM."

"What device? I see no—"

A slice of white light fractured away from the male's holographic projection, illuminating a twelve-by-thirty-inch oval canister set on a control panel.

"You must instruct the hovercraft to fly at an altitude of twenty thousand feet at a velocity of seventy miles an hour. Proceed east to the Holy City. The moment you cross over the crater's western border, press the control switch twice and the device will become active. Count eight seconds and release the device over the side, then instruct the hovercraft to turn around and execute a rapid descent to three hundred feet. The blast will be contained in the crater, shutting down and incinerating the computer and its brood."

"Wait . . . what blast? I thought this was an EMP?"

"Dr. Eisenbraun, the device you see before you is a fifteen-kiloton nuclear bomb, carrying roughly the same charge as the atomic bomb used on Hiroshima. The plutonium was salvaged from the *Oceanus* reactor."

"How did you recharge the plutonium? Never mind. I'm sure you've accomplished greater endeavors over the last twelve million years. But there's a problem with nuking the Holy City—the cephalopeds want the clones spared."

"They are unique creatures," the man said. "However, they cannot possibly comprehend the dangers of allowing their masters to live."

WARNING: LESS THAN TWO MINUTES OF AIR REMAINS IN YOUR TANK.

"Dr. Eisenbraun, there is much to discuss. Tomorrow night's lunar event will allow us to bring both you and Dharma Yuan to Alpha Colony so we may brief you in person. For now, it is imperative that you collect the explosive and leave the habitat before you lose consciousness."

I still had a million questions, but they would have to wait. Grabbing the sixty-pound lead capsule in both arms, I struggled with it up the aluminum ladder. My brain was operating in a fog and the egress passage was spinning by the time I made my way out the exit to daylight. I dropped to my knees, carefully laid the explosive down in the sand, and tore the suffocating mask from my face as Dharma rushed to my side.

36

The electrical storm had passed while I was inside *Oceanus*. Oscar used the break in the weather to locate his baskets of provisions. Alone with Dharma, I quickly briefed her on my contact with the Alpha Colonists, grateful our cephaloped friend was not around to question the nature of the device lying on the ground before us.

"Ike, you do realize that using a nuclear weapon to wipe out GOLEM violates your agreement with the cephs? They specifically wanted the clones spared."

"I didn't create the poison pill, Dharma. Right now, it's all we've got."

"Then inventory the rest of the ship. Have ABE create another option."

"And what if this is the best option?"

"Since when is mass murder the best option?"

"If you had seen how they torture the cephs you'd realize this is more like an act of self-preservation."

"Those you wish to preserve don't see it that way."

"Well, maybe I was placed here in order to act in their best interests."

"That is the spirit of the Hungry Ghost talking. The anger experienced during your past lives is dictating your actions."

"I don't remember any past lives. But if I could go back in time to World War II and wipe out the Nazis before they exterminated six million of my people, then I'd do it."

Before Dharma could respond, we both felt a deep reverberation in the sand.

"Ike, what was that?"

"Tidal waves, beginning their run on the shoreline. The ocean is rising with the approaching moon. We need to get to higher ground fast. This entire area's going to be underwater pretty soon."

Reaching into my sweat suit pocket, I squeezed the remains of Transhuman Andria's severed finger, praying the neurons within the digit were still active enough to allow us to communicate. *Andie, it's Ike. If you can hear me, baby, we need your help. We're at* Oceanus. *Please try to get to us.*

Oscar returned with the food basket. Dharma and I ate while the cephaloped examined the small nuclear device, pressing one of its sucker pads to the protective lead casing.

Touching my arm, he communicated—ABE translating the creature's thoughts internally for me: **IT IS WARM ON THE INSIDE. LIKE THE SUN'S HEAT.**

Yes. I replied, avoiding eye contact.

"Explain it to him, Ike. It's his species' future; let him have a say in it."

God, she could be annoying. "Oscar, we're going to use this device to destroy GOLEM—the ball of energy calling itself the Creator. We're going to stop your kind from being hunted down and slaughtered."

YES. THIS IS WHY YOU ARE HERE.

I glanced back at Dharma—catching sight of a seven-foot-high wave as it blasted its way up the beach like a wall of blue-green foam.

"Look out!"

Oscar was first to react—looping a powerful tentacle around each of us, clutching the nuke in another as it dragged us behind *Oceanus.* The sphere rattled as it split the wave, shielding us for the moment.

The tide rushed inland another two hundred yards before beginning its retreat. Oscar timed the back flow, maneuvering us around to the front side of the sphere to avoid the powerful suction.

When the roar of water had finally passed, we made our way back east toward the cliff face, careful to avoid the gurgling crab holes, the surface of the slowly draining pools shimmering beneath the clearing afternoon skies.

Oscar cradled the explosive in one of his sucker pads, still oblivious to its destructive power. There was no time to inform him—the next wave was minutes away—so my thoughts turned inward, using ABE to analyze my conversation with the holographic colonists.

Query: Were the transmitted projections of real people or holograms made to appear human?

ANSWER TO QUERY: UNKNOWN.

A distant thunderclap abruptly ended my internal conversation. The three of us stopped jogging, turning in unison to face an advancing ocean still too far away to see. From the sound, I guessed the wave bearing down on us in the distance had been three to four hundred feet when it broke; from my gut I estimated the source of the rumbling beneath our feet would be upon us within a few short minutes, its advance gobbling up beach at eighty miles an hour.

We sprinted to the periphery of boulders that formed a rise along the base of the cliffs. Escaping into the cave system was not an option—to get to the Holy City we needed the Hunter-Transport, which meant we needed to remain accessible.

It was like a bad déjà vu—we needed to climb.

Oscar made short work of the boulder field, carrying the two of us and the nuclear device three hundred feet to the highest perch—seconds before an eighty foot wall of water smashed like a freight train into the rocks below, igniting a blast of foam that splattered us like a cold, heavy rainfall. Shivering, Dharma and I held on to one another until the late-afternoon sun warmed us.

I gazed up at the journey still to come—an expanse of rock that had taken all my willpower to conquer. Oscar had descended the face with me weeks earlier, but that was down and this was up, and there was two of us to carry, plus the nuke.

Oscar remained on his boulder, no doubt exhausted from having just scaled the boulder field.

"Dharma, have you ever done any climbing?"

She looked up, her almond eyes widening. "You will teach me, yes?"

"One day. Not today." I reached out to Oscar. *Dharma can't handle the climb. Can you get her and the device up to the summit?*

ABE translated the reply. OSCAR SAYS YES. HE IS CONCERNED ABOUT ROBERT EISENBRAUN.

Tell him I'll climb as high as I can, but he needs to go. The waves are getting larger; the next one will easily reach this perch.

The cephaloped rose, extending one of its powerful arms around Dharma's waist.

"Ike, wait—"

"You take the elevator. I'll manage the stairs."

And up they went, Oscar's sucker pads adhering to the small crevices and creases in the rock, the cephaloped drawing four to five feet higher with each extension, the fatigued creature adding a second appendage to secure Dharma as the first one tired.

I watched until they melded into the stone, then reached up to find my first handhold—a four-inch wedge of slab that led to nowhere, forcing me to retreat back to the boulder.

EIGHTEEN MINUTES UNTIL THE NEXT WAVE.

"Shut up, ABE!" Taking a moment to survey the potential routes, I made my way to another boulder and reached up with my right hand to a crack in the rock . . . yet was unable to muster the strength to pull myself up.

Get your mind right. You're relying on Oscar. You need to climb . . . now!

I fought on scraped knees and elbows for the next perch, refocusing my eyes on the rock directly above me. For several minutes I bore down, no songs in my head, only ABE's intermittent warnings.

TWELVE MINUTES UNTIL THE NEXT WAVE.

The cliff face was still warm, the sun a yellow-white glare in the western sky. Sweat poured off my face and down my arms to my hands, forcing me to wipe them dry on my pants before feeling for the next ledge.

SIX MINUTES UNTIL THE NEXT WAVE.

ABE, estimate the height of the next wave upon impact. How much higher do I need to climb to be safe?

EIGHTY-TWO FEET.

My heart pounded in my chest. Reaching inside my pocket, I squeezed the transhuman's severed finger hard enough to drain pus. "Andie, I'm on the cliffs. Now would be a really good time to come and get me."

Pressing my face to the rock, I reached higher. Three successive ledges raised me a pitiful fifteen feet. I contemplated using the Superman protocol, but excessive adrenaline and free climbing made for a deadly cocktail.

TWO MINUTES UNTIL THE NEXT WAVE. FORTY-ONE FEET TO SAFETY ZONE.

Can't make it. Need to find a fissure . . . wedge your arms in and hold on tight.

Looking up, I scanned the slab above my head, spotting only a two-inch-wide jagged slice in the rock. With no other options, I wedged the toes of my left shoe onto a higher ledge and inched my way up, my muscles trembling.

ONE MINUTE UNTIL THE NEXT WAVE.

Balancing my feet on an uneven knob of rock, I shoved eight fingers two inches deep into the sharp fissure, feeling the faint rumble of the approaching tidal surge reverberate in the stone.

THIRTY SECONDS . . .

Unable to contain myself, I stole a glance over my left shoulder and nearly let go.

More tsunami than wave, the three-hundred-and-ninety-foot foam-spewing blast of ocean was approaching so fast and furiously that I knew it would flay me to the bone against the cliffs before I ever got the chance to drown.

Please God, quick and painless . . . Reunite me with my family.

Curled up against the slate, I hyperventilated my last breath against the echoing roar—as my fingers were torn from the fissure and my body violently pried from its perch.

Eyes closed, it took me seconds to realize the pain—a vise squeezing my armpits into my clavicle, was actually Oscar's tentacles and that I was being hoisted up the wall at a miraculous speed.

Make that near miraculous.

Looking down, I caught sight of the wave a second before it exploded into the cliff, igniting a geyser of grit and foam that blasted me full in the face. Blinded, I surrendered to Oscar's embrace—only to be swallowed by the eruption of ocean that ripped the two of us away from the rock and devoured us in its vortex.

I opened my eyes underwater in time to see the coffee-brown wall of rock accelerate into my forehead with a dull *thud* . . . clouded in blackness.

And then I heard my name and ABE summoned me back into consciousness.

I was racing backward along the surface of a raging river, my head and chest cradled by a thick bristle-haired tentacle, the cliffs retreating before me. I could feel Oscar's remaining limbs fighting to keep our heads above water, the bully ocean sweeping us into its agitated bosom even as it readied its next assault upon the land.

TRANSHUMAN ANDRIA IS BECKONING YOU.

Looking up, I located the platform flying overhead on my left—its biological pilot attempting to match our fluctuating course and speed as she descended. I remember thinking that there was no way she could rescue us, and then a coil of hemp shot out from a portal and Oscar snagged it.

The rope held fast as the Hunter-Transport peeled us free of the receding sea.

Oscar swung us onboard. I collapsed onto the platform, then crawled to the mutated version of my fiancée and verified that she was missing her ring finger. "Andie, thank you."

THE CREATURE IS HOLDING AN OBJECT. PLEASE IDENTIFY.

"It's a means to free you from bondage; it's why I needed your help. Before I explain what must be done, there's another member of the *Oceanus* crew on the cliff face. Can you locate her?"

The transport banked into a tight easterly turn, accelerating toward the rise.

Dharma was two hundred feet from the top, clinging like an abandoned puppy to an outcrop. Reaching out, I pulled her onto the transport and into my arms.

Big mistake.

Part biological, part machine, the transhuman female still had Andria Saxon's memories and her cognitive responses.

Wrenched from my arms, Dharma was violently splayed out on deck, her body pinned beneath three g's of gravity.

"Andria, let her go."

YOU HAVE SLEPT WITH THIS WOMAN?

"Of course not," I lied, quickly instructing ABE to adjust my biological responses to back my claim. "Dharma and the cephaloped are friends, they're here to help me free you and the others . . . to make you whole again."

She turned to me, looking at me through scarlet eyes that spewed a jealous rage. Reaching out, she gripped my wrist in her right palm, reading my pulse—ABE quickly slowing my racing heartbeat.

After a moment, her expression changed. **YOU SPEAK THE TRUTH.**

"I'd never lie to you. Search your memories aboard *Oceanus*. Access Commander Kevin Read. It was you who cheated on me . . . but I forgave you."

For several seconds her head twitched as she attempted to reconcile the contradictions between a life she believed she had lived and the dichotomy of existence she had been condemned to serve.

To my surprise, her lower lip quivered and she displayed emotions I would never have thought possible for a biological machine.

IKE, CAN YOU MAKE ME HUMAN AGAIN?

I could have lied, I could have simply told her what she needed to hear in order to get her to deliver the bomb, but suddenly she was no longer a genetic mutation to me, nor was she a random seed on an assembly line . . . she was a living being who aspired to be better than the warped depravity of her Creator.

"Andie, I can make your life better, only you have to trust me."

I TRUST YOU.

"Then release Dharma and take us to the Holy City. Most important, do not reveal our presence to the Creator."

37

An American monkey, after getting drunk on brandy, would never touch it again, and thus is much wiser than most men.
—CHARLES DARWIN

I had been born into a world of intolerance, a world where man's negative nature—fueled by the human ego—had determined that greed was good, that hatred could drive a political campaign as well as an entertainment medium, and that fear could be used to coerce a nation into war. I had grown up in a maelstrom of cynicism—democracy had been poisoned by the power brokers of extremism who were given unrestricted backdoor government access to perpetuate their own agendas, overseen by politicians who wore their religion like a convenient garment.

My father had been my moral compass. Though not religious, he was a spiritual man who lived by the creed. "Love thy neighbor as thyself." In 2003, he had spoken out against the invasion of Iraq and was labeled a traitor; in 2005 he had established a blog that foretold the future legacy of Peak Oil.

One of my lasting memories with my father was the two of us watching the 2016 presidential debates, the topic: How to deal with a nuclear Iran. "Listen closely, Robbie. You're about to hear two supposedly devout Christians invoke God's name to justify a future nuclear attack that will accelerate the end of civilization as we know it. And yet, it's not them I blame, it's the rest of us—the morally blind majority willing to consider the annihilation of millions of innocent people just because they happen to be Muslim, never realizing their indifference will destroy all of us."

Indifference. It was so easy when we weren't the ones being bombed or tortured. When it wasn't our job lost, our home foreclosed upon, our family living in a shelter.

When had caring about others become a debatable political issue? When had peace and love been labeled a weakness?

Where had we lost our way?

Soaring over the redwood forest, I realized that I had fallen into the same trap as the Washington bureaucrats who had authorized the nuclear "defense protocol" during the Great Die-Off, justifying the eradication of the transhuman population as soulless creatures hell-bent on wiping out the cephaloped species.

That GOLEM had to be shut down, I harbored no doubt. But nuking the Holy City and all its inhabitants suddenly seemed wrong. Remove the dictator from the scene and an oppressed people could flourish.

Transhuman Andria and her kind deserved that opportunity.

And so I instructed the transport pilot to land in an isolated field, seeking another battle plan. We had the Alpha Colonists' bomb, perhaps we could salvage some of its nonnuclear components?

Transhuman Andria, armed with telescopic claspers used during the cephaloped hunting expeditions, quickly dismantled the nuke. The device was a rudimentary design that used a battery to deliver a power surge to a blasting cap of C-4 explosive in order to blow one piece of plutonium through another, starting a chain reaction that would end in a nuclear explosion. Every part had been removed from *Oceanus*—including the plastic explosive that had been intended as a backup to destroy the ice sheet in the event the ship's rockets had failed to ignite when it was time to resurface.

ABE guided me in reassembling the explosive using only the C-4. Once Transhuman Andria verified GOLEM was in its lab, we'd drop the bomb into the facility, directing the transport's powerful gravitational field over the blast radius to confine the detonation and convert the fallout into a Terra-strength electromagnetic pulse.

One way or another, GOLEM would be destroyed.

It was 8:13 at night by the time we made our approach to the crater. The atmosphere was charged with static electricity, the elements playing havoc with the transport's guidance system. Whatever the lunar event to come was, it would be happening soon.

Dharma gripped my arm, pointing behind us to the western horizon.

The heavens had become a cocoon of shimmering emerald light, beckoning the Rebirth Moon. The rising orb seemed as big as a planet, it luminescent green color an effect created by the aurora australis—the first appearance of the Southern Lights since my awakening.

The green moon . . . where had I seen the symbol before?

Back on *Oceanus*—on Dharma's surcoat!

Is this a dream?

Before I could analyze this new epiphany, we entered the crater.

Moving to the transhuman pilot, I squeezed her shoulder from behind. "Andie, is the Creator present?"

THE CREATOR IS ALWAYS PRESENT. THE CREATOR IS OMNIPOTENT.

Uh-oh. "Andria, is the Creator in its lab . . . its palace in the Holy City?"

THE CREATOR SEES EVERYTHING AND KNOWS EVERYTHING. THE CREATOR KNOWS ABOUT ROBERT EISENBRAUN'S BLASPHEMY.

My heart pounded in my chest. "Andie . . . how?"

She turned to face me, her scarlet eyes blazing. **I TOLD HER . . . CHEATER!**

I leapt for the bomb, only my muscles were lead and my body crumpled to the deck. Pinned beneath what ABE calculated to be four g's, I attempted to crawl to the explosive, pressed to the deck three feet away.

Unable to push through the induced paralysis, I called out to Oscar. *We've been betrayed. Detonate the device before GOLEM captures us.*

But without physical contact the cephaloped could not hear my thoughts. It remained anchored to the hexagonal platform, along with Dharma, none of us able to move.

The transport banked, circling over GOLEM's lab, preparing to drop into a vertical landing through the open roof.

Lying on my back, utterly helpless, I stared at the emerald-hued heavens as a numbing anxiety battled my internal rage for control of my mind. I cursed my stupidity, my gullibility, my bravado. I cursed the ego that had given rise to GOLEM; I cursed God for allowing evil to flourish.

Closing my eyes against the sudden descent in altitude, I found myself back on the train bound for Auschwitz—a young Polish Jew crushed beneath the stifling embrace of his fellow villagers.

How did I get here? How did this nightmare enter my life?

Are You testing me, God?

The cattle car settled to a stop with a bone-jarring *thud*. I opened my eyes and was Eisenbraun again. The transport had landed inside GOLEM's lab, the cessation of its antigravitational field shunting the g-forces pinning me down, and in one motion I sat up, reaching for the explosive—but the device was already in the hands of a Monique De-Friend clone, one whose bizarre flesh bore the red, yellow, and black-striped scales of a coral snake. As she moved to the center of the room, a clear four-foot cube rose from the floor before her.

The three of us bolted from the platform, only to be pummeled backward by a nerve-rattling, eyeball-pounding surge of electricity. Flat on my back, I looked up to see GOLEM floating down through the ceiling, the sphere's internal DNA strands twisting into serpentlike coils, as if the AI had consumed the mythical head of Medusa.

The Monique clone placed the lead canister upon the cube, which appeared to be a sensory device activated by its creator.

In the blink of an eye the bomb detonated, the C-4's powerful blast radius contained within an invisible oval-shaped force field, the interior of the barrier outlined in sizzling violet discharges of light.

"A composite of cyclotrimethylene trinitramine, a diethylhexy plasticizer, and the odorizing marker 3-dinitrobutane. Eisenbraun's attempt to destroy the Creator has failed. The Creator is not of this world. The Creator is omnipotent."

"If the Creator is omnipotent," I ranted, "then how did I escape the last time? There is a flaw in the creation matrix——trace memories from your DNA donors that can be used to nourish the seeds of something innate in every human—free will. Release us now and those trace memories remain dormant. Harm us and those memories will spread like a cancer throughout every cloned being in the Holy City."

It was a bluff, but it was a good one (or so I thought), magnified by the computer's lack of recent experience in handling an intellectual challenge to its rule.

I anticipated a rebuff. Instead, GOLEM rose majestically up through the center of the lab, the facility's curved walls separating into five sections, peeling open like the pedals of a flower.

Exposed to the night, we watched spellbound as the glowing orb levitated three hundred feet or more above the lab, casting its light on the surrounding redwood hives and gardens, its presence demanding the attention of every clone, every transhuman, every being it had harvested with life.

"Robert Eisenbraun has sinned against the Creator. The punishment for blasphemy is harsh. Each one of you who shares memories of Robert Eisenbraun shall also receive a share of his punishment as a warning not to congregate with evil."

Without warning, Dharma, Oscar, and I were tossed onto the lab floor as GOLEM commanded the transhuman hovercraft to its side.

"This H-T unit allowed its memories of Robert Eisenbraun to manipulate it against the Creator. Each of you shall register a spark of retribution against this blasphemy as a vaccination against free will."

As we watched, billions of DNA strands began churning within the computer's enzyme vessel, the outer rim of its dark pupil-like gelatinous nucleus radiating with a golden hue as it downloaded a self-destruct program to its creation.

Transhuman Andria convulsed in silent agony, her scarlet eyes draining white, her mechanical circuitry fried into smoldering cinders.

Its gravitational field in flux, the biological machine dropped and hovered several times until it finally plummeted onto the roots of a thousand-foot-tall redwood tree.

A chorus of primal wails rustled the surrounding forest—phantom pain delivered by GOLEM to its children as if it were an abusive parent.

Dharma and I held one another as we listened to the animal-like cries. The image of Andria's clone dancing on meat hooks shook me to my core, and I knew we had to act quickly or we'd soon be trapped within the same eternal madness.

I turned to Oscar, gripping one of his tentacles to communicate. *ABE, instruct Oscar to kill us—quickly! Snap our necks . . . tear through our carotid arteries.*

OSCAR REFUSES. THE REBIRTH MOON IS UPON US. OSCAR ENCOURAGES YOU TO HAVE FAITH.

Faith? Faith in what? A full moon?

FAITH IN THE LIGHT THAT BRINGS THE REBIRTH MOON. THE SAME LIGHT THAT LED OSCAR TO FREE EISENBRAUN. THE LIGHT THAT WILL REMOVE US FROM BONDAGE.

ABE, are you sure you're interpreting Oscar's thought energy accurately?

Dharma, who had been listening to everything, touched my cheek. "Ike, the Light Oscar keeps referring to—it's not the moonlight, it is the energy of the Creator . . . the *real* Creator."

Before I could question her, GOLEM's feminine voice echoed across the crater valley, the computer's inflection decidedly more agitated.

"The Creator has shown mercy to Her children. There shall be no mercy granted to Robert Eisenbraun and Dharma Yuan. Their torture shall last an eternity as a warning to each one of you."

"Dharma, listen to me. I've seen the kind of cruelty this machine can inflict. I love you too much to ever allow that to happen to you."

"You wish to end my life?"

"Only to spare your soul."

"Please."

And suddenly it was the worst déjà vu imaginable, the moment when the SS had Andria and me trapped by the Virginia highway, my lover begging me to do the unthinkable.

Hugging Dharma from behind, I slid the crook of my arm gently beneath her chin. "Close your eyes . . . I'll be quick."

Her voice trembled. "What about you?"

"I'll have ABE induce a fatal stroke the moment I release you."

"Good-bye, Robert. I love you."

"I love you, too."

Tears flowed from my eyes as I kissed her hair, readying myself to violently wrench her neck sideways, praying for a moment's courage.

DANGER! SWITCHING TO EMERGENCY HIBERNATION MODE.

ABE, report! What emergency?

Oscar grabbed me by the skull, forcing me to look up at GOLEM. Something was wrong with the computer, its DNA strands darkening to ash, the sphere's altitude wobbling.

Directly overhead, flooding the forest with its surreal emerald light was the moon.

As we watched, the man-made machine that had fallen into madness fell from the heavens, crashing through one of the parted walls of its lab, its aero gel shell splattering upon impact.

38

Conquer the angry man by love. Conquer the ill-natured man by goodness.
Conquer the miser with generosity. Conquer the liar with truth.
  —*The Dhammapada*

In the end, I would learn that the Rebirth Moon was not a common lunar occurrence but a rare cosmic event that had actually begun forty hours earlier not in Earth space, but on the surface of the sun. Over the course of seventy-two hours, four massive sun spots, each larger than Jupiter and roiling with intense magnetic activity, had formed and were drawn together, their unification igniting a star-shuddering expulsion of charged particles known as a "coronal mass ejection" or CME. This once-in-a-billion-year event spewed a tsunami wave of magnetically charged gas bubbles that raced toward Earth on the solar wind. Channeled toward the poles by Earth's magnetic field, the titanic geomagnetic storm ignited brilliant curtains of aurora light from the Northern and Southern hemispheres clear to the equator, announcing a charged solar particle wave that swept down through the atmosphere—frying GOLEM's electronic circuitry into a molten mass of goo.

The computer—assuming it had ever been alive—was functionally dead, bleeding out gallons of adenosine-triphosphate fluid and trillions of strands of DNA. My bio-chip was off-line, having escaped the charged solar particles by shutting down into a dormant state known as "hibernation mode." There would still be superficial damage, just as there had been when I had been immersed in the cryogenic pod. It was impossible to predict when ABE would return.

The Hunter-Transports, having no such mode to escape the onslaught of magnetic forces, were permanently grounded, their transhuman pilots anchored to their vehicles in a state of paralysis. The aphaeresis machine draining the enslaved cephalopeds had been rendered inoperable, its freed prisoners staggering toward us like Auschwitz's liberated—the stronger survivors supporting those too weak to move.

Beneath a lunar spotlight, Oscar took center stage, expelling a long staccato blast of his breathing organ. Goose bumps rose on my flesh when I heard the cadence—the sound identical to the blowing of the shofar on Rosh Hashanah, the Jewish New Year.

My father's words spoke to me from long ago: *"The sound of the shofar awakens something supernal within us, Robbie, connecting us to the Light of the Creator, removing our desire to receive for the self alone. On Rosh Hashanah, our consciousness returns to the state of Adam before the original sin—a transformation that reveals the true state of existence—that every soul in the universe is part of the unified whole."*

Oscar continued mixing blasts and breaks, summoning more cephalopeds to join him. The exhausted, tortured creatures linked tentacles, gaining strength from the pack.

To my surprise, they were joined by the children of GOLEM. Winged transhumans fluttered down from their treetop habitats. Genetically mutated versions of Andria, Lara, Monique, and Bella emerged from the forest. Infants and toddlers cried out for the first time, igniting long dormant maternal instincts among the adults.

Taking my hand, Dharma led me into this growing congregation of lost souls, all of us beckoned by the unifying sound, desiring only to live in peace.

I awoke to the quiet of dawn, the air heavy with humidity. The aurora was gone, the moon waxing as it ventured once more on its elliptical circuit around the planet.

Dharma was curled next to me. We were in a meadow just outside the redwood city, the crater's southwest wall looming before us like the Appalachian mountain range. We were not alone.

Spread out around us were thousands of cephalopeds. They were sleeping in clusters of three to seven—brown mounds of entangled limbs in the dew-covered grass.

My left shoulder was sore, so I rolled over, Dharma following suit. Oscar was three paces away, his tentacles entwined around a female.

Sensing movement, he raised his bulbous head, his yellow eyes watching me, making sure I was all right.

I waved at my friend, assuring him everything was fine.

Of course, there were still questions to be answered. In the last eight hours an event of messianic proportions had taken place, and all indications were that it had been preordained. The cephalopeds were clearly the Chosen Ones on this rebooted Earth—Oscar their leader, an eight-legged Moses chosen to free his species from bondage.

Chosen by whom? God? Dharma had told me the cephalopeds had the ability to access the Light of the Creator; a theory I had too easily dismissed. But their desire to love their enemies demonstrated incredible faith, proving the cephs were not merely the next rung up the evolutionary ladder; in a sense they were everything humanity had aspired to be—loving, selfless, caring, nonjudgmental—they were clearly "connected" to a higher power.

Oscar had also been chosen to free me from my cryogenic purgatory. What role was I destined to play? Had I already played it?

Then there was the Rebirth Moon. Though caused by the sun, it seemed far more than a random celestial event. Dharma believed it was a connection between the spiritual and physical worlds.

I knew she was right. ABE was no longer functioning, but I didn't need the bio-chip to confirm that last night had been the eve of Rosh Hashanah. As my father had taught me, the Jewish holy days were not simply dates on a calendar, nor were they just for the Jews. According to the Torah, the holy days corresponded to certain times of the year when humanity could more directly access a connection with the spiritual realm. Rosh Hashanah was such a time—a day for atonement and transformation.

A time of rebirth.

If the cephalopeds had known it was coming, did the Alpha Colonists? Surely they possessed telescopes powerful enough to chart the sun's coronal activity; if so then they were well aware of the lethal effects the supercharged solar wind would wreak upon GOLEM. And yet, they had reached out to me with a nuclear weapon, requesting that I use it to destroy my machine and its genetically manufactured offspring. Why do this, if they knew the computer's reign of tyranny was about to end?

"It was a test."

I sat up, the holographic projection of the male Alpha Colonist was standing between Oscar and myself. "What kind of test?"

"A test of the human ego. To senselessly destroy another species is a primitive reflex. We needed to make sure you were not infected with the same character flaws that led to the Great Die-Off. We had to be convinced you and Dharma were worthy of the destiny that awaits you here on the moon."

Dharma was sitting up next to me, listening to everything. "What awaits us on the moon?"

The male smiled. "Immortality. Unbridled happiness. Nirvana."

The cephalopeds had gathered around us, all but Oscar bowing down to the strange glowing vision of the Alpha Colony male. My eight-legged friend seemed more agitated than awestruck. Grasping my wrist, he attempted to communicate, but without ABE there was only silence—Dharma's window of thought energy having closed as well with the Rebirth Moon.

Turning back to the hologram I asked, "Are we expected to live on the moon?"

"That will be a choice best made after we reveal to you the destiny that now awaits humanity, as well as your role in that future."

"How do we get to the moon? Are you sending a shuttle?"

The male smiled. "Simply step inside the hologram and you will be here."

Dharma and I looked at one another. "What do you think?"

She squeezed my hand. "The spirit of the Hungry Ghost has been vanquished with the Rebirth Moon. You are no longer destiny's castaway, Robert. A greater karma awaits."

"You'll come with me then?"

"Of course. After all, we are soul mates." She glanced at Oscar. "How do we make him understand?"

"You can't," replied the Alpha Colonist. "Oscar has no concept of who we are. Step through now, don't risk a long good-bye. Oscar may attempt to join you—his place is with his people."

Dharma and I held hands. Then we stepped through the hologram into a white haze of energizing light.

39

Animals, whom we have made our slaves, we do not like to consider our equal.
—CHARLES DARWIN

The sensation was similar to plunging down a roller coaster—gut-wrenching, flesh-tingling—and then we were through. Was our passage instantaneous? I had no way of knowing, but whenever and wherever we were going, we had arrived.

And where were we? Underground, I assumed. The shaft was dark, save for the horseshoe-shaped contraption we had emerged from and the proverbial light at the end of the tunnel—the tunnel being a rectangular passage of rock, specked with chunks of quartz crystal. With nowhere else to go we quickly covered the hundred yards, exiting through an archway of bright light—stepping into what appeared to be the grand lobby of a five-star hotel!

Two rows of gold pillars supported a three-story archway. Polished marble floors led us past lush gardens and trickling waterfalls. Blue neon recessed lighting escorted us to the end of the T-shaped chamber and a thirty-by-sixty-foot observation window that revealed the lunar surface nestled beneath the velvety black tapestry of space.

We stood there, awestruck by the three-dimensional visual evidence of our species' annihilation, frozen in orbit for all eternity yet animated by the Earth's gravitational pull. A debris trail high above the moon's surface formed a tail that was drawn to Earth by the planet's immense gravitational forces. Lunar dust glittered like diamonds, chunks of rocks as large as pickup trucks spun like rotating islands. And then there was the Earth itself, an image worthy of a thousand terabytes of information—a blue jewel occupying a third of the ever-changing skyline, its atmosphere doused with emerald flames and crimson-red highlights—fading remnants of the solar particle-fueled aurora.

As the moon's orbit changed and our home world gradually faded, the surrounding stars seemed to brighten. I could spend hours describing the tidal patterns forged around the churning vortex of the Milky Way or the distant clusters forming other galaxies and still never do them justice, but suddenly my flesh prickled and static electricity caused the hairs along the back of my neck to rise as I realized we were not alone.

Dharma shared the sensation, and yet we could see no one.

"Welcome to Alpha Colony."

From the darkened corridor to our left appeared two brilliant white specks of light. As they moved closer, the pale, almost luminescent faces of the couple who had communicated with me aboard *Oceanus* became visible, their black bodysuits having camouflaged their bodies in the recessed shadows.

"Dr. Eisenbraun, Dr. Yuan . . . so good of you to accept our invitation. My name is Douglas McEntyre and I am a senior liaison to the CCE, one of the three divisions on the moon. This is my soul mate, Lisa."

"My husband, Doug, understates our gratitude." She leaned in and kissed me on either cheek, her flesh warm and soft and to my relief quite real. "Your presence here honors us."

She repeated the gesture to Dharma.

Doug McEntyre smiled, observing my apprehension. "Our guest reminds us that he remains a man of science, his mind riddled with questions. You could learn a thing or two from your companion, Robert. Dharma's mind remains open and calm, thus unencumbered."

"Unencumber my mind with answers. Where are we? How did your predecessors construct all this with their limited resources? How many others are there? Have your people explored space? Colonized other worlds? What has humanity achieved over the last twelve million years?"

McEntyre motioned us down the corridor, his wife linking arms with Dharma. "You have so much to learn; for now we'll begin with the basics—the equivalent of your first day in kindergarten. Where are we? Technically, we're in a lunar cave system excavated beneath the Sea of Tranquility. As we discussed earlier, our ancestors were able to process water and air using the vast ice deposits found in the deeper caverns. Our marooned predecessors had seed banks and mining equipment, as well as the materials that were salvageable from the lunar shuttle. The historical records show that fifty-six scientists and crewmen survived the asteroid impact. How our predecessors built all of this involves million of years of history that pitted the challenges of living in near-zero gravity conditions with the greatest evolutionary adaptation since the first lobed-fin fish crawled out of the primordial sea onto land."

We continued down the corridor, my curiosity burning. At the time I had been frozen, modern man's intellect traced back a mere ten thousand years. McEntyre's people represented twelve million years of scientific advancements. Their sonic weapon had made fast work of the crocodilian monster; our transportation from the Earth to Alpha Colony had demonstrated their ability to transport living beings. Even with their limited resources they had to have colonized Mars, Europa . . . Certainly they had visited other solar systems. And yet an unanswered paradox was in play—*Why hadn't the Alpha Colonists returned to Earth?*

Specks of red, green, and white energy glistened like gemstones along the arched ceiling high overhead, glowing brighter as we approached the end of the corridor.

McEntyre continued. "Have we explored space? Colonized other worlds? And why did we allow GOLEM to rule the roost back on Earth? The answers are complex."

"Simplify it for me. After all, I'm only in kindergarten."

We had arrived at the end of the corridor and the double doors of a hotel suite. McEntyre nodded to his wife, who waved her hand along the wall to our right, causing a viewport to appear, the Earth still visible in the upper right corner of the glass.

"Robert, everything you see—the moon colony, the Earth, the stars and galaxies—all are part of the physical universe that came into existence with the Big Bang. Back in your time, quantum physicists asserted that the physical universe is merely one of ten dimensions—the lowest of the ten and the only one where time actually exists."

"I'm familiar with string theory."

"What if I told you the Big Bang was an event driven by a conscious purpose. What if I said the physical universe is an illusion . . . that it was created as an arena to test the soul."

"Test the soul?" I glanced at Dharma. "Do you have any clue what he's talking about?"

"Reincarnation," she whispered, as if mesmerized by his words. "Each of us must earn Nirvana."

McEntyre placed a reassuring hand on my shoulder. "I know you want to know everything right away. Before we go on, however, it's important that you rest."

Lisa opened the suite door. "Everything you can possibly want or desire can be accessed from these accommodations. There is a food replicator, baths, showers, privacy areas, exercise equipment, a therapeutic pool, and a king-size bed that will be far more comfortable than anything the land squids had to offer."

She kissed us on the cheeks and we entered the suite. Our eyes widened in amazement.

It was everything the female had promised and more, a four-thousand-square-foot palace, each chamber dominated by plush furnishings and floor to ceiling views of the lunar landscape, the bedroom closets containing a dozen outfits that seemed tailor-made.

I feasted on turkey and stuffing, Dharma preferring Eastern delicacies, the two of us agreeing on a double dessert order of chocolate mousse. We bathed together in a hot tub, made love on that magnificent bed, then curled together beneath a goose-down comforter and fell fast asleep.

Home, sweet home . . .

40

When the answer is simple, God is speaking.
—ALBERT EINSTEIN

I awoke, restless and disoriented from a dreamless sleep. With no daylight or evening to reference, just endless space, I had lost all concept of time—an unnerving feeling in *my* dimension.

I dressed, then headed for the exercise chamber, leaving Dharma sleeping in the bedroom. Climbing onto a stationary bike, I started to pedal. For six minutes I pushed myself hard, driving my heart rate up to 165 beats per minute as registered on the machine's built-in pulse monitor.

I stopped pedaling, coming to an abrupt stop. "This feels wrong. It feels empty."

RUNNING LEVEL-FOUR DIAGNOSTIC.

"ABE!"

RECALCULATING EISENBRAUN VITALS. A MAJOR DISCREPANCY EXISTS BETWEEN SENSORY INPUT AND BIOLOGICAL VITAL SIGNS.

Elaborate.

EISENBRAUN SENSES REPORT A PULSE RATE OF 122 BEATS PER MINUTE. ABE INTERNAL PULSE RATE REGISTERS EISENBRAUN'S HEART RATE AT 14 BEATS PER MINUTE. OTHER DISCREPANCIES INCLUDE BODY TEMPERATURE, OXYGEN VOLUME, BLOOD PRESSURE.

Fourteen beats a minute? How is that possible?

ANALYSIS OF RED BLOOD CELLS INDICATES THE PRESENCE OF A FOREIGN SUBSTANCE. CLASSIFICATION: ANESTHETIC.

Son of a bitch! ABE, isolate Eisenbraun sensory input.

SENSORY INPUT IS ORIGINATING FROM A FOREIGN CONDUIT FEEDING ELECTRICAL SIGNALS DIRECTLY INTO EISENBRAUN'S FRONTAL LOBE.

ABE, block those signals, then initiate an adrenaline spike powerful enough to wake me up!

WARNING: OVERLOAD COULD RESULT IN SEIZURE.

Do it!

Sound crackled crisply in my ear. Followed by a breath tainted with an acidic hospital taste.

Forcing a deeper inhalation, I used the airflow as a foothold, prying open my lead-sealed eyes—peering into a semi-dark chamber laced with streaks of neon-blue fluid seemingly hovering in the periphery.

I was naked, lying on my back on what ABE hypothesized to be a sensory pod, its pliant surface glowing a soft crimson beneath me. Quarter-size probes were adhered to my forehead and a dozen other neural junctions along my body. An IV feed line was threaded through my right armpit, a catheter protruding from my penis.

Turning my head to the left, I saw Dharma. She was unconscious, her nude body wired in an identical state, the surface of her thermostatic table more violet than red.

Raising my head caused my sensory pod to turn a yellow hue; tearing off the neural probes powered off the table, exposing the room in its soft white radiance. Gritting my teeth, I pulled out the catheter, then yanked out a six-inch wire feed from beneath my armpit. The effort made me nauseous, forcing me to lie back down.

ABE, search personnel files in 2028. Is there any record of a Douglas or Lisa McEntrye on board the lunar shuttle sent to investigate the helium-3 deposits?

TWO MCENTYRES WERE ABOARD SHUTTLE SEA-L29. DOUGLAS MCENTYRE: CEO AND MEDICAL DIRECTOR OF MILLENNIUM TECHNOLOGY RESOURCES. LISA MCENTYRE: GENETICS ENGINEER.

That's impossible. How can they still be alive? And what were they doing aboard that shuttle? They're not fusion experts. Who recruited them to the mission?

GENERAL DAVID SCHALL.

I closed my eyes, my mind plunging deeper down the "rabbit hole" with each new revelation. Willing myself to move, I stood on tingling, wobbly legs and groped my way past what appeared to be an aphaeresis machine, its clear lines transporting a neon-blue elixir. Following the fluid led me down a long corridor, the frost-tinged glass walls composed of pullout drawers—similar to what one might find in a county morgue. Pressing my face to the glass caused the internal chamber to illuminate, revealing the contents of each coffin-size compartment.

Humans. Their frozen bodies were grossly disfigured, evidence of living in low gravity conditions.

"That one was me."

I turned to find Doug McEntyre tapping the opposite wall, pointing at one of the drawers. "I was fifty-one when Lisa and I arrived on the moon; I think I look closer to thirty now, don't you agree?"

"What the hell is going on?"

"Your bio-chip woke you, didn't it? Damn impressive. But something gave the internal dreamscape away. Was it the food? The accommodations? We can alter any scenario, even return you to Earth if you wish—we want you to enjoy your life."

"While you do what? Harvest our bodies? What happened twelve million years ago? What exactly are you?"

"When the asteroid hit, it not only marooned us, it condemned us to a slow, agonizing death. What saved us were advances in genetic engineering that allowed us to harvest new organs from the original donor tissues—new red blood cells and bone marrow, even replacement flesh. For hundreds of years we continued to regenerate ourselves, anchored to our ever-changing bodies by the life force we call the 'soul.' And then we made the ultimate evolutionary leap—converting our consciousness to pure energy—a breakthrough that allowed us to abandon our physical bodies. What you see before you is a hologram."

"But you touched my shoulder . . . I felt you!"

"The hologram is wired into your senses. What you experienced was your neurological impulses reacting to an artificial stimulus."

I backed away, my eyes focusing on the speck of energy glowing from his chest. "What is it you want from us?"

"Do you know what the human body is, Robert? It's a vessel animated by the soul. When the body dies, the soul moves on. Only the body has to cease functioning before the soul can be released. We want to free ourselves from this purgatory of energy so that our souls can move on. To accomplish this we must die. Death is a physical event, requiring a physical vessel in which to inhabit. We tried capturing the cephalopeds in an attempt to occupy their bodies, only their genetics were incompatible and their souls refused to vacate their physical forms. We attempted to occupy your computer's clones, but GOLEM had tinkered too much with their DNA to allow us to inhabit their bodies. And then one miraculous day we discovered that both you and Dharma were still being kept in cryogenic stasis, and suddenly there was hope."

"You intend to preserve me and Dharma in a vegetative state so you can clone us, inhabit those bodies . . . and then what? Kill yourselves?"

"Suicide affects the soul's journey. Occupying your clones would allow us to return to Earth and live out our lives as physical beings before dying a natural death."

"Quite the happy ending . . . except for the two of us."

"You'll never know what transpired. Your minds will remain in a dream state, your consciousness maintaining free will. Had you not awoken, your mind would have found its way to a happier existence back on Earth."

"Another never-ending cryogenic dream? I don't think so."

A swarm of red, green, and white sparks of energy advanced down the corridor, surrounding McEntyre. "Unfortunately, Robert, you have no choice."

ABE, activate Hibernation Mode on my signal! Awaken me in thirty days!
EISENBRAUN VOICE-ACTIVATED PASSWORD IS REQUIRED.

I stumbled backward, the radiant entities spinning in my vision as I bellowed, "Vanilla sway . . . vanilla sway . . . vanilla sway!"

41

In the end, we will conserve only what we love. We will love only what we understand. We will understand only what we are taught.
　—Baba Dioum, African environmentalist

"Ike, open your eyes. Ike, if you can hear me, open your eyes!"

I opened my eyes.

I was sitting up, my body naked and trembling, my flesh sticky and wet from the tetrodotoxin, the liquefied gel draining from the open cryogenic pod. Before me was Andria, her dark hair short, her expression one of concern. Lara was next to her, smiling in relief. Jason Sloan was on my left, checking my blood pressure.

"Dude, you gave us quite the scare, it took us twenty minutes and two shots of adrenaline to revive you."

I struggled to speak, my throat parched.

Bella Maharaj leaned over, offering me a cup of water, positioning the straw in my mouth.

I sipped, too weak to move, my mind still in a fog.

Was this real? Could everything I had experienced simply been an Omega dream?

"Blood pressure's stabilizing," Jason reported. "Let's wrap him in a blanket and get him up to sick bay for an IV and a complete physical."

Reaching out, I grabbed the cryogenist by the wrist. "Asshole," I rasped. "What the hell happened to your emergency flush?"

"Sorry, dude. Commander Read found out I had set the system and deleted the program. There was nothing I could do."

"How . . . long?"

Andria smoothed wet strands of hair from my eyes. "Thirty days, six hours, and change. Ike, when I heard what Kevin did to you, I re-signed."

"You didn't have to do that."

"I wanted to."

"No . . . I mean you didn't have to do that because you and me—we're through. So please . . . go to Europa or the moon or Sioux City, Iowa . . . I don't give a rat's ass. Oh, and if you ever eat calamari again, I'm going to back over your Porsche with my pickup."

Lara snickered.

Jason whispered, "Ouch."

Andria stared at me, the hurt in her eyes tearing me apart. And then she left.

Two IVs, a shower, and a bowl of soup later and I was almost beginning to feel human again.

"So, the dreamer awakens." Dharma entered my room, sitting on the edge of my bed. "How are you?"

"Still wondering if this is real."

"Omega dreams often take several days to wear off."

"What about love?" I took her hand in mine. "I fell in love with you in my dream. I'm not sure I want to lose that feeling."

For the next hour I told her everything, sparing no detail.

When I was finished, she leaned in and kissed me on the cheek. "Your dream carries a theme of forgiveness. Just as the cephaloped forgave their oppressors, so too must you forgive yours if you are ever to find happiness. That includes the people who murdered your family, the enemies of your previous lives . . . and one more person—the keeper of your heart."

Ah . . . karma.

42

It took me a full day to recover from my thirty-day slumber, during which time I was relieved to learn that Asteroid 1997 XF11 missed Earth by 22,700 miles, Lara's pet squids were doing well, and that ABE, though stuck in hibernation mode from the cryogenic cold, would eventually thaw out and recover.

Andria and I had a long talk. Since then, she's yet to leave my side.

The next day, at precisely noon, GOLEM fired *Oceanus*'s rocket engines, the inferno coming from its four upper exhausts turning the refrozen ice shelf to slush. Forty minutes later we were back on the surface, surrounded by a convoy of trucks and all-weather terrain vehicles.

My uncle greeted us as we stepped off the habitat gangway arm in arm, my exhausted mind basking in the reassurance of subfreezing temperatures beneath a cobalt-blue sky. "So, Robbie, I hear you decided to take a thirty-day siesta after all."

"Don't even go there. What happened with the lunar investigation?"

"Preliminary reports indicate your computer was right, the helium-3 isn't active enough to generate a stable fusion reaction. Looks like it's on to Europa, although the crew's dropping like flies. First GOLEM determined Kevin Read was unfit for command, then the computer replaced every male crewman except Jason Sloan, then the Buddhist woman resigned. What the hell happened since we last saw one another?"

"Not much. Just an Ice Age, four-hundred-foot tidal waves, telepathic octopi that climb trees, cloned women who wanted to seduce me, and some nasty blue crabs."

"The women had crabs?"

"No, no . . . giant crabs. Never mind."

Andie kissed my cheek. "Tell him the news."

"We're getting married."

"Mazel tov," my uncle said, "but I pretty much assumed that when the two of you got engaged last year."

Andria slapped me playfully upside the head. "Not that news, the other news."

"Oh, right. I'm going to Europa."

Uncle David's eyes widened. "That must have been some dream."

"It wasn't the dream, it's that I love Andria and I want us to be together."

"For the record, General, I offered to resign. But your nephew insisted."

"Without Andie, I would never have survived the Great Die-Off. But having survived, the one thing I forgot is that life's too short . . . that each day is a gift. I've been too wrapped up in my work, and it's not fair to ask Andie to give up her dream. The way I figure it, I've witnessed the near end of humanity twice. This time around, I want to help secure our species' future the right way."

Andria kissed me, her lips cold. "We struck a deal with GOLEM. The computer agreed to push back the launch date to train the replacement crew long enough for us to take a month-long honeymoon."

Uncle David smiled. "Good for you. Tell you what—as a wedding gift I'll arrange round-trip air travel to anywhere you want to go. I just came back from Australia and it was beautiful."

"No more beaches for a while," I said, embracing my uncle. Andria hugged him, and then I led her to an awaiting helicopter, the two of us huddling against a sudden blast of katabatic wind.

EPILOGUE

A brahmin once asked The Blessed One:
   "Are you a God?"
      "No, brahmin," said The Blessed One.
   "Are you a saint?"
      "No, brahmin," said The Blessed One.
   "Are you a magician?"
      "No, brahmin," said The Blessed One.
   "What are you then?"
      "I am awake."
      —Buddhist saying

DECEMBER 7, 2028
ZHEJIANG PROVINCE, EASTERN CHINA

Located in a narrow forested valley in Hangzhou, the Lingyin Temple, known as the Temple of the Soul's Retreat, remains one of the largest and most visited Buddhist temples in China. Built in 328 A.D. by the Indian Monk Huili, the compound's main buildings are immense double-eaved structures with halls as high as sixty feet—a necessity when accommodating statues of Buddha that stand forty feet tall.

After nearly a month in China with my wife (I never get tired of saying that), I find I have settled into an Eastern biorhythm that has all but vanquished the internal strife that fueled decades of anger. Without the aid of ABE, Andie claims I have become human again. She has a point. Humanity has become so reliant on technology, we rarely raise our heads from texting to see the lotus blossoms. Having learned the usual tourist rhetoric of Chinese, I have enjoyed a newfound sense of accomplishment that was lacking with the "instant access" I had become so used to with my bio-chip.

The Lingyin Temple will be our last stop before returning to Hong Kong for the flight back to Cape Canaveral. Andria and I walk hand in hand through a vast outdoor courtyard, past shops and offices to Mahavira Hall. Within this chamber stands a massive image of Shakyamuni, founder of Buddhism. Painted in hues of gold, the sixty-two-foot figure is seated on a bed of lotus flowers, the entire creation carved from wood.

Andie excuses herself to use the restroom. Moving to a guardrail, I place my right heel on the four-foot-high section of steel, using the beam to stretch out my sore hamstring. Even after four weeks, all this walking . . .

"Oh, God—"

Doubling over in agony, I clench my teeth, gasping for air! My heart is racing. Sweat breaks out across my body, drenching my shirt.

SYSTEM ONLINE. INCREASING ADRENALINE.

The statue of Shakyamuni is staring at me, laughing silently at the foolish Westerner—a man who has sacrificed a lifetime of bliss for a principle governed by ego.

Sound crackles in my ear. I groan, fighting the sensation, fighting to remain here . . .

HEART RATE STABILIZING. INCREASING CORTISOL.

Nausea invades my senses, poisoning my efforts at salvation with its acidic breath.

OPEN YOUR EYES, ROBERT EISENBRAUN.

No!

OPEN . . . YOUR . . . EYES.

The chamber is dark, laced with streaks of neon-blue fluid. The sensory pod glows violet red beneath muscles long paralyzed with anesthetic.

A buoy of thought—happiness, vanquished by a simple command, can be restored by another—go back to sleep.

"You are destiny's castaway, Robert, a man who has witnessed the darkest days of existence. Now you live again, but only to change history."

I glance over at Dharma, her nude form stretched out on a sensory table, her features obscured behind her life-support modems. Unconscious and dreaming, yet unaware—a captive Buddhist princess, denied any chance of achieving real Nirvana.

"Seek justice or seek happiness. You cannot have them both."

Dharma or Andria?

Consciousness or an endless dream?

My anger swells at the injustice of our predicament, resuscitating the Hungry Ghost. I yearn for a lifetime of happiness with Andria, but Andria is dead, her soul has moved on.

Held in stasis, trapped in immortality, neither Dharma's soul, nor mine can ever be free.

I rise from the sensory table, tearing the electrodes from my flesh. *ABE . . . can you get us back to the lunar portal that brought us here?*

YES.

Then engage Superman protocol. We're getting the hell out of here.

A student once approached a sage who was well versed in the spiritual doctrines and mystical arts. He asked the master to teach him all the sublime secrets of life—to explain all the magnificent mysteries of the cosmos that are hidden in all the holy books. And he asked if all this could be done in the time that a person can remain balanced on one leg. The great sage carefully considered this request. He smiled and replied: "Love thy neighbor as thyself. All the rest is commentary."

—Kabbalist Yehuda Berg